Darling OBSESSION

Titles by Jaine Diamond

CONTEMPORARY ROMANCE

Dirty Like Me (Dirty #1)
Dirty Like Brody (Dirty #2)
2 Dirty Wedding Nights (Dirty #2.5)
Dirty Like Seth (Dirty #3)
Dirty Like Dylan (Dirty #4)
Dirty Like Jude (Dirty #5)
Dirty Like Zane (Dirty #6)
Hot Mess (Players #1)
Filthy Beautiful (Players #2)
Sweet Temptation (Players #3)
Lovely Madness (Players #4)
Flames and Flowers (Players Novella)
Handsome Devil (Vancity Villains #1)
Rebel Heir (Vancity Villains #2)
Wicked Angel (Vancity Villains #3)
Irresistible Rogue (Vancity Villains #4)
Charming Deception (Bayshore Billionaires #1)
Darling Obsession (Bayshore Billionaires #2)

EROTIC ROMANCE

DEEP (DEEP #1)
DEEPER (DEEP #2)

Darling OBSESSION

BAYSHORE BILLIONAIRES

JAINE DIAMOND

Darling Obsession
by Jaine Diamond

Copyright © 2025 Jaine Diamond

All rights reserved.

No part of this book may be reproduced, scanned, uploaded or distributed in any manner whatsoever without written permission from the publisher, except in the case of brief quotation embodied in book reviews.

This book is a work of fiction. Names, characters, places and incidents are the product of the author's imagination or are used fictitiously. Any resemblance to actual events, locales, organizations or persons is coincidental.

First Paperback Edition May 2025

Cover and interior design by Jaine Diamond / DreamWarp Publishing Ltd.

Published by DreamWarp Publishing Ltd.
www.jainediamond.com

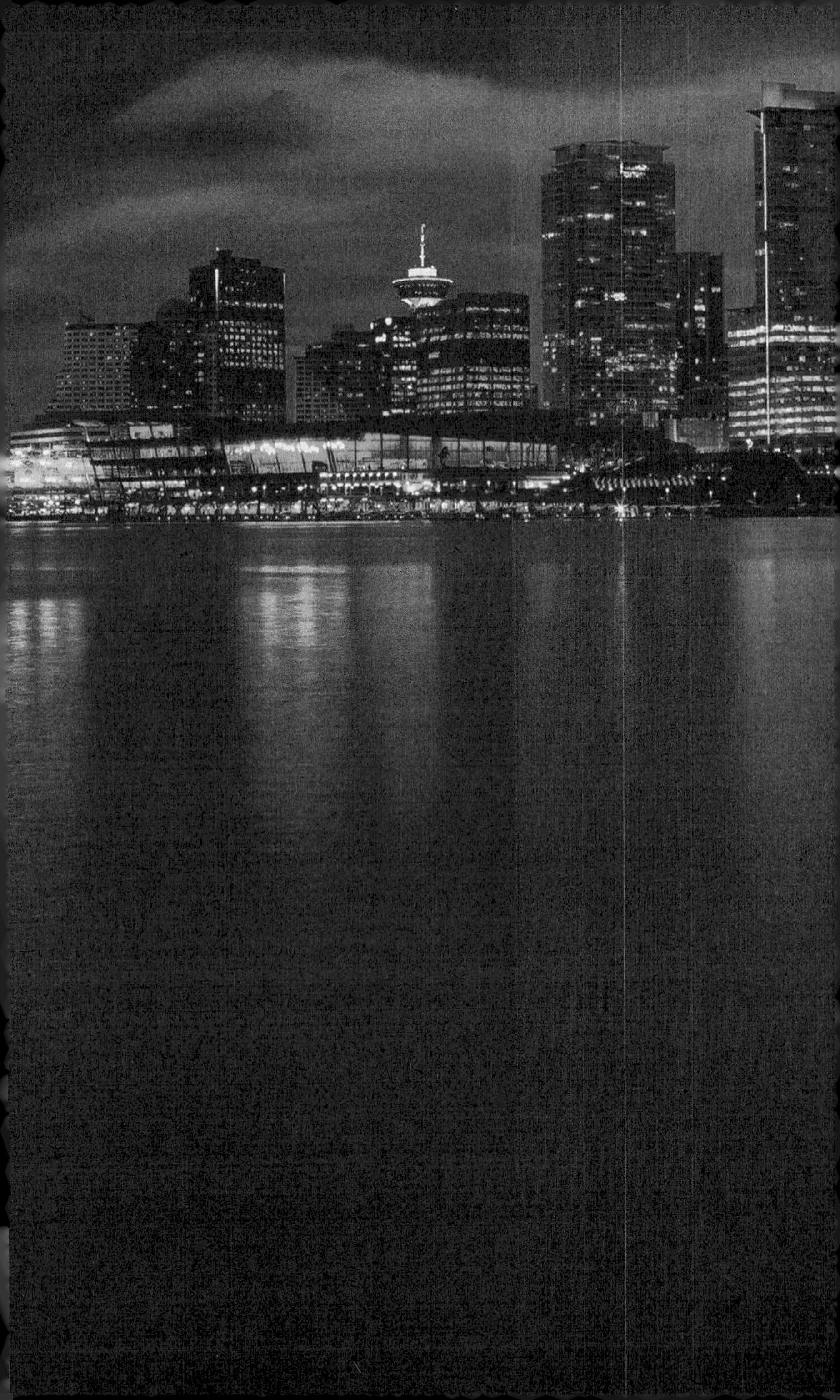

Prologue

Harlan

I walk into my brother Graysen's opulent living room at the Vance Bayshore resort with a familiar lump in my throat. It tastes like dread, and sticks like something sharp that I can never quite swallow.

The sun is high and bright through the towering windows, and my feet are hot in my shiny black shoes. I truly detest summer. Give me smothering low-cloud ceilings and pissing rain any day. Bad weather keeps people in their boxes and the hell away from me.

"Where the fuck is Jamie?" I grumble, tearing off my jacket.

Graysen, my oldest brother, stands at the wall of windows behind his desk, gazing out over the water of Coal Harbour. He's dressed as always in a three-piece suit, somber gray, not one dark hair out of place. "Harlan," he greets me with a frown. "Always a pleasure."

I grunt a hello. Our brother Damian smirks as I join my twin sister, Savannah, at the bar cart. She pokes me with her elbow in greeting as I start fixing myself a Manhattan.

"I see you're in a black mood," Graysen says as I add a dash of bitters to my drink. He's the only one of us without a drink in hand. He works here, lives here, does most everything here—instead of spending time with his fiancée. I assume he fucks his secretary here, too, but maybe that's because I find it rather soothing to underestimate people. It's a far better bet than hoping they'll surprise me.

"When is Harlan not in a black mood?" Damian quips.

I ignore them all as I cross the room to my favorite chair, pausing only to raise my glass to the wedding portrait of our grandparents over the fireplace. It's still there, the sharp thing in my throat. And now comes the burning in my esophagus, the acid reflux that kicks up every time I see Granddad's face.

Stoddard Vance, our billionaire grandfather, died only a few months ago. *Stoddy*. I was the only one of his grandkids who called him that. My granddad was the last soft spot I had left.

I pop open the top button of my shirt, trying to clear my throat of that sharp thing as I park myself in the big wingback chair I used to sit in while Granddad and I talked finances over drinks. I'd love to tear off my shoes, but that might reveal how uncomfortable I am, and I can feel my brothers watching me.

"Anything in particular piss you off today?" Damian inquires. He lounges on the sofa across from me in a stylish graphite-gray suit, suave as hell, but taking himself way less seriously than the rest of us.

"Can't stand that bodyguard of yours, Savi," I deflect. I don't need anyone digging into my private business, and that includes my mood. "Haven't we retired him yet?"

Savannah looks affronted and pauses in her stroll across the room, drink in hand. "What's your problem with Peter? You've never mentioned it before."

"The man's losing his hearing. What kind of bodyguard doesn't even hear me approaching in time to open a door? I could've mugged him if I wanted to."

She scoffs. "It's not my bodyguard's job to open doors for you."

"Don't take it personally, Savannah." Jameson saunters into the room, last and borderline late, like the prince he truly thinks he is; impeccable designer suit, wavy sun-kissed hair, magazine cover perfect. "You know Harlan hates everyone."

"Present company included," I mutter.

Jamie just smiles at me. He takes a seat next to Damian, not bothering with a drink. He's been in such a good mood lately, it's kind of revolting.

"Anyway, this isn't an employee review," Savi says crisply, annoyed with me, as she sits down. "We're here to play the game." She raises her glass to Jamie, and Damian follows suit. "As we all know, we have reason to celebrate. Jameson completed his challenge."

"How thoughtful of him to show up on time, then," I remark.

Savi frowns and sips her drink.

"Well played, Jameson." Damian shakes Jamie's hand in congratulations, eyes twinkling. "We all knew you could do it." We knew no such thing. But I genuinely think Damian's enjoying this bullshit. He always has loved a game, especially one he thinks he can win. Just like Granddad. "One down, four more to go."

"Yup," Jamie says. "Time to draw a new name from the box."

Granddad's cigar box sits on the coffee table between us. I'm trying to ignore it. But the straight edges of the box don't line up perfectly parallel to the edges of the table, and I've been itching to straighten it since I sat down.

We're here to play the next round of the game that we've been forced to play according to our granddad's will. We each need to complete a personal challenge, devised in secret by our siblings, that will "test what we're made of," in order to earn our inheritances, one by one. Today, the name of the next player in the game and their challenge will be drawn randomly from the box.

The stakes of the game are clear: win—or lose everything.

And I'm dreading my turn to play, more than I'd ever admit to any of them.

Because I can't even be sure that my siblings don't actually *want* me to lose this game.

Losing people you love makes you break or it makes you hard. That's what Grandma said years ago, just before she died, and I guess she thought it was fortifying wisdom. As if being hard is a virtue. My dad was already dead. Mom wasn't dead, but she was pretty much dead to me. And maybe Grandma knew I wasn't going to end up with some happily ever after. I wasn't Jameson.

Maybe she knew I was already hardening and she wanted to make it okay.

But just because you're hard doesn't mean you're not brittle as hell.

"So," I drawl, stalling. "Jameson slept with a sweet, small-town girl, who just happens to be beautiful, for *months*, while engaged to her, but didn't fuck her. This is the story he's selling, and we're believing it?"

"It's not a story, Harlan," Jameson informs me, his blue eyes cutting. "It's not a lie. You can ask Megan. She's an honest person, and she'll tell you the truth."

"No need. I'm sure your fiancée will tell the exact same story you do."

"Because it's the truth." The look on Jamie's face says he'd really love to punch me, if only he could. Kind of like when we were kids and I was still taller than him, and I'd hold his toys up high so he couldn't reach them, and he'd squeal at me until I gave them back. Even I couldn't resist giving him whatever he wanted.

Now he's taller than me, by like an inch, and I'm sure he loves it.

He stares me down for a stupidly long waste of time during which I ignore him, Savannah sighs, and Damian says, "Can we get on with this? Some of us have businesses to run."

I finally force out, "Congratulations."

"Thank you," Jamie mutters.

Savannah shakes her head at me.

It's not that I don't want to get along with our youngest brother. I just can't. It's chemical or something.

"Let's just get this done," Savi prompts.

"Let's." Graysen has joined us, and now looms over the seating area where the rest of us have gathered. As usual, everyone seems to be waiting for his lead.

I've always thought of our oldest brother as the mountain among us; solid and unmovable. Secure, right down to his molten roots and tectonic plates. Shaped by the forces that created him—our parents and our grandparents—Graysen is the glorious fruit of their best efforts.

I'm more like obsidian. Volcanic glass, jagged and hard, a scar coughed up on the landscape, forged in chaos and fire. Cooled. Solidified. Sharp. But weaker than you'd think.

Even solid black rock is vulnerable to the tides. To the smashing of other rocks against it. To all those forces beyond its control.

Paper and ink.

The will of those who want to see it break.

Graysen picks up the box. "Savannah. Do you want to select the next envelope? Might as well make it tradition."

"Sure." Our sister stands, and joins him on the far side of the coffee table. "Here goes."

As she slips her fingers into the box with anticipation, I get a glimpse of Savannah as a kid. We shared a room until we were eight. As twins, we went through school together. Went away to boarding school together. Mom even dressed us alike, sometimes.

She was my best friend, until she wasn't.

Sometimes I don't even know the dark-haired powerhouse of a woman standing in front of me in the smart blue dress, looking so grown up.

As she draws a small gold envelope from the box, I want to look disinterested. Bored, even.

I'm terrified.

Because I can't be the only one who loses this game. Who loses everything. My inheritance, my ownership in the family business, my place in the family. I'd no longer be Chief Financial Officer of Vance Industries.

My siblings could choose to hire me back, as an employee in *their* company. But really, would they hire me, if they didn't have to?

I'm not beloved like Jameson.

I'm not a mastermind like Damian.

I'm not utterly dependable like Graysen.

And Savannah? She's our only sister. Every one of us would kill for her. She'll never lose her place among us, whether she realizes it or not.

She reads the name written on the envelope.

"*Harlan.*"

Her eyes meet mine. I can't even tell if that's pure trepidation or sympathy I see.

I know Jamie's smiling. I was merciless with him during his challenge.

"Go ahead, open it," I say blandly. I refuse to appear fazed by any of this. "I'm sure we're all dying to hear what it is."

Savannah cracks the red wax that bears our family seal. V for Vance. Then she slips out the card inside. She reads it in silence. I don't like the worry that etches across her features or the way she seems to deflate.

"Well, *shit*." She blows out a hard breath. "You guys... I think we have a problem."

"We have enough problems," Damian says lightly, smoothing his tie, as if that changes anything.

"We have one year, collectively, to complete our challenges, right? But with this..." Savannah holds up my challenge card by one corner, barely touching it, like the ink on it is poisonous. The blank side is to the rest of us. "I'm getting concerned that we'll run out of time."

"Well, Jamie's challenge only took three months." Damian gets to his feet. "We still have nine months left." He moves to stand at her shoulder, reads the card, and chuckles under his breath. "Harlan could do that in one day. One minute." He gives me a look. "He could do it *tonight*."

"He could." Savannah meets my eyes again. "But he won't."

I say nothing. I won't bark at them to read me the damn card or hand it over, because that would suggest I care.

"The thing is..." Savi sighs. "The challenge I chose is going to be a long one."

Graysen sets the cigar box down. "How long?"

"Six months."

Jamie groans. "Savannah. What the fuck."

"I didn't know it would be used in this game, or that there would be a one-year deadline! Granddad never told any of us about the game before he died. How was I to know?"

"Does it have to be six months?" Graysen asks her.

"Yes. Just like Jamie's challenge lasted for a ninety day period, and we had to wait it out to see if he completed it... the one I chose will last for six months."

We all look at each other in the ensuing silence, wondering how fucked we are.

"Unless, of course," Savi adds softly, "the person who receives the challenge fails along the way first."

No one seems to know what the hell to say to that.

Savannah shows whatever's written on the card to Graysen, then Jameson. Graysen's jaw hardens at whatever he sees. Jamie kind of rolls his eyes.

And still, no one tells me what the hell it is. I slug down the rest of my drink in one go.

Damian eyes me, silently assessing.

Graysen's gaze razors over us, like he's deciding how best to wrangle a heard of wild animals who threaten to shit all over his living room. He has a habit of looking at us like that. "Okay, let's just think about the remaining challenges," he says. "This one, plus the three that are still in the box. Ask yourself, does the one you devised specify a length of time?"

"No," Damian offers. "Mine can be finished quickly."

"Mine, too," I admit. "But knowing the person I chose it for... probably not."

"Fucking great," Jamie says. "Mine *could* be fast, but yeah. Probably not."

"Well, Granddad gave us the one-year deadline, and he knew exactly what was on the cards," Graysen reminds us. "So he believed we could do it."

"If we put aside the ninety days for Jameson's challenge," Damian says, "and six months for whoever gets Savannah's challenge, that leaves three months for the rest, in total. So let's split it. One month each. That's the fairest way. Anyone finishes faster, it just adds more time for the others."

"Any objections?" Graysen asks.

No one objects.

Have they all forgotten that I'm the only one who hasn't

even seen the fucking challenge on the card that's still dangling from Savannah's hand like it's dusted with anthrax?

They all look at me, maybe waiting for me to take the card.

I struggle to still my finger; the end of a stiff upholstery thread, not a quarter of an inch long, pokes out of the seam of the chair under my fingertip, and I can't stop flicking it. Trying to run my nail over it in exactly the same spot with every flick. It's impossible to do. The thread's too soft. It just bends.

Does Graysen know about this thread? How does it not drive him crazy?

Because he's normal.

He's not like you.

"Anytime, Harlan," Jamie grumbles. "It's not like we have anywhere to be."

It's Monday afternoon. We all have places to be.

Graysen plucks the card from Savi's fingers irritably. "Remember, there are rules here, Harlan. Like it or not, you have to play by Granddad's rules."

I'm aware. And it won't be easy to cheat. Because ultimately it's up to my siblings to decide if I've successfully completed my challenge, if I win or lose the game. This in itself is a no-win situation for someone like me. I value privacy more than I value my next breath.

I won't live without it.

And having my brothers and sister all up in my personal business?

No.

"And even if it's the hardest rule..." Savannah adds gently, "you can't tell anyone about the challenge." This time, the sympathy in her eyes is clear. "Even her."

I swallow, the sick taste of dread gathering in my throat again. I don't even know why.

I don't know what "her" Savannah means. I barely talk to

Mom. And whether my siblings realize it or not, I swore off love long ago. There's no woman in my life.

Graysen thrusts the card at me. "One month," he says gravely.

I take the card.

Then I lounge back in my seat to read it, striving to look unaffected, as if the one thing I value most isn't about to be ripped away by a few handwritten words.

Introduce us to Darla

Chapter 1

Harlan

I watch the waitress across the room, standing at the bar, her back to me. Her turquoise hair dusts her shoulder blades in soft waves.

That color should look ridiculous on a grown woman.

But so should those tiny black shorts showing a quarter of her ass cheeks.

She turns her head, and I study the architecture of her nose in profile, perfectly proportioned on her pretty face.

Her eyes meet mine and I look down at my phone.

I thumb a text to my brother consisting of two words. *Fuck this.*

He doesn't answer.

I tell myself he's just in the elevator, coming down. He's almost here. I'll wait just ten more minutes.

Maybe thirty.

I never step foot in this place. I was just going to dip in for a minute. And now this. Damian has been pressing me for days to meet up; I know he wants to know how I'm doing with my challenge. When he texted me that he was in the office, I told him to meet me here at Velvet Lounge half an hour ago, and now he's left me waiting.

He must be loving this. Me, wasting my time for him. Waiting on him. Here, of all places. Yes, my family owns Vance Tower and everything in it, including Velvet, the lounge on the mezzanine level. But it's Damian who oversees our hospitality assets, and I'm not comfortable in Damian's playgrounds. The posh bars in our luxury hotels, the trendy hotspots, the private clubs. It's all the same to me.

A nightmare.

The cocktail waitresses wandering by in their skimpy black come-ons.

The wealthy elite who care more about what others think of them than what they think of themselves. The boasting of acquisitions, returns on investment, conquests. All of them desperate for attention, chasing it down with the perfect outfit, the perfect watch, the perfect business deal.

It's early evening and already the lounge is buzzing, three-quarters full.

Even the music oozes desperation.

I like music.

I don't like people who try too hard. And this place has the vibe of all my brother's bars, no matter the range of the patrons' ages and genders. It's the sticky, thick-liquid tension of older men with money chasing younger women with beauty, and those women so eager to be chased.

Damian has a habit of humblebragging about how "tiresome" it is that the waitresses here are always flirting with him. It's such a strenuous life he leads, spending most of his days fending off the advances of beautiful young women.

He'd probably literally die of loneliness if he spent one week in my life.

By the time he finally arrives, the whole place is giving me a headache.

Damian, on the other hand, looks totally at ease as he strolls through the room; the master of his domain. Fine Brioni suit, thick head of dark hair, perfect Patek Philippe watch. He loves this place and everything in it.

Especially the beautiful young women and the money that flows through them.

"I've been waiting for almost a fucking hour," I grouch at him, as soon as he reaches our table. "You've been hounding me all week, so here I fucking am."

"Lucky me," he says pleasantly.

He's barely sat down when our waitress is on top of us. Of course, she knows who he is.

"What can I bring you tonight, Mr. Vance?" Her voice is saccharine, eager. She has thick blonde curls and big, pouty lips. Her hip grazes the sleeve of my jacket, leaving floral perfume, as she reaches to set a cocktail napkin in front of my brother, offering him the obnoxious view down her cleavage.

I inch away.

"The bar knows what I like, sweetheart," he tells her.

"Are you sure I can't get you anything?" she asks me. It's the fifth time she's offered me a drink.

"Just leave us."

Damian chuckles as soon as she struts away. "Oh, she likes you."

I can't even tell if that's sarcasm or not.

"So, what brings you up from your subterranean lair?" he inquires, referring to my office on the lower level of the tower. "If not the view...?" His eyes follow the ass of a passing waitress. He'd be courting a harem in this booth in minutes if I weren't here. Damian Vance is a social creature.

Not like me.

I'm a lone wolf by design. But if I fail this challenge, I'll be *alone* in a way that terrifies me to the depths of my obsidian soul.

For the last sixteen days, it's been all I can think about.

I don't even want to do the math, yet the numbers are there in my head, all damn day and night. I'm past the halfway point now.

I have fourteen more days to introduce my siblings to Darla, or I fucking fail.

"You *know* what," I grit out. "I want to know who chose my challenge."

"Ah. So that's what the dark storm gathering in your atmosphere is about."

"Was it you?"

"Maybe you should ask yourself, if I did know, would I tell you?"

"Then it wasn't you."

"Time is ticking, Harlan," he says seriously. "Don't tell me you're still spinning. Trying to find some way out of this..."

Oh, I'm spinning.

I'm wound up so tight, I yelled at my assistant today, for no damn reason, and everyone on the floor heard me. I've never yelled at him before. I don't even raise my voice at work.

I literally try not to talk to anyone in person in the office, at any volume.

The best leaders listen more than they talk.

Gather data.

Review information.

Make decisions.

That's what I do all day, every day, as CFO of one of the largest privately held companies in the country. And I'm not used to problems I can't solve.

I've tried solving this challenge problem the way I always do —with data.

For sixteen days, I've had the one man on my team who I truly trust to protect me and my privacy—my head of security—work the data for me, and he's come up with an answer.

An answer I can't seem to fully swallow.

It's just too much of a risk.

Isn't it?

The turquoise hair across the room catches my eye. She stands at a table, smiling brightly at the male patrons who are probably flirting with her, directly in my line of vision over Damian's shoulder. I lean back in my seat so I can't see her, trying to focus.

I can't tell my siblings the truth.

I can't give them some bullshit story to try to explain why I can't introduce them to Darla, either.

Because either of those options will yield the same result: I fail to complete my challenge.

I've come to the horrifying conclusion that unless I find some perfect decoy Darla, I'm fucked.

I've lost endless hours to obsessing over this shit, and come up with nothing better.

I'm on the verge of completely losing my shit here.

Unless.

Unless Damian, the only person in my family besides myself who's more than willing to bend some rules, can help me with finding a loophole or something. "Do you think it was Jamie?"

He narrows his eyes at me. "You *are* spinning. This is your challenge, Harlan, not mine," he reminds me. "And not Jameson's."

"It had to be Jamie." Though the more I think about it, maybe it was Savi, and she's just a better actress than I thought.

What made me so sure it wasn't her in the first place? Just because she said the challenge she chose would last for exactly six months?

Okay, so she had no reason to make that up.

But still.

"What the hell does it even matter who chose it?" Damian says. "You're not going to convince Jamie, or whoever, to change the challenge. And even if you could, that's not how the game is played. Granddad had the challenges sealed in the envelopes, and those are the challenges we have to complete. Quit spinning your wheels, face reality, and save yourself the anxiety, Harlan."

While he speaks, my hand squeezes my thigh under the table. I rub my fingertip obsessively over the seam on the side of my pant leg, drawing small, quick letters, over and over.

The blonde waitress delivers Damian's drink, and he takes a long sip, assessing me with cunning eyes. Normally I'd appreciate that Damian is such a sealed vault. That brain of his is filled with the secrets of many a powerful man, and woman, in this city and beyond; pretty much goes with the territory when you host the rich and powerful at your exclusive private clubs—including a sex club.

But he didn't choose this challenge for me. I see it in his eyes.

At least I think I do.

"Do you recall when Graysen read us Granddad's letter?" he asks me. "The point of each challenge is personal growth."

"Fuck that. Granddad was a player. He's amusing himself with this shit."

"May I remind you that Granddad is dead."

That jagged shard materializes in my throat, sharp and bitter. "There has to be some kind of loophole. Or... what do they call it in gaming? Like a cheat code or something."

"May I also remind you that Granddad wasn't a cheat."

"Tell that to Grandma."

Damian doesn't exactly sigh, but he glances at his watch. Of course, he has beautiful women to entertain, somewhere. "Let me ask you. Why are you so upset about your challenge?"

"Do I look upset?"

"You look vaguely like a vampire who hasn't fed in weeks."

I scoff.

"Have you seen any sun this summer?"

"Not if I can help it."

"What's the big deal here? All you have to do is introduce a woman to the family. While that may seem unreasonable to you, I'm pretty sure Jameson's sex ban was much more uncomfortable."

"Why the hell does anyone want to meet her? It's not even serious."

Damian's dark eyebrow quirks. "Well, let's see. Maybe because she's the only woman you've mentioned to the family in years. Ever since what's-her-name? The one who ran off with her tennis instructor."

It was golf, but I don't correct him. I'd rather we all forget the details.

"All we're doing is fucking," I grit out. "It's hardly meet-the-family worthy. I haven't even seen her much lately."

Damian sits back, studying me with that annoying twinkle in his eyes. "You do realize that on several occasions, when one of us has asked you if you're seeing anyone, you've told us that you've been, and I quote, 'holding out for Darla.'"

"I recall," I mutter.

"It was quite a catchphrase for a while there. I considered putting it on a T-shirt for you, so you wouldn't have to keep repeating it."

"How thoughtful."

My brother chuckles. This must be amusing to him.

"Anyway, that was months ago," I mutter.

"Right. I believe the last time you mentioned her name was around the time that we all met with Granddad, and chose our challenges for one another, without realizing that's what we were doing."

Fuck. I really want to be pissed at Granddad. But I know he had no idea how this would come back to fuck me. My siblings wanting to meet the woman I implied I was interested in, possibly seeing, but refused to introduce them to probably seemed like an incredibly reasonable challenge.

"So, what is it between you and her, really?" Damian presses.

"Nothing. We had a thing, it didn't work out. The end."

"So, are you fucking her, or is it over? You're contradicting yourself."

"Can't it be both?"

He sits back and studies me in a way I don't like. I'm sure he's miles better at reading people than I am. "Harlan Vance. Are you in love?"

The way he says "in love," he makes it sound like some rare and curious disease.

Maybe to him, it is.

"Fuck love."

"She's important to you," he concludes. "More than you're letting on."

"What's important to me," I hiss, "is maintaining my privacy. You know I abhor anyone in my personal business. Including you."

"Oh, I know. You're extremely secretive. And yet here you are, looking awfully desperate for my help." He leans in with interest. "Who is Darla?"

I get the sense that it's actually starting to allure him that he doesn't know.

"The answer to that would fall under personal business."

"But I thought you hated everyone, little brother." His eyes narrow. "Or maybe you only hate what you can't have."

"Poetic."

He lounges back again, sipping his drink. "Has it occurred to you that if you keep hating on everyone, you'll end up alone? Forever. Is that what you really want?"

"Sounds like bliss."

He chuckles. Of course, that's the name of his private sex club. *Bliss.*

"Hate is just a front for fear," he says dismissively.

"More poetry. I didn't tell you to meet me here so I could watch you jack off to your own cleverness. I've actually got a fucking problem."

"What problem, exactly, do you have?"

"Well, let's see." I throw it back to him, playing to his ego, because I can't exactly tell him the truth. "Other than Savannah, you know me best, so you tell me. What problem would you have if you were me right now?"

He laughs a little. "Okay. If I'm you... I have literal OCD-level control over every detail of my life. And that control would evaporate if I lost my inheritance and my place in the family business. The news would go public, and I suppose I'd have some sort of nuclear-level meltdown."

Irritatingly accurate.

"And maybe," he probes, "I don't trust that if that happens, my siblings would protect me."

Maybe he's right.

I definitely don't trust them not to abandon me.

When I neither confirm nor deny, he says, "You don't give us enough credit. Just bring her around to a family dinner or something, and be done with it. You know Savannah would love to host." He holds up his hands in surrender. "We'll be on our best behavior."

"No."

"Then you do have a problem."

The blonde waitress drifts by to check on us, and Damian indulges her, flirting. I tune out, rubbing my fingertip over my pant seam, forming the letters. Performing the compulsive ritual, chasing the soothing that never quite comes. *B-E-A-U—*

"The poor girl," Damian says when the blonde leaves. "You won't even look at her."

I finish the word, because I can't not. *T-I-F-U-L.* "Can you take this seriously and forget about your cock for two seconds?"

"I'm not thinking with my cock. I'm thinking with my bank. She'd be good for Bliss, no? Those lips..."

I grunt with annoyance. "Maybe you're conveniently forgetting our fraternization policy."

"Oh, I don't forget."

"Then you know the full-blown fit Graysen would have if you got caught fondling the company goods. He'd never climb down out of your ass after an infraction like that."

Damian just chuckles. Of course, he's the sole owner of Bliss. He doesn't have to follow Graysen's rules for how he conducts business there. But he'd be stupid not to.

"How would he know, though?" he says. "Wouldn't it be my little secret? You know... like you and your Darla."

"And what if we *forced* you to tell us all your little secrets?" I growl back. Surely he can understand how fucked this position is I've been put in.

"I wish you luck with that," he says, eyes twinkling, "but I'd love to see you try."

"Not interested." I keep rubbing my fingertip over my pant seam, making sure to complete the word. *BEAUTIFUL.* "Keep your secrets. And I'll keep mine."

Damian studies me with open interest now. "Does Darla even exist? Is she a ghoul?" He leans in again. "Better question... Does she know *you* exist? You know, the way you'd talk about her, about 'holding out' for her, I halfway thought you were stalking her."

I laugh humorlessly, then realize he's not kidding.

"You have to admit, you do obsess."

I scowl. "About women?"

"How would I know? You never talk to me about women."

We stare at each other for as long as I can stand, before I start rubbing my fingertip on my pant seam again.

I don't like being out of control. Who does?

I tell myself this is a normal way to feel.

But there's nothing normal about the way I feel most of the time.

"I *can't* lose my inheritance, Damian," I growl.

"Then don't," he says. "Complete the challenge. By any means necessary."

I consider his words carefully. And I have to ask myself if Damian plans to use any means necessary—even cheat—when the time to complete his challenge comes.

I know he's right. That I have to do whatever it takes.

Even if it includes deceit.

Because what I've been asked to do is impossible. Even if I wanted to introduce my family to Darla, I couldn't.

"Good luck. Seems like you'll need it," he says. "And I look forward to meeting Darla." He gets up to leave, and the turquoise hair across the room catches my eye.

She's at the bar again, her back to me. My gaze instantly drops to her ass.

The blonde waitress blocks my view as she hurries to assist Damian. As he flatters her with a probably exorbitant tip, I check my phone.

I have a new text message from my head of security, and I open it immediately.

For sixteen days, I've been pressing him for a solution to my problem.

And for sixteen days, he's given me one answer.

Quinn Monroe.

Chapter 2

Quinn

I notice him right away.

The man in black in the corner booth. He's not even seated anywhere near my section, but from the moment I start my shift, he's watching me.

You don't miss a man like that. Especially when he's staring at you.

It's early Wednesday evening, and already Velvet Lounge is filling up with the after-work executive crowd; the wealthy elite and those who hope to meet them. The lounge sprawls across the mezzanine floor of Vance Tower, one of the tallest and most opulent buildings in downtown Vancouver. It's posh, expensive, and luxurious, and we, the cocktail waitresses, are an extension of the sumptuous decor.

I can't really blame anyone for staring at us in our tiny, black velvet shorts, and strapless black bustier tops. It's little more than lingerie.

But there's something different about the way he looks at me.

It's like he knows I'm just a lamb in disguise—because he's the wolf.

He's dressed entirely in black, a fine suit, no tie, crisp shirt unbuttoned at the collar. His brown hair is so dark it's almost black, too. His skin is pale, his features sharp, his lips lush, and even across the chandelier-lit lounge I can feel the force of his eyes.

"Ugh, he's alone now." The waitress standing next to me at the bar smoothes her blonde curls dramatically. "There is no way I can keep serving him. I don't care if he's in my section. I will explode in tears if he scowls at me one more time with those villainous cyborg eyes."

"So, make the new girl do it."

I don't mean to eavesdrop on my coworkers, but they're right beside me as I input a drink order. The blonde loads drinks onto her cocktail tray, sinfully voluptuous in her little black uniform. Her name is Alessandra, or so I'm told; maybe she'll tell me her real name once she gets to know me better.

We all have beautiful fake names in here. Mine is Dominique, which is weirdly exotic for a plain-Jane brunette with a passion for baking, even with the recent turquoise dye job. I'm told the fake names are to protect our privacy. But of course they're also because everything is a glamorous illusion in this place.

"Make the new girl do... what?" I inquire, sliding my empty drink tray onto the bar beside Alessandra's. Is she talking about Mr. Black? The man who's been watching me from the corner booth? He sure fits her description. Sitting alone. Scowling. The men in this lounge generally aren't doing either of those things.

"I'm sure he's an excellent tipper," she says, not sounding sure. "You probably won't ever have to see him again anyway. I haven't seen him in months. He, like, never comes in."

"Which really makes the new girl wonder why you don't want to serve him..." I say apprehensively.

"Did I mention he's incredibly, horrifically handsome?"

"Uh-huh. If you look past the villainous cyborg eyes." I bite my lip on saying any more. This is only my fifth shift at Velvet. I *am* the new girl, and I need this job.

"Owner's table," she says. "Don't bother trying to impress him. That man hates everything."

Hates everything...?

"Uh... okay. Which one is the owner's table?"

"Corner booth in my section." She picks up her drink-laden tray. "If I were you, I wouldn't leave him waiting." Before I can squeeze any more intel out of her, she hurries away with her tray of drinks, leaving me to collect my order.

After serving up the drinks on my tray, I walk through the room toward the corner booth where Mr. Black is seated. I didn't know it was the owner's table. Mr. Vance—or Daddy Damian, as the waitresses call him when he's not around to hear it—comes in a lot, or so I'm told. I've only met him once. He was in tonight, sitting at this table, but left a few minutes ago.

As the new girl, I've never worked this section.

I've also never felt so intimidated approaching any of the patrons here as I do walking over to *him*.

If he's sitting at Mr. Vance's table, he must be a VIP.

He's not looking at me right now. He's looking at his phone. He doesn't lift his eyes from the screen or show any sign that he knows I've approached the table, until I say, "Hello," and lean in to place a cocktail napkin in front of him.

He meets my eyes—and I almost jerk back. That dark look says, *Don't come near me.*

I think I startled him.

We stare at each other as my face heats. "Can I bring you a drink?"

When he finally speaks, he says one word to me, and that word is his drink order. "Manhattan."

His voice is sinuous and dark, like liquid chocolate.

Oh my god. He's so sexy.

Maybe the lighting is just that much more exceptional in this corner—I don't think so—but he looks about two-hundred percent more beautiful up close.

Moments later, when I've scraped my shit together and swing back with his drink, I find him typing on his phone. I can't help peeking at his phone screen, the object of his attention.

It looks like a text message, but I can't read it.

"What are you working on?"

He stops typing.

I've casually asked other patrons what they're working on, when they're on their laptop or phone. They don't seem to mind. If they don't want to talk business with me, they just deflect to something else. Often, they take the opening to flirt.

But when Mr. Black's eyes lift to mine, his prickling silence tells me that his business is not my business.

"I'm so sorry." And now my face is heating all over again. "I don't mean to interrupt you." When I put his drink down, I notice that the cocktail napkin has been moved directly in front of him, the edge perfectly parallel with the straight edge of the table. I didn't place it like that; it's so purposeful.

I meet his gaze again, and find myself struggling for words. "Uh, my name's Quinn, if you need anything."

His stony eyes seem to say, *Turn around and walk away, Quinn.*

So that is exactly what I do, feeling a little wobbly in my high heels. I shouldn't have hovered. Maybe he thought I was sniffing around for tip money?

Yes, I'm here for the money. But I've never felt so cheap about it.

At the bar, I stack cocktail napkins on my tray and try not to stare at him across the room. I just gave him my real name. That's a first.

It's also against the rules.

He just had me all flustered. It's because he's at Mr. Vance's table, that's all.

God, I hope he doesn't complain about me.

I wonder why he stayed when Mr. Vance left. And why he didn't have a drink in front of him until now. And why he's not socializing with the other patrons, or flirting with the waitresses.

And most of all, why do I keep feeling his eyes all over me, every time I look away?

I dip into the staff room to make sure there's not a huge piece of lettuce in my teeth, because I'm seriously starting to wonder what the man is staring at with such distaste. At least, I think it's distaste.

I really need to pull myself together.

I decide to check the group chat on my phone labelled *Squad* for a quick pick-me-up, and find that my girlfriends have been chatting. I'm the only one working tonight.

But there's also another message waiting for me.

Justin: Need you to work late tomorrow. Big catering order.

In my email, I find the cake order, which will take me hours to fill. The order came in this morning, and he's just telling me about it now? I'm sure I told him I was seeing the girls tomorrow night.

I pop back into the *Squad* chat and tell my girlfriends, *So sorry but I can't make it tomorrow night, have to work at the bakery,* with a wailing sad face emoji.

Which instantly gets a stream of replies.

Dani: NO. Full stop.

Nicole: But we never get to see you!!!

Dani: He better be paying you this time...

Nicole: As if you don't have enough to do!

I definitely do. And I so desperately wanted this rare night out with the girls. But my car isn't going to repair itself, and my landlord definitely isn't getting talked out of raising the rent next month—I've already tried.

I text back quickly to quell their worries.

Me: He's definitely paying me. There's a huge catering order.

Nicole: Is this about Lorraine?

A knot tightens in my chest. If it weren't for my incredibly ride-or-die girlfriends holding me together, I'd probably have fallen to pieces so many times over the last few years. But I've leaned on them enough.

Me: Mom is okay. Don't worry.

Dani: I'll stop worrying when you leave that man for good.

Dani is blunt like that, but I wouldn't have it any other way. I've known Daniella Vola for many years as the most confident alpha female in any given room. She's a total man-eater. Meaning she's everything I'm not, but need in my life. And I know she disliked Justin from day one.

It took me a while, but I finally see why.

Five days ago, when I woke up at his place at four-thirty in the morning to get ready for my morning shift at the bakery, his phone was lighting up in the dark on his bedside table. I went to turn it face down, so he could sleep in a bit, and I saw the text. At least part of it. I also saw who it was from. And all the pieces just fell into place.

It's so obvious now. That he's been cheating on me with that cute girl who delivers the chocolate. And looking back at his behavior... it's probably been going on for a while.

I don't even know which hit me worse—the cheating, or the fact that she's always been so nice to me. She even kinda looks like me.

Does she know about me and Justin?

Am I the only one being lied to, or is he lying to us both?

I know that a workplace relationship can get messy. That's why we've been keeping ours a secret. Justin said we should, to protect me, because I'm dating the boss and that might cause problems with my coworkers.

But maybe he just wanted to make it easier for himself to keep fucking around.

Me: I'll make it up to you girls another night. I promise.

Dani: It's not that. How can you let him take advantage of you like this?

If only she knew the half of it.

I was planning to tell my girlfriends about Justin's cheating in person, tomorrow night, because I know they won't take it well. I wish I could say that even one of them will be surprised to find out that he did me so dirty.

But they won't be surprised at all.

I really can't get into it now except to say...

Me: It's complicated.

Dani: You really need to quit. There are other bakeries.

True. But sadly, there's about a zero percent chance I'll quit *this* bakery, no matter how complicated things are between Justin and me.

Justin: Are you coming over?

I read the new text that pops up, and my stomach sinks. This is the first time he's asked to see me in days.

Because he wants to know if he's getting laid tonight, right?

I guess chocolate girl is busy.

He might as well have just said *Wanna fuck?*

It's a lot less than I'm looking for after spending six months with a man. He probably doesn't even remember that I'm working a night shift at Velvet on top of my day shift at the bakery.

There's no *Where are you, sweetheart? I miss you.* No *How did your day go? Can I take you to dinner?*

I text him back.

Me: Not tonight. I'm working late.

Then I message my girls again.

Me: Have to get back to work. Thirsty tippers. XO

Nicole: Go get it girl. And I don't just mean the tip!

She punctuates that with a tongue-out hungry emoji.

I shake my head with a smile and toss my phone back into my purse.

Nicole is a cocktail waitress, too, and it was her idea that we both apply at Velvet last month, after dragging the squad here for a girls' night. She was envious, I know, but not at all sore about it when I was offered a job and she wasn't—because the best friends are supportive like that. The tips at this place are insane, and she knows I need the money.

She'd also love it if some hot new guy—or three—caught my eye here, and I left Justin in the dust. Attractive men are Nicole's love language.

I wonder what she'd have to say about Mr. Black.

When I head back out on the floor, I run into Alessandra at the bar. "How's it going with my favorite customer?" she says sarcastically.

"You mean Mr. Black? Well, I'm not sure if he hates me and/or wants to eat me alive, and not in the good way."

Her eyebrow creeps up. "You don't know his name?"

"Why would I know his name?"

Pity flashes across her face. "It's Harlan, honey. Harlan Vance. He's one of Daddy Damian's brothers." My stomach tightens as her voice lowers. "The Vance family owns this whole building." She adds ominously, "And everything in it."

Of course, I know who the Vances are. They employ me.

What I did not know is that *he* is one of *them*.

I've only met Damian Vance. Until now.

I did not know that I just served a drink to one of my new bosses—and judging by his response to me, made a terrible first impression.

"So... why don't you want to serve him?"

"Isn't it obvious? He's grouchy as hell, ice-cold, and unbelievably arrogant," she says breathlessly, like she's majorly turned on. "He probably wouldn't touch me to save his life. I'm hopeless. Just keep me away from him."

"You can take table twelve, in my section," I offer. She really does seem stressed out. "Looks like they just sat down."

"Thank you. And if you're smart," she warns, "you'll stay away from him, too."

"You told me to serve him!"

She shrugs, like, *Sorry!*, and heads for table twelve before I can change my mind. I sigh.

Drama. Cakes don't give drama. I miss my cakes.

If only they paid better.

I swing through my section, stopping to chat with a group of men at one of my tables.

When I approach the owner's table again, Mr. Black—Harlan Vance—is watching me. His eyes look unholy black. That hateful smolder of his could burn a city down.

"My glass has been empty for five minutes," he tells me.

I scoop up the glass guiltily. "I'm so sorry. I'll get you another."

"You didn't ask me if I want another."

We stare at each other as my heart tries to hammer its way right through my ribcage. "Would you like another?"

"What I'd like is for you to notice that I'm sitting here."

I blink, astonished. "I did notice."

"Did you?"

"Yes. Of course I did."

His expression is unforgiving. His eyes roam down, linger on my little shorts, then climb all the way back up my curves. I'm steaming by the time they drag over my cleavage. It's like his fingers are all over me. His hot coal eyes snag on my throat, then my mouth, before meeting mine again.

"Bring me another drink, Quinn."

"Yes, sir."

I'm sure I feel his eyes burning into me as I beeline straight to the bar and collect his drink. I never call people *sir*. Even in here.

As I return directly to his table, he watches me approach. He's fixated on me now, and I feel the pull like hot, sticky glue.

What the hell is going on?

I lay down a fresh cocktail napkin, perfectly parallel to the edge of the table, the way he did it, and set his Manhattan down. "May I get you anything else?" Not *Can I. May I*. It's like I'm begging him to let me serve him. I don't recognize the needy tone of my own voice.

Or the thirst I feel.

His gaze flicks down to my hand, which I realize is pressed to the table. I'm leaning over him a little. Hell, I'm holding myself up, he's got me so twisted.

His eyes meet mine and hold for one excruciating moment. "Not right now."

I stand up straight, nod politely, and walk away to check on my other tables. Breathing deeply. He's not that intimidating. He's just a man.

A man who employs me and thinks I'm an idiot.

I need to keep an eye on his table. On his glass. Or maybe find someone else to serve him? Avoid him altogether?

Not only is he one of my new employers, he's a man-sized red flag. And that red flag reads: *danger*. The Vances are billionaires. They're powerful. My life is complicated enough without attracting the attention—or the animosity—of someone who could destroy me.

Mom needs me, and I can't fail her.

But when I circle back around to check on him, he's gone.

His drink sits on the table, barely touched. I find two crisp one-hundred dollar bills lying beside it.

"Thank god." Alessandra comes up behind me. "Is he gone?"

"Uh-huh. He left me two hundred, for two drinks." I show her the money. "He didn't even drink the second one."

"That's not for the drinks, hon. The Vances don't pay for drinks here. That's for *you*."

"Oh." I can't understand why he'd leave me so much after he reprimanded me like that. "Maybe he made a mistake?"

She regards my turquoise hair with curiosity. "Or... maybe the man who hates everything finally found something he likes."

Chapter 3

Quinn

"Mr. Vance would like to see you in his office," says the man with the haughty voice over the phone. "Can you come in at eleven?"

This is not good.

This is so, *so* not good.

Yes, I can come in at eleven. But hell no, I don't want to.

"Um, any chance we could reschedule?" *For, say, never.* "I have a lot of—"

"Mr. Vance is a busy man, Miss Monroe," says the man, now with an even haughtier voice, who identified himself as "Brant, calling from the office of Harlan Vance," when I answered my cell. "You wouldn't want to know the level of disappointment that would cause."

Oh-kay. That's terrifying.

I get the feeling that by *disappointment* he might actually mean *punishment*.

"I understand. Yes, I'll be there."

"Wonderful. Vance Tower. Financial office. Tell security you have an appointment. Don't be late." He hangs up on me.

I guess Harlan Vance's staff are about as friendly as he is.

I maybe shouldn't have answered when the call display said *Vance Industries*.

But what good would avoiding him do?

The Vance family owns this whole building. And everything in it.

While they don't own *me*, per se, the insinuation was clear.

The Vances have the power. At least, if I want to keep working for them.

It's Thursday morning, Crave bakery opened a couple of hours ago, and I'm in the back room, filling cream puffs with pastry cream. Or at least I was. I have my iPad set up on a stand while I work, and I've been chatting with Nicole all morning, too.

Now, I panic text the squad, *He just called me into his office!!!* And while I wait for their replies, I proceed to sweat about it while filling cream puffs and replaying my coworker's words from last night.

Maybe the man who hates everything finally found something he likes.

And my personal favorite: *If you're smart, you'll stay away from him.*

Believe me, I'm trying.

I thought it would be easy enough, considering he's a billionaire and I'm just a baker/waitress. But I had an unnerving feeling that our paths would cross again.

Maybe because my girlfriends seem so convinced of it.

Ever since I messaged them early this morning to tell them what happened at Velvet last night, Nicole can't seem to come down off this cloud she's on that Harlan Vance is going to get down on one knee for me. I adore Nicole, but she is desperately delusional when it comes to attractive men.

Dani sent me a detailed rundown of what to say to my

employer—any of them—if he threatens my job. There are a lot of colorful swear words in it.

But now that Harlan Vance has called me in for a meeting, I'm seriously thinking I might need them.

My plan to break up with Justin tonight after I put in that overtime for him—while asserting my position that I'm staying here at Crave whether he likes it or not, and I expect no animosity at work from him—has taken a distant backseat in priority to my growing worry that I made a terrible first impression on one of my new employers, and my job at Velvet is now on the line.

Fearing that I'm about to imminently get fired is somehow worse than finding out Justin is screwing someone else. At least I haven't seen Justin yet today. He hasn't even come in yet this morning, but that's not unusual.

For all I know he's sleeping in late with chocolate girl.

Finally, my iPad chimes with a *Squad* response.

Nicole: SQUEEEE. He probably wants to ask you out!

Damn, it's just Nicole. Again.

Me: Please. I'm his employee, not a Tinder match.

Nicole Lalonde is way too boy-crazy blind to help me with this. Dani said she'd be pretty tied up with a client today, though, so I guess I'm shit out of luck.

Me: I'm freaking out. He was supposed to be too busy with his very important life to remember the weird girl with turquoise hair who tried to read his text!

Nicole: You mean the dazzling hottie who crushed his will to live without her? Who melted his ice-cold heart into a roaring crotch fire?

Ugh. The ice-cold thing. As it turns out, that reputation precedes him, big time.

Not only did I serve drinks to a member of the Vance family—and piss him off—it had to be *that* member of the Vance family. The one who seems the scariest.

I don't exactly have oodles of time to dig into it myself, but Nicole has all morning, apparently, and has been alerting me every time she finds something interesting online. Which isn't much. It seems the Vance family is ultra private. Even Nicole, whose friend Megan is engaged to one of the Vances, and who was the reason I even heard about Velvet and the Vances in the first place, knows nothing about Harlan.

Except now that I met him and he tipped me two hundred bucks, she's fully on board with Team Harlan, if he wants to marry me.

My iPad jingles with another *Squad* message.

Nicole: Finally found a clear pic of his face. He's stone cold gorgeous!!

As if I didn't know.

Though Nicole is usually a pro at stalking men online, she's been struggling to come up with a decent photo of Harlan's face. In the rare few public images of him with his family or at some event, he's always way in the background, out of focus, and/or turned away.

You'd think he was a legit vampire, she texted me early this morning in frustration. *Like no one ever gets a photo of him!*

Now, she sends me a photo.

I click on it. And holy Christ, he's *smiling*.

He wears a dark suit with a white collared shirt, the collar splayed open to reveal a hint of collarbone. His arms are draped around the two people standing on either side of him. One is a dark-haired woman I now know is his twin sister, Savannah, thanks to Nicole. The other is Damian Vance. The two other Vance brothers flank them. Harlan isn't looking at the camera; none of them are. It seems like a candid shot.

I really shouldn't be feeling what I feel when I look at—and save—this photo of him.

I close the photo and get back to work, carrying several large trays out to the front of the bakery, restocking the display cases with filled and glazed treats. Then I get set up in the back room to decorate a new dummy cake—a fancy but fake cake that will sit in the window display. I change it out every few weeks.

As I take out some fondant and start kneading it, I have to stop myself from looking at that photo again.

I've already learned the brutal life lesson that dating your boss *sucks*. Because it gives him way too much power over you.

And anyway, I don't even know if Harlan Vance is single.

Nor do I care to.

I mean, Nicole says he is, but what does she really know?

It doesn't matter.

I am not crushing on him in the slightest.

How could I crush on a man who detests me?

The employees-only door at the back of the room opens, and Justin hurries in. His blondish hair is still damp from his morning shower.

I wonder if he had to wash her off of him.

I wonder if he feels guilty when he says, "Hey, babe," barely meets my eyes, and brushes a hand over my arm as he strides past me.

"Morning," I say as neutrally as I can, pretending to be

laser-focused on rolling out fondant. I was the first one in this morning, which means I got to set the music for the day. Thanks to my mom, I've got a sweet spot for the music of her glory days. But I'm deeply regretting putting on my *Lorraine Forever* playlist as the man who's cheating on me slides into his white chef jacket to the tune of Honeymoon Suite's "New Girl Now" playing over the bakery's sound system.

I pretty much hold my breath until he heads out front to micromanage his other employees.

Breaking up with him now, while imperative, will be even stickier. After what happened at Velvet last night, I shouldn't be doing anything to endanger this job. But I really can't continue on like this.

When my iPad jingles, I can't resist checking it. What if it's another photo?

Nicole: I can ask Megan about him for you.

It's not the first time she's offered. Her friend Megan recently became engaged to one of Harlan's brothers, Jameson Vance. But I feel icky about the whole thing.

Me: That's okay. I don't think even she could save me if he already hates me.

Nicole: Fine. Then just show some cleavage. Lead with an apology and next thing you know... you're getting railed by a billionaire!

I can feel her excitement through the iPad.
But maybe she's right about one thing.
Maybe I should lead with an apology.
I finish my dummy cake and check the time; it's almost ten

o'clock. The fake, three-tier cake is covered in a sleek flat-black fondant, and dusted with some edible gold leaf. It's darkly elegant. Manly, even.

It only occurs to me when I stand back and look at it what inspired me. It's not the approach of October and Halloween season. It's Harlan Vance. If ever there was a cake for that man, this would be it.

Too bad it's not a real cake.

On that thought, I slide the completed dummy cake into the window display, then head into the back room again to pull a fresh cake out of the fridge. It's a vanilla cake, already stacked, filled with white chocolate ganache and crumb coated with pale-pink strawberry buttercream.

I place the cake on my turntable and smooth it with more strawberry buttercream, to get a perfect finish, and nice, sharp edges.

While I'm working, Justin disappears into the small back office, without a word or a glance in my direction. I can tell he's in a bad mood. He's always stressed out at work.

I pull a tray of my signature buttercream roses from the fridge, these ones turquoise, and start adding them in a swirl across the top and down the side of the cake, watching the time as I go.

I pop my head into the office, to tell Justin I'm running a cake over to a client. He frowns distractedly, and I hurry out the back door before he can complain. I carry my pink-and-turquoise cake in a Crave-branded bakery box, and wear my cleanest white chef jacket with the Crave logo embroidered above the breast. I smell of cake batter and sweat. I wish I could shower, but at least I look official.

I've learned that even the grumpiest people get excited and open doors for you when they see baked goods coming.

It's three blocks from Crave bakery to Vance Tower, along busy sidewalks and busier streets filled with workday traffic. The drive in front of the tower loops away from the street to the black glass entrance, where the name VANCE stretches in gold above the triple set of tall doors.

As I approach the grand main entrance and glance up, I can see all fifty-six floors of the tower soaring above me, a spear of black glass thrust into the sky.

I enter through one of the glass doors, recalling how nervous I was the first time I had to approach one of the doormen, and show my ID for my first training shift at Velvet.

I'm way more nervous now.

Maybe because that time I was getting hired, not fired.

This time, the doorman sends me over to an elevator bank on the far side of the enormous, polished lobby. A gorgeous woman in yoga wear walks a well-dressed chihuahua past me and out into the sun. I know most of the upper floors of the tower are residential, and several of them house the head offices of Vance Industries. The lobby and sprawling mezzanine feature luxury retailers, a fine restaurant, and of course, Velvet Lounge.

When I tell the security guard at the desk by the office elevators that I have a meeting with Harlan Vance, he calls ahead to check that I'm expected, then presses an elevator call button for me.

The one that points down.

Once I step into the elevator, he presses the LL button labelled *Finance* for me, sending me down.

I didn't even know there was a Lower Level.

As the elevator sinks, my stomach lifts. I ponder the mindset of a billionaire whose family owns a majestic tower in downtown Vancouver choosing to locate his office in the basement.

The elevator doors slide open to reveal a small, empty lobby with dark walls.

As I step off the elevator into the enclosed space, I feel like I'm entering the underworld. A security camera watches me like a dark eye from the corner.

I ask myself for at least the dozenth time since I was called in for this meeting what the hell I'm even going to say to Harlan Vance. He has to be planning to fire me or reprimand me or something. Why else would he summon me to his office?

I don't know this man. But I do know he has power.

Which means he could be capable of anything.

I enter through the solid wood door in front of me into the office space—which is nothing like I expect it to be. It's bright and inviting. Past the reception area, a wall of glass separates the receptionist's desk from a sea of cubicles, the entire office bathed in daylight. The ceiling is transparent; it's the glass floor of an exterior courtyard above.

I can see people walking on it.

Like the rest of Vance Tower, this office space is beautiful and has probably been featured in architectural magazines.

Before I have a chance to approach the reception desk, I notice a man approaching me with intent from a single, distant desk at the far end of a long hallway to the right. I wait obediently.

Through the glass wall, eyes flicker my way with interest. The bakery box is drawing attention.

"Miss Monroe?" The man greets me. "I'm Brant. We spoke on the phone." He looks at the box in my hands. "And what's this?"

Might as well go with the truth. "It's an apology cake."

He raises a sharp eyebrow. "Well." He looks me over. "You

seem... sweet." He lowers his voice. "Let me prepare you that Mr. Vance is not."

"It's okay. I totally get it, and I can handle him. I've met him before."

What am I saying? I'm so nervous, I could pee. Right here. In the immaculate reception area of the gleaming subterranean financial offices of Vance Industries.

Brant seems surprised to hear that I've met his boss, and completely unconvinced that I can handle him, but leads me along the hall toward the single, imposing door at the far end nonetheless. This man walks fast. I hurry to keep up as he remarks on the nice day we're having. Somehow he makes even that sound haughty.

I'm too nervous to make small talk.

The door at the end of the hall is black. It's not encouraging.

Brant knocks crisply, then opens the door and leans in. "Mr. Vance, your eleven o'clock is here," he announces, then steps aside and shoos me into the room.

The door shuts behind me with a heavy thud as Brant abandons me here, alone, with Mr. Black. I mean, Harlan Vance.

He's sitting approximately a mile away from me across a cold expanse of gleaming polished concrete floor, behind a massive desk. His dark eyes meet mine like a switchblade opening, and my breath lodges in my throat like a wad of bubble gum.

"Good morning," he says curtly.

It practically echoes in here.

If it's such a good morning, why isn't he smiling?

I swallow the gob of trepidation in my throat, thinking of Mom. "Good morning."

I glance around with discomfort. This room is not bathed in daylight. The ceiling is a regular ceiling and there are no windows. There's a small sitting area to the right of his desk with dark, stiff-looking furniture at sleek angles, that looks like no one's ever used it. To the left, a wet bar is inset into the seamless dark cabinets that line the wall.

It's compulsively neat and pretty much empty. No art on the walls. No plants.

There's really nothing much to look at.

Just him.

I cross the empty expanse of the room toward his desk, my sneakers squeaking a little on the shiny floor. His gaze drops to the bakery box in my hands.

"Before you say anything," I blurt, "please let me apologize. For last night. I work with cakes in the back room at a bakery most of the time, alone, so I'm rusty with front of house service. But," I add hastily, realizing he could take that as yet another reason to fire me, "I've waitressed before. It was only my fifth shift at Velvet last night, though. I'll get better."

"Get much better," he says grimly. "Fast."

"For sure. I mean, I will."

He leans back in his seat, regarding me in sharp silence. Probably wondering why I appear to be delivering him a cake no one ordered.

I'm starting to sweat in my chef jacket. Maybe Nicole was right about showing cleavage; if I'd done that, maybe I wouldn't be overheating right now.

"Also..." I press on, determined to right my wrongs. "I shouldn't have given you my real name. I thought you were just a regular patron, so I should've given you the fake name I'm supposed to use at Velvet. It's Dominique."

"And who decided that?" His voice is low and resentful. "My brother?"

"Um, I'm not sure. The name was just sort of handed to me along with my uniform."

"It doesn't suit you," he informs me. And I swear I feel the touch of his gaze, his strong fingers sifting through my hair from across his desk.

Does he suddenly look thirsty, or is it just me?

I feel mildly panicked as heat starts to prickle between my thighs.

No. Damn it, *no*.

I am *not* crushing on my new boss.

I haven't even broken up with Justin yet. Dating one boss at a time is more than enough.

"You know what... this is really heavy. Do you mind if I put it down?" I edge forward to rest the box on the edge of his desk.

"What is it?" He regards it as if it could very well be a bomb.

"Oh. It's a cake. Here." I peel open the box to show him the lovely pink-and-turquoise cake with the words *I'm Sorry* piped onto it in turquoise icing. It is, in a word, gorgeous, but at total odds with the vibe of his sleek, cold office; the room and its furnishings are minimalist and masculine, and this cake is everything but.

I really should've gone with a black one.

"I work in a bakery," I repeat, feeling awkward.

Has anyone in history ever been less excited to see a cake?

Damn, it's hot in here.

Why did I think I could sweeten his opinion of me? What did I expect him to do, thank me profusely for the flowery cake he didn't ask for, and lavish me in promises of job security? Offer me a raise?

"Why don't I put it in your fridge for you," I suggest. I take the cake to his impeccably clean—actually, empty—little bar fridge, and set it carefully inside. "There. You can enjoy it whenever you like. It'll keep for a few days."

When I turn to face him again, his eyes are dragging over my white jacket.

Okay, wait.

That.

That thrill across my skin.

I'm not supposed to be feeling *that*. Not right now. Not here.

Not with *him*.

"The thing is..." I clear my throat. "I really like working at Velvet." Okay, just a small lie. "I'd like to keep working there." Truth. "I really need the job. And I'm afraid I made a bad impression." More truth.

His eyes narrow as he takes that in.

He emits the empathy of a blade, the kind that resharpens itself every time you withdraw it from its case. I get the feeling that if he reached out to touch me, he'd slice right through me.

I don't know why it turns me on.

"So you think I'm going to fire you. And that cake, it's a bribe?"

"It's an apology cake." When he just stares at me, I add "It's a thing."

"And what am I supposed to do with an entire cake?"

My face must be as pink as the cake now. "You could share it with your family? Or your staff? Or... your... girlfriend?"

We stare at each other for an uncomfortably long stretch of time while I wait for him to say something, I try to think of something more to say, and his office phone starts ringing.

Without breaking eye contact, he picks up the receiver and sets it back down, hanging up on whoever was calling.

"You're busy. I'll go." I turn to leave.

"We're not finished here, Quinn," he says in that low, sexy voice of his.

The heat that whooshes through my body like brush catching fire when he says my name is insane.

I take a breath and turn to face him again.

Right. He called me into his office.

Probably to fire me.

I kinda hoped we'd forgotten about that.

"Am I being fired?" I ask him. "I'm, um, just wondering if I should be contacting my lawyer." I choke out that last bit on Dani's advice. She was very up my butt about my legal rights this morning.

I don't even know why I bother. I don't have a lawyer, nor can I afford one.

I'm sure the Vance family's legal team would make dog meat of any lawyer I could scrounge up anyway.

"No, you are not being fired," he says. "Quite the opposite. You're going to do a job for me."

Chapter 4

Harlan

An actual half-minute passes before my words seem to fully sink in, and Quinn Monroe's brain rearranges itself around the concept that she's being given a new job to do.

"Oh," she says, looking stunned. "What?"

I suppose the last thing she expected walking in here with her "apology cake" was another job.

"You will meet my family," I inform her. "And you'll pretend that you're my lover, Darla."

I hear the words, but I still can't believe I'm saying them out loud.

If she hadn't signed an iron-clad NDA when she was hired by Vance Hospitality, I wouldn't be.

"But... my name isn't Darla," she says slowly, struggling to make sense of this. "And I'm not... your lover." Her voice cracks a little on that last bit.

I try to ignore the way her cheeks flame.

"That is what 'pretend' means," I tell her, deadpan.

"Wow. Can I sit down?"

"Go ahead."

She seats herself on one of the stiff chairs in the sitting area off to the side of my desk that no one ever uses.

My whole office smells like her now. Like a spring meadow and something faintly edible. Like cupcakes.

I've always hated cupcakes. Too sweet.

Her turquoise hair is twisted up in back, her eyes are clear and blue, and her lips are like succulent berries without a drop of makeup. She looks precious and pathetic, like something you instinctively want to protect.

Kind of like a scared baby bunny.

I don't know what this annoying flutter in my gut is all about. My breakfast must not be sitting well.

Ever since she walked in here wearing a chef jacket and sneakers and somehow looking even sexier than she did wearing next to nothing in Velvet Lounge, blathering apologies and trying to give me a pink cake, I've felt... *off*.

I concentrate on taking slow, deep breaths as I get up and round my desk. I stand in front of her, and she looks up at me.

She seems to be struggling to breathe right, too.

Maybe she really thought I was going to fire her.

Good.

"This is a joke, right?" she says, still struggling to digest the situation. "I saw this in a movie once. Demi Moore and the billionaire... *Indecent Proposal*, right?"

What a nice time to discover that she has a sense of humor.

I slide my hands into my pockets, a stance of calm control, but my fingers are feeling twitchy. "This is not about sex. I'm not paying your husband for a night in bed with you."

"Oh, good. You've seen it, too. Then you know how ridiculous what you just said to me sounds."

"I'd caution you to take me seriously."

She frowns. "Doesn't the billionaire lose in the end...?"

"I am not trying to win, or buy, your love," I grit out. "Pay attention. You will attend a family dinner with my siblings and I. All you have to do is pretend that Darla is one of your names. It shouldn't be a problem. You seem to have several of them."

"Several of what?"

"Names. Identities."

She shakes her head, confused. "I... what?"

"Your name is Allison. You told me it's Quinn."

Her full name, according to her employee file, is Allison Quinn Monroe.

"Quinn is my middle name," she says. "Everyone calls me Quinn. I literally only use Allison when I have to."

"You go by Dominique at the club."

"Because I was told to."

"And I'm telling you, your name will be Darla, for one night."

I can see it's sinking in, slowly. That I am serious.

"Why, though?"

"I don't owe you an explanation. I'm your employer. But," I force out, "I broke up with Darla and didn't tell my family. They've never met her. So, you're her, for one night."

That should be explanation enough to satisfy her, true or not. It's all I'm willing to give.

Maybe the undertone of this whole conversation is becoming clear to her. That I'm in control of this situation, and I'm not giving her a choice.

I'm not asking.

"But... how can you trust me to pretend to be someone I'm not in front of your family?"

"Because I told you you're going to."

"But if you call it a job," she pushes back, eying me like I might be some part insane, "usually there's payment involved."

"Your payment will be keeping your job at Velvet."

"Oh." Her voice is small when she says, "I see."

My eyes narrow as a prickle of something like sympathy creeps up my spine. I replace it with irritation. "If that isn't enough for you... I can assure you that I'll also keep your secret."

A dark, silent pause stretches between us, before she manages to ask, "What secret?"

"That you're sleeping with your boss."

Her eyes widen.

To my surprise, she doesn't even try to deny it. "Dating him, you mean," she says, with a note of indignation.

I slip one hand from my pocket and rest it on my desk, sliding my fingernail purposefully across the edge. Back and forth, back and forth, in a restless pattern. Spelling one word over and over in the back of my thoughts.

It shouldn't bother me that she's carrying on a relationship with her boss, when her willingness to keep secrets only contributes to the fact that she's the ideal candidate to pull this off for me.

But it does bother me.

Those surveillance photos of her and her boss at the bakery walking out of his apartment in the early morning, after spending the night together, bother me.

Finally, I feel in control enough to speak. "Do you think that's appropriate?"

She raises her chin. "So this is blackmail."

"It's respecting your privacy. No one needs to know that you're involved with your boss."

"Except the man who's using it to blackmail me. And I'm supposed to trust you?"

"I'll remind you that I own the bar where you just said you'd like to keep your job, and I just assured you continued employment. All I'm asking for is one evening."

"And now we're right back to that *Indecent Proposal* vibe

again," she says smartly. "But like you said, I'm already in a relationship. So your proposal is highly inappropriate."

"A secret relationship." I can't seem to resist asking, "Do your coworkers know you're sleeping with him?"

"*Dating* him. Secret or not, I'm not a cheater."

"It's not a real date. And he doesn't have to know. In fact, you won't tell him."

Her eyes widen again as she takes that in.

Then her gaze drops to my hand, where my fingernail slides across the edge of the desk in a restless pattern. I still my finger.

"If I do this," she says carefully, "I don't want it getting back to people we work with."

"It won't. Because you're not going to tell anyone about it, and neither will I."

"The dinner can't be in public."

I frown. "I don't do public."

"It's just one dinner, right? One lie?"

"Just one."

She's silent for a moment. Then: "Why me?"

"You need your job. I need this."

"Why, though? Who is this Darla person? Does she look like me?"

"It doesn't matter what she looks like. You signed an NDA when you were hired, and this is just another job. All you need to know is your role here."

"Which is... Darla."

"Correct."

"So... your family thinks you're still with her? But you're not. And they've never met her before?"

"Correct."

"Then why do they need to meet her now?"

I grind my teeth. I don't love the inquisition. But I need this girl to play along.

I just need to get this done.

"Because they've asked to meet her."

"But... it's over?"

"Right."

"But won't it bother them that I work for you? I mean, do you think that's 'appropriate'?" She serves my word back to me.

I don't like it. She's proving feistier than I expected her to be.

Was the data wrong?

My finger continues the restless rhythm across the edge of the desk, dragging my fingernail back and forth.

"It won't matter," I growl. "It's just a quick dinner. Then we'll 'break up.'"

"I see."

That's the way it has to be. After the dinner, I'll tell my siblings we're through.

Neat and tidy.

Why does it not feel neat and tidy?

Maybe because we're alone in this office, and I underestimated how appealing she would be when we actually had a conversation. She has backbone. She doesn't like that I'm making her do this thing, making her go on a fake date with another man who isn't that baker guy.

Maybe she's in love with him.

I've never been so irrationally jealous of a man I've never even met. But I don't know a thing about him, nor do I care.

"Dinner will be tomorrow night," I inform her, trying to stay on track. "I'll have a car pick you up here, at Vance Tower. Brant has your number and he'll let you know when to be ready."

"But I can't do it tomorrow night. I have cakes to prep for the weekend. I have a cake design business on the side, and I have a wedding and a baby shower."

I consider this, my finger pausing briefly then resuming the pattern, back and forth over the edge of the desk.

She waits for my response, her eyes locked onto me.

We're playing with fire here, aren't we?

Or am I just imaging the way she looks at me? With those wide-open blue eyes...

"We'll do it Saturday, then," I growl.

"I can't. I work at Velvet that night."

"I'll take care of it," I tell her. "It has to happen this weekend. All my siblings are in town. You'll still be paid for the shift."

"But I'll miss out on the tips."

"I'll make sure you're compensated."

"Oh. Well... okay, then. I guess." She gets to her feet, slowly. She's still eying me like she can't tell if I'm just dangerous or completely insane. "I guess I'll see you on Saturday."

"Yes."

She heads for the door, but turns back.

"Uh, what should I wear? I've never dined with a billionaire before, much less a family of them."

My gaze sweeps over her chef jacket, the jeans beneath. "What does it matter?" I head back to my desk. "You're not actually Darla. In case I wasn't clear..." When I glance at her, she's still watching me warily, and I force the words out. "After Saturday night, we'll never see each other again."

Chapter 5

Quinn

I'm working at the bakery on Saturday morning when I get a random text.

Unknown: Where are you?

I consider deleting it, but reply, *Who is this?*
When the answer comes in, I just about drop my phone.

Unknown: Harlan

Oh. My. God.
I'm not even sure why I text back an answer—What business is it of his where I am? But my fingers actually shake when I do. The level to which this man excites me is beyond sensibility. I try to convince myself it's terror.

Me: I'm working at the bakery.

He doesn't reply, but I save his number to my phone and label it *Harlan*.

There's something deliciously intimate about that.

I shouldn't like it as much as I do.

Luckily Justin isn't in today, because I'm stupidly distracted, and drop an entire cake on the floor in the back room.

Does this mean I can text him now whenever I want to?

Not that I want to.

About an hour after he texts me, a courier arrives.

Wear something presentable.

Those are the three incredibly daunting words scrawled onto the envelope the courier hands me. Inside the envelope is a prepaid credit card with ten thousand dollars loaded onto it.

Ten. Thousand.

That is a hell of a lot of money to spend on a dinner outfit.

I guess Harlan changed his mind since we spoke in his office and he said it doesn't matter what I wear.

So... not only am I getting paid for the shift I'm missing at Velvet tonight, he's buying me an outfit for this dinner that will cost more than my entire existing wardrobe. I guess he assumes whatever I was planning to show up in won't be good enough.

This *is* a job.

The whole thing suddenly feels so transactional, I'm disappointed and simultaneously pissed at myself. This man does not have a thing for me. He didn't pick me because he actually likes me.

I still don't know *why* he picked me; surely there are oodles of employees at his many companies who need their jobs as badly as I do, who could be paid, blackmailed or otherwise compelled to do his bidding.

But I need to remind myself that no matter how chiseled-ice-sculpture-handsome he is or how many times I've wondered since meeting him what he's like in bed—and if he wants me in *his*—that this is just business.

Business *and* blackmail.

I'm tempted to get myself a fifty-dollar dress and spend the rest on my desperately outdated kitchen at home.

But that would be wrong.

So instead, as soon as I'm finished my shift at Crave in the afternoon, I call Dani while delivering a cake to West Vancouver for a wedding reception, then hustle it back downtown to meet her. Dani is a personal stylist with a social media following in the hundreds of thousands, in other words, way more qualified for this task than a woman who buys most of her clothes pre-loved and as cheaply as possible.

I spend the next two hours just trying to keep up as my most beautiful and fashionable friend—who should probably be the one going on a date with a billionaire, quite frankly—stalks through Holt Renfrew, yanking designer items from racks and tossing them into my garment-laden arms.

"What does 'presentable' even mean to a billionaire?" I lament as Dani stuffs me into a fitting room for the fourth time and tosses in shoes.

"Oh, we'll make you presentable, all right," she mutters. She sounds lowkey pissed, as if the scrawled command on the envelope was a personal slight against her.

"I'm sweating so bad, I can't get this dress on," I pant, my voice muffled from inside the Givenchy dress that's stuck over my head. I glimpsed the price tag and I'm terrified of ripping it.

Dani helps me pull it on. "This is just him exerting control. It's a power play. Don't let him win."

Maybe she's right.

Maybe he's exerting control because that's just what he does.

Or maybe he's more worried than he let on about my ability to pull this off, and the clothes are supposed to help.

That finger thing he did, picking at the edge of his desk? It seemed like a nervous tic, but who knows. Maybe he had an itch.

I'm nervous as hell. It's not just the prospect of having dinner with Harlan Vance's billionaire siblings that freaks me out. Or the part about lying to them, pretending to be this Darla person.

It's very specifically the part about pretending to be *Harlan's lover.*

Maybe because I can't even seem to decide if I'm more afraid of him or intrigued by him. It's not on purpose. I can't help it if my sex parts are curious about the man.

The rest of me still finds him ridiculously intimidating.

And extremely confusing.

Though he ordered me to do this job for him like there would be no taking no for an answer, he was quick to accommodate my needs when I said I couldn't do the dinner last night. He respected my boundaries and my cake business.

Justin never does that. He seems to think my employment at his bakery means he owns me and my time, for a fraction of what I'm worth.

The panic is real and it's growing.

What if I actually *like* Harlan Vance? As in, want to bang him?

A *lot*?

What does that even say about me?

I don't know.

But I definitely don't tell Dani that he blackmailed me into this. Just that he ordered me to do it. Fine line.

I know I wasn't supposed to tell her anything. NDA and all. But come on. I tell my besties everything. I'll tell Nicole, too, when I see her in person; some things just don't belong in a text.

And like the ride-or-die friend she is, Dani proceeds to calmly assist me in procuring a new dress, shoes, lipstick, liquid eyeliner, a satin handbag, and finally, when she realizes we have almost five grand left, a diamond tennis bracelet.

I personally think the bracelet is a bit much. But when I express this to Dani she replies, deadpan, "Well, I think that your boss ordering you to lie to his family that you're his woman because he doesn't have one is a bit much."

We spend the remaining balance on a blow out for each of us, the two smoothies we slurp at the salon, and an Uber back to Crave bakery, which is now closed but conveniently close to Vance Tower.

Dani puts on "Love Is a Battlefield" courtesy of my *Lorraine Forever* playlist and does my makeup; while Dani couldn't give a crap about eighties music, if any woman truly believes love is a battlefield, it's her.

Then I get dressed in the cramped staff washroom.

When I step out for the big reveal, she looks triumphant. "You look gorgeous. Way too good for some spoiled billionaire boss." She takes me by the shoulders and instructs me, "Make sure he works for it before you serve up any sugar. You're too sweet for your own good, Quinn Monroe."

I roll my eyes a little, way more nervous than I want to let on. "I'm still in a relationship with Justin. Technically. There will be no serving of sugar."

Now Dani rolls her eyes.

I am in a relationship, but only because I haven't told Justin yet that the relationship is over. He didn't ask me how I'm doing, or how Mom is doing, the last time I saw him. Or the time before that. Or any of the times before, in weeks. I barely see him. He rarely takes me out.

All he does is call me over to his bed in the middle of the night, when he feels like it.

Harlan was right. We are sleeping together.

Rarely are we actually dating.

I used to tell myself he just doesn't have time because he's so focused on making a success of his bakery business. That used to be a good thing. Admirable.

I don't have much time for a relationship, either.

I keep telling myself I don't want anything serious. And Justin was the perfect casual boyfriend. Successful in my field, easy on the eyes, and he doesn't judge my music preferences.

But Justin has never given me a hot flash with just a look in his eyes or a lowering of his voice.

I've never lusted after him.

Suddenly, I don't know why I thought that was okay.

When did I set the bar so damn low?

I mean, maybe it's still low if I'm now lusting after a man who would blackmail me into a fake date with him, but we'll sort that out later.

I retrieve the cake I stored in one of the fridges, ready to go, then Dani walks me over to Vance Tower, hugs me goodbye, and says, "Remember. Don't let him win." Then she turns me by the shoulders and sends me off toward the gleaming entrance.

She definitely thinks I'm going to fuck him.

That this dinner is just a ruse. Foreplay. That he's inviting me to dinner with this fake-date scheme just to get me into bed.

I guess that's more believable than the real explanation.

As I approach the giant gold VANCE sign, a driver mobilizes from his post near the valet stand, and strides over to a black Mercedes SUV that's parked in front of the entrance. He opens the rear door and nods at me.

On second glance, he looks more like an assassin than a chauffeur. I think I can see his eight-pack through his suit. All the security guys around this building look like this; like they take their jobs very seriously.

"Miss Monroe," he greets me.

"Oh. Hi." It's truly pathetic how disappointed I am that it's not Harlan himself who's here to meet me. He's not waiting in the back of the car, either; it's empty. As I slide into the backseat, I wonder what he told the driver about me.

Though I don't know where we're going, I'm surprised when we leave downtown. From the sleek black glass tower we head southward, over the Granville bridge, straight down South Granville, then make a couple of turns as we wind into Shaughnessy. It's barely more than a fifteen-minute drive, but it feels like we're in a completely different world.

I've only driven through this tree-lined neighborhood a few times over the years, ogling the huge estates and mansions, both old and new, many of them walled-off and gated.

We stop in front of an ornate black iron gate, and it opens for us. Then we roll past the stone wall that looks like it's been there for a hundred years, and up the gently curving drive, past lush, formal landscaping. The house is immense. Old stone, a sprawling two stories.

Harlan told me our dinner wouldn't be in public. But I didn't expect it to be at someone's home.

The driver parks us in front of the entrance and comes to open my door for me. He offers to take the cake box for me as I slide out, but I prefer to carry it myself. It feels like a sort of security blanket as I follow him up the wide front steps.

The door opens from inside before we get there.

Harlan Vance has opened it himself, wearing a black suit and black collared shirt with a black tie. My breath lodges in my throat.

This feels intimate, too. Him. Me. Seeing each other outside of Vance Tower.

And in his home, presumably.

"Hello," I say nervously, when he doesn't greet me, just stares. I'm getting maybe one percent used to his staring. It's like he's too busy running calculations in his head to speak. "You live here?"

"I do."

I feel the driver ebb away, leaving us alone, as Harlan's eyes rake over me—from my hair, side-swept in a loose knot, and down my new black sheath dress, which features zero cleavage, a knee-length hem, and just a slight side slit. It's flattering, classy, but Dani insisted he hasn't "earned" anything sexier. I tend to agree with that.

"I brought cake," I say quickly, before he can comment. I'm not sure I want to hear a compliment *or* a critique on my appearance. Either one would just make me more nervous. "It's a vanilla cake, always a crowd pleaser, but it's layered with decadent white chocolate ganache," I babble, "drizzled in more ganache, piled high with fresh fruit, and topped with edible flowers."

"I didn't ask you to do that," he says warily. The man is more guarded than one really needs to be, what with all the security.

"It's just what I do," I say awkwardly. "It's for your guests. I mean, your family."

I step inside. He hasn't exactly invited me in, though he does step aside a bit in a suggestion of welcoming.

He closes the door behind me, shutting out the evening sunlight as I wander into the massive foyer.

The floor is gleaming marble. The chandelier above is vast, the lighting dim and elegant. A massive double staircase curves up to the second floor on either side. The house isn't modern and sparse like his office, but like his office, I can already see that it's masculine, meticulously neat, and clean. It's also hella fancy.

"Please, allow me, miss." I startle as a middle-aged man in a tidy suit appears like magic at my side. He whisks away the cake before I can recover.

"Was that... a butler?" I say, astonished.

"Of course." Harlan appears confused, if not slightly irritated, by my wide-eyed awe.

"Oh. I guess I was expecting more of a talking teapot situation."

We stare at each other.

I guess the *Beauty and the Beast* reference went right over his head.

I clear my throat, extremely uncomfortable, and look around again.

"My family will be here any minute," he says. "We should get settled."

He leads me into a formal sitting room off the foyer. This place is intense. It feels like a vampire lives here, except for the lack of cobwebs and coffins. It's still bright outside, but all the heavy drapes are drawn. It's like I'm in another world, or another time.

A place where the same rules don't apply?

Maybe it's okay to be bad in here, a little voice inside me says.

I'm pretty sure it's Nicole's.

The sitting room opens into a grand dining room through a set of wide double doors. I can see the table lavishly set for our meal.

The sitting room itself is dark, luxurious, and furnished like a relic lives in it. I wonder if some elderly but now deceased relative previously owned the house, because it doesn't suit a totally fuckable man Harlan's age. According to Nicole and her internet sources, he's thirty-three.

There's not one spark of life in the room, except—

"Oh, you have a cat. I love cats."

"I don't have a cat," he says.

"Um. There's one right there." I point to the petite black cat lounging on the fancy sofa.

Harlan frowns, and promptly shoos it out one of the French doors into the yard.

"What's its name?"

"It's just a stray," he mutters as he shuts the door, then draws the heavy curtain back into place.

Okay... it sure didn't look like a stray. Its coat was glossy and lush, and it was chilling like a little royal on the sofa when we walked in.

But Harlan looks stressed, so I don't mention it.

"Do you have something against sunlight?"

"What?"

"The drapes. It's gorgeous outside right now."

"Well, we're not outside."

We stare at each other again. So awkward.

"Let's prepare," he says tensely.

"Okay..."

"Dinner will be in the dining room," he informs me, as if I didn't notice. "We'll eat, and after dinner I'll have you driven home. My siblings won't be bringing dates. It will just be the four of them."

"Okay."

"Jameson is the youngest. He may seem like a flirt, but that's just how he is. Don't let it go to your head. He's happily engaged."

Wow. Do I seem that easy?

"Okay," I say carefully. "Uh... I actually know who Jameson is. My girlfriend Nicole is pretty close with his fiancée, Megan. They grew up together."

His jaw does this clenching thing that doesn't seem like a good sign. "You didn't mention that."

"I didn't know I should. I've only met Megan a couple of times since she moved to Vancouver this summer. I don't know her well."

"You haven't met Jameson?"

"No. I doubt he even knows who I am. But Nicole's the one who encouraged me to apply for a job at Velvet."

He glowers, and I can practically feel his brain processing this new information. I get the distinct feeling he doesn't like not knowing everything.

Control freaks are like that.

"I've never met any of your siblings," I try to reassure him, "except Damian, at Velvet, briefly. He might remember me. The turquoise hair is kind of memorable."

His eyes move over my hair the way they did in his office; like his fingers are sifting through it.

"It's fine," he says tightly. "As I said, none of them have met Darla. As far as they know, I've been keeping you—her—a secret. Which will explain why I didn't look at you when he saw me at Velvet, and you were there."

"You did look at me, though."

His eyes darken as they hold mine.

In response, blood courses through me, hot and fast. My skin prickles, and I take a deep breath.

Oh, boy. I *am* lusting.

"If Damian recognizes you," he says, diverting the subject, "I'll handle it."

"Okay."

"My sister, Savannah, is my twin. She doesn't like anyone I date. Don't take it personally."

"I mean, how could I? I'm not actually dating you."

He doesn't seem to appreciate my attempt to chill things out with humor.

"Graysen is the oldest. He's a stickler for the rules, so he'll be watching you."

"What rules?"

"All of them."

I swallow.

Am I really doing this?

"Any questions?" he asks.

So many.

"Yes." I have one incredibly burning question, which he never really answered to my satisfaction. "Why me? I mean, there must be someone better for this role. Someone else who could play your lover more convincingly than I can. Someone else you can trust."

"No," he says darkly. "There isn't."

Could this man get any more intense?

If he doesn't stop staring at me like that, and saying things like that, I'm going to get it all twisted, and start feeling flattered that he picked me.

"Well... can you tell me more about Darla? Like what does she do for a living?"

"It doesn't matter."

"It might help."

"Just be yourself."

"Is she like me?"

"I don't know you." His switchblade eyes sweep over me. "But I doubt it."

Yeah. *Me, too.* "What does she look like?"

After a moment's hesitation, he says tightly, "Black hair. Green eyes."

"Is she beautiful?"

"Yes."

"How long were you lovers?"

His jaw does that clenching thing, and I can tell he's impatient with the questions. "A while."

I try to imagine her, dark and sensuous and utterly lovely. *Darla.* I imagine her getting fucked by the infernal creature in front of me and my mouth goes dry. "What a lucky woman."

Shit. Pretty sure I said that out loud.

Yup. Definitely.

Harlan studies me, tilting his head slightly like I might make more sense to him that way.

Maybe he thinks I'm being sarcastic.

Wish I was.

"Uh, let's see." My cheeks are flaming, and I struggle for a topic change. "You already know I work at a bakery," I offer, filling the tense silence. "And I have my own little cake design business on the side, with my mom. I make celebration cakes, and she makes cupcakes. Like for weddings, baby showers, birthdays. Engagements. Reunions. Mitzvahs—"

"I get it," he growls.

Why does he look like he's reacting allergically to that list? Does he have something against celebrations?

"So... if you ever need a cake, you know who to call."

"I already told you. We won't be seeing each other after this."

We have another brief staring contest, which he seems to win.

"Right. Well, what else can I tell you? I live with my mom. I never bought a pair of shoes for more than fifty bucks before today, and I have a pretty serious addiction to salted caramel."

He looks confused. "Salted caramel *what?*"

"Anything."

"Why are you telling me all this?" He seems both suspicious and annoyed.

"I thought you might want to know me? At least a bit. Like, learn a few details about me to make our connection seem more genuine?"

"I don't need to know you," he says, his voice low and sincere. "I told you, it's just a dinner. I'll introduce you as Darla. We've been seeing each other on and off for a while. You like me or you don't. It doesn't matter. You can be as vague about our relationship as you want. I've always been."

"Oh. Okay..."

"Just answer their questions, be polite, and that's it. Then you won't ever have to see them again," he says, reminding me that I'm little more than a prop, stage dressing for the lie he's about to tell.

The doorbell rings, and he orders, "Wait here while I bring them in."

When he leaves, I take a deep breath.

I don't know why I find him so attractive. Yes, he's handsome, and he looks hotter than hell in a suit.

But he's a liar.

He's lying to his family. He's got a secret about this Darla woman, and he's going to some pretty extreme lengths to cover it up. The man is obviously a cautionary tale. The villain in his own fairytale.

And he didn't bring me here because he wants me.

It's not lust I feel in the air between us.

It's power. Ruthless, uncompromising, and total, drugging in its potency.

It's *his* power.

I tell myself there will never be anything between Harlan Vance and me but this brief, shady business deal.

But maybe I'm a liar, too.

Chapter 6

Quinn

"I always wanted a big family," I tell Harlan's sister, Savannah. "You know, lots of kids running around. A whole little band or soccer team."

I immediately catch my foot in my mouth and wash it down with wine, realizing that I might've just implied a desire to have "lots of kids" with Harlan. You know, my lover.

I glance at him. He's sitting next to me at the dinner table, watching me, and looking tense as ever. His jaw is doing that clenching thing.

This man needs a massage or something.

If he didn't want me to bond with his sister, he really shouldn't have provided so much wine. This is what women do. We bond over rosé.

"Well, how old are you, Darla?" Savannah asks me, sipping the rosé that she had the butler pull out from what I can only assume is some wine cave beneath this castle, after she asked me what I like to drink, and I told her that I'm a rosé all day type of girl.

"Thirty-one."

"Plenty of time for kids, then," she muses. "Just don't wait too long, if you want that band."

"Right. Better get on that," I quip, feeling bubbly. Even the dark clouds gathering over the man next to me can't dim my mood. Savi—as he calls her—and I are having a moment.

When he introduced me to his siblings, they all seemed to accept that my name is Darla, and we sat right down to dinner, quickly moving on to friendly conversation. His brothers are all gentlemen—way better manners than Harlan—and I find myself especially intrigued by his twin sister.

Maybe it's all the wine, but Harlan's family is kind of amazing.

His brothers are handsome, well-spoken, and intelligent, and Savannah is fabulous. She's self-possessed, accomplished, and surprisingly cool.

She reminds me a bit of Dani, actually, except warmer and more voluptuous. And with dark hair and a massive fortune.

I shift the subject away from babies, though, so Harlan doesn't have a cardiac event right next to me. His brothers are all listening to my conversation with Savannah, too. "What was it like growing up with Harlan?" I ask her, feeling his eyes scorching the side of my face. "I can't really picture him as a little boy."

"Well, aren't you in luck. I happen to have a photo right here." She slips a photo out of her wallet and hands it to me.

It's a photo of four boys I can only assume are Harlan and his three brothers. They stand in a row, facing the camera, arms slung around one another, oldest to youngest. Graysen, the oldest and tallest, has his hand buried in Harlan's hair, which is tousled into a dark froth. Harlan, maybe six years old, is grinning, his eyes pinched into happy slits.

They're all smiling. Damian appears to be in the middle of laughing.

It looks like happy chaos.

"You carry this around? Why?"

A small smile hooks the corner of Savannah's mouth. "Because I love them."

"Oh." My cheeks heat. "Of course." What a dumb question. I'd just wondered if there was some funny story there.

"And it reminds me not to murder them when they piss me off," she adds.

I smile and hand the photo back to her. "Brothers must be fun."

"Oh, they're something." She tucks the photo back into her wallet. "You don't have any?"

"No. No sisters, either."

"I always wondered what it would be like to be an only child. Hard to imagine when you're smack in the middle of five, and a twin, too."

"Overrated," I tell her wistfully. "I always wondered what it would be like to have lots of siblings."

"Overrated," she says, and we each take a sip of our wine, smiling at one another.

I like her.

A lot.

"What about your parents? Are they cool?" I lean in and lower my voice. "Or chilly like Harlan?"

She glances at him, and her smile turns nostalgic. "He wasn't always chilly."

"I'm sitting right here," he mutters.

Savannah ignores him. "What can I tell you? They wanted great things for us. They loved us the best way they knew how. They screwed up. We still loved them." She laughs shortly.

"Sounds like most families I know."

"Yeah." Her smile fades. "Dad died when Harlan and I were fourteen. In a helicopter accident. Mom remarried shortly after. She lives just outside of Paris. So, it's really just the five of us now."

"Oh... I'm so sorry. I know what it's like to lose your dad. I lost mine when I was seven. He also died suddenly. He was a tree cutter, and there was an accident at work."

Savannah softens. "I'm sorry, too. I think that might be worse...? Not getting a chance to really know him..."

"I remember him, a bit. But not much. I have all these stories my mom has told me, and now I don't know which parts are my own memories and what are the parts I've heard from her. The way she tells it, he was some kind of superhero. I think she wants me to remember him that way, but I have no way of knowing how much she made up."

Savannah takes that in. Her eyes flick to Harlan, who seems to be listening intently.

"I think Mom did something similar," she says. "It's how they cope. Can you imagine having to walk your children through the grief of losing their father, then have the hard talks that come when they find out he wasn't a saint? Wouldn't it be tempting to just put him up on a pedestal and be done with it?"

I get what she's saying. Mom did that, for sure.

But there's something sad in her tone.

"Who knew we'd have so much in common," I joke.

"Who knew," she says kindly. And she doesn't seem like she's joking. She gazes at me thoughtfully. "And who knew my brother had such great taste in women."

"Oh, wow. Thank you."

"Please. You should see the one he brought home last time. That was years ago. God, what was her name?"

"Chelsea," Jameson supplies.

"Yes. *That* bitch."

"Savannah. We're at the dinner table," Graysen says seriously.

"Oh, you know she was," Savannah says. "The way she screwed with Harlan—"

"We're not here to talk about that," Harlan says tightly.

"Okay, listen," Savannah says to me, unbothered. "I don't think anyone should butt into someone else's love life—"

"Right," Harlan grouches, throwing back wine.

Savannah ignores him. "I don't have much time, or much patience, for a love life myself. But Harlan's been existing just this side of Hermitville for too long now." As she speaks, I can feel the cloud cover next to me growing black. "I'd be lying if I said I wasn't getting worried about him. After what happened with that bitch—"

"Savannah," Harlan growls.

She ignores him again. "It's been quite a while now that he's been telling me, every time I ask him when he's going to leave his house and start seeing someone, that he's been 'holding out for Darla.' But he's always so private, I couldn't get anything more out of him. Who is this Darla woman who's seized my brother's attention? He just seemed so obsessed with you. That's all I'm trying to say. And now, I can understand why."

"Thank you," I say again. I know I'm seriously blushing, which is ridiculous, because I'm not even Darla. I'm not the actual object of Harlan's attention or obsession.

"Honestly, I kind of thought he was full of shit," she goes on. "You know, making you up, just to get us off his back. But maybe he really was waiting for you."

"Well... that's sweet." I'm getting nervous now, because everyone's attention has converged on me. Like, no one is even eating anymore. "And really, the obsession is totally mutual."

That's the right thing to say, right?

So why does it feel like there's a storm about to break right next to me?

"Really?" Savannah looks intrigued.

"Of course. Harlan is..."

I try not to look at him. I can't. I don't even need to. It's eerie how I've already memorized the angles of his face. I can even guess the look in his eyes right now. I can feel it. It's the same dark intensity with which he stared me down at Velvet.

"... deeper than you think. He's so attentive, so thoughtful, and he takes care of everything, so I don't have to worry about it." I mean, it's true enough, from what I've gleaned of him so far. If slightly exaggerated. "He's generous, and he just makes me feel special, you know?"

It's easy enough to describe a man I don't really know, actually. I think I just described the man I really wanted Justin to be.

When no one speaks, and Damian and Jameson exchange a look I can't quite interpret, I feel the need to fill the empty space immediately and exuberantly.

"From the first moment we met, he was just such a gentleman." Okay, now I'm laying it on thick. "How could I not want to spend my time with him? He's amazing."

Am I getting *too* into character here? I mean, I'm even starting to believe myself.

Savannah looks surprised, but amused. "You'll have to excuse us if we seem shocked," she says. "We actually call Harlan 'the beast.' On account of how warm and friendly he totally isn't."

Well, yikes. I can see that.

Maybe she's never seen any of the qualities I just mentioned in her twin. But she's his sister, not his lover.

Am I overselling this?

"So tell us, Darla," Graysen says. "How do you spend your time?"

"And now that we're finished eating," Savannah tells me, "this is the part where Graysen requests your resume. But don't let him intimidate you. He's not as difficult to impress as he seems."

"He is, actually," Jameson says, but smiles at me. He's been friendly, not flirty like Harlan warned, and I get the distinct feeling there's some sort of rivalry between the two of them. Between all of them, really.

"That's okay." I glance at Damian, who hasn't mentioned seeing me at Velvet. Maybe he doesn't recognize me? "I'm happy to tell you anything about myself that you want to know. I make cakes," I tell Graysen. "I actually brought one for all of you, for dessert. My big dream is to own my own bakery one day. In the meantime, I work full-time at a bakery as a baker and cake decorator, and sometimes I waitress for extra money. Recently, I started working at Velvet Lounge."

Graysen frowns.

"I was wondering when Harlan might mention that," Damian says slowly. "I thought I recognized you. You were there when we were at Velvet the other night."

"Oh, he was just worried about what you all might think," I offer quickly.

Why is Graysen frowning like that?

Is it just me, or is the whole vibe in the air changing?

"This is why you didn't want us to meet Darla?" Savannah asks Harlan, looking slightly concerned. "Because she works for us?"

"Isn't it interesting." Damian's eyes twinkle in a way that I'm not sure how to take, though an uncomfortable feeling is gathering in my gut. "She's an employee." The way he looks at Harlan, like a cunning cat with a juicy mouthful of canary, makes my stomach turn.

Uh-oh. Is this bad?

Yes. Judging by the displeased look on Graysen's face, it's very, very bad.

"Um, only for a few weeks now," I say quickly.

"So, we hired her well after you started sleeping with her?" Damian ventures, looking amused. "What a relief."

"Damian," Savannah warns as Harlan slides his chair back, getting to his feet.

What's happening??

"It was definitely after." I glance nervously at Harlan. "I mean..."

"Let's get that cake." Harlan takes me by the elbow, guiding me to my feet. "I'll help you." He ushers me through a door, the one his staff have been using to serve us all night, and down a long hall—then pushes me gently up against the wall.

"What was that?" he demands in a low voice.

"What?!" I whisper-shout. "I panicked. I didn't know what to say! Why didn't you jump in? You said you'd take care of it if Damian recognized me."

"How could I? You answered so fast."

"When was I *supposed* to say we started sleeping together?"

"It doesn't matter. Just stop talking so much."

"You told me to say whatever!"

"I didn't tell you to talk incessantly."

"How can I not? You never say anything!"

He glowers. "How can anyone get a word in when you chatter away all the time, telling everyone your entire life story?"

"I barely told them anything. And you told me to answer their questions!"

"Correct, I said *answer*. Yes, no. How hard is that?"

"Well, how does anyone get to know anyone if all they supply is yes or no answers?"

"They don't need to know you. They just need to believe you."

I take a frustrated breath. "And do they believe me now that

I totally stumbled over answering the simple question of how long we've been seeing each other?"

"It's fine. I'll just tell them you're nervous because you know that I've been hiding our relationship, and you didn't know what you were supposed to say. They'll just think you're covering for me. They'll believe me." He adds distractedly, wandering away into his calculating brain, "This isn't exactly the first time I've kept something from them."

"Well, I'm not used to lying. It feels weird lying to my employers, who I happen to like. Savannah's cool. "

Harlan refocuses on me. I'm breathing hard.

And we're standing really, really close.

Alone.

"I'm sorry." I try to calm down. "I choked. Damian just seems really interested that I'm an employee. Is it a problem that I work for you?"

"Yes. But it doesn't matter," he adds, when I press my hands to my face in panic. "Because our relationship is over after tonight."

"Maybe it doesn't matter to you. But are your siblings going to fire me now?"

"No. Quit panicking."

"Easy for you to say! You're a billionaire. And you still get a paycheck whether or not they believe your lies tonight."

Something dark and unreadable passes over his features. "It's just one little lie, Quinn. And it'll soon be over."

My heart is pounding. I take another breath to steady myself. He seems so calm. Irritated with me and my "performance" as his lover, but calm.

"They believe you," he says firmly. "You're overthinking it."

I press my eyes shut. "Okay."

I feel him as he shifts even closer to me; his body is surprisingly hot.

Just breathe.

"Your job is secure. You have to trust me."

"Okay."

"If it comes to it, I'll protect you." He adds in a dark voice, "No one touches what's mine."

Oh, god.

In a lower voice, he says, "I'm going to touch you now."

My eyes fly open. "Wh-why?"

"Someone's coming."

I hear the approaching footsteps as he wraps a warm, strong hand around the side of my neck, and cups my jaw with his thumb. He touches me like he's already claimed every inch of my body.

The reaction between my legs is extreme and immediate.

"W-wait. Okay. I just don't think we should—"

"Stop. Talking." His lips are at my ear, his words low and soft. Velvety liquid chocolate, pouring over my senses and down my spine, right to my—

"But—"

Then his lips seal over mine, hot and demanding, and the world goes dark.

Chapter 7

Harlan

Quinn closes her eyes, instantly succumbing to the kiss.

As soon as my chef strides past, pretending not to notice us, I rip myself away.

I retrieve her cake from the fridge in the chef's kitchen myself and let her plate it, just to keep her busy. And after dessert with my family, I see everyone out the front door. I need all the people out of my house. My siblings take off, and I have Quinn driven home.

I don't think about that kiss one more time.

I think about it many, many times. All damn night, and the next day.

And for many days after.

Obsessively.

She touched her tongue to my lip.

She licked me.

Tasted me.

You don't use tongue unless you mean it, right?

On Thursday morning, I go into the office early, as usual, but I can barely focus on work. The morning is half over before

I realize I've gotten little done. I stared at the wall through two meetings.

The only thing I hate more than meetings are parties—and basically any occasion that Quinn makes cakes for, including awkward apologies—but I've had my team book me solid with meetings this week. I'm trying to occupy my mind with work and other people's voices, instead of the incessant one in my head that keeps telling me to replay that kiss.

It's not working.

Alone in my office after useless meeting number two, I try to focus on the financial statements for Crave bakery that Brant placed on my desk.

Printed out on paper.

I've been avoiding the internet and every device I own, because the temptation to look at Quinn online or pore over those surveillance images on my hard drive is too strong.

I just want to forget about her, and my entire challenge. Move on with the next person's challenge. I keep telling myself I'll feel better then.

But Damian left town after the dinner at my place, and Jameson left the next day. Apparently, no one put much stock in the idea that I'd actually finish my challenge eleven days early. We can't draw the next name from the box until they both get back, the day after tomorrow, and we can all meet up. We agreed to draw each challenge together.

It's making me uneasy, the waiting.

As far as my siblings know, I successfully completed my challenge five nights ago, well within my allotted thirty days.

I introduced them to Darla.

Jameson even called me the next day to congratulate me more sincerely—and admit that he was the one who devised my challenge. He actually told me he was impressed that I came through.

But is the challenge really complete? I've earned my inheritance in my siblings' eyes—but at what cost? The challenge was completed on a lie. A lie that's much worse than the original lie I told them that I was "holding out for Darla."

Because what if they find out?

It's not the lie that troubles me, exactly. It's not knowing if it will hold. Or if my siblings will somehow glean that my relationship with "Darla," the woman they met at dinner, doesn't exist.

It's been eating at me ever since the dinner. I've barely slept. I can't stop thinking about the lie, the truth, the things Quinn said to my family at dinner.

Her.

I like things black and white.

I don't know why I can't stop thinking about this chatty, cheerful woman with turquoise hair.

I just don't like loose ends.

I run my thumb over the diamond tennis bracelet in my pocket, over and over. The one she left behind at my place, in the hallway, where I kissed her.

Where she kissed me back.

This bracelet is a loose end. But only if she asks for it, which she hasn't. I haven't heard from her. Maybe she doesn't know that she dropped it at my place.

I don't know if she'll reach out, looking for it.

I don't even know if she left it on purpose. How do I know what devious lengths a woman might go to if she wanted to see me again?

Wishful thinking.

I don't know her at all.

Her feelings for me, and how she'll deal with me or my siblings when she runs into any of us again—if it ever happens—are uncertainties, and I don't like uncertainties. Uncertainties are shades of gray, and they send my mind into endless spirals of *what if*.

I can't live with what ifs.

I need answers.

Clear data.

Facts and figures.

Not embellished desserts with no function but to overindulge the senses.

Even lies are better than uncertainties, as long as they're fully received. Believed.

Black lies.

White lies.

It doesn't matter. Black or white is always better than gray.

I decide I need to disrupt my spiraling with another meeting—before I break down and start scrolling Quinn Monroe's TikTok like a Gen Z with a crush—and have Brant call Savannah's assistant to find out where she is.

Then I stalk out of my office, heading straight for the executive elevator. My head of security, Manus, gets up from his desk and strides after me, diving into the elevator just before it closes. Maybe it's the look on my face that has him running.

He straightens his tie. "Are we in a hurry?"

"That special assignment I gave you?" I growl. "You gave me bad data."

"I don't see how that's possible," he says carefully. "The search was exhaustive, and thorough."

That may be so.

But the data *was* bad.

I don't care how well Quinn Monroe checked *most of* the boxes on my list. Do I have leverage over her as my employee? Check. Does she need to retain her job for financial security? Check. Is she willing and able to pretend to be someone she's not, to bend or break rules, and to keep a secret? Check, check, and check.

The problem is, there was that one last box that she also seemed to check, but fucking didn't.

Is she emotionally unavailable?

Big nope.

I was very specific that she was not supposed to get attached to me in any way, or want anything from me other than her continued employment and the paycheck it provides. She was not supposed to develop any feelings for me whatsoever.

This was not supposed to get personal.

But that kiss...

The way she looked at me after?

No.

I don't have time for this.

Manus is talking, offering to have our team run the data again, run more surveillance, find someone else. He doesn't understand that it's too fucking late. Because he doesn't know *why* I had him seeking an ideal candidate for some secret—and probably unethical-sounding—job.

I just cut him off. "Never mention this again."

"Of course."

"I'm meeting with my sister. You won't be needed."

I step off the elevator, alone, letting it close behind me.

The thing about Manus that I appreciate the most is that he does what he's told—with efficiency, and without questioning my orders. Security personnel who come from a military background tend to perform like that.

Which is why I hire them.

When I stalk into Savannah's office, she seems surprised to see me outside my usual habitat. I normally don't stray far from my office or my house. This whole Darla/Quinn mess is really fucking with the order of things.

"What a rare and unexpected pleasure," she remarks. "My twin brother, storming into my office."

"About as rare as you being in your office."

"I'm always in my office," she says grimly.

She is. But not in this office. These days, she practically lives in her new office over at the resort.

We're a block from the water in Coal Harbour, and through the wall of windows looking northeast, I can see the waterfront property where the Vance Bayshore resort sprawls, mid-renovation, just two blocks away. "Can't get away from it, can you?" I remark. I know she can see it clearly from the window of her penthouse apartment upstairs, too. None of my siblings are married yet, but my sister is definitely married to her work.

"Down time is overrated," she mutters.

I couldn't agree more.

I pace over to the massive vision board on her wall, where she or her assistant have tacked up hundreds of images, everything from bits of maps and blueprints, to sales forecasts and newspaper clippings, to color schemes and fabric samples. As Vance Industries' Chief Revenue Officer, Savannah's talents lie in sales, marketing, and revenue generation, but she recently took a step back from that role to focus on the resort's opening, and the gala that will launch it.

I don't think any of us knew how much the completion of the resort—Granddad's final labor of love—would take over our lives, especially hers and Graysen's.

"So what brings you up from the depths?" she asks me. "Don't tell me I submitted my lunch receipts too late."

"I heard you were looking for me."

"I was. Tried to meet with you yesterday. And this morning. Your team is incredibly adept at concealing your whereabouts and dodging my calls."

"Good. Then they're doing their jobs."

I don't know why she's been trying to reach me, but hearing whatever she wants to say—hopefully not that she can't wait for me and the chatty cake baker she met at dinner the other night to make "lots of kids"—couldn't be worse than being alone in my head right now.

"You lied to us," she says, shocking me out of the rhythm: I was starting to zone out in front of her vision board, picking at the diamond bracelet, spelling out the word with my thumbnail. B-E-A-U-T-I—

"About what?" A second after it comes out of my mouth, I realize that's not the most convincing denial.

"Her name isn't Darla."

Oh. That lie.

—F-U-L.

The next lie slides out easily. "It's Allison, but Darla is an old nickname." I wander over to one of the plush armchairs facing Savannah's desk and sit down. "She likes to be called Quinn, her middle name."

"Why Darla?" Savannah inquires. Innocently, I think.

I anticipated this question. "I don't know. She told me once. Something about... darling? It sounds like Darla, maybe? I wasn't paying attention."

Savannah laughs under her breath. "Sounds like you."

I am a proficient liar. It's not something I'm proud of, it's just a fact.

And my family is proficient at butting into my personal life, wherever they can. It doesn't surprise me that they've already done their research on "Darla." After hearing that she works at Velvet, Savannah probably had her head of security, Peter, look into her immediately, pull her employee file and her background check.

It's what we do. None of us trust outsiders easily. Which is why I no longer introduce my siblings to any women I might get involved with.

Just look at the disaster when they found out—before I did—that Chelsea was cheating on me. My family didn't stop gossiping about it until long after the relationship ended.

It's like they truly believe my love life is somehow their business.

"What's going on with you?" Savi scrutinizes me. "You're especially twitchy today. As you were at dinner."

I stop picking at the bracelet in my pocket. "So?" I say flatly.

She frowns.

Twitchy is one way to put it.

It started creeping in after the dinner, when I stayed up way too late going over and over the events of the evening. What Quinn did, said, wore, how she ate, the way she laughed. Was she a convincing Darla?

It only really hit me Monday morning when I found myself unable to concentrate on work that it was starting.

Or maybe it started when she walked into my office with a cake.

Or when she served me drinks at Velvet.

Or when I saw those photos of her sucking face with her boss outside his apartment.

Or when Manus first gave me her name, and I pulled her employee file.

I don't even know.

But I've been down this road before. Never over a woman, exactly. It's not about her anyway. It's about the lie she told for me, and my fear that the truth will be discovered. I think.

All I know for sure is that poring over information about her, looking at pictures of her, and even thinking about her is triggering the "reward pathways" in my brain, and—if I keep doing it—will become habit forming. Therefore, thinking about her will lead to obsessing about her, and obsessing about her equals literally overthinking about her.

It's a cycle for which *vicious* is not an adequate descriptor.

I've always thought of my obsessive disorder like a flesh-eating disease for the mind. If I'm not careful, I'll be losing more sleep to it, losing my appetite, losing countless hours of my life as it spreads, killing my ability to focus on anything else.

"So, Darla... Quinn... was rather impressive at dinner," my sister prompts, still studying me. Like she's waiting for me to go on. But what more is there to say? I've never felt the need to fill the silence in a room. And she was the one who wanted to talk to me, right?

"That cake she made was divine," she goes on. "I'd order some for the gala if the whole situation weren't so... problematic..."

Again, she seems to be waiting for me to pick that up where she left off.

I don't.

"She's very pretty. Well-spoken. Vivacious. And she handled our questions without breaking much of a sweat. She was... effervescent."

Agreed. She was far too bubbly for my liking.

I didn't ask for bubbly.

I didn't ask for Champagne, or worse, some overly sweet rosé with a cutesy label featuring a cupcake or high heels, the kind women bring to book clubs and bachelorette parties.

I thought it was obvious that I was looking for more of a straightforward chardonnay; not too dry, not too exciting.

I never would've told her to just be herself if I knew she'd be so... sparkling.

When she behaved more like a love-struck girlfriend than a casual lover, it messed with my head more than I'd like to admit. She made our relationship sound more serious than I meant for her to, considering I was already planning for us to "break up" immediately afterward. Hadn't I made that clear?

"You two make an interesting couple," my sister concludes.

"We're not a couple."

"Could've fooled her."

I struggle not to take the bait, but I can't resist. "And by 'interesting,' you mean...?"

"Things that you keep quiet about, she was vocal about. And things that you seem to be unemotional about, she was emotional about."

I notice she said "seem to be."

"And that is precisely why we would *not* make a good 'couple.'"

"You don't think so?" Savannah actually seems surprised. "I mean, even I was starting to buy into the act that you hate everyone. It's very convincing. But clearly, you don't hate her."

"I never said I hated her. But do I look like I'm about to commit myself to a hyperactive woman with turquoise hair and a sweet tooth? And make hyperactive babies?" I almost shiver at the thought.

Instead of laughing like I might've expected, Savannah frowns.

She gets up and walks over to the window, gazes out toward the resort.

"You've changed over the years, Harlan."

"I hope so. Haven't we all?"

She glances at me, arms folded across her chest. "Change isn't always for the better." She gazes out the window again. "We used to share a bedroom. And do you remember when we were about eight, Mom said it was time we had our own rooms? So we did. But then sometimes you would come into my room in the night with a blanket and pillow, and sleep on my floor? You did that for years."

"I remember."

"You did it a lot just before France."

She doesn't say *after Dad died.*

But we both know what she means.

"You didn't like sleeping alone in your own room, so she'd put you in with Jamie."

"Jamie flopped around too much and always woke me up."

"So you've said." She turns to face me. "You were much nicer to him back then. You were nicer to everyone. That was just before you really started hating school, I think. I was worried you were going to get kicked out, and we wouldn't be in the same school anymore."

"What does this have to do with anything?"

"Maybe nothing. I just never thought you'd be the brother who wouldn't tell me anything."

"I tell you things."

She scoffs. "That I've blown the budget on the gala, I know. You tell me at least once a week."

"It's a fact."

"It might be nice to hear the truth."

"About what?"

"About what you're feeling."

"About what?" I repeat.

"About Darla, for example. Quinn. Whatever you want to call her."

"If there was something to tell you, I would."

"Hmm," is all she says.

I don't think she could pay me enough to tell her about my love life, and maybe she knows it. I have more than enough money, for one. No one on earth has that kind of leverage over me. Or her.

I don't need to tell anyone anything. None of us really do.

It's better that way.

Black.

White.

"Isn't it interesting that she lost her father as a child, too?" she says.

"We don't really know each other very well," I say disinterestedly. I don't want to discuss Quinn. Everything I say about her is just another lie to my sister.

But I've been thinking about the things she said about herself at dinner, too.

I didn't have Manus dig that much into her past.

I wanted to know her present.

If I saw Quinn Monroe without knowing a thing about her, I wouldn't have guessed that the two of us had a thing in common.

Turns out we have one of the most formative events in our lives in common.

"Well, maybe you could've known her," Savi says. I'm not sure how to read that tone. Wistful? It's like she feels sorry for me.

"Meaning?"

Her shoulders drop. "Look, Harlan, I'm actually sorry you have to give her up. But you do know you can't continue a relationship with her, don't you? It goes against company policy."

I do know. But it's actually kind of a relief to hear it from my sister.

I've been flailing around in this gray bog of *what if* and uncertainty for the last five days, trying to come up with reasons to see her again and knowing that I can't.

"I'm aware," I force out. "And I'm sure Graysen would fire me if he could."

"It's not a joke, Harlan. Graysen is fucking *pissed*."

"So this is you being his messenger, saving me from a confrontation with Graysen?"

"This is me trying to save Graysen from a heart attack. The opening of the resort wouldn't survive our CEO dropping dead," she says smartly. "You don't seem to understand how much pressure he's under, and how seriously he bears it all."

She's right. I don't really want to see it. I have enough of my own issues to deal with.

But I don't like to think of Graysen struggling. He's our leader.

Our unmovable mountain.

"Well, you can all calm down," I say cooly. "No heart attack necessary. I already broke up with her."

Savannah blinks. "You did?"

"You demanded to meet her. Or rather, Jamie forced my hand, with the challenge. So, you met her. But we're over. I broke it off after the dinner."

"Oh." Clearly, she did not see that coming. "Well... that's some good news, then."

And now I feel guilty for lying to her, yet again. She believed me so fast.

But I expected her to believe me.

Quinn really oversold our relationship at dinner, but my family is used to me being secretive, antisocial. And single. It probably won't surprise any of them to hear I dumped a woman directly after introducing her to them.

Really, it's too easy to lie to them. They trust me, even when they shouldn't. And they definitely shouldn't when it comes to my personal life.

"I knew that's what you'd all want," I go on. "For me to end it with her." I keep telling myself that it *is* over. I can't have my lie exposed, my family finding out that Quinn is not Darla. It would only be dangerous to see her again. "But it was over between us anyway. She's not right for me. And now you can just stay out of it. It's done."

"That's good," Savi says carefully. "But unfortunately, it's not good enough. She also can't work for us anymore, Harlan."

I start picking at the diamond bracelet again. "What do you mean? I told you. I'm not seeing her anymore."

"I mean, it's bad enough that we hired a woman you've been sleeping with. She can't remain an employee of any of our companies. Graysen wants every trace of any connection between you two *erased*. Fortunately, Peter couldn't find any evidence of your relationship online—"

"Peter?" She had her geriatric bodyguard snooping on *me*?

A vein in my head starts to pulse, and I grit my teeth.

"Does anyone else know you've been seeing her?" she asks, ignoring my anger.

"No."

"Good. Then the last connection to cut is her employment with us."

I stare at my sister, willing the rage to subside, but it's only rising. "And how do you expect to accomplish that? We can't exactly fire a woman because I fucked her, can we?"

"No. But we can, and we must, convince her to quit."

Fuck.

This is bad.

I promised Quinn that her employment is secure. After she brought an apology cake to my office, fighting for her job.

And then I blackmailed her into lying for me.

I take a steadying breath. I can't allow emotion to override logic here. I have to keep control.

"That may be easier said than done," I say calmly. "You heard her at dinner, when she said she takes waitressing jobs when she needs to. Which means, she needs the money."

"She's a baker and a cocktail waitress," Savannah points out, unmoved. "Those jobs are abundant." She sighs. "And I've already had Damian arrange a position for her at the Crystal, to soften the blow. Don't be mad."

The Crystal. A luxury hotel in downtown Vancouver, with a five-star restaurant—which is not owned by us. It's owned by Damian's best friend.

I draw a deep breath through my nose and grit out, "No."

"Why?"

Because the Crystal is nowhere near my office.

Because I won't know when she clocks in and out.

Because I can't watch her on the security cameras.

The swiftness with which these facts come to me is disturbing.

"She'll be full-time as a baker," Savi says. "And she can sling cocktails in the bar, too. You can talk details with Damian, then give her the news. Phrase it like it's a promotion. If she wants more hours, a bit of a raise, just tell Damian."

"I don't like this side of you."

"Which side?"

"The one that gives me orders."

"Ha. I've been bossing you around since the playpen. Nobody tells you what to do and gets away with it like I do."

"Don't gloat."

"Because no one loves you like I do, Harlan," she adds, with a fake-sweet voice that makes my skin crawl.

"Don't overdo it."

She drops the sweet act. "Out of discretion, you should give her the message yourself. If you think that's wise. If you don't..." I'm not sure what the look she gives me is all about. Wariness? "I'll do it for you."

I scowl. "I don't need you to fight my battles for me."

"So you think it's wise for you to see her again?"

What the hell is she getting at?

"I told you, it's over between us. I'll meet with her in private, and get it done."

"And you're sure it's over?"

"How many times do you need me to say it?"

My sister stares at me for a moment too long.

Then she sits down at her desk, picks up a file folder, and drops it in front of me. "What's this?"

I open the cover and glance at the first page, where a few words grab my eye. *Crave bakery.* And my name.

I close the folder and dead-eye my sister. "This has nothing to do with her."

"I don't believe you."

"It really doesn't matter, does it? What Graysen wants, Graysen gets," I add bitterly.

"Are you going to talk to her," she presses, "or am I?"

"I'll do it," I growl. I get to my feet.

"Fine. The sooner the better."

"And what about Graysen?" I growl. "He'll stand down?"

"I'll make sure of it," she says. "It won't be hard. He'll trust you to be discreet, because the only one in the family who wants a scandal even less than he does is secretive, antisocial *you*. Just make sure she's pleased with the new job arrangement. We need her leaving happy."

"That won't be a problem."

"Good." She sighs wearily. I'm sure she doesn't love being in the middle of this. Or being the messenger. Any more than I love receiving the message. "Then never mention her again, and you know Graysen won't, either."

"Deal."

The thing is, I also need Quinn to be happy. So she won't ever feel the need to mention Darla, or the fact that I blackmailed her, again.

But fuck the Crystal. I'll arrange a new job for her where I don't have to worry about Graysen's rules, and it will go without saying that I could take it away. She'll know I still have the upper hand.

I'll make sure she knows that it's in her best interest to take the new job and run.

And I'll still have control.

I pick at the diamond bracelet in my pocket as I leave Savannah's office.

I'd planned to leave no loose ends with Quinn after our dinner, so none of this could ever come back to fuck me. That plan meant never seeing Quinn again.

But now I have to.

One last time.

I need to handle this quick, keep it professional, and get it over with, then put the whole thing behind me. Then I really won't see her again, which I keep telling myself is what I want.

I don't like loose ends. Relationships are all or nothing, and all is way too messy. I prefer to be alone.

And I don't need these incessant thoughts of her.

By tonight, I'll have cut all ties with her; severed all loose ends.

Black.

White.

I'll kill this budding obsession when I see her one last time, and I'll give her back her bracelet.

And my family will never find out the truth about Darla.

Chapter 8

Quinn

I'm deep in my *Lorraine Forever* playlist, ridiculously dance-mopping the floor of the bakery to Gino Vannelli's "Black Cars" like a woman who thinks she's completely alone, when I realize that I am not.

Because the front door is open, and a dark figure is standing in it. Staring at me.

I shriek.

The music is so loud, I didn't even hear the electronic jingle that signals the front door opening. Or notice the man in black who opened it to watch me dance-mop. Like a freaking stalker.

It's Harlan Vance.

He frowns at me, and my stomach twists into a hungry little knot.

I slap at my phone, which is sitting on the counter, to shut the music off. It's Thursday afternoon, the bakery just closed, and I'm the only one still in. How did he even know I was here?

I haven't seen him or heard from him since dinner at his place on Saturday night. I really never expected to see him again. But maybe some small part of me knew—or at least hoped—that I would.

As he lets the door shut behind himself, he scowls at the *Sorry We're Half-Baked, Please Come Again* sign.

"Cute sign," he says, like the sign is not cute at all.

Justin thinks it's cute. I told him it sounds like we're getting stoned in the back room. I can see Harlan agrees.

"My boss picked it out," I say, heart thudding, as I move to lock the door behind him. I thought I already locked it.

Our eyes connect.

We're now standing way too close for a super hot boss and an employee he blackmailed and then kissed who are suddenly alone together in a room. Yet neither of us backs away.

"You mean your other boss," he growls, in a low, displeased voice.

"I mean the man I'm seeing."

Unfortunately, that's still present tense. Technically. Though to my girlfriends' delight, it's about to become past tense, officially. They all know about Justin's cheating by now. He still hasn't said a word to me about chocolate girl, or made any attempt to repair the broken state of our relationship. In fact, he seems grossly oblivious to it. So, I've decided to put my big girl panties on and tell him that it's over. Tonight.

He's swinging by to pick me up soon. He thinks we're going on a date—a date that I insisted we go on, to a decent restaurant. Which means he probably thinks he's getting laid afterwards. It was the only way I could ensure he'd show up, the man has been so tuned out lately.

None of which is Harlan Vance's business.

"What are you doing here?" I ask him warily. "I have dinner plans."

He wanders around the bakery, and even looks into the back room, like he owns the place.

While I stare, unfairly fascinated with his every move—wolfish, predatory, commanding—in that black suit.

"Yes... I see life is good." His eyes drag over the mop handle that's still in my hand, with what I think is resentment.

"What, this?" I tip my chin up. "It's called making lemonade." I tuck the mop away, embarrassed, but clinging to my dignity, and trying to appear unfazed that he caught me dancing with it.

I have every right to try to make lemonade out of the lemons I've been dealt lately. I don't have to justify it to him.

The truth is, it's been a sucky month, the highlight of which was dinner at his place. I have to admit that I kind of liked what happened that night with his family, when we pretended to be lovers.

It was a nice fantasy for a few hours.

So, yeah.

Sucky.

"Are you here alone?" he asks me, frowning as he completes his nosy lap of the place.

"Yes. Why?"

"You should turn the volume down when you're working alone."

"Good idea. I wouldn't want any overstepping employers creeping up on me."

His frown deepens. But what can I say? Ever since he kissed me at dinner, then ignored me through dessert, then rushed me the hell out of his house—after I did everything he told me to do, against my better morals—I'm feeling pretty over his whole just-do-whatever-I-say-because-I'm-your-employer thing.

Or maybe I just didn't like it that he told me—repeatedly—that we'd never see each other again.

I don't like this feeling, either, that I don't *want* to never see him again. I know I'm in danger of wanting too much, things I can't have, with this man. I feel drawn to him, and I don't know what to do about it—except never see him again.

"We need to talk," he informs me.

"Yeah. We probably do." I take a breath. "I feel like we should clarify things."

His eyes narrow. "What things?"

"I appreciate what you did, promising me that I can keep my job at Velvet. But we can't see each other."

"I realize that." He adjusts his collar, like it's too tight, but it's already unbuttoned. "I told you that."

"I just wanted to be clear. Because it felt like there was something left unfinished between us..."

"Like what?"

Just say it. "Well... it felt like you *wanted* to kiss me."

His eyes darken hotly. "Yes. And you kissed me back."

"You pressed me up against a wall!"

"You used your tongue." His heated gaze drops to my lips, and stays there.

I clamp my mouth shut.

Okay... I did not expect him to bring that up.

And who can remember whose tongue did what? It was hot and wet and *fucking good*, and how was I supposed to keep track of such things?

I turn away, trying to gather myself, then turn back. "Do you have any idea how freaked out I was to find out that I'm not *allowed* to be involved with you? You knew that, and you still introduced me to your family as your lover. You could've warned me."

"Yes. And you could've read your employment package, and the contract you signed."

"Yeah. I guess I could've."

I mean, I did. Mostly. That contract was *thick*.

I guess I can see why now. Life lesson learned.

"And that is why you need to quit," he says.

"Uh... pardon me?"

"Let's sit down." He pulls down one of the chairs that are turned up on the tables, then another, and waits for me to sit. I slide into a chair nervously.

What is this new flex? He's here to tell me that kiss meant nothing to him? That it was just some kind of test, which I failed... and now I've lost my job, because I broke the rules?

I try to bite my tongue as he sits down, but I can't. "Couldn't you have just fired me in the first place, if that was where this was always headed, and saved me the trouble of lying to your family?"

His jaw clenches. I suppose he doesn't appreciate my tone. "That wasn't where this was headed. But my family isn't comfortable with our relationship, even though I told them it's over now. Which is why I got you a new job."

"What new job?" I ask skeptically.

"A better job. At an exclusive private club that I do not own."

"That is not what we agreed on."

"I know. But we both know this is what's best. You and I..." His gaze snags on my lips again. "We can't be a thing."

My heart thumps wildly. He feels it too, is that what he's saying?

This dark, sweet, sticky pull between us...

Nope. I am not getting side-tracked here. I don't care how hot he is.

Or how delicious he tastes.

Stand your ground.

"So now I'm being punished, because I broke the rules and slept with you? You're the one in the position of power. And it's not even true! And *you* kissed *me*."

"It's a better job," he repeats.

"You said you'd protect me!"

"And this is me, protecting you," he says calmly.

"How can I trust you? You already made me a promise, that I could keep the job at Velvet."

"You want this job," he says simply. "It means a pay raise."

Okay, I'd love to tell him where to go right now. But, shit. I'm curious.

"What private club is it?"

"I can't tell you until you're officially hired and you sign the NDA. *That* private."

I don't want to be intrigued. *I am not intrigued.*

So he's connected to other business owners in town. Who are probably just like him. Bossy. Manipulating. Endowed with big-dick energy and out-of-control god complexes. Thinking they can just walk into your life and tell you what to do...

"You know, you can't just control other people's lives like some puppet master."

"Can't I?" he says flatly.

"No. You can't. And just because you're handsome doesn't mean you can demand whatever you want from a woman, and expect to get it."

He stares at me, and I stare right back, unflinching, even as my cheeks heat.

"So you don't want the job. Would you rather find your own new job?"

Ugh. *I am not daunted by the prospect of job searching right now.*

Yes, yes I am. And by his tone of voice, he knows it.

"That's not what I said."

"Good. You seem like a smart girl. Which means you understand that this is the best job offer you're going to get."

"Woman. You mean, I'm a smart woman."

"Did I mention that you can set your own wage? Within reason."

I'm not intrigued, I'm stunned. "How does that work? Who owns this club?"

"My brother Damian owns it. Just him," he clarifies. "No one else in my family, including me."

Okay, so I'm intrigued, just a bit. "And it pays even better than Velvet?"

"Yes."

"So what's the catch?"

"There is none. The job is already yours. But you do have to quit working for Vance Industries. To protect us both. Then we'll just pretend that this"—his gaze rakes over me, like he's trying not to look, but can't help it—"never happened."

I don't know what to do with that look.

He's pushing me away. But maybe he doesn't want to?

I wonder if he thinks he needs to.

"Are you getting rid of me because you made me lie to your family, and you think I might tell them? Like, if I you piss me off enough?"

He glowers at me.

"For the record, I would never hold it over you like that," I tell him honestly. "That's called blackmail. And it's not a nice thing to do."

We stare at each other in silence. For way too long.

I can't quite tell if he wants to strangle me or kiss me.

Then he abruptly breaks the spell. "My office will be in touch, to connect you with your new employers." He starts to rise.

"I'm just wondering..."

He stops. He doesn't ask what I'm wondering. He looks annoyed. But he settles back into his seat. "Yes?"

"If I don't work for you anymore," I say, "then it wouldn't matter if we're in a relationship."

"We're not."

"Right. Because I'm not Darla."

His jaw does that clenching thing. "I'm not with Darla. I told you, that's over."

"So, you're single."

He stares at me, but he doesn't answer.

Justin is going to be here soon. I have a relationship to end, and a busy day tomorrow that involves working for my ex. I really don't have any time or energy for Harlan Vance and all his red flags, which only seem to multiply every time I see him.

I don't know why I don't just tell him to leave.

Instead, I say, "My coworker Alessandra is deeply into you."

"I'm not sure what you expect me to say to that."

"Why don't you like her?"

"I don't know who that is. Nor do I care to."

"How did you meet Darla?"

"My private life is just that. *Private.*"

"And yet you let me into it."

"No. I did not."

"Really? How many people know the truth about Darla?"

His frown deepens. "I suppose... just you."

"And why is that, again?"

He considers me for a moment. "You want to know why I chose you."

"Yes. I really do."

"You won't like the truth."

I sigh, fucking tired. I was up at four this morning, worked overtime, and I still have a floor to finish mopping, a boss to break up with, groceries to pick up, and laundry to do. "I'm a grown-ass woman, Harlan Vance. I can take it."

"Okay. I chose you because you needed it. Because you're taking care of a loved one who's unwell."

His words hit me like a punch in the gut.

"And I chose you because you have an impeccable work ethic. But your other ethics are... questionable," he finishes.

"Wow. You don't pull punches, do you?"

I get up, turn my back to him, and walk over to one of the display cases. I press my hands to the cool glass surface, trying to stabilize myself, as anger and something like humiliation flood my veins, hot and kind of nauseating.

It feels like he just opened me up and looked inside.

The fact that he used my need to care for Mom... to manipulate me...

I turn to him as he gets up and walks slowly toward me. "But... how did you know anything about me?"

"I had my staff search our employee database," he says calmly, "to find an employee who met the specific criteria I gave them."

I seriously can't believe what I'm hearing.

Who does that?

Oh, right. A man with a serious god complex.

"You told them to find you a fake lover to accompany you to a family dinner?"

"No. I told them to find someone who needed to keep her job, badly, so I have leverage. And someone who would be able to do what I needed her to do. Your situation at home, your secret relationship with your boss, and the fact that you already go by different names made you an ideal candidate."

"And how did you know," I say quietly, "that I was in a relationship with my boss? Or that my mom is sick?"

"Surveillance."

I almost choke on my next words, I'm so shocked. "And is that how you find all your dates? You just go shopping in the employee database? Then stalk them? What a disgusting abuse of power."

He tilts his head, regarding me for a moment. "You find me disgusting. Is that it?"

"Is that... what?"

His eyes burn as they hold mine. "The reason you don't want to see me again."

And I just say it. Because at this point, what does it matter? I can't lose my job anymore. He's not my boss anymore if he's already forced me out. "I didn't say I don't want to see you again." It's barely a whisper.

"I didn't say that either," he growls, and a shiver runs down my spine.

Jesus Christ. This man has me spinning in circles. He wants me? But he can't have me. Is that what it comes down to?

And he still chose me to pretend to be his fake lover.

And put my job in jeopardy.

After running *surveillance* on me.

"That's why you came into Velvet while I was working. You knew who I was. You were watching me. Stalking me. Deciding if I was *the* ideal candidate."

"Yes," he says. Not a trace of shame.

"And was I?"

He frowns. "No, as it turns out."

I laugh humorlessly. "You would've preferred someone who doesn't talk back so much?" I guess.

"I would've preferred someone who doesn't interest me so much."

Oh... *no.*

This is so fucked up.

He stares at me like he doesn't know what the fuck to do with me.

The feeling is mutual.

He made it clear we can't be together. But he just came in here to personally offer me an even better job than the one I have at Velvet, and if I'm totally honest with myself, I'm getting this gooey, dangerous feeling that maybe he actually cares. Like maybe he's not just here to cover his own ass.

Maybe he's really looking out for me, too. Protecting me, like he said he would.

Maybe he even likes me a little.

And if he does... what do I do with that?

Maybe I'm just desperate to know what it feels like to have a man look out for me because it's never happened before. But I definitely don't hate it.

Just standing here talking to him about how I *interest* him, yet we're not going to have a relationship, is more exciting than the last six months I've spent dating Justin. Having sex with Justin. Waking up next to Justin...

I barely even know this man, but it strikes me as the electricity crackles between us that I don't really know Justin, either. He never really let me know him.

That man is married to his work, and he has no room for a woman in his life.

He's so much like me. Too much like me.

Why didn't I see it until now?

I seriously have the worst man picker.

For example, the man standing in front of me. Nothing but a bad idea, right? And yet I can't stop thinking it.

What if I really never see him again?

"So... when do I quit Velvet?"

"Right now."

I can see he's not kidding.

"Well, when do I start at the new place?"

"Whenever you want to. Day shifts, evenings, whatever you like."

"I can't work days. I work here at the bakery six days a week."

"Not anymore."

Dread seeps into my gut. "What do you mean?"

"I told you, you can't work for Vance Industries anymore. Which means you need to quit Velvet, and quit Crave, too."

"But your family doesn't own this bakery. Justin does."

Harlan makes a disgusted sound. "I don't know what he's been telling you, Quinn, but clearly he hasn't told you the news. As of three days ago, your lover boy sold this bakery. To me."

Chapter 9

Quinn

I slide into my dress and zip up the back, getting ready for my final date with Justin in the staff washroom of the bakery. It's a cotton candy color, a fun, strapless bouffant with a poofy chiffon skirt. I got it for a party years ago, and pull it out sometimes when I need a mood lifter.

I swipe on a matching pink lipstick.

I'm definitely in a mood right now.

Outwardly, I'm calm and collected, which I need to be for this conversation. My plan is to respectfully tell Justin, over dinner, that our relationship... situationship? Whatever the hell it's really been between us... is over.

Which is more than he did for me.

Instead, he let our connection—and the promises he made to me—fade into oblivion, without telling me.

I doubt I'll even ask him about chocolate girl. But I do want answers. I need to confront him about what Harlan told me.

That Harlan and his family now own Crave bakery. That the transaction was finalized days ago.

Meanwhile, Justin never even mentioned to me that he was thinking about selling it.

I'm angry, because I'm hurt. Justin knows how important my job at Crave is to me; how essential it is to my own cake design business, Quinn's Cakes. He'd even talked about promoting me to management. Did he even consider how selling the bakery might impact me?

He owned it, so it was his to sell. But he could've at least given me the respect and compassion of a heads up.

Didn't I deserve that much from all the times I kissed him, shared a bed with him, encouraged and supported him in his business? I was decent to him, even if I wasn't his dream girl.

Fuck. I just need to keep calm.

I can't let this turn ugly. I can't afford to burn any bridges with the man who employed me for the last eight months. I might need him for the glowing reference I surely deserve after the work I've done for him.

But inside, I'm crushed. Because all my carefully laid plans of the last few years are threatening to unravel. All the shit jobs, working my way up to ones that at least pay better, and afford me the slightest chance to actually achieve my dream of owning my own bakery one day.

I couldn't bring myself to explain my whole situation to Harlan, beg for my job here, because why bother? I can't work here anymore. He made that clear.

Because his family thinks I fucked him.

The whole thing is humiliating.

If I actually had slept with him, maybe there would've been some kind of twisted silver lining in all of this, at least.

As it is, the whole mess just feels like a disaster of my own making.

Maybe Harlan screwed me over, without meaning to, when he dragged me into his personal shit, but I'm the one who made the mistake of counting on Justin when I shouldn't have.

Ultimately, I screwed myself.

I leave the staff washroom at Crave for the last time, and walk through the bakery, past the table where Harlan and I talked just half an hour ago. I wonder how we looked, drawn together across the table like a couple of magnets. Our attraction seems undeniable at this point, but futile.

A cruel joke.

It's just past six o'clock when I step outside, but Justin isn't here yet. Of course, he's late. I sit down on one of the wooden benches in front of the bakery to wait.

I'm still waiting at six fifteen, and decide to text him. *Are you coming?*

A few minutes later, while scanning traffic for Justin's car, I notice the black Mercedes SUV that's parked in front of the storefront next door, partly obscured by some trees along the sidewalk. I can see the driver, sitting behind the wheel.

He seems to be watching me.

Heat prickles through me, a heady mixture of shock and exhilaration, when I realize it's the same man who drove me to Harlan's house for dinner.

I take a breath, and check my phone, which still shows no word from Justin.

I blink back the tears that sting my eyes.

What the fuck, Justin.

When I look at the SUV again, the driver still seems to be watching me. I wave hesitantly.

My heart pounds when he nods back.

I get up and start walking toward the vehicle, thinking this is crazy. That Justin will pull up any moment. He'll come rushing out of his car, serving up excuses for his lateness, and whisk me off to dinner at that Caribbean place he loves.

But that doesn't happen.

Instead, the driver steps out of the SUV as I approach, and

comes around to the passenger side. "Miss Monroe," he greets me.

"Hi again," I say tentatively as he opens the rear door.

This time, Harlan is sitting in the backseat.

When his dark eyes connect with mine, the only word for this feeling coursing through my blood is *fire*.

Or maybe *insanity*.

He's been watching me, too?

How long have they been parked here?

"Hi," I say, feeling weirdly shy as his gaze roams over my dress.

Did he see me almost crying on that bench, like a sad, dejected wad of cotton candy?

"What happened to your dinner plans?" he demands. There's an air of murderousness about him, and I'm really hoping it's not for me.

Maybe it's for the man who was supposed to take me to dinner. I told Harlan I needed to talk to Justin tonight.

But I don't want to talk to Justin anymore.

"I don't know," is all I say.

"Well, where is he?"

"I don't know." I glance over my shoulder, where I still see no sign of Justin or his car.

"Get in," Harlan growls. "We'll drive you home."

Suddenly, I want to be anywhere but here, waiting for a man who can't be bothered to show up for me.

I slide into the backseat and murmur, "Okay," fighting back the pressure of tears.

I give the driver my address, wondering if he already knows it. *Surveillance*.

And I wonder what this would look like to Harlan's siblings, if they happened to see me getting into his car with him. But if he doesn't care, I guess I won't, either.

What does it matter? I don't work for Vance Industries anymore.

As the driver shuts the door, my phone chimes with a text message.

I tell Harlan, "I guess I should check this."

He says nothing, just clenches his jaw, but the tension rolling off him is extreme. I'm not sure how I'll handle sitting in this small space with him, I'm so flustered already.

At least we're not alone; the driver is right there in the front seat. My place in East Vancouver, just off Victoria Drive, is only about twenty-five minutes away. I can survive that without saying or doing anything embarrassing, right?

I check my phone.

Justin: Sorry babe. I can't make it tonight. Reschedule?

I stare at the words, letting them sink in exactly as they are. For once, I don't even try to sugarcoat the way he takes me for granted. I see it for what it is.

I close my eyes. "He can't make it." I add quietly, "I was going to break up with him at dinner."

Harlan doesn't reply.

I take a deep breath. "He's been sleeping with someone else, behind my back. I don't think he even knows I know."

"Turn off your phone." His voice is low and deadly.

When I look up, there's a quiet fury in his expression that leaves me breathless. "If a man doesn't give you the attention you deserve," he growls, "don't give him yours."

I decide he's right.

I turn off my phone, and breathe through the pinched feeling in my chest. Justin really doesn't fucking care. He's been showing me so, in so many ways.

Why has that been so hard to accept?

He's not the man I hoped he'd be.

I don't think he's a bad person, either. I just think I'm incredibly low on his priority list.

Maybe Harlan understands that I'm going through it here, because he doesn't say anything else. We drive in silence, leaving downtown over the Georgia Viaduct and heading south along Main Street, then eastbound on Broadway.

All the while, I can feel his restless energy next to me, tense as hell. It's like sitting next to a wolf who's struggling to be tame.

"You really bought Crave?" I finally ask him, when I think I've settled enough that I can talk about it without melting down in waterworks.

"Yes."

"I don't understand why he'd keep that from me."

"Same reason he didn't tell you he was sleeping with someone else..."

I'm afraid to ask what that is, but I don't have to, because he doesn't pull this punch, either.

"So he could keep getting out of you what he wanted. Also," he mutters, "because he's a coward."

I blink back tears as I let that sink in. Because I know it's true.

No more sugarcoating.

I force myself to hold Harlan's gaze. It's not easy looking at him this close. "Do you have any idea how terrifying you are?"

He frowns, like that genuinely confounds him. "Terrifying?"

"Intimidating."

I can see that the computer in his brain is struggling to process. "Right now?"

"Always."

"I'm not trying to intimidate you," he says uneasily.

"What were you doing in your car in front of the bakery just now?"

He scans my face. "You were upset."

That really doesn't answer my question.

But my pulse races. I feel one of those Harlan-induced hot flashes coming on.

He was concerned about me?

"Of course I'm upset. He lied to me."

It's about so much more than that, though.

The tears are creeping up again, burning in my eyes. Everything I've been holding together so tightly feels like it's seeping through the cracks, as all the pressure I've been under for months on end finally begins to unravel me, right here in Harlan Vance's car.

Shit.

I'm a mess.

The tears spill over before I can stop them this time.

Next to me, Harlan stiffens as I dab the tears from my cheeks with the hem of my poofy skirt.

"Tissue?"

I look up to find the driver handing a box of tissues over the seat.

I reach to take it. "Thank you." I'd forgotten he was right there and could hear all of this. "I'm sorry," I sniffle, dabbing the tears from my face with a wad of tissues. I don't know what I'm trying to save my makeup for anyway. "I didn't even say thank you for driving me—"

"Don't thank us," Harlan cuts me off.

"But I appreciate—"

"Stop now." His tone is so cold, it's like an icy hand around my throat.

I swallow my words.

"He didn't mean that as rudely as sounded," the driver says.

I catch his eye in the rearview mirror, and he gives me just the hint of a smile. There's empathy in his eyes.

I glance sidelong at Harlan. "How can you be sure?"

"Been working for him for years," the driver answers. "You should see him when he's in a *really* bad mood."

I swear I can feel the man next to me ticking like a bomb about to go off.

"I hope not to."

"You're a smart woman, Miss Monroe."

"What's your name?"

"Manus, ma'am."

"Well, thank you for the ride home, Manus."

"My pleasure, Miss Monroe."

I watch as a partition of blacked-out glass rolls up between the front seat and the back, cutting us off from Manus. And sealing me into the back with Harlan.

"What was that for?" I ask him. "We were having a conversation."

"Yes. I enjoyed being discussed as if I'm not here."

"You could've joined in."

"*Quinn.*" It's a low, warning growl that probably *should* intimidate me.

Instead, it turns me on. The response between my legs is unmistakable as he stares me down. It's like now that we're truly alone, my sex parts think it's time to play.

I can't blame them for being confused.

I've never met anyone so obnoxiously controlling and so sexy at the same time.

I lift my chin and force myself to maintain eye contact when I ask, "Do you like me?"

"That's a childish question."

"It's a straightforward question."

He seems to consider his options, then answers. "No, I don't like you."

"You're a liar."

"Yes. I am."

Jesus. It's like talking to the Riddler. "Is everything a game to you?"

"No. Everything is a problem to solve."

"That's how you see me?"

"That's how I see everything."

"Then what problem were you solving when you bought Crave from Justin?"

"Frankly, I paid more than it was worth. I suppose he needed the money. The bakery was struggling, financially."

I knew that. Though I didn't know it was *that* bad.

Just another thing Justin didn't tell me.

"Okay... so that's *his* problem. Why would you care?"

"I didn't say I care."

Ugh. I'm getting dizzy from these circles he spins.

"Why did you buy the bakery, Harlan?" I press.

He glares at me, nostrils flaring. I'm determined to win this standoff, though. I want an answer.

Finally, he blinks. "Because you worked there."

Oh. *My god.*

Did he just speak the truth? It stuns me every time he does it. But I swear, I'm starting to be able to tell when he's not bullshitting.

"You bought it because of me?"

His jaw works for a moment before he answers, "Yes."

"Why?"

He looks at a loss again, like the computer upstairs just crashed. And he forgot his password.

"I don't know."

We stare at each other.

His fingernail picks at the armrest on the door.

"Ummm. You just told me I can't work there because you and your family now own it. I lost my job because of you. I'd appreciate a little more explanation than 'I don't know.'"

His gaze drifts to my mouth. "I felt... compelled."

I blink at him. "Compelled?"

His eyes narrow with intensity, locked on my face. "Do you have any vices, Quinn? Like... a bad habit that you have a particular inability to resist? A weakness. Say, when you want to do something that you know you shouldn't? And then... you do it."

What is he talking about? And what does this have to do with the bakery?

"I mean... I guess so. If you put salted caramel ice cream in front of me, it probably doesn't matter how full I am. I'm gonna eat it."

"Yes. That. That indulgence that feels beyond your control. It's like... a compulsion."

"So you're saying... this is your vice? You have a compulsion... to acquire businesses in the blink of an eye?"

He hesitates. "Something like that."

Why do I get the feeling that he's the one who's sugar-coating now? Trying to make the truth behind his words more palatable, for me...?

"But you said you bought it because of me. So, you felt compelled... to own another business where *I* work? You *want* to be my boss?"

He seems to war with something in his head, before finally answering, "Yes."

I consider this, trying not to freak out. Trying to convince myself that this is not at all alarming.

"But... then your family said you can't be my boss."

He's glowering again.

"You don't like that they have power over you," I conclude.

"My family doesn't control me, Quinn," he says darkly. "I'm the one in control here."

Then why do I get the distinct feeling that whatever's really going on, he's losing control of it?

When we turn onto my street, I have Manus take the back alley and pull up behind my house. I thank him again, thank Harlan—which earns me a scowl—and open my door.

I'm pretty sure that if I never see Harlan Vance again, it would be a great idea.

Very healthy.

"Well, it's been really weird knowing you," I tell him. "Good luck with solving all the problems."

I scoot out before he can say anything else, planning to hightail it to the house, but then the music hits me. Mom has Loverboy's "Turn Me Loose" absolutely *cranked* in the house. The screen door is shut but the solid inner door is open, so is the kitchen window, and I can already smell the marijuana.

I turn to shut the SUV's door, but I'm too late. Harlan is getting out, presumably to walk me to the door.

He has to pick *right now* to decide to be a gentleman?!

Trying to stuff him back into the vehicle would just be awkward, not to mention futile, so I do the only thing I really can and march onward. I cross the small backyard and climb the old steps to the tiny, rickety porch.

Harlan walks slowly up the steps behind me, probably wondering why I live in a frat house circa 1980.

It's not a frat house. It's just an old rental house. Mom and I occupy the main floor, with other renters above and below. But if you could only hear it and smell it... frat house.

Except for when cupcakes are baking in the oven, which they currently are not. Unfortunately.

There's no way I'm inviting Harlan in, so I turn to face him, blocking the way. "You really didn't have to walk me to the door. But thank you."

He frowns as he looks past me through the screen, into the kitchen. I cast a glance over my shoulder.

Yikes.

My cozy but crazy kitchen looks like a tornado whipped through it. And tore the oven out of the wall.

That tornado would be named Lorraine.

I don't see Mom; she must be in another room. But it appears that she's been "organizing" again.

"Uh, it's not usually like that." *Sort of.* "The repair guy came today to try to fix the oven. And we've been reorganizing. It's really not as crazy as it looks."

I look at Harlan in his fine suit, so sharp and precise, and completely out of place on my sagging, plant-covered porch, piled high with mom's pottery projects of yore.

"I just don't exactly have a place for everything," I ramble, "so the kitchen is a bit... overflowing. I bake here sometimes, and Mom bakes amazing cupcakes for our clients here. And I store all my extra baking supplies here..."

I'm immediately flooded with stress at the prospect of having to bake *all* my client cakes here. Which I now will. The number one reason I took the job at Crave, *before* Justin and I started dating, was because he gave me permission to use the ovens for Quinn's Cakes on the side, after hours.

I don't want to tell Harlan how much I depended on those damn ovens. Or how much trust I put in Justin, when I shouldn't have. He doesn't need to know how many mistakes I've already made, how many poor decisions and backwards steps, while struggling to get Quinn's Cakes off the ground.

It's embarrassing. He's the CFO of a multibillionaire dollar company, and I can barely make ends meet.

But like he said, problems are for solving.

The oven issue is my problem, and it's mine to fix.

Just like all my other problems.

"It's kind of been a work in progress," I conclude. *For six years.*

Maybe I expect criticism. But Harlan looks more bewildered than judgmental.

"I know what you're thinking," I say, "but there's a system to it."

He's been studying every inch of the kitchen he can see, but his eyes finally meet mine.

"I can assure you," he says in a low voice, "you don't know what I'm thinking."

I blink at him while my cheeks heat. Why did that sound so sexual?

Maybe it's the guitar solo wailing behind me.

We're still talking about my kitchen, right?

I swallow. "It's messy, not dirty."

"It's chaos."

"It's not chaos," I protest.

"How do you get any work done in that?"

I shrug uneasily. "Cakes are my passion. I can just focus on what's in front of me, and everything else just… falls away."

He stares at me. "I believe that's called obsession."

"It's prioritizing."

He's silent for a long moment, and I know there's something going on in that brain of his. I just don't know what it is.

Problem solving?

"Hey, um, this is embarrassing." It is, but since this might be my last chance to mention it, and I kind of forgot with all the drama going on… "I lost a diamond tennis bracelet at your place.

I think. I don't know for sure where I dropped it. But I got it at Holt Renfrew. It was pretty expensive."

I don't even want to admit that he actually paid for it. If I find it, I should really drop it off at his office.

He stares at me for a long moment, and I have no idea what he's thinking. But I hope he's not thinking this is just some ploy so maybe I get to see him again.

"I'll have my staff alert you if they come across it."

"Great."

"I wish you luck, Quinn Monroe," he says softly. I almost don't hear it, under the blaring music. "With your bakery, I mean."

Okay... He remembers what I told his family at dinner, about my dream of one day opening my own bakery? That's kind of... sweet.

"Thank you." *I'll need it.*

"Goodnight, Quinn. And goodbye."

"Yeah. Goodbye."

I watch him walk across the backyard and get into the SUV, and for some reason, I hold my breath. He glances at me before he closes the door.

Then Harlan Vance drives out of my life, for good.

Chapter 10

Quinn

It's just after dark and pouring rain as I dash out my front door with a Quinn's Cakes box in hand. I'm making a run for the Uber that's waiting for me at the curb, when a black SUV screeches up like a giant bat out of hell.

The rear door opens and Harlan lunges out, grabbing me.

I shriek in surprise.

"It's me," he says, like that's supposed to make me feel any better.

"Um—but—where are we going?" I splutter, as I find myself moving involuntarily toward his vehicle.

"Get in the car," he orders.

"But... my Uber rating..."

"Get in the car, Quinn," he growls, propelling me there with his man strength.

The uber driver puts his window down, craning his neck, probably to see if I'm being abducted.

"Sorry!" I shout at him. "I have another ride! I'll five-star you—!"

Harlan tosses me into his backseat and follows me in, slamming the door. I barely hold onto my cake. He takes the box from me and sets it on the floor, on the far side of him, as we pull away from the curb.

Then he crowds me in, leaning all into my space.

The black separator is up, so I can't even see Manus or whoever is driving.

"Where are we going? Did I just get kidnapped?"

"I'm asking the questions," he says, fuming. "Where were you going just now?"

Why is *he* fuming?

And what is he doing, showing up out of nowhere to snatch me off the street?

I haven't seen him in almost a week. According to him, I was never supposed to see him again.

I take a moment to catch my breath, trying to calm my pounding heart, but it's impossible to stop the heat that rushes to my face in embarrassment as he stares me down.

"To your house," I admit.

He blinks at me, raindrops clinging to his dark eyelashes. He swipes a hand over his face. "My house," he repeats angrily.

"Yes. I made you a cake."

He glares at me, incredulous. At least his furious breathing is slowly getting under control.

"A cake?"

"Yes. That box you practically threw on the floor? It's a thank-you cake."

Now he looks even more pissed. "What the hell for?"

"Jeez. Don't they send you to, like, etiquette school or something when you grow up rich?"

His dark eyebrows twist irritably.

"Manners. You could really work on yours, you know."

His nostrils flare like an angry bull as he inhales deeply. "What is the cake for, Quinn?" he asks, a little calmer and maybe five percent nicer.

I'll take it. Baby steps.

"I wanted to thank you for what you did for me. You know, arranging that job for me? I know you were trying to help. It was... considerate of you."

"You were supposed to start there tonight," he growls.

"I know."

"But you blew off the job. Why?"

Seriously? That's what he's so riled up about?

"Because it's at a sex club, Harlan!"

He clamps his mouth shut and fumes in silence, the computer upstairs working overtime.

"Yeah. You *should* be ashamed."

"I'm not ashamed," he says darkly.

Okay, now I'm annoyed.

"Well, I'll tell you what. The situation you put me in was *embarrassing*. Your assistant Brant put me in touch with this very nice woman named Monique, and I met her at a café downtown. She was so lovely, we chatted, she told me how highly recommended I came, and how happy she was to welcome me to the club. I signed the NDA she brought for me, and then she told me all about the job. Wherein I'd be serving cocktails to rich sex fiends in the fancy bar at a *sex club* called Bliss."

"There is no way she said 'sex fiends,'" is Harlan's calm reply.

Oh, *now* he's coolheaded?

"I'm paraphrasing!"

"It's a completely safe work environment. The waitresses aren't there for sex. Club members know that."

I frown. "You seem to know a lot about it..."

He frowns back. "It's my brother's club."

"Are you a member there?" It just slips out before I know it's going to. Because I've been dying to know.

I can't believe he actually answers. "No. But there are rules in place. You won't be preyed upon. I wouldn't have you work there if it wasn't safe."

"That god complex of yours is really shining through again."

His eyebrows furl. "God complex?"

"I can't work there, Harlan," I say firmly. "It's not who I am."

"What? A waitress? The employment contract is clear. I read it. You'll serve drinks, that's all."

God. He does not listen well.

"Even if I wanted to work there, I wouldn't. It's all the way over in West Vancouver. When you said you arranged a job for me at some private club, I assumed it was downtown."

"What's wrong with West Vancouver? The club is in a very exclusive, upper-class neighborhood, and has rigorous security. You'd be safer there than working anywhere else in town."

"I'm sure it's very posh. But I can't afford the commute time or the expense. I have to rely on transit and Uber when my car breaks down, which is often."

He considers that. "I can provide car service as part of the deal."

Is he for real?

Yup. He seems deadly serious about all of this.

I still don't understand why.

I shake my head. "No. I... I don't want to make a deal. What I'm saying is thank you, but no thank you."

A muscle along his jaw spasms, and he skewers me with those switchblade eyes of his. "You're being stubborn."

"I'm being independent. In other words, true to myself."

"No, you're being obstinate."

"You know what? This is on me. It was my mistake for trusting you."

His gaze drops to my lips. "Mulish."

Okay, now I'm getting pissed. "I never should've let you arrange a job for me. I'm perfectly capable of finding employment myself."

"Employment that pays as well as Bliss?"

"I already found another waitressing job," I inform him, sidestepping that. "It's much closer to home. And I won't have to worry that any of the clientele mistake me for a sex worker. We actually get to wear pants while we serve people alcohol. It's revolutionary."

I'm actually kind of bracing myself for his wrath. I can't imagine he enjoys my sarcasm.

Instead, he seems to be struggling to process what I just said.

Then he says the weirdest thing. "Are you still angry with me?"

I struggle to understand where he's coming from. He's got me spinning in circles again. "About what, exactly?"

"About losing your job at Crave."

Huh. I thought we were ramping up. But he doesn't seem quite as furious anymore.

"I... it's not that I loved working at the bakery." *Ugh.* Am I getting into this, really? "I needed access to the ovens, okay? Justin let me use them, to bake cakes for my own business on the side. That's why I was so upset to lose the job."

Harlan stares at me for a long, intense moment. Calculating.

"Are *you* still angry?" I ask him.

"I'm not angry. I'm regretting my decision."

I'm not sure what decision he means, so I wait for more as he silently simmers, looking gradually less angry.

"I should've offered you the job Savannah suggested in the first place," he says tightly. "At the Crystal hotel, in the restaurant. It was a baking position, and you could waitress there, too, if you wanted. It was the perfect job for you." He adds solemnly,

"I'm sorry. I should've given you that opportunity. I'll call her immediately, and have it set up."

He stares at me expectantly, like it's all wrapped up now, and he's waiting for that thank-you cake.

"I just told you," I say carefully, "that I don't want to make a deal. I don't need you to find a job for me."

"But it's the perfect job," he repeats. "I can make sure you're allowed to use the ovens to bake your cakes."

Well, shit.

Do not cave to temptation, Quinn.

This is just the same damn situation I had with Justin, isn't it? Though possibly worse.

I can't owe this man anything for doing favors for me.

I can't rely on him and his network.

I need to be strong myself.

"I don't think you understand," I say softly. "I'm not taking any job at the Crystal. My friend Nicole works at Champagne nightclub. They're hiring wait staff right now, and they scooped me up. I'll be okay."

"But what about the oven situation?"

"I have an oven."

He blinks at me. "That ancient relic in your kitchen that's not even attached to the wall?"

"It's reattached now," I say stubbornly.

He shuts his eyes for a second, and I have no idea what's going on.

"I'm sorry you can't work at Crave anymore," he says. "I shouldn't have bought that bakery."

He seems sincere.

I sigh. "Why did you, really?"

He opens his eyes, and locks onto mine again. "I told you." His voice is low and unexpectedly warm, like silken, melted chocolate. "Because you worked there."

I don't even know what to say as heat coils in my gut and spreads throughout my body.

He wants to keep me close, is that it? Somewhere that's under his control?

Somewhere he has access to me, knows where I am and what I'm doing, can even have me driven to and from?

Is that what this is all about?

He drags a hand through his hair, looking uncomfortable. "I'm truly regretting buying that bakery." Then he grits out, "I screwed up."

Wow.

I can't imagine he admits *that* very often.

"Harlan Vance. Was that the first time you've ever uttered those words?"

"It might be." He adds in a rough voice, "Don't get used to it."

"How can I get used to it when we're never seeing each other again," I deadpan.

A fraught silence stretches between us.

He's sitting closer to me now. So close, I can feel the heat off his body. And the tension in his muscles.

How did we end up so close?

I can see every fleck of darker gray in his dark-gray irises, every slight line at the corners of his eyes. Every perfect, dark eyelash.

I can feel his warm breath on my skin.

I can smell him under his clothes; faint soap, and warm, naked male.

"It's okay." My voice is soft, the words choked with longing. "You probably did me a favor. I was kidding myself that I could keep working with Justin."

His eyebrows draw together. "You don't want to work with him anymore?"

"Why would I want to work with him?"

He stares at me as my heart pounds.

His eyes are on my lips again. I can practically taste his hunger.

"You said you don't like me..." I whisper.

"I know."

"Harlan... are you obsessed with me or something?"

His eyes meet mine, darkening.

His voice is dangerously low, almost vicious, when he says, "I am not obsessed with you."

"Oh... kay," I say, the way a little bird might agree with a wolf who said he wasn't going to eat her.

Then he scoops me up in his arms, drags me onto his lap, and kisses me.

My whole body catches fire.

I'm in Harlan's strong arms, and *he's kissing me*. I'm breathless as we smash together, sucking, tasting. He buries one hand in my hair, and the other grabs my ass. He drags me closer, shifting his hips under me—so I'm sitting on his erection.

Oh my god. *He wants me.*

What the hell am I doing right now?

I can't stop making out with him as if my life depends on our bodies fusing together. *Red flags be damned.*

He groans. And breaks the kiss.

"Tell me you broke up with him," he pants against my lips.

"I broke up with him."

I did. The day after he stood me up for the last time.

The day after Harlan said goodbye to me.

His lips are so fucking luscious, and I dive back in. I bite his lip, and he groans again.

His hand slides under my dress, and grips my thigh, hard. It's like he's trying to resist sliding it higher.

"I can't get involved with you," he says huskily, even as his other hand holds me trapped against his thick hard-on. And now he's making out with my neck, licking the pulse point on the side.

Mixed messages much?

"Uh-huh..."

"I'm no good for you, Quinn."

"I'm... aware..."

"Even though you no longer work for Vance Industries..." he says between sucking on my throat, then my lips, "I told my family I stopped seeing you. It's important... they believe... I've distanced myself from you. You know, cut all ties..."

"That's fine," I say breathlessly as we suck face. "I never asked you... to wander around town with me... holding hands..."

"But you can't just show up at my house... and pry into my life," says the man with his hand up my skirt and his mouth on my throat again.

"Uh, I didn't."

His eyes, gleaming with lust, meet mine. "You were coming over with cake."

"You showed up and threw me in your car!"

When he doesn't have a comeback for that, he kisses me again. With a lot of tongue, and so much hunger it takes my breath away. I melt around him like caramel.

"I need to fuck you," he growls. "Please, let me fuck you." His hand slides deeper up my skirt—and grabs my panties.

"Oh. *Whoa.* Okay, um... we're in your car. Can we, just... go somewhere..."

I don't want to say, *go to your house so you can grope me in private*, when he just told me not to show up there. I have no idea where we are. For all I know, we've been driving in circles.

I really don't want to do this in his car, with a driver three feet away.

But I *really* want to do this.

The way he just said *please* and *fuck* made my insides melt and my lady parts gush. I squirm in his lap, trying to keep space between my pussy and his fist, which is gripping my panties like they're denying him a delicious snack and he's fucking starving.

He draws a breath, his chest rising as he collects himself.

Then he releases my panties, regretfully.

He reaches to press a button. The black divider slides down, revealing Manus in the front seat.

"Oh, shit," I squeak, feeling vulnerable now that Manus can see me, all wrapped around his boss.

Harlan dumps me off his lap.

He drags his hand through his hair and orders his driver, "Take us home."

Chapter 11

Quinn

When we get to Harlan's place, Manus drops us at the front door. The nice butler greets us as Harlan drags me inside by the hand. I guess I don't walk fast enough for his liking, because he picks me up—and tosses me over his shoulder, carrying me upstairs.

Holy shit. Men really do this?

Upside down, blood rushes to my face. My hair is all over the place. I'm glad I can't see the butler. I really hope he's not watching this, but hell, I would if I were him.

On the drive here, Harlan drilled me with questions. Am I on birth control? Am I sleeping with anyone else? Did I really break up with Justin?

I guess the answers I gave satisfied his computer-brain's need for information, because he takes me straight into his bedroom, and tosses me down. I scream. I can't see where he's tossing me, so until I land on the king-size bed, it's startling.

He closes the bedroom door, and tears off his suit jacket, stalking over to me.

I scramble up to a sitting position as he stands over me, unbuttoning his black shirt.

"Hi. Um, this is fast," I say nervously.

"It's not fast," he says with intensity. "I've wanted this since I first saw you."

Mind blown.

"At Velvet?"

"At the bakery."

"Oh..." My brain scrambles to make sense of this new information, and file it in logical order. Which is more challenging than it should be, as Harlan peels his shirt off in front of me. He's wearing a tight black undershirt, and I already know he's strong, but he's surprisingly cut under his suit. I see pecs, hard nipples, and a rippling six-pack hugged in black fabric.

Before I can even rip it off with my eyes—or my hands—he grabs me under my knees. I'm yanked toward the edge of the bed. Then he spreads my knees, dropping me flat on my back. He towers over me, his hands traveling up my inner thighs.

"Wait." I blink up at him. "You came into the bakery? Before that night I served you at Velvet?"

His hands pause in their exploration, his eyes meeting mine. "Yes."

Oh, boy. How deep does this stalker rabbit hole go?

"When?"

His eyes darken, as if with the memory. "As soon as I was told that you were the one."

Then he leans down and kisses me. Soft and hot, then deep and scorching. And with so much hunger, I'm soon melting into a tingling, horny mess as he ravages me with his mouth like he wants to swallow me whole.

The whole time, he hovers above me, making me long for his body to press down on mine.

God damn, he knows how to kiss.

How can someone so cold kiss so hot?

I can't believe I'm here, on his bed, and he's kissing me like this. I could make out with him like this for *hours*.

But... what were we talking about?

I find my spine in the puddle I'm rapidly becoming, and force myself to wrench away, because I need to know this shit. "The one... what?"

He draws up above me, and his hands land on my breasts, squeezing. His eyes hold mine, hot with desire. "My perfect, decoy Darla."

"Um..." I struggle to make words as he massages my breasts, then pinches my now rock-hard nipples through my dress. "Did you really break up with her?"

He pauses the massage, unfortunately. "That's what you want to talk about right now?"

"I told you about Justin."

"I already told you I broke up with her."

"Yeah. But we've established that you're a liar, so..."

His expression darkens warningly, and one hand slides down my body—and over my panties. I quiver as he squeezes my pussy. And when his fingers brush my clit, I jerk involuntarily. My ovaries squeal.

His hand is so *warm* through the cotton. *God, that's good.*

"Careful, Quinn," he warns. "I like it much better when you say nice things to me."

When have I ever said nice things to him?

His eyes gleam at me as I try to remember. I think I said it was nice that he got me a job? Maybe I called him handsome at some point...?

Did that go to his head?

That's probably the last thing anyone needs here.

But I'm melting as he gently massages my pussy through my panties. I swallow, lest I start drooling on his expensive bedspread. My whole body warms as his thumb rubs gently over my clit, back and forth, and I figure he's earning a compliment.

"Um. Okay..." My voice shakes. "You're very, very good at that."

"Thank you."

"Is Darla really out of your life?"

He scowls, annoyed by the distraction, as he manipulates my clit with focus. "Yes," he growls, as my eyes roll back in my head.

"How... serious were you? Um, you have nice hands."

I can tell he finds the questions tedious and annoying, but maybe he's tolerating them because I'm asking so nicely.

"Not serious," he grumbles as he teases his fingers up and down the lips of my pussy through the thin fabric.

"It's just that... *oh, god...* your sister said you seemed to be obsessed with her. That you said you were 'holding out' for her. What does that mean?"

"What does it matter?"

"I just want to know. It sounds like... you were saving yourself for her."

"I'm not a virgin," he says dryly, "if that's what you mean."

"But maybe you were saving your heart for her?" I gasp as he pinches my clit through my panties. "Did you... love her?"

"Quinn," he growls softly. He tugs at my hard nipple at the same time he fondles my clit, and a little moan slips out. I tremble, really trying not to completely lose it here. His eyelids lower. "Are you jealous, beautiful?"

My cheeks burn. *He called me beautiful.*

"Yes."

He laughs, a low, sexy chuckle that makes my nipples even harder.

"That's the first time I've heard you laugh," I say nervously.

"That's the first time you've said something hilarious."

"Why is it hilarious?"

"Because," he says hotly, pulling at my panties, "there's no woman you should be jealous of right now." He manages to slide them down and right off, tossing them across the room before I can fully process that I'm half naked. My dress is up around my hips, and he's got me spread open again.

He lays his hands on my inner thighs, gently spreading me open with his thumbs, and says roughly, "This sweet pussy of yours is the only one that's getting my mouth."

He kneels down, his hungry gaze between my legs, and his mouth follows.

I gasp when his tongue flickers over my opening. And when it thrusts inside, I choke back a cry.

I mewl helplessly as his luscious lips meet my clit, followed by his devilish tongue. I buck from the sheer pleasure, and he presses me down with a hand flat to my belly.

Then he proceeds to ravage my clit and my entire pussy with his hot, ravenous mouth, as if the devil himself possessed him to do it.

He spears me with his tongue, then laps hungrily.

I moan and pant.

When he starts suckling my clit with intent, pleasure converges on that one sweet spot so fast, I'm shaking.

I dare to look down, and when I see his gorgeous face between my legs, his mouth on me, his cheeks hollowing as he sucks, I don't think I can withstand the rush of desire. This bossy, controlling man on his knees, all his power focused on sucking me toward climax...

I make a ragged, desperate sound of pure pleasure and helplessness, and his eyes drag up my body to lock on mine.

The look of lust and satisfaction on his face does me in.

My pussy shudders, aching to be filled, and my clit pulses in his mouth.

He groans.

"Oh, god. Harlan. *Fuck*. I'm gonna—"

He stops completely, just before I explode.

He swipes his tongue over his lips as he stares me down, like he's daring me to go off. *Do it,* that look says, *and see what happens.*

My heart pounds. I'm shaking all over.

I swallow, and try to catch my breath.

He gives me a moment's reprieve, and pulls me up to sitting, deftly unzips the back of my dress, then tears it up over my head and tosses it away. My bra goes next, and I'm completely naked.

He's not. It doesn't seem fair, but it doesn't seem like it's up for negotiation, either.

He's singleminded about it as he pushes me onto my back again, and sucks my nipple into his hot mouth. Suckling, with the same focused intensity, and what can only be called *tenderness*, that he used on my clit. It's so delicious, all I can do is moan and take it.

His fingers slide over my clit, swirling in leisurely circles as he tongues my nipple, then dives onto the other one. He sucks harder now, and I'm right there with him. When he sinks his teeth into my breast, I squeal and arch, so ready for it, I could almost climax.

I've never had a guy bite me like that before, but I am instantly here for it.

He snarls. It's a hungry, feral sound that makes my core clench with need.

He releases me, grabs my hips and flips me over like I'm weightless. I'm folded over the side of the bed, and he yanks my hips so my bare ass tilts up, toward him.

Then he smacks it.

I yelp. It stings, and heat flashes through my core, fading into a tingling warmth.

My mouth hangs open. I'm shocked by my own arousal.

I've been spanked before. And kissed. And eaten out. But this man just does it different.

He does everything *better*.

I hear fabric shifting, the unzipping of his pants, and desire courses through me.

"You want more?" he taunts, in the silkiest, hottest voice, it sets me on fire.

I don't know whether to be more embarrassed about my reactions, shy, or just fling myself open in abandon. I cling to the bedspread, squeezing it in my fists, holding on for dear life when I whisper, "No?"

"Oh." He clucks softly. "Well, then I guess I'll put this hard cock away, and let you get dressed."

I make the most embarrassing *eep* sound, and he *tsk*s at me.

Then he waits, a long-ass minute, for me to get up. Not touching me at all.

But I don't move. I can feel his ferocious heat and want. I can hear him breathing. I know his eyes and all his attention are locked onto me, and it's fucking intoxicating.

"Did you just lie to me, Quinn?" he says softly.

I mumble something into the bedspread, hiding my face against it.

When I don't really answer him, he grips my ass in both hands—and shoves his bare erection against my pussy. It's long, hard and silken-hot, and I immediately rub up on it, practically purring like a cat.

"You said no to me." His voice is deadly soft. Low, controlled, and hotter than hell.

I've never wanted anyone so badly.

Not even close.

I try to breathe like I'm not totally losing my mind. I just want him to take over, so I don't have to think about it.

But he won't let me avoid his questions. He grabs my jaw, and gently turns my head so he can see the side of my face.

"Answer me. Yes or no?"

I nod, *yes*. It's all I can manage. He can probably feel my pulse slamming against him.

When he flexes his hips and rubs himself against me, my clit spasms. And I know he feels it.

He groans softly.

"You've been a very bad girl, Quinn," he says gruffly, but he sounds happy.

Have I?

"You talk back." He smacks my ass again, sending a thrill through me. "You defy me." He notches his cockhead right into the opening of my pussy. Just the tip. "You lie to me." I feel him throb, and I shudder.

It's maddening, and I buck, trying to take him deeper.

"I'm afraid you've earned yourself some punishment," he says softly, and I can hear the fucking glee beneath his words.

Monster.

He spanks me, one stinging blow followed by another, then over and over, until I'm humming with pleasure and heat, and my cheeks sting.

Then he smoothes his hand over them gently, and I push up into him, wanting his touch.

In answer, he slides his hand to my lower back, another to the back of my neck, pinning me down to the bed. Controlling me.

"But tonight..." He teases me with a couple of shallow thrusts. "You're going to do exactly as I say."

When I just gurgle helplessly in response, he prompts, "Aren't you?"

Whatever this game is he's playing, I'm loving it.

I have never in my life had a man take control like this in bed. Taunt me. Punish me with pleasure.

What the hell have I been missing?

"Answer me."

"Yes," I choke out. Because clearly that's what he wants to hear. And I just want him to keep doing what he's doing.

More.

"Yes, what?"

Umm. *What?* He wants me to come up with something, right now? He wants me to *think*?

Impossible.

I have no idea what he wants me to say.

"Yes, *what*, Quinn?" he prompts, his low tone a warning.

Finally, my mind spits out an answer from somewhere in my memories of him.

"Yes... sir?"

As my reward, he mutters, "Good girl." Then he shoves himself deep, filling me with his swollen cock. The feeling is so intense on so many levels, I cry out.

"Beg for it," he orders.

"Please!"

I moan helplessly as he fucks me, with long, leisurely thrusts, his hips battering against me. He groans with satisfaction as he does it.

I think I've legit died and gone to some heavenly version of hell. Harlan is the devil, and he plans to fuck me for eternity while I beg.

Right now, I'm beyond okay with it.

Suddenly, he stops. I squirm and pant, wanting more.

"More?" he demands.

"Yes," I gurgle.

"I don't hear you, pretty."

"Yes!" I gasp. "Sir!"

I'm rewarded with a deep thrust. But then he stops again, just the tip nestled into me.

I growl, a desperate, guttural noise, as I try to force my hips back, and he presses me down, holding me off with that one hand on my lower back, the other still gripping my neck. He's owning me. Playing me like an instrument.

He chuckles, a sound of pure male pleasure.

"You're gloating," I pant. "It's not sexy."

My pussy flutters helplessly around his dick as he nudges it deeper, totally betraying my words.

"Is that how you talk to the man who's going to make you come harder than you've ever come in your life?" he purrs.

I laugh, but it's a nervous, starving sound. I struggle to maintain some dignity. "How can you be so sure?"

He answers darkly, "Because neither of us is leaving this room until you do."

His tone is so ferocious, so intent on his objective, I feel mildly panicked.

I've never had someone so fiercely focused on getting me off. But any nervousness is whisked away into oblivion as he proceeds to fuck the hell out of me... until my moans and cries bleed together into a filthy song of ecstasy. I'm seeing stars, my whole body is quaking, and there's a river of my juices streaming down my thighs.

When he pauses, panting over me, his cock seated deeply within me, I feel him spasm. I know he's fighting back his arousal, hanging on, so he doesn't come before I do.

He takes a steadying breath.

The thrill of knowing he's so turned on, over *me*, sends me to a high I've never known. My whole body flushes with excitement. My core tingles, aching with the need to come.

Then he starts fucking me again.

The friction of my clit rubbing against the bed, combined

with the pressure of his cockhead rubbing my insides as he pummels me, is pure insanity. I think I'm going to come while getting fucked from behind for the first time in my life.

Hard.

I groan and rub myself against the bed like an animal, dying for it.

But Harlan slows his thrusts. He slips his hand around my throat, and folds over me, so his heat envelops me. He's heavy, his body hot and slick with sweat.

His fingers gently squeeze my throat as he purrs in my ear, "I could slide my fingers over that sopping wet pussy of yours, play with your swollen little clit, squeeze it, slap it... tease you however I like until you come for me." All the while, he fucks me, slow and deep, his swollen cockhead driving me mad. The angle has intensified, and he's rubbing into my front wall, sending tingling warmth through my clit.

I'm humping the bed in response, what little I can maneuver under his weight.

"But I'm not going to," he mutters, dragging his luscious, hot lips along my neck. His tongue caresses my ear, and I shiver.

My clit throbs incessantly.

"I want to feel you come, from the inside out, while I fuck you. I want you to climax on my hard cock because you love the feel of me inside you. You're going to come all over my dick like the good girl I know you really are, sweet Quinn."

I'm sobbing now, the feeling is so exquisite. So raw and hot. So excruciating, as he drags his cockhead through my swollen lips, then pounds into me, again and again.

"Tell me now," he growls softly into my ear. "Tell me you want to come for me."

"Yes. I—I want to come. Sir."

"For me," he growls.

"For you," I gasp.

"It's nice when you call me sir," he murmurs. "But I prefer my name. Say it."

"Harlan," I choke out.

He squeezes my throat, gently. "Now beg me. Beg for release, pretty girl."

"Yes," I gasp, shuddering as his hips keep ramming, forcing me higher and higher. His swollen cock inside me... The friction of the bedspread against my clit... His hand wrapped around my throat.

"Yes, what?" he demands.

"Yes. *Please. Harlan.* I want to come."

He chuckles softly, with satisfaction. "You're going to, sweet girl. You're going to come so hard. But not until I allow it."

Oh, fuck.

Heat is coiling tight between my legs. Pleasure surges in my core, even as I try to hold it back. To delay the inevitable. To make it last...

"I can't," I choke out. "I can't stop..."

"Shh. You will. Not yet, baby. You're going to hold it until I say."

Oh, no. My pussy clenches around his dick when he speaks like that. It just fuels me higher.

Maybe I am a bad girl.

"Shh," he murmurs again, and I realize I'm getting louder, practically screaming with each thrust.

He slows his pace again, fucking into me deep, but so slow, as if that will calm me down.

It does not.

"Quiet now," he says, but he's gloating again.

Heat expands through my chest.

I gasp for air, trying to calm down. I'm hyperventilating.

"That's a good girl. You're not going to come until—"

"God. Harlan! I can't..." I squirm and buck, tears running down my cheeks now.

"Did you just interrupt me, darling?" he whispers hotly in my ear.

And that does it. Something about him calling me *darling* while holding me by the throat and fucking me with such control, and telling me *not* to come... sends me over the cliff.

I scream and hump the bed like a mad woman, my pussy squeezing his cock, as I implode. I'm sucked into a black hole, screaming. And when I'm spit back out, my core is spasming wildly and Harlan is grunting above me, fucking me *hard*.

"That was very naughty of you, Quinn," he grunts. "Coming before you're told..." But he sounds delighted about it.

I couldn't care less if he's mad, glowing as I am, trembling with aftershocks and splayed like a wet noodle beneath him.

"You want my come, Quinn?" he growls.

"Yes!"

Do I. There's literally nothing else I want more in life right now than the feeling of Harlan Vance losing control, right in my pussy. I'm floating in euphoria as he starts to shudder, losing his rhythm.

He pants in my ear, almost helplessly, "Fuck, baby. You're making me come so hard..."

He sinks his teeth into my neck with a growl.

I can't even respond. I'm whirling into utter space again as my pussy clenches suddenly and hard, and he pumps into me, both of us coming. I feel the jerks, the hot pulses of his pleasure deep inside me as I groan deliriously, my pussy shuddering and pulsing right along with him.

I'm just lying here, rolling in orgasm as he comes in me. *Because* he's coming in me.

When he finishes, he swears and sags against me.

I pant beneath him, too stunned to do a thing.

I've never come like that before—in response to a man coming inside me. Without any other stimulation.

I mean, he was still gripping my throat and he bit my neck... but that was new, too.

What is this black magic he's cast on me?

I can't even move, I'm so boneless as I drift back to earth, trying to find myself in all of this.

And when I do, I feel a strange stinging sensation, deep in my chest.

With crystal clarity, it hits me what just happened here.

I just crossed a giant, dangerous line. The one that I drew for myself when I promised myself that I'd bring him the cake, thank him for the job, let him know I wasn't taking it, and gracefully exit his life, forever.

I promised myself that I wouldn't keep seeing him. I wouldn't seek him out again. And if he ever crossed my path, I'd walk the other way.

Now I'm trapped beneath him, naked, he's still half in his suit, and his cock and his come are deep inside me.

I just leapt over the line, naked and screaming, begging him to let me come for him. Without a parachute.

Or a condom.

As he settles against me, his face pressed to the back of my neck, neither of us speaks.

I know I need to be sensible here. I can't get confused about what this is. Because what just happened between us was sheer, horny madness.

I need to be clear with myself about what this is: hot, *hot* sex. And what it isn't: a budding relationship.

To ground myself in reality, I try to remind myself what's important. The only things that truly matter. Mom, and our bakery dream.

I can't get distracted by a man.

Especially not one like Harlan Vance.

Even if the sex between us is mind-blowing.

I need to heed the warnings my intuition has been waving in my face, the giant red flags that won't let me forget his lies. His power. His ability to hurt me.

He's not my boss anymore.

But if I'm not careful, he could be something else.

Something with far more power to ruin me.

Lying here, crushed beneath his weight, my internal warnings feel like ominous whispers of truths to come.

As his heart beats against mine, I warn myself not to like this feeling too much.

Men like Harlan are thrilling but volatile, like the most dangerous ocean currents.

You think you're safe in the shallows, keeping them at a distance.

You don't even see it coming before they take you under.

Chapter 12

Harlan

I'm on my laptop in my home office when Quinn nudges the door open and leans in.

"There you are!" she says, like she's happy to see me or something. "This place is *huge*. I thought I might never find you."

Then she wanders right in without an invitation, looking around, at the books lined up perfectly on my shelves, all the dust jackets removed so that they appear more uniform. There isn't much else to look at in here. I don't like clutter around me while I work.

"I'm surprised you don't turn them backwards," she marvels, "so the white pages are showing."

I stare at her.

"You know, so they all look the same."

She's reaching to touch a book, maybe pull it out and browse, when I snap, "I'm working."

She stops abruptly. "Oh. Good idea." She pulls out her phone. "I should take care of some emails for Quinn's Cakes this morning."

I can only assume she's making herself comfortable when

she sits down and stretches out like a cat on her belly—on the floor.

I didn't know grown adults did that.

I suppose the absence of any chairs besides the one I'm sitting on didn't get the message across that I don't want company in here.

I allow my eyes the indulgence of traveling up her bare legs and over her dress to her ass. The ass I smacked and squeezed last night, while I fucked her.

I'm glad to see she's at least wearing the same blue polkadot dress, and didn't help herself to one of my shirts. She was still sleeping when I woke up, so I decided to do some work while I waited for her to get moving.

But it's put me on edge, leaving her in my bed, like she belonged there.

When she looks up at me, I fix my gaze on my laptop screen. But all I can seem to see is her face in profile as she gasped, choked and screamed while I pounded into her, and I whispered filth in her ear.

And now I'm uncomfortably hard, and my mood is turning black.

I have work to do.

But she's talking, making morning-after conversation, like we're fuck buddies or *friends* or something. "I have to say, that bed of yours is amazing. I don't even remember falling asleep."

I do. After fucking her senseless, she was quite a mess. I dragged her into a warm shower and soaped her off, and she was barely conscious when I carried her to the bed, where I tucked her in.

I wasn't planning to keep her overnight, but she was asleep before her head hit the pillow.

I slept beside her, off and on, but not well.

When I don't respond, she says, "I hope I'm not making it

weird. I think we can be cool around each other, right? We're both adults."

I grumble something I hope satisfies, but it's definitely not words. I'd rather we didn't talk at all.

"Also... thank you for the shower," she says carefully.

Maybe she's finally picking up on the fact that I don't want, or need, her thank you's.

When I say nothing, and hopefully appear to be absorbed in work, she hums softly to herself as she presumably checks email on her phone.

I can't concentrate, too obsessed with the curve of her lower back. I can handle less than a minute of it before getting up and telling her, "I need to make some calls."

She looks up. "Oh. Of course. Should we have breakfast after?"

"I don't have time." I leave the office, and head through the family room and out to my backyard.

I stalk across the patio, and settle onto one of the stools along the bar by my immaculate but unused pool, in silence.

Something brushes against my leg, and I glance down; black fur.

I stroke the cat absently as I consider that last item on the list of criteria I gave Manus with his special assignment. *Emotionally unavailable.*

Logically, I understand why she appeared to meet that criteria. She wasn't single. Presumably, she was emotionally involved with her boss at the bakery. Dating her boss was a risk. Dating him in secret was yet another risk. And those risks she was taking, for him, suggested a depth of connection.

Clearly, that part was wrong.

And maybe the biggest mistake I made was not taking into account that *I* might get attached.

However, there is no world in which I can afford to attach myself to Quinn Monroe.

If my family sees me with her, they'll ask more questions about her. They'll dig in, because they can't help themselves. And even if they can look past the fact that she *used to* work for us, I'm sure they'd love nothing more than to gossip about the love life of the brother they nicknamed *the beast*—because they decided, years ago, that I was too ill-tempered for any woman to put up with.

And if they dig enough, maybe they'll find out the truth; that Quinn is not Darla.

I can't have that.

I met with my siblings last weekend so we could draw the next name from Granddad's cigar box, and the next challenge. Now, it's Savannah's turn. My one-month deadline officially passed yesterday. So, my allotted time to complete my challenge is now finished, and Savannah's challenge is underway.

My lie is sealed. It's far too late to ever go back on it now.

I wonder, suddenly, what Quinn thinks of me lying to my family. Which is fucking annoying. I've never wondered that before.

Maybe it's just the guilt that's getting to me. I don't feel great about lying to my family, that's all.

And what would Quinn think if she found out the truth?

Would she hate me for lying to *her*?

It bothers me that I care.

I shouldn't care.

We fucked, and now it's done.

Maybe we were both denying our attraction from the start, because it was inconvenient, but now we've taken it to its logical conclusion. We released all that pent-up lust.

Closure.

We have no reason to ever see each other again.

I make a couple of calls, and when I finally head back into the house, the cat tries to follow. I make her stay outside, closing the sliding door.

What the hell is that smell?

The house smells sweet and inviting, like cinnamon and maple syrup.

And what the hell is that music?

It's coming from the chef's kitchen. But that is not my chef's music. He sometimes listens to classical music while he works, but this is eighties pop.

I push the door open, and find Quinn making pancakes to "Hungry Like the Wolf."

"What are you doing?"

"Pancakes," she says cheerily, lifting one on the spatula to show me before adding it to a pile of them on a plate. "I was going to bring some to you. You really shouldn't skip breakfast."

I can't even respond to that. I'm too thrown off by this whole scene. Her, flipping pancakes, in her polkadot dress, with one of my chef's aprons on. Where the hell is he?

What did he do, hand her the keys to my house and leave?

She can't get comfortable here.

"Don't they smell good?" she goes on. "It's a family recipe. My mom makes the best pancakes. The secret is a little real maple syrup, right in the batter, amber if you have it, and Ceylon cinnamon. I was so happy to find you have both. That pantry is well-stocked! Apparently the recipe actually came from my dad. Mom said he made them for her on their second date, and that's when she knew she was in love. Although... maybe that means she spent the night with him on their second date? I never really thought that through before. Is that TMI?"

Yes. Yes it is.

All of it.

This woman is the queen of TMI.

Once again, she just told me way the fuck more than I ever wanted or needed to know. Because the more I know, the more I have to think about, and the more I think about her... the more I need her out of here.

"I don't have time to eat. I'm needed at the office." Mostly, I need to get away from her. "I'm leaving."

"Oh." She turns to me. "Well, just let me finish cooking these last ones? And I could catch a ride with you? I have a cake order to fill, and then I'm starting my new job tonight."

And now she thinks I want her itinerary?

But fuck, *I do*.

There's something seriously wrong with me.

She chews on the side of her lip, like it's finally occurring to her that she might be oversharing. "You can warm up the pancakes later."

"Fine. I'll have the car ready out front."

When she turns back to the pancakes, I go put my shoes on. Manus pulls the car up for me, and I get in, waiting for her in the backseat with the door open.

A few minutes later, she emerges from my house, disturbingly beautiful in the morning sun. Bright turquoise hair, blue polkadot dress. She slides in next to me with a cheerful "Thank you!" to Manus as he shuts the door for her. "What a beautiful morning," she says to me.

"I want to make it clear," I tell her as we pull out of the driveway, "that last night was a one-time thing."

Her bright expression fades a little. It's like clouds drifting in front of the sun. "Okay. I was just trying to be nice."

I look out the window. "I don't like people in my space."

"I know," she says softly. "I can tell."

That night, I work late, trying to bury thoughts of Quinn and what we did last night—and failing. When I get home, I find the dinner my staff left for me in the chef's kitchen, as requested.

Her pancakes are on a plate in the fridge, along with a handwritten note with warm-up instructions.

I refuse to get used to this. I won't eat her pancakes. I won't let myself start missing her. Craving her niceties, longing for her attention.

You can't start counting on things like that.

I knock on the door of Manus' apartment over the garage, and give the pancakes to him.

I should've just given her bracelet back when she mentioned she'd lost it. Or before that, like I told myself I would. Lying to myself.

I don't know why I lied to *her* and kept it.

I don't know what I was thinking having Brant run it over to my family's jeweler today. The diamonds in my pocket are a terrible reminder that I can't control these things like I need to. That I'm already out of control.

I already want to see her again.

Every time I let myself think of her, remember how she feels, how she smells, the way she reacts to my touch, I get hard.

When I go up to bed, I can't sleep.

I end up folding clothes in my walk-in closet. Folding and rearranging the socks and underwear in my drawers in perfect lines, because no matter how long my housekeeper has worked for me or how neatly she puts them away, I have to redo them.

Not because they're wrong.

Because they're not quite right.

Meanwhile, I keep telling myself I won't see Quinn again. That she's out of my system. Now that I've fucked her, I don't want or need anything else from her.

I meant it when I told her that last night was a one-time thing.

I know it's becoming hazardous to my health to even think of her at all.

I just can't stop.

I'm still awake at almost one in the morning when Manus texts me, to ask if I'm still up. He tells me I have a visitor.

I stare at the text, absorbing his meaning.

Manus: I wouldn't have bothered you, but it's her.

There could really only be one *her*.

One woman who he'd let into my house at this hour, without my permission.

One woman he's seen me with lately.

One woman he thinks I hired for some dubious job after running surveillance on her, then made out with her in the back of my car, brought her home, and let her stay the night.

I head downstairs to find Quinn standing in my foyer.

Manus is nowhere to be seen.

She grips her purse and jacket, wearing a little black dress, with a short skirt and juicy cleavage.

Did she wear that for me?

She already took off her shoes and stands barefoot on my floor.

I stand on the bottom stair, leaving space between us. Her eyes rake over me. I'm not wearing anything but a pair of black pajama pants that I pulled on when I received Manus' text.

And with her eyes all over the front of my pants, I'm already getting hard.

"Hi," she says softly.

My heart is thumping, blood is rushing to my dick, and I'm not sure she understands what she's getting into here. If she thinks she came hard last night, that was nothing.

I've spent countless hours today vividly imagining ways to make her scream.

"I thought you were starting your new job tonight," I say evenly.

"I did. I went home after my shift. But then I just couldn't sleep, so..."

Her unfinished sentence hangs in the air between us.

I wonder what panties she put on for me.

Or if she's wearing any.

"This is stupid. I should go."

But she doesn't go. She just stands there, gazing at me with those wide-open blue eyes.

"Has anyone ever told you," I ask her, stepping down the last stair and stalking slowly toward her, "that you have lost kitten energy?"

"Uh... no."

"I told you not to come here."

"I heard you."

"You should leave."

"I know."

I stop in front of her, and she makes no move to leave.

"I was just thinking that maybe we should do it again, you know?" she says tentatively. "I mean, you're really good at it..." As she speaks, she inches closer to me, her eyes roaming hungrily over my bare upper body. "And it seems kind of lonely in your house. It's a shame." Her pretty eyes meet mine. "You really shouldn't let such talents go to waste, all alone in here..."

I swallow. "Careful, Quinn. Talk like that will get you fucked." I mean it as a warning.

But her eyes flare with heat.

My pulse is slamming in my cock.

I'm wrestling with whether to throw her over my shoulder again or throw her out, when she launches at me. Her mouth slams against mine, and I catch her.

She moans, sliding her sweet tongue into my mouth.

I'm supposed to say no to this?

Send her away?

I'm already drowning in the way she kisses me as she climbs me like a tree. Like she's been thinking about this all day.

The way she sucks on my lips, like she's hungry for it...

"Just one more time, okay?" she breathes.

"Yeah," I manage between kisses. "Just one."

The next thing I know, I'm carrying her up to my room and kicking the door shut.

Chapter 13

Harlan

When I set Quinn down by the bed, her purse drops to the floor. She tosses her jacket aside, and we stare at each other. I'm fucking panting.

Maybe I just need to have her again, to purge myself of this growing obsession with her.

One night just wasn't enough.

I've never tried to fuck a woman out of my system before her. I've never had to. But it's worth a shot, right?

"You broke my rules," I growl.

Her eyes open wider. "I... I guess I could text you first, next time..."

"There won't be a next time," I remind her. "And you learned last night what happens when you break my rules, didn't you?"

"Uh..."

"Take off your dress."

She hesitates. Maybe she's feeling shy. It just makes my cock harder when she finally strips it off.

"Panties," I say.

They're tiny and black, and match her bra. She shouldn't have bothered.

She slides them off, too.

She takes off her bra without being told, as I watch. It's a stretchy, lacy thing without stiff cups or an underwire, and it inspires me. I take it from her hand before she can drop it on the floor.

"This time, you don't come until I say you can," I say sternly.

She eyes the bra in my hand warily. "Yes... sir?"

"You know what I like to hear."

"Yes... Harlan."

"Good girl." I set about tying her wrists together with the bra.

"Um," she says, as I cinch it tight, "that's a nice bra you may be ruining."

"I'll buy you a new one. Lie down on the bed."

She climbs awkwardly onto the bed and I instruct, "On your back. Arms over your head. Legs spread."

She does as she's told, her cheeks flaming. The mixture of shyness and eagerness is stunning.

I've never met anyone like her.

I've never had my cock and balls throb all day just thinking of someone. Except maybe when I was a teenager.

I'm both fascinated and disturbed by the hunger I feel.

The only sensible solution to this problem is to satisfy it with a thunderous orgasm, while deep in her pussy. Or so my body tells me.

All the blood is rushing away from my head.

I slip my pants off and toss them away, and kneel on the bed between her legs. I push her thighs farther apart as her gaze drops to my erection. She licks her lip.

I feel a surge of animal pride.

"You want that?"

She nods.

"Say it."

"Yes," she whispers.

"Don't move," I order, and give my cock a leisurely, gratuitous stroke as she watches. "Be good, and you might get it."

Lies. She'll get it no matter how good or bad she behaves.

Cock as reward. Cock as punishment.

It's really all the same, isn't it?

Win/win.

Maybe she knows it, but she's desperate for this little game we play.

"Why did you come here, Quinn?" I demand.

She swallows. "Because… I liked what you did last night."

"You want more?"

"Yes."

"Ask me nicely for what you want, Quinn."

The flush creeps down her chest. "I—I want you to take control."

"You want me to tease you and spank you and fuck you and call you a good girl while you come on my dick," I correct her. "Because you love it."

"I love it," she forces out. I can't tell if she's more aroused or embarrassed.

I run a finger up her inner thigh, and she trembles.

Aroused.

I can feel it, beating in her frantic pulse, as I skim my hands up her curves.

I lower myself over her with purpose, taking my time as I consider her pretty body and which part to feast on first.

This time, I start with her breasts. Squeezing them together, then cupping them with my palms, stroking her gorgeous, hard nipples with my thumbs—and watching the way her eyes change as arousal courses through her body.

I suckle each one, stimulate it with my tongue, then bite a little, making her gasp.

Her hips buck.

"Naughty girl," I chastise her. "Tonight, you'll keep your hips completely still while I make you climax. And when you do…" I flicker my tongue over one cherry-bright nipple. "You'll earn yourself another orgasm."

She swallows, and bites the side of her lip.

I kiss my way down her belly, placing a kiss between each word. "Not… one… twitch." I glance up at her. "Do you understand?"

"Y—yes, Harlan," she breathes nervously.

When my fingers drift toward her pussy, her whole body tenses.

"Just try to relax," I say soothingly, my breath teasing her clit. "And enjoy your punishment."

"Th-this is punishment?"

"Yes. Good girls get to come. Bad girls have to wait."

"Oh, god," she moans.

I start playing with her pussy. Teasing with my fingers. Tasting with my tongue. Sucking. Kissing.

I listen to her answering moans like sweet, sexy music.

I tease her clit until it's nice and swollen.

Then I play with her tits for a while. Plucking at her swollen pink nipples. Taking my time. Licking. Nibbling.

"Making you suffer with pleasure…" I tell her, "just makes my cock throb harder."

She groans.

I play with her clit some more, alternating between licking and suckling, until her cries of pleasure mix with sobs of ecstasy.

Her hips twitch, just barely, and I sink my teeth into the softness of her upper thigh.

She squeals a little.

"You moved."

"I did not," she pants.

I suck her clit into my mouth and flicker the tip of my tongue over it, hard. Tears run down her temples as she quivers. Her tits jiggle with the effort as she hyperventilates.

But her hips don't move.

"That's much better," I murmur, and reward her with a much gentler lashing of my tongue.

She presses her lips together, muffling a soft scream.

Then she gasps, "I think I hate you, Harlan," her voice drunk with pleasure.

"Is that any way to talk to the gentleman who's eating your pussy?"

I slide my middle finger into it, making her groan deliriously.

She trembles, but her hips remain flat on the bed as I fuck her in long, slow strokes with my finger. She's trying so hard. Taking her orders like a very good girl.

"And by the way, your pussy is *soaked*."

"You're a monster," she moans, her pussy pulsing around my finger.

I chuckle.

"A big... bad... monster," she huffs, eyes squeezed shut.

"I'll take that as a compliment," I tell her.

Then I lightly slap her clit.

Her eyes fly open, meeting mine. I slap her again, and she cries out again, her face flushing pink.

Her pussy ripples on my finger.

"You're very easy to read when you're naked in my bed," I tell her.

I'm sure she'd love to call me a monster again, but I pinch her clit, and her eyes close halfway. I tug, and she moans, her body tensing against the pressure. She's struggling so hard for me. Barely holding it back.

Which is good, because I don't know how much more I can take.

I'm sweating, and I'm rock fucking hard.

I pinch her clit again, and she jerks under my fingers. *Fuck, yes.*

"Please, Harlan, *please*," she sobs.

"That's a good girl. Come for me."

I feel her falling apart and quickly withdraw my finger, getting myself lined up. I shove my cock into her as she starts to come, pinning her hips down with mine. She's impaled on me, and climaxes with a scream.

I don't move, just basking in the wet heat of her. Her pussy spasming, tugging on my cock. Breathing through it and trying not to blow.

I watch her beautiful face in ecstasy, her eyes rolling closed, her open mouth. I lean down and kiss her, driving my tongue inside, and she sucks on it desperately.

I resist the pull of every pulse and twitch until she lies still, panting.

Then I start fucking her, deep and hard.

"Don't move," I tell her. "Just take."

She moans a response as I pound into her. And all my dirty thoughts come pouring out.

"You loved it when I spilled in you last night," I utter in her ear. "When I came, you came."

She pants as her arousal builds again.

"You want my come, don't you, Quinn? You want my hot seed."

She moans again, not really words, but I think she's beyond that now.

I would be, too, if I just came like that.

"You loved it when I filled you with my come. When I left myself inside you, and you could feel me, running down your thighs..."

She whimpers as I suck on her neck.

"I bet you could feel me all damn day."

She makes a strangled noise when I shift my angle—so I'm ramming harder against her clit, my ball sac slapping against her as I pump. I'm hammering her, and she's loving it. She's screaming now, those pretty little helpless cries of hers, totally lost to the pleasure I'm giving her.

I have to murmur my dirty words right in her ear, so she can hear me.

"My balls are so full for you, pretty girl. They're so fucking heavy with come. And if you're very good for me... I'll let you have it."

She shudders when I lick her ear lobe, then bite.

"That's a good girl. Don't you move a muscle unless you're coming for me."

She whimpers as I pick up the pace, fucking her faster.

"This is the last time," I tell her, desperate to believe it myself. "The last time I ever fuck this sweet pussy. So I promise you... I'll make it good."

"Oh... *fuck*..."

I pump into her a few more times, grinding my hips, and when I feel her tense, hear the change in her breathing, I know she's almost there.

"That's it, sweet girl," I pant. "Come for the big bad monster who fucks you so good."

She climaxes on my dick again, and the heady rush is too much to withstand.

I manage a few more deep thrusts as she convulses beneath me, whimpering through her orgasm. I can see the intensity of her pleasure all over her face, and I come with a final thrust and a shout I was not expecting.

The climax rocks me, and I fill her in long bursts. I keep rutting into her with a groan, shaking with the pleasure as my balls empty.

I get the dizzying sensation that for the first time in my life, I'm not pouring myself out. I'm being pulled.

Jesus. *Fuck.*

I collapse against her, savoring the aftershocks as they tremble through me.

I don't mean to crush her, but she seems perfectly content, panting and warm beneath me. And I'm momentarily unmovable.

I catch my breath.

Once again, Quinn is filled with my semen, and I don't feel finished.

I feel like this is exactly where I want to be.

It's primal, this need to have her take me into her body. To seize control of her. To fill her. Possess her.

Obsess her.

For just a few minutes, to try to make her feel the all-consuming *want* for me that I feel for her.

Chapter 14

Harlan

I lie sprawled on my back under the sheet, too warm for blankets, my heart still pounding. Quinn lies next to me, snuggled into my armpit, her head on my chest.

I don't know how we got here. I just kind of fell over after the sex, untied the bra from her wrists, and we ended up like this.

I can't move.

But my thoughts are racing.

Obsession never rests. It only feeds, which just makes it more hungry. And now mine needs to be fed—with more data.

"Are you looking for another bakery job?" I ask her.

"Oh. We're doing this, are we?" She gazes up at me with wide eyes, ridiculing me. "Pillow talk? Really?"

"Humor me," I growl.

"Why would I do that?"

"Because if you don't," I say silkily, "I'll hold it against you."

"That was a very sexy-sounding threat," she says. "I thought we weren't having sex, ever, ever again." She rolls her eyes.

I consider that. And how I should spank her for sassing me in my bed.

I know what I said to her.

I'm not sure my body agrees with my words.

My words were a lie meant to force us apart after we fucked. Clearly, since she's laying in my arms, it didn't work.

I war with it for a moment.

Then I tell her, "We aren't. Since that's the case, you might as well answer me."

She considers, but seems too tired to argue further.

"Yes, I'm looking for another bakery job. I'm not desperate about it, though."

"Don't you need somewhere to bake your cakes?"

"Yes. But I've learned from experience. I've been desperate about jobs before. And I'd rather be in a good working situation than a bad one out of desperation."

I'm not sure how to take that.

"Was it bad at Crave?"

"It... wasn't great. There was a lot of pressure. And Justin was a very stressed-out boss."

I'd rather she never mention another man's name in this bed, especially one she was fucking so recently. I'm a jealous man. But I'm also compulsively curious when it comes to her, apparently. It's an itch I need to scratch.

"He didn't treat you well?"

"As an employee? No. As a semi-girlfriend, or whatever I was to him? No. I mean, yes, he let me use the facilities at Crave so I could make cakes for my clients. But the trade-off was that I was at his beck and call. I was always working overtime for him last minute. Doing him extra favors without being properly compensated, while he strung me along with vague promises that he'd promote me."

"I should fire him."

She lifts her head, looking up at me with wide eyes. "He's working for you?"

"We kept him on after buying the bakery. He's still running it."

"Ugh." She settles her head onto my chest again. "Well, please don't fire him on my account. If he's the best person to run the bakery for you, so be it. He's good at his job," she adds grudgingly. "That's why I wanted to work for him. To keep learning."

I make a vague, grumbly noise.

After a moment, she says, "Harlan? I know tonight was just a one-more-time thing... but can you please not fire him now? I know you want to."

"I never said that."

"You just said that," she says patiently. "I realize ethics may not always be your first priority in business, but it really wouldn't be ethical to fire him because a woman in your bed talked shit about him."

"Thank you for the business advice, Quinn," I say evenly.

"Do it for me?" she says softly. "Please?"

I think it over. "Okay."

"Can I trust you?"

"About this? Yes."

"Hmm," she says. "Look, it was my fault for buying what he was selling, and letting him take advantage. But he did make unrealistic demands on my time and energy. That said... he's a great baker."

I don't agree that it's totally her fault. She seems to take on responsibility for things that don't always need to be on her.

But it's admirable that she's so self-sufficient and responsible. I suppose.

Admirable and irritating.

"Why did you put up with it?"

She blinks up at me. "Okay, maybe this isn't a reality that you can comprehend, but some of us don't have ten-digit bank account balances. We get these things called jobs and we rely on them."

"Thank you," I tell her, equally condescending. "I didn't actually go to business school or learn math. My family just handed me the job of CFO straight out of high school."

Her eyelids lower, unimpressed. "I'm sure you worked very hard to prove yourself."

"I did, actually."

"But you have to admit you had a giant head start."

"I'm not denying that."

"Anyway... I'm used to supporting myself. It's not that big a deal. It's just that..." She hesitates, then says quietly, "When I had to start supporting Mom, too, that's when things got hard. I wasn't ready for it. But my new job at Champagne has been a huge help. They already offered me six nights a week, if I want them."

"But doesn't that take time and energy away from making cakes?"

"Yes, but it puts money in the bank. The tips are worth it. Right now, I need money more than I need to make cakes."

I don't like that. "You're not giving up on Quinn's Cakes, are you?"

"No. But there's only so much of me to go around. And only so much I can get done in our cramped kitchen anyway. Mom's cupcake orders take up space, too."

I consider this. And the fact that she was very adamant that she didn't want me to arrange a job for her. I'm still calculating if I can work around that.

"What would your ideal job be?"

"One that pays enough to cover my bills, and that I don't hate. And frees me up to make cakes. That's all I want. To make Mom's dream a reality."

"You're talking about the bakery thing?"

"Yeah."

"You just said it's your mom's dream. I thought it was your dream."

She sighs. "It's both. She's always wanted her own bakery. There's no way that's happening now, if I don't make it happen."

When she's silent for a moment, I ask her, "Do you want to talk about it?"

"About what?"

"Her illness."

She takes a deep breath. Then says, "I forgot that you knew about that."

"It was... evident. But I don't really know why you were taking her to the doctor's office."

She looks up into my eyes. "You really had surveillance on me?"

"It's just what I do. I need to have all the information about something, all the facts, before I make a decision."

"And what decision have you made about me?"

I don't have an answer for that.

I mean, I do.

I just don't feel like sharing that I've decided she's a threat to my sanity. I've already made it clear we've fucked for the last time. That there can be nothing more between us.

She doesn't need to know how completely mixed up I am about it.

I can't stop wanting to fix all her problems, control her life, make her do dirty things in my bed. But *that's* the problem. It's better if we just say goodbye. But that doesn't mean it's easy.

I'm indulging myself here, lying in bed with her, drilling her for information, when I know I shouldn't be.

"I already know," she says softly, when I don't answer. "That we're not going to see each other again."

We lie here, naked and entwined, and the futility of that declaration, which I've made so many times, feels grossly obvious.

She's kind enough not to mention it.

"What's her prognosis?"

She doesn't reply, but I feel her heart beating against me a little faster.

"Since this is the last time we'll ever talk like this... you might as well tell me."

"You didn't uncover that while stalking me?"

"Your mother's private medical files? No."

"Just checking. You do seem to have godlike powers."

"Thank you."

"That wasn't a compliment, Harlan."

"Sure it was."

"No wonder you have such a large house for one man to live in alone. Your ego wouldn't fit in a regular-sized one."

After a moment, I say, "Some of my staff live here."

Quinn is silent for a long moment. Her breathing deepens, and I actually wonder if she's falling asleep.

"Her prognosis isn't good. But what do doctors know?" she says softly.

"Sometimes very little. Sometimes a lot."

"Yeah," she says sadly. "Sometimes too much."

"We don't have to talk about it. You can go to sleep."

The words are out of my mouth before I really hear myself.

I expect her to make some sarcastic remark about how I just gave her permission to sleep.

And get up to leave.

She only seems to enjoy my orders when we're having sex.

But she doesn't do that.

"For the last three years," she says quietly, "I didn't even make her a birthday cake, until after her birthday had passed. I just can't stand the thought of her not getting to eat it. And I cry on her birthday, because she made it to another one. Then we make a cake together, and go down to the waterfront to eat it. Her birthday is in summer, so at least there's that."

We lie in silence as I try to picture Quinn and her mom sitting by the water, eating birthday cake.

I've never had a moment like that with my mom. It seems foreign to me.

And utterly beautiful.

I think, when I was a kid, I wanted that kind of life more than anything. But even then, maybe I knew it was an impossible dream.

I just didn't have that kind of mother.

But I don't long for that anymore.

I wonder, when was the last time I actually had a dream like Quinn's dream about her bakery?

"If you could have anything," I ask her, wanting fiercely to know, "what would it be? Even if it seems impossible."

She considers for a long moment, then says, "A view of the water."

"Really?"

"Yes. My dad used to love the water. He never had a boat or anything. He always wanted one, but we never had that kind of money. So he would take me down to the waterfront as often as possible, and we'd look at the water, and talk about the boats going by, imagine the lives of the people on them and where they were floating off to. And when I'm feeling overwhelmed or scared, I still go down to the water. I walk along the beach, or on the Seawall. And I feel close to him. And everything just feels… better."

I take that in.

I never had moments like that with my dad, either.

"My granddad was obsessed with the water," I find myself

saying. "He told me that when he was a teenager, he met a man who owned a skyscraper downtown. It was some friend of his grandparents'. And he got to go up to the top and look out at the city, and he could see these buildings all along the waterfront. And he decided that one day, he was going to own them."

I pause for a moment, considering. "He had no reason to think he could do that. His dad owned a modest auto repair business and his mom was a librarian. And those buildings he saw out the window weren't the actual buildings he ended up buying, but before he died, he'd acquired an entire waterfront neighborhood in downtown Vancouver. All the properties along Bayshore Drive, and others close by. And the arena, too, and a resort on the ski hill. Every one of them with a water view. He not only achieved what he set out to do, I think it became his obsession."

Quinn takes that in.

"That's wild," she says after a moment. "Like, what makes one person see a waterfront neighborhood and think, 'I'm going to own all these buildings one day,' and then go *do it*, and another person just sit on the shore and watch the boats go by?"

I consider what she's saying, and I don't have an answer.

I've always felt my own success was driven by a desire to dominate in business.

But more and more, I'm understanding that it's a distraction.

The need to dominate keeps me focused. An extreme work ethic and the demands of perfectionism give my obsessive compulsions an outlet. I work hard. I work a lot. I expect perfection from myself and everyone around me, and when I don't get it, I keep pushing for it until I get it.

The thing is, there is no perfection, so, it's an endless pursuit.

It's also a selfish pursuit.

Maybe Quinn's father wasn't selfish enough. He prioritized his family, and forfeited his chance to acquire boats.

Clearly, Quinn is driven by her love for her mom. She wants to take care of her.

She also wants to achieve their shared dream.

But there's no reason she can't do both.

"You're not going to let the boats go by, Quinn," I tell her. "You'll get your bakery, if that's what you set out to do."

I'm not even sure if she hears me.

She seems to have fallen asleep in my arms.

I know this dream well.

It has the familiarity of a well-worn nightmare, one that never changes.

But it's still deeply disturbing every time.

I've just come home from school.

I'm standing in the foyer of my family's home. I'm alone. But I can hear sounds in the distance, coming from upstairs—a door closing. Then the muffled voices of my siblings. My mom.

More than I can hear them... I can feel their sorrow.

I'm supposed to be there, with them.

I climb the stairs to the second floor.

When I get to the top, I see the door to the room where the terrible thing is going to happen, and I know they're waiting for me.

I walk toward it.

When I finally reach it, I start to open the door.

But before I can see what's inside, I wake up in a panic. I feel the whole bed shake as I jolt awake, panting.

"Hey. Harlan?" It's Quinn. Her soft, sleepy voice next to me in the dark.

I swear and rub my hands over my face. "I was just dreaming," I mutter, disoriented. "I was in my house. The one I grew up in. I haven't been there in years. In my dreams."

I don't know if I'm making sense. The dream is still so vivid in my head and my body. That crushing feeling, of being too late...

"Just try to breathe," she says gently. She sounds concerned.

I take a deep breath and try to relax.

My heart is racing.

I feel her warm body against me, and it's grounding.

"What happened?" she says. "You had a nightmare?"

"Graysen still lives there," I try to explain. "But... the house was different back then. It feels different, in the dream. It sounds different. My mom is... crying."

When I don't say anything else, she asks softly, "Are you okay?"

"I'm okay."

The dream was the same as it used to be. It was always the same. How can it be exactly the same, after all these years?

She slides a hand over my chest, maybe trying to soothe me, and I reach for her. I roll toward her, right on top of her.

She sighs a little, her hands sliding around my back and down to my ass. "Harlan," she whispers, and it's all I need.

I kiss her, hot and slow. Deep. Losing myself in the feel of her. So soft and warm beneath me. I dig my cock into her thigh, already getting hard. And she shifts her hips to accommodate me.

I find her opening, slick and ready for me, and push inside.

I swallow the soft sounds she makes as we kiss, needing to consume her. To possess her again.

To lose myself in her body, completely.

In the back of my mind, I know what I'm doing. I'm fucking her again, when I said I wouldn't.

But I don't care. I sink into her again and again. I don't fucking care.

It's dark in here, and the hunger between us is insatiable. And all I want is the feel of her, sucking me in. I thrust into her again and again, drowning in the sweet oblivion.

But no matter how deeply I fall into her, I know I need to be careful.

I can't let her in.

I can't start to need her.

Need this.

No matter how good it feels.

No matter how many times we come together tonight, I just have to make it clear to her that this won't last.

Chapter 15

Quinn

I feel a warm, strong hand sliding down my back, seeking. Harlan grabs a handful of ass cheek and squeezes.

"Morning, sunshine," he murmurs in my ear, with that liquid-chocolate sex voice of his.

I grumble, face first in a pillow. "Nuh-uh."

"Oh, my." He squeezes again. "Is my sunshiny little friend a grump in the morning?"

"Very funny," I grumble. "We are not friends." I push myself up, turquoise hair everywhere. "And what did you expect me to do, spring out of bed singing 'A Spoonful of Sugar'? I'm not Mary Poppins." I toss off the covers. "I need a coffee and some breakfast. Then I'll be a much better human."

I start sliding off the bed, but he catches me around the waist and drags me back. Right up against his warm body.

His erection, long and eager, pokes me in the ass. "You were much nicer yesterday morning when you woke up in my bed."

"Yesterday I was walking on eggshells, worried about pissing you off or making it awkward or hurting each other's feelings."

"And this time?"

"This time I don't care. Because we already established that this isn't happening again. Which means..." I squirm out of his grip, eel-like, and break free. "We're done here." I give him a winning smile that's the equivalent of the middle finger.

He smolders at me.

I pick up my clothes and my purse from his bedroom floor. "So, thanks for the orgasms," I add casually. "I'll be going now."

"Whoa. What about that coffee?"

I'm heading for the bathroom, but turn on my heel. "What coffee would that be?"

"The one I'm making for you in the kitchen right now?"

I lift an eyebrow.

"Okay. The one I'll have my staff make for you. Do you want it or not?"

"When you put it so sweetly, how could I say no?" I say sweetly. "I'll take it to go."

He lowers his eyelids. "Are you sure you don't want some more of what you had last night, first?"

"Oh, no time for that. I've got a busy day. Cakes don't bake themselves."

With that, I turn and breeze into the lady bathroom, shutting the door. He has two en suite bathrooms, and this one, which would be for his partner, is sadly unused. So, I go about making myself at home.

I really like the idea of making him question whether he made a stupid move telling me that it was the last time we'd ever fuck, *while* we were fucking.

I didn't love it.

I'm thinking yes is the answer to that question, and he now knows it.

Since he screwed me when he woke up in the middle of the night, then woke up with a hard-on this morning and thought it would be a good idea to grope me again, maybe he changed his mind?

Nice try, buddy.

Let him miss my ass, when I take it home and keep it there a while.

This whole shtick of his—the one where he tells me over and over again that we'll never see each other again, and then ends up inside me—is getting old.

I take my time in the bathroom, getting all freshened up to start my day. This time I came prepared, my purse stuffed with supplies for an overnighter, just in case when I showed up at his door he let me in instead of denying me entrance.

The man is all talk.

But actions speak louder than words. He doesn't want to get rid of me as badly as he pretends.

I'm not sure who he thinks he's fooling, but it ain't me.

I take a long, luxurious shower, just because, then do my hair and makeup, and get dressed in yesterday's clothes. I even brought fresh panties.

When I emerge from the bathroom, Harlan is gone.

When I emerge from the bedroom, I hear Tears for Fears playing.

I head downstairs, to the tune of "Head Over Heels," which seems to be emanating from the back of the house. I follow the music through the foyer, and down the grand hallway in the middle of the house, the one that I know leads to a big family room at the back, because I stumbled upon it yesterday morning before finding Harlan in his office.

The music is coming from even farther back, so I continue past the entrance of the family room.

I smell fresh coffee.

The hall ends at the entrance to another room.

I step inside; it's a giant kitchen that's flooded with light from the big wall of windows along the back. It looks out into a lush, green backyard.

The room is gorgeous, and looks utterly untouched.

Except for Harlan, who appears to be making coffee at the counter. Actually, he's making espresso at an espresso machine.

"What's happening right now?"

He looks up, turns the music down to conversation volume, and continues watching the espresso pour into two latte-sized glass mugs.

"Just making your coffee."

"What happened to the staff making it?"

"Thought I'd do it myself."

Okay... he's making coffee for me. I fucking love it when guys do that.

I don't know quite what to do with this. Harlan, freshly showered and fully dressed in a fine black suit, making coffee for me. While Tears for Fears plays.

"What's with the music? You don't seem like a music guy."

He frowns. "I'm not sure what that means. I like music."

"This music?" I say doubtfully.

He shrugs. "Eighties pop seems to be your thing."

I watch him pour milk into a metal jug, the kind you steam milk in, reeling a little over the facts that a) he noticed the music I listen to, and b) he's playing it right now... for me?

"Actually, it's my mom's thing," I say uneasily. "She's been listening to the same songs for decades, which means they've been infused into my DNA. I can't not listen to them."

He glances at me. "You don't like it?"

"I do like it. It reminds me of her." I change the subject; that's really all I'm willing to say. We got personal enough chatting in his bed last night. I don't even know quite how that happened. "And by the way, where are we?"

"I thought you were a baker," he says dryly. "Is a latte okay?"

"You can make a latte?" I exaggerate what is legit surprise. "And clearly it's a kitchen," I add, equally dry.

"There's a machine," he says, taking the jug of milk over to the steamer, where he starts foaming it.

"Since when do you have two kitchens?"

"Since the people who built the house put in two kitchens?" he says, deadpan.

"I don't think I like you in the morning."

The monster smiles at me as he foams our milk.

"I was thinking," he says.

"Great."

"What?"

"Well, last time you did some thinking, you decided it would be grand to blackmail me into being your fake lover. And we both know how that turned out for me."

"It may surprise you to know, Quinn Monroe, that I've actually done other thinking since then. I do it daily."

"How impressive!" I bat my eyelashes.

He frowns. "As I was saying, I was thinking. We could keep having sex. If you want to."

"Oh. *Wow.* How generous. Thank you so much for that offer." I could not put more sarcasm into that sentence if someone had a gun to my head.

He looks slightly affronted. "You don't have to be rude about it. You can say no."

"I can? Gee, thanks for the permission."

His eyes darken dangerously. "You have no idea how much I want to put you over my knee right now."

"Too bad I don't have time for that," I say breezily, running my hand over the waterfall marble island. Jesus. It must be nice to be rich.

"What I'm saying is, we could maintain a casual, just-sex situation. Nothing more."

"Cool. An awkward, surface-level situationship. It's the dream every girl dreams," I say, distracted by the lovely brass faucet on the island sink.

"You can think about it."

"Golly. So many choices."

He seems to let that one go by. Or maybe he just doesn't want to burn himself with any sudden movements. You've really got to keep an eye on that steamer.

"I was also thinking—"

"I can't wait to hear this one."

He glares at me warningly. "You need a kitchen. I have an extra kitchen." He stops there.

"Uh, I have a kitchen. As I already mentioned. There's one in my house, as there is in most houses. I'm starting to think you may need to get your hearing checked. And your eyes, since you saw my kitchen yourself."

"Yes, I saw it. Which means I know how badly you need one for your business. You can't make cakes for clients in that place."

I can, actually. It's just extremely difficult and unenjoyable.

"So," he presses on, "you can use this kitchen. For Quinn's Cakes. You know... just for now."

I'm shocked, truly. I can't even believe he just said that.

"You want to trade sex for a kitchen?"

He glowers. "No, Quinn. I'm not mistaking you for a sex worker. The two offers are independent of one another."

"How wonderful. Penis *and* appliances. It's not even nine o'clock. This must be my lucky day."

"How about this," he says darkly. "If you sass me one more time, I'll consider it an invitation to that spanking I mentioned. And it will be *thorough*."

I ignore my lady parts as they beg me to sass him one more time.

"Look, I warned you that I need coffee. I'll be much more

equipped to handle the penis and appliances talk with caffeine and sugar." He's still glowering, so I add, "Sir?" There's absolutely no deference in it, like there was when I said it while he was pounding me, but it's the thought that counts.

He's still frowning, but doesn't pull me over his knee, so I think we're good.

He pours the milk into our mugs, slowly. "So, sugar?"

"Yes, please."

He stirs in sugar, then starts spooning in the foam like he's gunning for some barista of the year award as I continue my wander around the room.

"So what do you think about the kitchen?" he asks me. "Will it work?"

Is he insane?

It's absolutely gorgeous, and huge. The appliances are Miele. And the endless countertops, floor-to-ceiling cupboards, and ample shelves are a baker's dream.

"I think I just need a minute."

"Take all the minutes you need. I only have back-to-back meetings this morning."

I guess I'm not the only one who can be sassy.

"How perfect do you need to make those? I really don't need the foam." I've barely gotten the words out when he hands me a beautiful foamed latte. "Oh my god, thank you." I take a sip, and assess.

It's divine.

I don't tell him so.

He's waiting, staring me down while he drinks his latte.

"Okay. Are you serious about this?"

He gives me this dry look, like *When am I not serious?*

"Because I'm not sure you've thought this through."

"Try me," he says evenly.

"Well..." I look around again. Am I even entertaining this?

"I would need full access. I can't be seeking you out to ask permission every time I need to get in here and work. I get orders sporadically, and often without warning. So one week it's two cake orders and the next it's five..."

As I'm talking, he reaches into his pants pocket and pulls something out. He lays it on the counter between us. It's a beautiful antique key.

On a diamond keychain.

"This key opens that door." He points at the beautiful French door that leads to a stone path through the backyard.

I don't know what to say.

He actually thought about this, like, ahead of time?

"That actually works?" I hedge nervously. "I would've thought you'd have something more high tech."

"Well, it's prettier than the passcode you'll need for the deadbolt, and for the front gate. I thought it would make a nicer gift."

Did he just say *gift*?

He's giving me... a gift?

"But yes, it works to unlock the old doorknob, then you put in your code."

"I see." I'm still stuck on that word, *gift*.

This feels personal. It's his house, and he's giving me access to it. With a beautiful key.

I don't know how to process this.

I gulp my latte.

"So, you can come and go, use the kitchen anytime you need to," he prompts. "You don't need to check with me. Consider it a business professional helping out a start-up. I've done it before," he adds, as if to make the offer seem commonplace.

"You're trying to make this sound casual. It's not."

"It is. Don't take it personally. It's not personal."

Uh-huh. Whatever he says, there is nothing casual about a

man who fucked me three times in the last forty-eight hours giving me a key to his house.

"It's a key to your house, Harlan."

"It's a key to this kitchen," he corrects me. "Which no one uses."

"Why?"

"My staff uses the chef's kitchen. It's the one that's stocked, so if I need anything, I go in there. This is the family kitchen. I don't have a family."

Right. Okay.

When you think about it logically...

"I guess it is kind of a waste that it's not getting used..."

"It's up to you," he says. "But it's just sitting here. It's a fifteen-minute drive from your place. Much closer than Crave was."

That is true.

And it's a way bigger space.

And it has free parking.

I pick up the key, examining the gold keychain laced with what appears to be real diamonds. They can't be real, though, right?

Wait.

"This... matches the tennis bracelet. The one I lost. I mean, it literally matches it."

He hesitates. Then he pulls something from his pocket again and lays it on the counter. "Then I guess you have to keep it. It's a set."

I stare at the diamond tennis bracelet he just pulled from his pants.

"Can you please stop doing that?"

"What?"

"Please tell me there are no more diamonds in your pants."

"There are no more diamonds in my pants."

I pick up the bracelet, and examine both items. "You're telling me... this keychain is real diamonds?"

Now he looks insulted. "You seemed to like the bracelet."

"Jesus." And now I feel bad. "Um, Harlan... I should tell you. You paid for this bracelet." My face heats with embarrassment. "I bought it with that prepaid credit card you sent me."

"Okay."

"Uh... aren't you mad?"

"Why would I be mad?"

"Because I lost a forty-five-hundred dollar bracelet that you paid for, like the day I got it? And now you're giving me this?" I hold up the keychain, as it really sinks in that I'm clutching close to ten-thousand dollars of gold and diamonds.

"You're a grown-ass woman, Quinn Monroe," he says, quoting me. Is he amused right now? "I'm sure you can handle it."

With that, he finishes his latte, sets the mug by the sink, and starts toward the door.

"Where are you going?"

"I told you, I have meetings."

"But. Where did you find the bracelet?"

"In the hallway." His eyes darken a fraction. "Where I kissed you."

"You had the keychain made to match it?"

"I had a jeweler customize a similar bracelet, make it into a keychain for you."

"I don't know what to say..."

"You don't have to say anything. Just treat this like you would any kitchen for your business. The only rule is, keep it clean. My staff will help with that. You can communicate with them regarding any comings and goings, and anything you need. I'll put them in touch with you."

"Um... okay?"

I can't believe I'm actually agreeing to this.

But how can I not agree to this?

I hear what he's saying. I think. The kitchen serves no real purpose for him, so it doesn't matter to him if I use it. And maybe he's even pawning me off on his staff to deal with, so he doesn't have to.

Maybe this doesn't even mean we'll have to see each other again. I'll be here baking during the day while he's at work, right?

And if things go south, I'll just leave, no worse off than when I came.

I don't know what else to say, except "Thank you."

He frowns a little. I don't know why my thanks always make him grumpy. "It's no problem." He hesitates at the door, his eyes holding mine. "I think we both know... this doesn't change anything. Between us."

Oh, god. This again.

"I think I made it clear where that line is drawn," he finishes.

"Right. I know. Sex only. And coffee. And diamond jewelry."

I manage that with a straight face.

But this man is ridiculous.

Maybe he's been a billionaire too long to understand normal human interactions and boundaries.

He checks his watch, then says far too casually, "I'd have a lot more to say about your smart attitude, with my hand on your perfect ass and my cock in your throat, if I had more time."

Heat flushes through me.

Perfect ass? I don't want to be flattered, but damn.

I consider the kitchen he just offered me. And the preplanning it took to have this keychain made for me.

And the generosity with which he lavished me with orgasms over the last two days.

And this delicious latte.

I decide to reverse my position on denying him more sex.

You know, *for now*.

Because overall, considering how poorly mannered he is, he's been quite nice to me lately.

I set my mug and the diamonds on the counter, and look him right in the eyes.

"What man doesn't have time for a blow job, though? You might need to rethink your priorities, Harlan."

He blinks at me, caught off guard. Perhaps I've stunned him.

I rather like it.

I walk over to him, get down on my knees, and unzip his pants—stunning him further, I'm sure.

He actually loses his balance for a second.

When I suck his thick, half-hard cock into my mouth and start going to town on it, he groans, loudly, hardening in my mouth. And he definitely doesn't stop me.

He moans my name, almost gratefully, and sinks his fingers into my hair.

I guess those meetings weren't so important after all.

Chapter 16

Quinn

When I arrive home, through the back door, Mom is still in bed, so I go about packing up a couple of bins and a cooler in the kitchen as quietly as I can.

Her voice floats in from the hallway. "Quinn?"

"I'm here."

She shuffles up the hall and into the kitchen wearing the giant South Park T-shirt she's been sleeping in. I think some thirty-something guy she had sex with recently left it behind.

Lorraine Monroe looks a lot like an older version of me. People used to think we were sisters, sometimes. But that was before she got sick the first time. She's aged a lot in recent years.

She takes a seat at the breakfast bar, blinking at me sleepily. "I slept in."

"I noticed. It's like I'm living with a koala." Right on cue, she fires up a joint. "Do you really have to smoke in the kitchen?"

"What? You're not baking right now."

"I'm breathing."

She smiles. "Doctor's orders. Cancer has to have *some* perks."

I shake my head at her, like I'm the parent and she's the

unruly child. I have nothing against pot. I just don't believe in smoking it with my mom.

Maybe because it makes me emotional, and I don't like getting gushy with her. I'm too fragile around her for that these days, and I don't like her to see it.

She offers me the joint. "It'll enhance your creativity."

"I'm creative as hell, Lorraine. You should see how creatively I keep our bills paid," I quip.

She frowns a little, and I deflect. "How are you? There's lasagna in the fridge for lunch."

"I'm just fine. And thank you." She turns on some music from her phone, because my mom and silence aren't friends. Bowie's "Let's Dance" blares through the house, and she turns down the volume. She probably had it cranked while I was out last night. "Why are you packing?"

"Because I met Prince Charming and he's whisking me away from all this," I say cheerily. I'm halfway serious, but she doesn't know it.

"About time."

"Unfortunately, his castle kitchen doesn't stock enough butter." I pluck several blocks of it from the freezer and pop them into the cooler. "I'll be out of your way when you make your cupcake order this afternoon." It's a not-subtle reminder that she has an order to fill. I point at the overstuffed cork board where we keep track of orders. "The client is coming by to pick it up when she gets off work, but you need to text or call her to confirm the time."

"Yes, ma'am."

"And don't forget, your dirty book club is coming over tonight."

Mom is in about eight different clubs, and they all have something dirty about them.

"It's called erotica, Quinn. Don't be such a pearl clutcher."

I clutch my imaginary pearls. "It's not the books that disturb me. It's the women who read them."

"Women over fifty enjoy sex," she says dryly.

"As you remind me daily." She's actually become a raging cougar since her cancer diagnosis, like she's afraid her time will run out before she gets to shag all the young hotties in the neighborhood. I guess I can't blame her.

"Speaking of which," she says. "Did you see that delivery guy the other day? In his little uniform, with the shorts? Those legs."

"Wow. The electrician's coming to look at that wonky outlet this afternoon," I remind her, neatly avoiding chatting about men's body parts. It's another thing I don't do with my mom.

"I have a calendar app, Quinn."

"Oh, I'm so sorry," I tease. "I didn't realize women over fifty knew how to use such things."

"Brat. Are you working today?"

"I'm not at Champagne again until tomorrow. But I did go pick up one of my turntables from Crave this morning. I just realized I'd left it there."

"And how did that go? Was Justin there?"

"He was. He's still running the place, apparently. And it was uncomfortable. But we didn't really talk."

"Do you need to talk?"

"No. I already said everything I needed to say to him. He wasn't exactly heartbroken when I ended it. He only mildly freaked out when I quit the bakery because it means he has to find another cake decorator willing to work for him around the clock." I hesitate, but decide to tell her, since it's over now. "I guess when he decided to sleep with someone else, it killed the romance for me anyway."

"Oh, Quinnie. Shit. I didn't know."

"It's fine," I tell her.

But she finishes her joint and gets up, comes over and gives me a Mom hug. The best kind.

"I'm all good," I assure her.

She scoops my face in her hands and tells me, "You deserve better."

"I know." I return to packing. "The romance was dead already. I mean, maybe that's why he slept with someone else," I joke. Before Mom can worry that this is false bravado, I add, "I'm moving on. I already found a new place to bake my cakes."

"Really?" She starts filling our ancient kettle with water for tea. "I thought you were kidding."

"Nope."

"Prince Charming?"

"That part was the joke."

"So where's the kitchen?"

Here goes. "Well, it's the luckiest thing. Nicole's friend Megan has this brother-in-law with a great, incredible kitchen he's not even using. Isn't that amazing?!"

I know I'm overselling it with brightness, but I've gotta try.

Mom arches an eyebrow at me, clearly not buying. "Megan... the one who's marrying the billionaire?"

"Yup! That Megan."

"So this brother-in-law... Would he be one of the Vances?" Lorraine Monroe is no dummy.

"He might be."

"I see."

As with most everything that I'm afraid might make her worry about me, I breeze past it. "I've only met him a few times. It's no big deal." I decide against showing her the antique key on the diamond keychain, which might suggest otherwise.

She settles onto her barstool again. "Really? I'd say any man who gives *you* a kitchen either understands you very well or likes you very much. And very possibly both."

"He didn't give it to me. It's just a loaner," I say lightly, which is true. Harlan made it clear that the kitchen is only temporary.

And that our relationship is only temporary, and sexual.

Which means I won't be telling Mom anytime soon that I'm screwing him.

While she might be into casual sex for herself these days, I'm not sure she'd be thrilled about any man wanting to fuck me while constantly telling me we're never going to see each other again.

She never believed Justin was the one for me, and I know she worried that I was giving way more than I got in that relationship.

Of course, she was right.

But I don't want her to disapprove of Harlan.

As much as it annoys me, I always want her approval. She's my role model.

She had a beautiful relationship with my dad. She's the queen of cupcakes, and taught me almost everything I know in the kitchen. And maybe it took me until I was an adult to really appreciate it, but she worked hard as a single mom to make my life as worry-free as possible after Dad died.

I want nothing more than to do that for her now. The last thing I want her to waste her precious energy on is worrying about me.

"Don't worry," I tell her, snapping the lids on my tote bins shut. "The kitchen is amazing and there are no strings attached." *I think.* "I'll send you photos of it."

"I'd love to see it," she says cheekily, and I know she wants to see *him*. She probably thinks I like him. "And does this mysterious kitchen benefactor have a first name?"

"It's Harlan," I admit. Then I add hastily, "Please don't look him up." Nicole didn't find much, but you never know.

The man doesn't exactly give "someone you want your daughter to date" vibes in spades.

"I make no promises," she says.

"Have a lovely day, Mom. Eat that lasagna." I give her a kiss on the forehead, then scoop up a bin and head for the back door.

"And where are you off to?"

"I'm setting up my new kitchen!" I can't hide my joy. "I have two client cakes to make this week. And I have to get settled and figure out my new ovens. They're Miele!" I practically skip just saying it.

"Uh-huh. And does your new kitchen come with a bed?"

I pause in the doorway, doing my damnedest not to blush. I balance the tote on my knee, blinking innocently at my mother and feeling sixteen. "Why would you say that?"

"I just noticed that your bed went mysteriously unused last night. And the night before."

"I'm thirty-one, Mom. And you're sounding very judgmental for a woman who has *Eat Me* tattooed on her thigh."

She does. It's one of those details about my mother that I could've died happily never knowing.

She blinks back at me innocently.

She's happy, and it makes me crack a smile. *Damn it.*

"Just don't ask, Lorraine!" I hurry out the door.

"Oh, I will!" she calls after me. "And you better send me those pictures!"

"Please do let me know if there's anything else I can do for you while you get settled," the butler says formally.

"I will. Thank you so much."

I'm standing in the middle of the gorgeous family kitchen that's flooded with light at the back of Harlan's otherwise gloomy mansion, and I'm still having trouble believing this is real. And that I have a butler at my disposal, so to speak.

His name is Carlisle. He's standing just inside the doorway that leads into the grand hallway in the middle of the house, having just walked me in. I have the key and security code, but I still rang the buzzer at the gate when I arrived.

It felt weird not to.

Carlisle formally introduced himself as he escorted me in here, helping carry my bins and cooler. He's so nice. I guess he's paid to be nice, but still.

I wonder if he knows I blew his employer in here this morning.

If he does, I can already tell he's way too proper to let it show.

I also wonder what kind of gossip he has on Harlan. Though I guess there's a zero-percent chance he'd breathe a word of it to me.

"Have you eaten lunch, Miss Monroe?" he asks me politely.

"I haven't." I glance at my phone and realize it's past noon.

"I'd be happy to have Mr. Vance's chef prepare a lunch for you. Would that suit?"

"Oh. That would suit just fine. Thank you. Maybe just something snacky?" I'm not all that hungry. The truth is, I'm too excited to eat.

But who says no to an offer like that?

"How about a charcuterie board?" he suggests.

"That's literally my favorite, Carlisle."

The man beams.

"I'd like a little time to get some cakes into the oven first, though." I hesitate to ask, but Harlan told me to treat the kitchen like I'm literally running my own business here, and if—*when*—I open my own bakery, you better believe my girls will be there to check it out. "And also... I was thinking of having a girlfriend over to see the kitchen, and taste some of my test cakes. Would that be okay?"

"Of course!" He straightens, like he's just been awarded a delightful task. "And will she be joining you for lunch?"

"She will if I tell her Mr. Vance's chef is making it for us."

"Wonderful. Shall we say two-thirty?"

"Two-thirty is great."

"And would you like coffee, tea or wine with your lunch? Cocktails, perhaps?"

"Uh, yeah. Cocktails would be grand."

"Margaritas? Mojitos? Mimosas?"

"You read my mind, Carlisle. I love all the M ones. Surprise us?"

"Very well. And would you like to entertain in the dining room? Or would you prefer a more casual setting, out by the pool, perhaps?"

This just gets better and better.

"Pool, please?"

"Of course."

I add, with hesitation, "You're welcome to taste my cakes, too. I mean, if you want to. I'd love to have your opinion."

"It would be my absolute pleasure."

He says it with such dignity, I believe him.

He leaves me to get settled, and I take a moment to look around the room in awe.

I take a couple of photos, making sure to include the ovens and the lush green view out the back windows. I send them to Mom.

I send them to Dani, too, along with Harlan's address.

Me: Cocktails and charcuterie at 2:30! Bring a bikini!!

She's been on standby for more details ever since I called

her this morning on my way home; I told her I'd have her over to see the kitchen as soon as possible.

On second thought, I send another text.

Me: Bring a swimsuit for me too?!

I didn't exactly think to pack one with my kitchen stuff.

Then I compose a text to Harlan. It's my first time messaging him since we started screwing, and I feel weirdly nervous. Considering that thing I did to him right here, like a total lady boss, in broad daylight, just hours ago, you'd think I'd be over it. Cool as a cucumber.

I can practically still taste him.

But just thinking of him gives me an almost sickening thrill.

Me: This kitchen is beautiful. You don't know how happy I am right now.

I get myself unpacked, move food from my cooler into the fridge and freezer, and lay out everything I need to make a couple of standard cakes. Vanilla and red velvet. I brought my own mixer, which Carlisle carried in from my Uber, and I want to run a couple of cakes through my new oven to get the baking times just right.

I'm just putting the vanilla cake in the oven when Harlan replies. When I see his name pop up on my phone, I get a sweet thrill in my chest.

Harlan: I hope it satisfies.

Oh, wow.
Is he flirting?
I decide not to text him back. I don't need to be *that* eager.

I poke my head into the hallway. I hear faint noise that I think is coming from the direction of the chef's kitchen, on the far side of the dining room, but it's otherwise quiet. I move along the hallway toward the foyer, just wondering if maybe I should take a look around.

In the foyer, I don't see or hear anyone, so I creep up the curving staircase to the second floor. Why not? Harlan's already taken me up to his bedroom. Twice. If anyone sees me, I can just pretend I'm looking for a lost earring.

Harlan didn't expressly say that it was okay for me to roam around when he wasn't here, but when he gave me a key to his kitchen, he had to assume that I might poke around the house, right?

And he never told me not to.

It's not like I'm going to dig through his office or anything.

All I really want is a closer look at his bedroom.

The door is shut when I reach it, and I open it quietly, slipping inside and closing it behind myself. My heart is pounding. Because this feels naughty, but in the good way.

If Harlan found me in here without an invitation, he'd probably just spank me.

I'm very okay with that.

I take in the king-size bed in the middle of the room, the sumptuous, dark bedding and the heavy drapes drawn over the windows. Other than the matching nightstands, which have nothing on them but a lamp, there's no other furniture in the room. No art on the walls.

I've already noticed that while the house is kind of stuffy and formal, a definite neat freak lives here.

I wander across the room, toward the open closet.

When I woke up here this morning and yesterday, I didn't really have the luxury of snooping around either time. He was home, and I wasn't going to do it in front of him. Now, I can't resist wandering into his walk-in closet.

I only glimpsed inside before. But now I see I was right. It's like a designer boutique in here. Not just the subdued lighting, glass shelves, and display cases, but the clothing, arranged so perfectly, it seems unreal.

There's a row of identical black suits on hangers that could've been lined up with a ruler. There's a row of identical black dress shirts hung with the same precision, white dress shirts, black T-shirts with both long and short sleeves, and white T-shirts, too. All hung with the same anal-retentive degree of neatness.

And an array of ties in a glass case, all of them black except one that's gray. I guess that's his party tie.

I run my fingers over it.

I slide open the drawers in the large island in the middle of the closet. Cufflinks and designer watches. Dozens of them. Leather wallets. Tie clips. Pocket squares.

And his underwear. Obsessively folded rows of boxer briefs, all black.

In the built-in drawers along one wall, I find his workout clothes. Sleeveless T-shirts, shorts, jogging pants, all black. And white athletic socks.

What's most striking is the absolute meticulousness, the arrangement of every single flawlessly-folded item.

There isn't a loose thread or a speck of dust anywhere.

I wonder, do his staff arrange it like this for him? Or does he come in here and perfect it himself?

"Miss Monroe?"

I startle when I hear Carlisle call my name.

I hurry to close the drawers and dart out of the bedroom, where I find Harlan's butler in the hall. Clearly, he knew exactly where I was.

I shut the door to Harlan's bedroom behind me guiltily, heart thudding. "Um, hi. I lost an earring," I blurt, before realizing that I'm wearing an earring in every hole in my ears, and my hands are empty. "I mean, I found it. And put it back in." I've barely squeezed out the lie when I cave. "Actually... I was admiring the very nice suits in Harlan's closet. Mr. Vance, I mean." I lower my voice to a gentle conspiratorial tone. "We don't have to mention this to him, though, right?"

"And yet, we probably should," he says, matching my tone.

"Right. I'll do that."

I swear he looks amused. "Your guest has arrived."

"Oh. Great!" I hurry downstairs to find Dani standing in the foyer, looking pool-ready in a flowy, see-through cover-up and a hot yellow bikini, her butterscotch hair swept up in a ponytail, gazing up at the massive chandelier.

"If that thing fell right now, I'd be so dead," she muses.

I give her a hug. "I'm so glad you're here."

"I brought you a bikini." She pulls a string bikini from her tote bag and hands it to me. "And reinforcements. She's creaming herself on the front lawn."

I go to the front door, which stands open, to find Nicole on the driveway, watching some guy with noise-cancelling headphones on and no shirt, mowing the lawn. How many people actually work here?

"Psst! Nikki!" I wave her over, and Nicole hurries past me into the house.

I follow her inside.

"Wow." Nicole gazes up at the antique chandelier. "Megan will die. She says Harlan is sooooo secretive. I think she literally thinks he lives in a cave in the mountains somewhere. That's what Jameson keeps telling her."

"Well, now you can set her straight," I say lightly. I've

already gleaned how private Harlan is. But I'd rather my friends didn't think he was some kind of reclusive freak.

I invited Dani over so she could see for herself that I'm okay here. But now I'm nervous. What if Harlan gets upset that I invited people over when he wasn't here?

"And why do we need reinforcements?" I inquire as Carlisle closes the front door behind us.

"I'm really not sure yet," Dani says, looking me over. "An intervention? An extraction? Blink twice if you need us to bust you out of here."

"I think I'd just let him hold me prisoner." Nicole runs a hand along the banister and gazes up the stairs. "It's so big, you could live here and not even see him if you didn't want to."

"I'm fine, you guys, really." I glance at Carlisle, who's standing by politely, holding the tote bag Dani handed to him like he's some kind of coat tree while she looks around. "No one's holding me hostage. And I don't need an intervention. I promise, this will all make sense when you see the kitchen."

The truth is, I'm kind of hoping baking in his kitchen will mean that I actually *do* get to see more of Harlan.

But if I'm barely admitting it to myself, I'm definitely not saying it out loud.

Chapter 17

Quinn

After two rounds of mimosas, I'm already worrying ninety percent less about what Harlan will think of this as I float on an inflated popsicle in the pool, wearing the outrageously slutty bikini Dani brought for me, along with a cropped T-shirt. She's floating on a sprinkled donut next to me. Nicole is flopped on a rainbow floatie, and the three of us have formed a floating island, arms and legs flung over one another's floaties to hold us together.

Nicole also has one leg flopped onto the side of the pool, next to the tray with what's left of the charcuterie board and our latest mimosa pitcher, anchoring us.

"I thought you were insane when you said bikini," Nicole says lazily as she basks in her bikini and a cropped sweatshirt, her wild brown curls spilling over into the water. "But this is actually amazing."

"Ditto," Dani says, downing her mimosa.

It's the first week of October, which means cool, but the sun is blazing and the pool is heated, and it's actually quite nice. I could laze here all day.

"Who wants a refill?" Nicole offers, and I hold up my plastic champagne cup.

Because how badly have I needed a break like this?

Badly.

I even turned off the oven after I pulled out my perfectly cooked vanilla cake. I cut it into cubes and piled them into a bowl, which sits next to the mimosa pitcher. I can bake more later.

"Okay, ladies," Dani says. "Before we get too comfortable here—"

"Too late," Nicole says, passing us our refills.

"Let's just remember why we're here," Dani goes on. "Which is to get the goods on Harlan Vance. The man who just gave Quinn *a freaking kitchen.*"

"He didn't give me a kitchen, Lorraine," I say. "Jeez, my mom said the exact same thing. You can't *give* someone a kitchen in your house. It's his house. I'm just baking in it."

"And you're not defensive about him at all," she observes.

"Well, we can also talk about that guy you've been seeing. Shit. What's his name?"

"Exactly," Dani says. "I'm currently in the blocking-him phase. Hence the song."

Nicole brought her waterproof portable speaker, and when we rock-paper-scissored for it, Dani won the right to pick the music. Sabrina Carpenter's now singing about how much better life is without some bitch. I think the bitch is a guy.

"Oh. I'm sorry it didn't work out," I offer.

"I'm not. And don't think you can avoid this. It's high time we discussed this Harlan guy, and decide if he's worth the fuss."

"What fuss?"

"Um, hello?" Dani looks at Nicole like, *Jump in here.*

"I love how she always thinks who we date is a group decision," Nicole says to me.

"We're *not* dating."

"Either way. You, dear Quinn, are *obsessed.*"

"I'm not!"

"Girl. I know an obsessed woman when I see one," she says. "You know the way you eat a salted caramel chocolate bar?"

"Um... no?"

"Well, I've seen you do it. And it's the exact way you look when you talk about him."

"Ew. Really?"

"Yes, really. I'm jealous, actually."

I know she means it. Nicole is perpetually single, perpetually looking, and has worse luck than I do with men. She'd love to fall madly in love. Until then, she'll happily live vicariously through her friends' relationships.

"Come on, Quinn. Give us the goods," she says.

"Okay, okay. Fine. Here's the goods." I pause, considering how to put it, well aware that the mimosas are scrambling my better sense.

I'm also aware that anything I do or say might get reported to Harlan by any one of his many staff. But we've got the music playing loudly enough for some privacy, and Carlisle only pops out of the house now and then to check on us.

"The thing is, it started out as that weird fake date scenario. But I guess it kind of became something more?"

Nicole knows about the whole fake date thing now. I had to tell her I went to dinner with him, obviously. She's my girl. And what if it got back to her, via her friend Megan, that Harlan introduced me to Jameson as someone I wasn't? If Nicole and Megan got talking, Harlan's lie about Darla might unravel, and Megan might tell Jameson, and then Jameson would confront Harlan... And I'd have screwed this up for him.

I didn't mention Darla's name to Dani or Nicole. But I did make Nicole swear to me up and down that she wouldn't get involved. As in, she wouldn't tell Megan what I told her in confidence—that the date was fake. And I trust my girls with my life. Nicole would never betray my trust.

This floatie island here? This is a zone of trust.

Anyway, Nicole's not particularly interested in the fake part. All she wants to know is the *real* part, if there is one.

"How much more?" she presses, waggling her eyebrows at me.

"I mean, we've seen each other a handful of times. Even though we weren't supposed to after that one night."

"Says who?" she asks.

"Him. He said he'd never see me again, and the next thing I know, he's showing up at the bakery, and then he's driving me home, and then he's showing up at my place to abduct me, and—"

"Abduct you?" Dani says, eyes narrowing. "I *knew* it. He's blackmailing you again, isn't he?"

I broke down and finally told them about the blackmail thing, too. Maybe not the best idea.

I don't know how Dani will get past it.

Not that I need her to. He's not my boyfriend or anything. And he's never going to be, obviously.

"It's nothing like that. He's actually letting me use the kitchen just to help me out. Like, one very successful business person to another not-so-successful business person."

Dani looks skeptical.

"You know, Megan did this whole fake-engagement thing with Jameson when they first met," Nicole says. "I don't think she'd mind if I told you that now. Just don't repeat it." She shoots us both a zone-of-trust look. "So what is it with these guys? Can't they scare up any legit dates? They're hot as fuck and rich, which is totally my type. And none of them asked *me*. I'm just sitting here, like, waiting on my billionaire to arrive."

I giggle, but Dani's too busy trying to figure out Harlan's evil ulterior motives to be amused. "What do you think his issue is?" she says.

"Well, he's a twin, right?" Nicole ventures. "And we know twins are fucking nuts." She splashes Dani lightly with her foot. Because Dani's a twin, too.

"But boy-girl twins can't be identical, obviously," Dani says, "so that means they're just fraternal twins, which are really nothing more than a brother and a sister in the womb at the same time..."

"True," Nicole says. "It's the identical ones that are batshit."

Dani, who is an identical twin, splashes her back. "He's hiding something. For sure."

"Maybe he's secretly into men or some such thing, and he wants it kept secret?" Nicole suggests.

"Maybe he's into some weird-ass fetishes he doesn't want his family to know about," Dani says.

Then they look at me for my take.

I'm blushing, but maybe we can blame that on the mimosas. My friends look pretty pink right now, too. "He definitely strikes me as a man with secrets," I admit.

"We're overthinking it," Dani concludes. "Maybe he just can't get it up."

"Oh, he can," I tell them.

At which point they find out that I've had sex with him—and freak out.

Loudly.

"Shh!" I hiss-laugh, realizing, when I can't stop giggling, that I'm fairly drunk.

"I will flip your noodle," Dani says, jerking my floatie threateningly, "if you withhold one detail."

"It's a popsicle," I protest, snorting as I try to stop laughing. "Okay. *Okay.* Don't flip me. All I'm going to say is that he has this very sexy way of focusing all his attention on me. And it's... intoxicating."

"Yeah, I'm sure he really puts the *toxic* in intoxicating," Dani mutters.

"Clever!" Nicole says.

"Come on, Nicole," Dani presses. "I know you've gossiped with Megan about Jameson's brothers. Tell us. There might be something you've heard that Quinn needs to know."

"There isn't any gossip about Harlan. Believe me, I've tried," Nicole laments. "All Megan says is that apparently he *never* dates. According to Jameson, he's super antisocial. They call him 'the beast.'"

Dani frowns. "Who does?"

Nicole shrugs. "Everyone. His siblings. His employees. That's what Megan said that Jameson said. And it tracks, right? I mean look at this gloomy castle he lives in."

"Hey. He has a pool, though. And these fun floaties," I say defensively.

"These things?" Dani says. "That his butler pulled out for us? They had price tags on them, because no one's ever used them."

"The house isn't gloomy," I protest. It totally is. "It's Gothic-esque. In a cool way. He wears all black. It's a vibe."

"Well, just remember this is not some fairytale," Dani says. "If he's doomed, you're not gonna save him."

"I'm not looking to save him. It's not like that. He's just... hard to resist. In a nice way." *I think.*

"Even with all the red flags?" Dani presses.

"Red flags are *so* my color," Nicole says.

"There was a disturbingly aspirational tone in your voice just now," Dani notes.

"I just never thought they'd be Quinn's color," Nicole says.

"They aren't," I insist. "And there's more to him than red

flags, guys. We actually have something pretty major in common. His dad died when he was young, too. Fourteen."

"Oh, good," Dani says. "So he has daddy issues? And this is what you're leading with? His childhood trauma?"

"Hey, I don't have daddy issues," I protest.

"Because you had a great dad. What was his dad like, before he died?"

I actually don't know the answer to that.

And I do think my friends have reasons to be concerned.

Maybe Harlan is damaged. Maybe he really doesn't want anything more than dirty but casual sex. But when he gave me the key to his kitchen, it gave me a spark of hope that maybe there *is* something more going on between us.

And maybe what worries me the most is that I'm not as scared of him as I should be. That I'm not running for the hills.

"I don't know why," I tell my girls, "but I just feel weirdly at ease here, in his home. I can't explain it."

"Maybe you don't have to," Nicole says supportively.

"Maybe he just matches my crazy," I suggest. "We do kind of get along..."

"So what do you think happens when two crazy people fall in love?" Dani inquires.

"We're just sleeping together," I say.

"When do you ever just sleep with a guy?" she counters. "The moment your ass hits his mattress, you're making him breakfast and organizing his closet for him. You start nesting. Nurturing. You get attached."

"There's nothing wrong with it," Nicole adds. "It's your nature."

"I'm not getting attached." I hesitate, but then admit, "He said our relationship is sex-only. Like, we can keep sleeping together, if I want to, but nothing else."

"Oh, hello, red flag," Dani says fake-pleasantly. "Thank you for waving in my face so I couldn't possibly miss you. Oh, no, thanks, I'll find the exit myself. Fast."

She gazes at me expectantly.

I frown. "You love sex-only relationships."

"For *me*. Not for *you*. Know thyself, woman."

"I think Lady Gaga said that," Nicole quips. Then she says, "Oh, hello, kitty," totally throwing me off. I look over to see her reaching out for the little black cat that's wandering over to the edge of the pool. It has to be the same one I saw in Harlan's sitting room, the first time I came over.

It sniffs Nicole's fingers, then rubs its little cheek against her.

"I see his cat is black, too," Dani says dryly. "Is this part of the vibe? He's a witch and this is his familiar? Oh, since he's a man, I guess he'd be a wizard or a warlock, right?"

"Actually, 'witch' is gender-neutral," Nicole provides helpfully. "The use of wizard and warlock to mean male witch is more of a fantasy thing and not really accurate."

I roll my eyes. "He's just a regular human, ladies. And that's just a stray cat from the neighborhood."

Nicole's eyebrow spikes. "This neighborhood?"

"It does seem weird..." I consider the cat. "It looks so healthy. Someone must be taking care of it."

"*Don't* feed her."

I startle at the sound of Harlan's voice. I look up to find him standing at the opposite edge of the pool in his suit, glowering at us. "And especially don't feed her cake," he says.

Nicole withdraws the piece of cake she was offering the cat. It's stretched out on the side of the pool now, soaking up the sun and the attention.

"She has a special diet," he mutters.

"I thought she was a stray," I say. Is he pissed that I have friends over?

His dark gaze shifts to me. "She is. She throws up people food."

"Oh."

I notice Dani and Nicole exchanging a look.

"These are my best girlfriends. Dani and Nicole."

"Hi," Dani says.

"Nice to meet you," Nicole says.

"This is Harlan," I add, when he doesn't introduce himself to my friends.

"Hello," he says gloomily.

"I must've lost track of time," I tell him. "What time is it?"

"About four o'clock. I came home early. I'm going to take a shower."

With that, he turns and heads into the house.

I'm not sure how to take *I came home early*. Does he often come home early, or did he hope to see me?

As soon as he's gone, Nicole says, "She?"

"I guess it's a girl."

"Well, is it a stray or not? He seems to know a lot about her."

I break away from the floatie island, and paddle my popsicle toward the side of the pool. "Sorry, girls. I think you need to head out." I know they're both politely ignoring the elephant in the pool right now, namely their first impression of Harlan, but that won't hold. "I want to make him dinner tonight for being so nice to me."

"See?" Dani says. "Nurturing. Next thing, you'll be adopting the cat."

"He does seem really nice," Nicole says with wide eyes that say the exact opposite.

I frown. "You don't know him. Maybe he had a rough day at work."

"And doesn't he have someone who cooks for him?" Dani says. "I thought you said there was a chef."

I haul myself up on the side of the pool. "There is, but that doesn't mean I shouldn't put in the effort."

"Uh-huh. And what effort is he putting in?" she inquires.

I throw out my arms, indicating his luxurious home, which he's welcomed me—and them, by extension—into.

Dani just says, "Please."

My girls climb reluctantly from the pool. And after we dry off, I walk them to the front door to see them off.

They hug me goodbye. Then Dani holds me by the arms, fixes me with her shrewd blue eyes, and says seriously, "Real talk. What happens if things get rough? If Lorraine gets sick again? Do you really think he's going to be there for you?"

"I'm just making him dinner, Dani, really. It's casual. I swear. Thank you for your concern, but I've got this."

Then I shoo them gently out the door.

But the truth is, I'm already asking myself those same questions.

Because the way I'm feeling whenever I'm in the vicinity of Harlan Vance is anything but casual.

Chapter 18

Harlan

After my shower, I head downstairs and find that Quinn's friends are gone. And Carlisle tells me that Quinn is preparing food in the chef's kitchen.

I pause in the kitchen entrance, where Quinn is at the sink, her back to me. She's the only one in the room, which smells of fresh cilantro.

She's washing tomatoes, humming to herself. There are onions and bowls on the counter, a bottle of olive oil.

It's extremely odd, coming home to someone who isn't employed by me.

It's never felt so welcoming in here.

I just stand and watch her for a long moment, tying to comprehend this warmth that emanates from her at all times. Drawing me to her.

It's not just the way she looks, though that's part of it. It's the way she *feels*.

The way I feel when I'm close enough to sense that warmth.

She's changed into a little black-and-white checkered dress. Her turquoise hair is up in a loose bun, with pieces falling out.

It bothers me that I couldn't resist the urge to leave the office early today, and come home after Carlisle informed me that she was here. With guests.

I knew that the surge of jealousy I felt when I heard she was in my pool with people—just women, even—in a bikini, and I wasn't here, was irrational.

I knew that thinking about her all day while I was at work was unhealthy.

I knew that my compulsion to come home and see her was dangerous, if I indulged it.

But that's what I did.

That's what I'm doing.

Watching her, because I can't fucking stop.

I take a step deeper into the room.

"What's going on?"

"Oh, hi!" She glances at me over her shoulder. "I'm making us dinner. I hope you don't mind? I asked Chef Edward if I could. I just wanted to thank you for letting me use your other kitchen. Without *saying* thank you." She glances at me again. "You don't seem to like that."

I drift closer to the counter where the ingredients are. "What are you making?"

"Chicken tostadas. There's some chicken breast already cooked, because Ed was going to use it for your dinner, so this will be easy."

I absorb this, not quite sure how to interpret it.

Not quite sure if I should be jealous. But I am.

She's calling him Ed.

I don't even call him Ed.

"You don't have any actual tostadas," she goes on, maybe misinterpreting my perplexed look. "But we can use taco shells." She makes a hopeful face. "Do you like cilantro, though? Be honest."

"Cilantro's fine."

"Oh, thank god. It's kind of a key ingredient. Did you know some people can't eat cilantro because it legit tastes like soap to them?"

"I've heard that."

"It's because of a genetic variant that affects some people's olfactory sense. I learned that in culinary school. I'm much better at baking than I am cooking, but this dish is served cold, and it's so delicious. It just takes a lot of chopping." She lays a cutting board in front of me and holds out a chef's knife. "Can you chop?"

I take the knife. "Can't we just throw it all in a food processor?"

"Ugh, no. The Romas will turn to mush." She piles a handful of ripe tomatoes in front of me. "I know I said I'm making you dinner, but you've heard that saying, 'If you can lean, you can clean'?"

"Uh... sure."

"Well, Mom always told me, 'If you can look, you can cook.' Dice them up small. After that, I've got cilantro for you to cut up. I'll handle the red onions, so you don't have to cry in front of a girl." She grins at me.

Then she takes an onion to the island and starts cutting.

We chop for a minute in companionable silence, which is fucking weird, while I tell myself to relax. Let down my guard. I'm in my own damn house, in my kitchen.

It just feels like it's been invaded by a sweet, sexy chef I never asked for.

A little voice in the back of my head warns, *Don't get used to it.*

"So... you're a two-shower-a-day guy," she says.

Observant. I'm not sure how I feel about her making observations like that about me. Other than uncomfortable.

"Usually," I mutter. *Sometimes three.*

"I guess you hate this," she observes further. Presumably, referring to the disaster the counter is quickly becoming.

"It's okay. As long as it gets cleaned up right after."

"Hmm." She doesn't say anything else as she takes that in.

I've never felt the need to justify my cleanliness and orderliness to a woman. But I've never lived with a woman.

I rarely even have them in my house.

Maybe that's so I don't have to justify, or explain. Normally, I don't have people anywhere near my personal space unless they're on my payroll.

I wonder how much of my house her friends saw.

"Your friends are... interesting."

She considers that. "They are. But what makes you say so?"

"The conversation you were having when I got home. Something about me being a witch?"

She cringes. "You heard that?"

Her face says, *What else did you hear?*

"Don't worry, I didn't eavesdrop."

"My girls speak their minds, but the mimosas didn't help."

"I guess it's good to have friends who tell you what they really think," I say neutrally.

I really wouldn't know.

"They're just looking out for me. We're like family."

Yeah. I still wouldn't know.

It's not that my family doesn't tell me what they think. I'm just usually not listening, when it comes to their thoughts on my personal life.

Usually, I don't even give them the opportunity to voice them.

"So... can I ask you something?" she says.

"Maybe."

She laughs a little. "Why did you lie to your siblings about Darla, really?"

I take a deep breath. This, again.

"I don't like anyone in my private business."

"Even your siblings? Your twin sister?"

"Even them."

"Huh. So... you were never in love with Darla, though?"

"No. I told you that already."

"But you were sleeping with her?"

"Yes."

She's silent for a moment, but I know we're not done here.

"I lied for you, Harlan," she says carefully. "I'd appreciate more than a one-word answer on this. Like, why can't you just tell your siblings who she really is, and that she's not *me*? Why can't they know the truth, now that your relationship with her is over? Why the secrecy?"

Shit.

I know what she's doing.

And I knew this might happen.

That if we kept seeing each other, she might ask about Darla again. She already told me she was jealous. She knows I lied to my siblings. The deeper I let her into my life, logically, the more curious she might get.

And the closer she might get to discovering the truth about Darla.

That can't happen.

And now, to complicate things, it's clear that her friends don't trust me. They joked—I think it was a joke?—that I'm a fucking witch. So maybe they think I'm working some kind of black magic on Quinn, tricking her?

I have no idea what she told them about me, but logically, she trusts them more than she trusts me. Combine that with the fact that she knows I lied to my family, and she's probably come to the conclusion that I'm not trustworthy.

As in, she trusts me to get her naked, wrists bound, in my bed, but not to tell her the truth about my ex-lover. So, she's going to probe a bit to figure out where the line is, between my lies and my truths.

I've been trying to come up with a solution to this possible problem ever since I realized that she wasn't going to stay away. And that maybe *I* wouldn't be able to stay away. To prepare myself for this moment.

I hoped it wouldn't have to come to this. But here we are.

"Because," I tell her, "she's famous."

"Oh." She sounds... intrigued. Like, way more intrigued than it occurred to me she might be. "Like how famous?"

"Very."

Maybe I should've known it would never be that simple.

"Well, shit, Harlan. Now I need to know."

"I really can't say who she is."

"But you must know by now that you can trust me not to say anything. I didn't mention her to anyone, even my best girlfriends."

I give her a look. "I told you not to."

"I mean... full disclosure, I did tell them you blackmailed me into a fake date."

I stare at her. "Are you kidding me?"

"Um. No?"

"Fuck. Quinn... You told your friend Nicole?"

"Yes. But don't worry—"

"She knows Jameson's fiancée. What if it gets back to him, through her?"

"It totally won't. Nicole is a sealed vault when it comes to me. She won't say a word."

"How do you know that?"

"Because we're *friends*." She gazes at me expectantly. "We're *besties*. We're *girl squad*."

I don't know how that's supposed to reassure me, but she seems to think those terms are sacrosanct or something.

"You should've told me."

"I'm telling you now. So we can build trust." She blinks at me hopefully. "Come on! How could I not tell them? I wasn't going to just go off on a date with you and not tell anyone where I was. You were *scary*. You *blackmailed* me."

I consider that.

"But I never mentioned Darla. Because I don't know her, and she's really none of my business. But..." She bites the side of her lip. "Now that we're having sex... it's different. I'd like to be able to trust you."

That's fair.

I just don't know how we'll accomplish it, if she won't stop asking me questions to which she's not satisfied with my answers.

"So... is she in business, like you? Or like, *really* famous? Like a supermodel or actress or musician?"

Fuck me. Telling her that Darla is famous seemed like the perfect excuse, the best way to make Quinn understand why I would never reveal her identity. But I can see that I was wrong. Her eyes are literally gleaming with excitement.

"It's not for me to say, Quinn."

"Harlan, come on. I'm trustworthy."

She gives me those big blue eyes of hers.

"You're ridiculous," I tell her.

"Please!"

"Why would you even want to know?"

"Because I'm a slight masochist? And I really, *really* want to know."

"No."

"Okay, fine. Just give me some clues and I'll figure it out. Is she like household-name famous? Or like only-in-certain-circles famous?"

She waits, her bright eyes blinking hopefully.

I shake my head.

But the sick taste of dread is gathering in my throat. Her interest in this topic is giving me a glimpse, maybe, of how badly she'd take it if she found out the truth.

She truly cares about this. For some reason I can't fathom.

"How many Instagram followers does she have?" she presses. "Just ballpark." When I don't answer, she says, "Has she won any major awards? Like Oscars? Grammys? Does she have a sex tape?"

I roll my eyes.

"Does she have an album on the charts? Is she on TV? Headlining her own tour? Has she starred on Broadway?"

"Quinn."

"Has she dated other celebrities? Is she internet famous? TikTok famous? Does she get oodles of free stuff to wear on the red carpet? Has she had cosmetic surgery?"

Jesus.

I have no idea what a celebrity's life would be like, nor do I fucking care, because I would never date a celebrity. The whole idea of dating someone famous, who lives so much of their life in the public eye, makes my skin crawl. It offends every fiber of my being.

But... Jamie's an attention whore. He's dated famous women.

Who was that actress who was all over him several months ago? Before he met Megan...

Quinn is still drilling me with questions—"Does she have her own celebrity makeup brand? Has she performed at the Super Bowl?"—when I finally cut her off.

"She's an actress, okay? Her name is Geneviève Blaise."

That finally shuts her up. But her eyes widen, telling me she knows exactly who Geneviève Blaise is. "Oh. Wow."

"Darla is just a pseudonym, for her privacy. Let's leave it at that."

"Okay…" she says. And I can tell it's going to be very hard for her to leave it at that.

But she actually stops talking.

She's looking at me differently, though. Like this new information about my ex-lover is giving her way more food for thought about me.

I don't love it.

What does it matter who I was with in the past?

The past is the past.

I have no interest in hurting her by talking about any previous lovers of mine. It's pretty evident from this inquisition that she's the jealous type. I get that. So am I.

But I'd rather throw her a bone than have her just keep searching.

To my surprise, she doesn't ask any more questions.

Maybe now that I've given her a name, it's uncomfortably real.

"I wanted to be an actress when I was little," she says tentatively.

"So, what happened?"

"Thin skin. I couldn't take all that rejection. So then I wanted to be… wait for it. An accountant."

"Really?"

"Oh, yeah. But all the CFOs I'd have to work under were these horrible, controlling tyrants, absolutely *obsessive* about bossing me around—"

"Watch out," I warn. I can't believe she suckered me in. "You'll get another spanking. Tyrants don't like to be lied to."

"But then I found cakes," she says, ignoring the threat. "They're much sweeter. And sooo chill."

"Well, that's a real loss for all the CFOs out there."

"Hey." She tosses a piece of onion at me.

"I'm serious."

"Sarcasm and seriousness are not the same thing."

"I can't believe you just made up that crap about wanting to be an accountant. And I thought you were the honest one."

She snickers. "Hey. I never said I'd be honest about *everything*." After a moment she adds, "We probably have a lot more in common than either of us would've thought, huh?"

"Such as?"

"Well, for one, I have kind of an obsessive personality myself. Or so my friends tell me."

I consider that.

"Do they really know you, though?"

"Yes. They really do. Better than I know myself, sometimes." She's quiet for a moment, pensive. "I'm thirty-one years old and sometimes I feel like I've already lived nine lives. And I still haven't figured myself out. Do you ever feel like that?"

"No. I know exactly who I am."

I can feel her staring at me.

"Maybe that's why I'm so drawn to you," she says softly. "You're as precise as a razor blade."

Actual tingles run down my back. She's *drawn* to me?

Maybe I knew that, but hearing her say it is different.

"You make me sound so warm and cuddly," I say gruffly.

"You're not. But..." She glances at me, and our eyes connect. "I like how hard you are." She shrugs. "I've always been soft."

"You say that like it's a bad thing."

We stare at each other as my heart thuds in my chest.

She *likes* me? Is that what she just said?

I don't even want her to say that.

Her eyes are glistening, but maybe it's just the onions.

I swallow.

I'm supposed to be in control here.

But I can feel the equilibrium tipping. And I don't even know how to stop the downward slide we're on. The one where we both get wrecked at the bottom.

Maybe because I've never been here before. Wherever this is.

"Quinn. This thing between us... It's just sex."

For a moment, I think she's going to reply with sass. But she says softly, "You made that clear."

"I can't offer you more."

"I know."

But she's probing at my sharp edges, seeking more.

The thing is, she wouldn't like me, if she knew the truth.

That I've lied to her about Darla all along.

And that I'm not going to stop.

Chapter 19

Harlan

When I leave my office mid-afternoon for the second time in a week, headed for home, Brant looks at me strangely, and Manus asks me if I'm unwell.

But Carlisle has informed me that Quinn is at my place, and I haven't seen her in six days.

After we ate chicken tostadas the other night, then she insisted on cleaning up the kitchen herself rather than letting my staff do it, I took her up to my bedroom, peeled off that black-and-white dress and the lacy panties beneath, and ate her out. Until she begged for release, which has now become my favorite thing.

I know this, because it's taken priority over all other thoughts.

The way she moans and pleads, giving herself over to me.

The way she says my name when she's desperate, and I'm in control of her pleasure.

The way she comes for me, so hard, when I tell her she's a good girl.

The next morning, I dropped her at home on my way to

work, and ever since, it's been slightly killing me that she hasn't come back for more.

Every night, I've worked late at the office. When I come home to my silent house, I lay out by my pool or pace the length of my family room, staring at the stars or the ceiling or the floor, lost in thought. I even had Manus procure me some weed so I could smoke a joint; an old habit from college, but something I haven't done in years.

I've also been drinking too much, maybe to try to fill the void she left.

It's like there's something missing that I never thought I needed, never wanted to need, but now that I've had a taste of it, I've stumbled upon this deep, cavernous emptiness I never noticed was there before, just lurking under the surface.

But maybe it's always been there. Like a crack in the floor you step over so many times, and maybe throw a rug over, and you pretend it's not there for so long, you actually start to forget.

Maybe I'm just a spoiled brat, deep down, and I don't like being deprived of my favorite thing.

But as soon as I get home, and I know she's there, I take a quick shower. I put on fresh clothes, though my home clothes are pretty much the same as my work clothes. Black pants and a black collared shirt, just no suit jacket. I roll up my sleeves a bit to make it more casual, wondering what Quinn thinks of the way I dress.

Which is not the kind of thing I wonder about women.

I want to get into her head almost as much as I want to get into her body, which isn't right. It isn't my thing.

But I can't stop it.

The thoughts are there in my head, insidious little compulsions, these wonderings about her, even when I don't want them to be.

I head downstairs and find her in the family kitchen, where

it looks like a bakery exploded. I'm so glad to see her, I'm not even that bothered by the incredible mess of baking supplies and ingredients that's covering almost every surface.

I just try not to look at it.

She's wearing a little lavender-colored dress, her turquoise hair up in a messy ponytail.

She looks like dessert. Sweet, and good enough to eat.

She has music playing quietly, and I ease in behind her. She's measuring what looks like powdered sugar into the big bowl of her standing mixer. I say in a low voice, close to her ear, "Can I get extra sugar in that?"

"Oh! Jesus." She startles, and I give her a wicked smile. "Don't creep up on a girl like that!"

I give her what I think is the closest to a sad-puppy face that I can make. "But I'm so good at it."

"You're a creep."

Oh, but she's smiling.

"So what you're saying is, you've missed me." I settle against the counter as she turns the music way down with her phone.

She glances at me almost guiltily. "This week has been a blur. What day is it?" she jokes as she measures a bit of cream into her bowl.

"You haven't been baking much?" She hasn't been back to use the kitchen until today. I don't want to be disappointed, but I kind of am.

"I've been working so much at Champagne, and I don't have a cake order to fill until the weekend. But I offered to make some cupcakes for Mom because we need a few batches for tomorrow."

"How's the job at Champagne going?"

"It's like nine straight hours on my feet, and I'm not getting home until three in the morning. The tips are excellent, though."

Yeah. That waitressing job is really interfering with my ability to screw her as often as I'd like to. I even went in there last night when she was working, just to see her—and maybe see if I could take her home after. But it was so crowded, so loud and filled with obnoxious drunk people, I had to leave, before she even saw me.

The idea of watching men leer at her became unpalatable as soon as it was right in my face. I don't know what I was even thinking arranging a job for her at Bliss. I've examined it a few times, and can only conclude that I was so focused on the need to keep control of that whole transaction, and make sure she was safe and content—while working somewhere I could keep tabs on her—that I was in denial about the rest of it. And how much I would utterly hate it.

It's for the best she's working at Champagne. It's a nightclub, and I'm sure men hit on her there. But at least people aren't fucking on the premises.

Probably.

I'd really rather she didn't work in a bar at all. But maybe we'll get to that.

"What are you making?" I inquire. I can't even tell, there's so much to look at, and I'm really trying not to.

"Buttercream," she says, and turns on the mixer.

"Why is it so... disorganized?"

"It's not."

"I don't know how you get anything done like this. How do you even know what you put in there?" I eye her buttercream suspiciously as she adds pink coloring.

"Please. I'm a pro. I had to buy more ingredients, but I haven't had time to organize more thoroughly. I will, though." She eyes me curiously. "Why does it bother you so much? You don't have to come in here."

Because you're in here. So, yes, I do.

"It's my house. I like things my way. I think I've earned that right. I pay for it."

"Yeah..." She gives me an uncertain look. "That reminds me. I was supposed to tell you. Carlisle might be upset if I didn't. So, here goes. He caught me snooping in your closet. Like, a week ago. I told him I'd tell you. I was just looking at your suits and stuff," she adds quickly. "I was curious."

"About what?"

"About how freaking perfect everything is in there! And *everywhere* in your house." She shuts off the mixer and removes the bowl.

"It's not perfect."

I watch as she starts loading buttercream into an icing bag. "There's not a crumb or a speck of dirt or a piece of lint anywhere, Harlan. Your staff tiptoe around like little cleaning ninjas, rarely being seen, but making everything flawless for you."

"It's not flawless. And like I said, I pay for it."

"It's more than that. It's not *their* standards they're adhering to." She goes over to a big tray loaded with cupcakes, and puts one on a little turntable thing. She starts icing the cupcake, spinning it on the turntable to make a perfect pink dollop on top.

I don't know what she wants me to say. So I just watch her ice cupcakes, one by one. She *is* a pro. The cupcakes look photo-shoot-ready.

She keeps throwing me looks while she does it, like she's waiting for me to explain my high standards or something.

I don't.

"I've caught you doing it, too, you know," she says. "You wipe down the counters behind my back when you think I'm not looking. You straighten books and mugs and shoes so they line up perfectly. You adjust chairs and doors and windows. You shower in the morning *and* when you get home from work—"

"I like things clean."

"It's more than that, Harlan. I'm not blind."

In the ensuing silence, I consider whether to tell her or not.

It's not something I tell anyone.

My siblings know, because they've lived with me. I'm sure many of my staff have figured it out, too. I don't hire stupid people.

But I don't volunteer the information to them.

Quinn's not stupid, either.

And maybe if I tell her, it'll be another step toward gaining her trust?

"I've been diagnosed with OCD."

She looks at me. She doesn't seem surprised by this, exactly. More like surprised that I told her.

"In the past," I add. "It's not a problem. I have it under control."

"I'm not judging," she says. "I'm kind of fascinated, actually."

"Why?"

"Because. That's another piece of the Harlan puzzle, solved," she muses.

"If you say so." I can't imagine how anyone would find something like my OCD interesting in the slightest. It used to feel like a fucking curse before I tackled it with major therapy.

"What kind of OCD do you have? I know there are different kinds."

"And how do you know that?"

She shrugs. "My roommate in college had it. You know, when I was in culinary school. That was the most hyper-organized kitchen I ever worked in. She'd get mad if I put a cereal box back in the cupboard 'backward.' Let me guess. Orderliness and Symmetry OCD?"

"Correct."

"That's the same as my roommate. I wasn't sure if you were just, I don't know, controlling and perfectionistic."

"I also have Perfectionism OCD."

"Oh. Wow." She considers this for a long moment. "So, I imagine it probably really bothers you when I do this." She takes a scoop of her pink buttercream and blobs it on the counter.

I stare at it, and draw a deep breath. It's not so much the blob of buttercream that's irritating me. It's her conscious attempt to irritate me.

Actually, it's both.

"The rule was," I remind her in a low voice, "that you keep this kitchen clean."

"Don't worry, I'll clean it up. Of course. But first, I want you to taste this." She picks up the cupcake she just iced and holds it out to me.

"You're feeding me cake, now?"

"It's a cupcake, Harlan. And I'd like you to taste it, and tell me if it's good."

"I can already tell you it'll be too sweet for my liking."

"Just taste it." She puts it right in front of my mouth.

I eye her suspiciously.

Then I open my mouth to take a small bite.

She smooshes the whole thing in my face. Half of it sticks to me, and half of it falls to the floor.

I suck in a breath through my nose and glare at her.

"Whoops. My hand must've slipped." She bites her lip.

"Are we doing this?" My voice is dark with warning. "How old are you?" I grab a dish towel, and swipe buttercream and cupcake from my face. "And I thought you wanted to build trust."

"It's exposure therapy," she says innocently. "My roommate did it for her OCD." She picks up another iced cupcake and offers it to me. "You want another one?"

"Don't you dare."

She starts backing up, but she doesn't put the cupcake down.

"Put the cupcake down, Quinn."

I advance toward her and she whips the cupcake at me. It hits me in the chest.

I stop abruptly.

"You just got that buttery shit on my shirt. That'll leave a grease stain."

"Good thing you can afford a new one." She scoops up three more cupcakes, and dives behind the island.

"*Quinn,*" I warn.

She whips another cupcake at me, but misses.

I pick up the whole bowl of buttercream and advance on her.

She screams, drops her cupcakes, and runs.

I chase.

She does a full lap around the island, screaming, almost laughing, and starting to hyperventilate, then makes a run for the door.

I catch her by the hips just before she can leave the room, and haul her against me with one arm.

I drag her over to the kitchen table, in front of the big bay windows. I kick out a chair and set the bowl on the table. Then I undo my belt, unzip, and shove my pants and underwear down as she tries to scramble away.

I sit down, and she squeals as I drag her over my knee, face-down—and my hard-on digs into her hip. I yank up her dress.

"You're being a very bad girl, Quinn. You know that?"

"Yes," she says breathlessly. Defiantly.

It makes my blood boil. In the best way possible.

"You want to be punished?"

"Maybe," she says smartly.

I yank her panties down her thighs, baring her ass.

Then I spank it, thoroughly, as she gasps and wriggles.

When I'm satisfied that I'm now in control, I squeeze, then smooth my hand gently over each reddened cheek.

She's panting now, and I'm rock-hard.

I take a scoop of pink buttercream with my bare hand, and slather it onto her ass.

"That's for a baby shower!" she cries.

"Then I guess you need to make more."

She moans a little as I smear it over both cheeks.

"Any more complaints, little baddie?" I murmur.

She keeps her mouth shut.

I lift her off my knees, then yank her onto my lap so she's straddling me. And sitting directly on my hard cock. She wraps her arms around my neck, eyes shining with lust.

I grab her by the hips, and fill her in one deep thrust. She arches, crying out, and shoves her tits in my face. I pull her dress down, and yank her bra out of my way.

I pinch her clit with my buttercream-coated fingers.

"You've been a very bad girl making my kitchen so dirty," I tell her, nuzzling between her breasts. "Are you a dirty girl, Quinn?"

She mewls a response.

"Words, kitten. I need words."

"Yes," she pants.

"Say you're sorry for being so naughty."

"I'm sorry for being naughty."

She whimpers as I drag my stubble over her skin, making her shiver.

"Because you know what good girls get, don't you?" I pluck her clit with my fingers and lightly bite her breast.

She gasps.

"Good girls get to come," I murmur, "so hard."

I suck a hard nipple into my mouth. She moans.

This. Fuck, I needed this.

I grasp her hips again in both hands and start jerking her up and down, making her fuck me. I suck harder, and she starts to take over, riding me in a frenzy.

My thumb slides over her clit, rubbing insistently, as my other hand squeezes her ass, which is slippery with buttercream. It's all over my thighs. I don't even care what a mess we're making, laser-focused on her pleasure now.

My cock is impossibly hard as she rides it, and I tell her, "That's a good girl. Fuck that cock, Quinn."

She moans. I cup her breasts with my buttercream-coated hands and feed them into my mouth. The more I suck, the more her rhythm stutters, the louder she moans. I feel her pussy contract, squeezing me, and my balls throb as she bounces on them.

"Harlan," she pants, "can I... I need to come. Please?"

It's so fucking sweet when she asks me for permission.

So fucking hot when her pussy pulses around my shaft.

I'm right there with her.

"Yes, baby. You can come. Put a big, juicy come on that dick."

I've barely got the words out when she's grinding against me and shuddering, crying out. She crushes her face into my neck, hips jerking, and I lose it. I slam her hips down on me and release with a growl of pleasure, filling her in hot bursts.

We're still coming when her phone starts to ring.

It must be her phone; it's an annoying electronic jingling, coming from the kitchen counter.

We both ignore it. Eventually it stops, and we cling together, panting, a sweaty, buttercream-smeared mess.

Then her phone chimes a few times.

She lifts her face from my neck and meets my eyes. Her

pretty face is flushed, and awash with sated pleasure. "Well. That was messy," she says dreamily.

I pull her to me and kiss her soft, swollen lips.

And her phone starts ringing again.

She moans, but not with pleasure this time.

"Is that your phone?"

"Yes. Shit." She gets up, awkwardly extracting me from her body as she stumbles a bit. I catch her. "I should see if it's important. It could be Mom."

I smack her ass, and she flashes me a dirty look before darting across the room.

I struggle to stand myself, and debate whether to pull my pants back up right over the buttercream, or try to slip up to my shower, pants down, without running into any of my staff.

"Oh my god."

When I look up, Quinn is staring at her phone, and her face has gone pale.

Her wide blue eyes meet mine across the room, and she looks panicked.

"It's my neighbor. She's driving Mom to the hospital."

Chapter 20

Quinn

I'm decorating a forest-themed kid's birthday cake in Harlan's kitchen, while watching a movie starring Geneviève Blaise. It's playing on my iPad, on a stand next to the cake.

It is extremely difficult trying to mix all the different colors of buttercream that are required when I'm barely looking at what I'm doing.

She is terrifically, uncomfortably beautiful. And a good actress, too.

I'm almost convinced that she's actually fucking that guy on-screen. But it's a pretty big-budget Hollywood movie, not a porn, so I'm guessing not.

She's playing the seductive mistress who lures a wealthy married man into a steamy affair, and then very bad things happen. It's a thriller. There are many murders.

And many, many sex scenes.

In which she wears very little clothing.

I'd probably stop watching, to protect my mental health, if she weren't so mesmerizing. It's both fascinating and maddening picturing her with Harlan. Which is remarkably easy, since I've now seen them both undressed.

I make excuses to myself about why I'm doing this. The movie is new on Netflix, so why not? I need the movie to keep me company; I'm not used to working completely alone. Usually when I'm baking, there are other employees coming in and out, or I'm with Mom.

I could put music on, which is what I usually do.

But instead, this.

When it ends, I put on another movie starring Harlan's gorgeous ex-lover. Now she's playing a hot college professor who seduces her hot jock student. Then bad things happen.

I'm noticing a pattern here. They definitely typecast this woman, but when you look that good in garters and stilettos, I guess it's an occupational hazard.

I can't believe Harlan fucked her.

I can't believe he hasn't fucked *me* in almost two weeks.

That's how long it's been since the night he drove me to the hospital, after we messed up his kitchen. When I was finally able to get back here five days later, it was pristine.

The staff cleaned up our mess.

Well, mostly my mess. I started that cupcake fight.

Though Harlan really finished it...

I wonder if he was more bothered by the mess than he let on. But I really don't know for sure why he's been so withdrawn.

When he stepped up to drive me immediately to the emergency room—with buttercream down his pants, no less—it made me want to draw closer to him. But it seems to have had the opposite affect on him.

The man's mood swings are dizzying.

I've been trying to decode his mystifying behavior, but he really hasn't given me a whole lot to go on. It's like every time I lean in, he tells me I shouldn't, but then he leans in, too, and harder. Then he pulls back.

And now he's pulled way, way back.

When I haven't been at home helping Mom, I've been working at Champagne a lot, and the few times since that night that I've come over to work in his kitchen, he's been at work. And I've barely heard from him.

I've texted him almost daily, subtly flirting, making little jokes. He responds, but not quickly, and not with more than a word or two.

I've even tried looking for him online, desperate for a little hit, but on the internet it's like the man barely exists.

I'm so fucking confused.

I've been trying to distract myself from my obsessive worries that maybe he's over me and our sexy little fling, already, by busying myself with work. It's easy, when there's always so much work to do.

But I still can't stop thinking about him.

Missing him.

And now here I am, scrutinizing his former lover, as if that will help me understand him better.

The lover he's trying to protect by not even telling his family he was seeing her.

I just don't get it.

He says he didn't love her, but maybe that's not true? Because he's gone to some pretty extreme lengths to protect her privacy.

I check the clock. It's four-thirty, and I wonder if I'm going to see him today. Or if he won't even come home until after I'm gone. Which seems to be his thing now.

Finally, I decide to text him.

Me: I'm baking at your place today. What time do you think you'll be home? I can make dinner.

Ugh. When I read it back—after sending—it sounds like something a clingy, wannabe girlfriend would say.

At least I don't have to sweat it very long. By the time the hot jock finds the sexy professor he's banging in bed with his father, and a naked fist fight ensues, Harlan texts me back.

Harlan: Not sure. I have a meeting.

I decide to believe him.

And try to lure him with sex, because I'm getting that desperate.

Me: Too bad. Sounds boring. And here I am all alone in your kitchen wearing an apron and not much else.

His reply is immediate this time.

Harlan: Shut... your... mouth.

Excitement tingles through me.

Me: Come home and shut it yourself.

He doesn't answer.

Since that night at the hospital, I'm really not sure how to interpret these silences of his.

He didn't actually come in and meet Mom, but when he dropped me off at emergency, he told me to call him if I needed anything.

I didn't, because I didn't need anything from him.

Mom is fine, thankfully, except for a broken ankle. She tripped on our rickety front steps, which I suppose anyone could've done, while carrying a box of cupcakes out to a client's car. But she should've been more careful. She never asks for help when she needs it, and she's weaker than she used to be. She's tired more. She gets lightheaded, even dizzy.

And I should've been there to help her, to make sure that didn't happen. I felt so horribly selfish about it, I didn't leave her side for days.

Harlan sent us food, takeout from some amazing restaurants, for the whole week afterward. So neither of us had to do much cooking.

But when I asked him to come over for dinner as a thank you, and meet Mom, he made an excuse not to come. Something about a business dinner he couldn't get out of.

I mean, it could've been legit. I have no way of knowing.

I tell myself I should just give him whatever space he needs, but maybe I'm trying to protect myself. I know my mom's illness is a tall order for anyone to handle.

I try to stop checking my phone, hoping for a reply, and focus on my work. While torturing myself with the rest of this steamy, twisted movie.

It seems to be reaching the climax when Harlan suddenly walks into the kitchen.

Geneviève Blaise is on-screen, making out with yet another male actor. I think he's the hot jock's coach. I've lost the plot.

Harlan totally sees it.

"Uh, hi." I quickly close the cover on my iPad. Where the sex sounds continue to play. "*Jesus.*" I flip it back open and jab at it. "Doesn't this automatically... pause...?"

I set the now-silent iPad aside, and pretend that never happened.

"Welcome home. Hungry?"

"What're you watching there, Quinn?" he inquires.

"Porn."

He gives me a wicked look. "Liar." Then his gaze moves over me hotly. "How disappointing. There are a lot more clothes than I expected under that apron."

I try to act cool. "Yeah. I got cold, so I had to put some on. Sorry you missed it."

He *tsks* at me. "More lies."

"What can I say? You're a bad influence."

Heat rushes through me when he looks at me like that. Like he's thinking very carefully about how he's going to punish me for that sass.

I guess it's time for another mood swing? Distant Harlan is now horny Harlan again?

But he seems to be in no hurry to pull me over his knee as he strolls over to the counter, where he places the bottle of wine he's carrying. Then he proceeds to pull out two glasses.

"Wine?" he asks me, starting to pour.

"I would love some. But not yet. I don't like to drink while I'm doing client work. There's a lot of precision going on in this forest. No one wants *Happy Birthday Henry* misspelled."

"Especially not Henry."

"Well, in this case, Henry is three. He might not notice."

He smiles, just a little.

Interesting.

I'm not sure I know what Harlan in a good mood is like, but I think I might be meeting him for the first time.

Post-sex Harlan? That's maybe the nicest mood I've seen.

He picks up his wine and takes a sip, leaning a hip against the counter.

Relaxed Harlan?

I don't really know this guy, either.

"How's Lorraine doing?" he asks.

I like that he calls Mom by her first name, even though he hasn't met her.

"She's doing fine," I tell him. "Hobbling about on her cast. We argue daily when I catch her doing things she's not supposed to, like getting out of bed when she needs rest. But she'll recover. It's her dignity that took the biggest hit. She says falling down stairs and breaking an ankle is 'old lady shit.' She keeps bitching that next time it'll be a hip, and I'll have to put her out to pasture."

I give him a look that I hope conveys how much shit that woman puts me through.

"Sounds reasonable. And like she hates being treated like a sick person."

"Hey. Don't you take her side."

"Wouldn't dream of it," he says indulgently, in that silken-chocolate voice that makes me melt. "But maybe sometimes what she needs from you is space more than smothering."

I gape at him. That might not've hit so hard if I didn't get the feeling he wanted the same thing from me.

I compose myself. "Am I being smothering? I just offered to make dinner..."

His eyebrows pinch together. "What? No. I'm just saying... your mom may be battling an illness, but she's a grown woman. And so are you. You can't be there all the time. She probably doesn't want you to be missing out on anything because of her, right? And you shouldn't feel guilty for having a life, especially when you're working so hard to try to support you both."

"Hmm. How did you know I feel guilty?"

"It's written all over you, Quinn."

Great.

"Have you ever thought about getting in-home care? Someone to be there, cook for her, just make sure she has what she needs when you're not there?"

"Of course. But I can't afford that." I don't really know how to explain this to someone who's never had to worry about money. "She took care of me for a long time, by herself. After my dad died. And now that I'm the one who's the caretaker, I know that wasn't easy. We never had a fancy life or a big house, but she worked hard. She sacrificed. All that. The least I can do is the same for her."

He considers that.

"You don't like asking for help," he says, "because you're a lot like her, right? You feel like you need to do it all yourself. And you want her to be proud of you for it."

I study him. His perceptiveness is unexpected. "Since when are you so knowledgable on interpersonal relationships? I thought you were, like, a hermit."

He scoffs. "Even hermits have parents."

"So you're saying you work your ass off to try to impress your mom, too?"

Whatever trace of a smile I just glimpsed on his face is now gone. "If I did... it would be a waste of energy."

I stare at him. "You're hard to figure out, Harlan Vance."

"Am I?"

"Yes. I really thought you were a run-of-the-mill tyrant. Don't go getting complex on me now."

"Tyrant or hermit, which is it?"

"Can't it be both?"

"No. Tyrants rule over people. Hermits lock themselves away from people."

"Okay. Then I choose tyrant. Because you might seem to hate people, but you *love* bossing them around." His eyes narrow at me, and I wonder if I'm just earning myself a longer spanking. "And you are a frightening boss. I mean, I truly thought I was about to lose my job when I brought you that cake."

"Which one? There have been so many cakes..."

"The first one. The one I brought to your office when I begged you not to fire me."

"I don't believe there was actual begging involved." His eyes darken. "I would remember that." He wanders closer to me. "And if I was going to have a waitress fired, it would be the one who tried to serve me a drink... like this." He demonstrates by picking up his wine glass with just his fingertips clasping the rim, right where his mouth would touch it, then setting it down on the counter in front of me.

"Urgh. Nasty."

"I know. Where have those fingers been, and why would I want them in my mouth?"

"I don't know," I say, disturbed. "I'm not a clean freak, but that is definitely a fireable offense."

He looks forlornly at his wine glass. "Honestly, *I* can't even drink out of that now."

I laugh. "Then why did you do it?"

"To paint you a picture of what a bad waitress actually looks like."

"Wait." I blink at him. "Are you implying... that I'm a *good* waitress?"

His eyelids lower seductively as his gaze roams down my body. "The only thing you did wrong that night was leave my sight."

My jaw drops. "You gave me such a hard time! I thought you hated me. And I *wanted* that job. You wouldn't believe how much I made in tips on my first four shifts. It *blew* to think I might lose it. I was *sweating*."

"Sure," he says, eyes meeting mine again. "That's why you were sweating."

I narrow my eyes at him. "I should've just licked your glass right in front of you. You fired me anyway."

"I did not fire you."

I make exaggerated air quotes as I speak. "Forced me to quit." I frown. "Wait again. You said you didn't even fire the waitress who put her dirty little fingers on the rim of your glass?"

"No. I complained to management. They fired her."

I laugh. "Ah. There it is."

"Her days were numbered anyway. Anyone who works for Vance Hospitality should know far better. However, my brother Damian tends to get distracted by... other talents."

I gasp dramatically. "You're saying Daddy Damian screws his employees? I thought that was a no-no."

Harlan's eyes flash to mine. A muscle along his jaw spasms. "What did you just say to me?"

"Um..."

"Daddy what-the-fuck?"

I clear my throat. "Daddy... Damian? That's what the waitresses call him," I quickly explain. "Not me."

"You just did," he growls.

"Aaand I'll never do it again?"

His eyes linger on my lips for a moment, then meet mine. "Good girl," he murmurs, and my ovaries fucking shiver. Heat and lust course through me.

What did he tell me the other day? *Good girls get to come... so hard.*

I think there's a buttercream leaf getting smushed into oblivion in my hand right now.

"As I was saying," he goes on. "He gets distracted. But I'm not saying he screws employees. I'm saying he hires pretty girls because they look good in whatever skimpy uniform he's devised for them to wear." He looks at my nipple area like he can see right through my clothes. "Then, if needed, he has them trained. The training doesn't always take."

He brushes my hair away from my throat with his fingers, making me shiver, and says in my ear, "Some people just aren't as malleable as one might hope."

"Well then, won't you be disappointed when you discover that I'm not malleable at all," I say breathlessly. "I'm very, very stubborn."

"Hmm. That really hasn't been my experience."

"Okay, but... only when I'm naked..."

"Then we should get you naked." He draws back. "After I have a shower."

"Seriously?"

He heads for the door. "I always have a shower when I come home."

"Come on."

"The world's a dirty place, Quinn Monroe."

I don't know how he made that sound so sexy. Maybe because he's starting to unbutton his shirt.

"I'll have Edward make us dinner tonight," he says, "so you can relax. You can't be working all the time." Then he heads out of the kitchen to take his shower.

I wash the buttercream from my hand with a stupid smile on my face. I can't help it.

Whatever this mood of his is, I like it. Because it seems to be telling me that he likes *me*. Enough to hang out a bit, and not just when we're having sex.

Maybe I don't understand him, and maybe he's moody, but the one thing I know for sure is that he's nothing like Justin—who couldn't be bothered with paying attention to the things that matter to me, yet pretended to want a relationship.

At least Harlan isn't lying to me about what he wants from me.

Or... maybe he is?

My smile is gone as I think it over. He's told me, many times, that our relationship is only sexual.

Is it? Or is it not?

I don't even know, yet here I am, offering to make him dinner again. And trying to bring him home to Mom.

Dani was right. It's my nature to nurture.

I finish decorating the birthday cake and store it carefully in the fridge. That cake took way too long, thanks to Harlan's unfairly sexy ex-bedmate. I still have a batch of cupcakes to bake for tomorrow. So I whip up Mom's recipe for cookies and cream cupcake batter, pour it into my cupcake trays, and get them in the oven.

As I'm cleaning up a bit, I open my iPad, and swipe away Geneviève's movie with a pang of embarrassment. I'm about to update my grocery list when I notice a couple of alerts from my calendar.

Alerts I somehow missed.

No...

I read them carefully, even though it's crystal clear what they're telling me. And what they're telling me is that I've missed something important.

Crucial.

I check my calendar, scrolling back a few weeks.

I tell myself not to freak out—as I start freaking out.

I go peek into the hallway to make sure no one is around as I call Dani.

As soon as she answers, I tell her, "Help me, I'm freaking out!"

"Whoa, babe. What's wrong? Where are you?"

"I'm at Harlan's. I have cupcakes in the oven, so I can't leave." It's beyond surreal when I hear myself say the words. "Is there any way you can come over with a pregnancy test?"

Chapter 21

Harlan

"Your friends were welcome to stay for dinner," I tell Quinn as we sit down to eat the tagliatelle Bolognese that my staff has served for us in the dining room, with a Caprese salad and wine.

The two of us are alone, and she seems tense.

"I know," she says. "Thank you. Carlisle told me so. But I thought we could eat alone."

When I came downstairs after my shower, she'd insisted that she had work to finish before dinner. She was adamant about it, barely looking me in the eye as she rushed around the kitchen. Minutes later, her girlfriend Dani arrived, and they disappeared into the house somewhere. So I went to do some work in my office.

Soon after that, Carlisle informed me that Quinn's girlfriend Nicole had also arrived, and that the girls were out by the pool.

I went to the family room and saw them through the windows, sitting on lounge chairs on the far side of the pool. I could see the furry little black body stretched out beneath

Quinn's lounge chair; taking a cat nap while the girls huddled together above, talking.

Their closeness made me uneasy. Because I was excluded from it.

Now, I watch Quinn picking at her food. I'm not sure what happened to the woman I came home to after work. She had such a sparkle in her eyes.

Now she just seems anxious.

I wonder if she and her friends were talking about me again. And why.

"Don't they ever work?" I ask her lightly.

"Sometimes." She smiles a little, but it's forced. "Dani is a fashion stylist. But she works mostly on social media these days, so her hours are generally flexible. Unless she's working with some rich, demanding client." She glances at me, like maybe that was rude. But I'm not offended. "Nicole works at night. Waitressing."

Of course, I already know what her friends do for a living, and a whole lot else about them. I had my team run a security check on each of them after the first time I found them in my house.

Quinn doesn't know that, though.

"And when they're not working, they just hang around?"

She meets my eyes. "I told you before, they look out for me."

"Do they have some reason to be worried about you?"

"What makes you think they're worried?"

"I saw you talking, out by the pool."

She's silent for a moment, still picking at her food. Maybe considering what it means that I was watching them. "Does it bother you that they came over? I don't have to have them over here."

"It's fine. If you wanted to see them. I'm just not accustomed to reporting to a team about my personal life. I don't see a reason for it."

"We're girlfriends," she says, as if that explains it. "We share. They care about me."

"Then maybe they should respect your privacy."

"Uh..." She looks uncertain. "That's not really a thing for us."

I raise an eyebrow.

"I think you and I have very different ideas of what 'friend' means." She sips her water, then frowns. "Come to think of it, do you have anyone you talk to about personal things?"

"No."

"But there must be someone you trust like that. A confidante of sorts?"

"Manus."

"He's your bodyguard, though."

"Which means I trust him with my life. And he signed an NDA."

She seems to be considering what this says about me.

"Harlan. Do you not have friends?"

I hesitate before answering. "If I didn't, would you think less of me?"

"Honestly, I don't know what to think. It never really occurred to me before that someone like you wouldn't have friends."

"Someone like me?"

"Successful. Smart. So handsome."

I study her, and she avoids my eyes.

"I find friendships complicated, and messy," I say. "That's why I don't have them. As you know, I like things clean."

"Of course." She bites her lip a little, glancing at me. "It has nothing to do with the fact that you hate everyone..."

"How could I possibly hate everyone," I counter, "when you're so cute and likable?"

Her cheeks turn pink. But she doesn't look happy. "I'm cute?"

"Adorable. Why else would I tolerate your friends? I'm fairly certain not one of them is house-trained."

She laughs out loud. "I would pay money to see you tell Dani that she's not house-trained."

"I promise, I won't."

"That's probably for the best."

I wait for her to eat something, but she's barely touching her food.

"Is there something wrong?"

I can tell there is. I've never seen her this uneasy, just talking to me. Even when I was blackmailing her.

"I wasn't going to mention this," she says hesitantly. "Because it's not really my business. But I looked up Geneviève. You know, Darla? There was nothing online about you and her. But there were pictures of her with your brother Jameson."

Great. She just had to go looking.

This is another reason I don't like people digging into my business. They never find anything that makes them happy.

"I guess that's another reason you didn't want to tell them about her, huh?"

"Guess so," I say.

There's an uncomfortable silence when she doesn't respond.

"Are you upset?"

"I have no right to be upset," she says. "It has nothing to do with me."

That really doesn't answer my question.

"I'm just feeling... stressed out," she says.

"You work too hard. You should quit the waitressing job. You don't need it now."

She stares at me. She looks kind of alarmed. "Why would you say that?"

Because the more time I spend with her, the less I want her working that job.

But I can't say that to her.

Instead, I tell her, "You can keep using my kitchen, and I can help in other ways, to take some pressure off. Maybe with an investment. And I can help you with transportation."

"What do you mean?"

"You have to deliver your cakes around town, right? I didn't see your car in the driveway when I got home. Did it break down again?"

She stares at me. "How do you know my car broke down?"

"You took it into the shop when I had you under surveillance. How often do you have problems with it?"

She takes a deep breath and doesn't answer.

"You need a reliable vehicle, Quinn."

"I'm aware of that. Obviously."

"You must be making some kind of profit from your baking. And if you're not, you should be. It might seem like a scary move, but it'll be easier for you to grow your business if you give up waitressing and focus on it."

"That's not really for you to decide."

"Right. What do I know about business?"

"Well, maybe if my grandfather left me a billion dollar empire, and I had four siblings to help me, I'd be business savvy too."

I'm not sure how this is turning into an argument.

"I'm sorry," she says. "That wasn't fair. I'm a little on edge right now."

"It probably was fair," I admit. "But I was just trying to be supportive."

She doesn't look happy, and I'm confused.

I thought what she truly wanted was to focus on her bakery business. She said that was her dream. But she appears to be getting more stressed out over this conversation.

"I didn't think you loved being a waitress, or having to work in your kitchen at home."

"I don't. I can't do this, Harlan. I—"

"Then why don't you—"

"I'm pregnant."

She stares at me, with tenderness and fear and so many emotions in her eyes, it overwhelms me.

I struggle to absorb those words.

I don't know what to say. And the look on her face tells me it's taking me way too long to say anything.

There's a bitter, sharp shard that's suddenly stuck in my throat, making it difficult to swallow.

"Are you certain?" I force out.

"Well, I took a pregnancy test. Two, actually." She draws a shaky breath, and her eyes shine with tears. "Honestly, I can't be one-hundred percent sure that it's yours and not Justin's. But," she adds quietly, "timing would seem to indicate that it's yours."

Something dark and ferocious stirs in me.

"You slept with Justin again?" My voice is low and rough as I struggle to keep calm. "While you were sleeping with me?"

"No. *No.* I had a period in-between him and you. But, I mean, you can still bleed when you're pregnant. There's a small chance. And he and I were, you know, kind of recent. I just want to be sure, before I tell you one-hundred percent."

I set down my cutlery, too loudly. "I thought you were on the pill."

"I am."

"And if you're bleeding while you're pregnant, you need to see a doctor."

"Of course. I will. I just found out, like half an hour ago."

She adds softly, "The blood was probably just my last period. Before I got pregnant."

"Jesus, Quinn." I swipe my hand over my face. Is this happening?

What the fuck is she even telling me?

"Should I not have told you until I know for sure?"

"Know *what* for sure?"

"That I'm actually pregnant and that it's yours!"

I pinch the bridge of my nose and focus on breathing.

"Are you mad because I'm pregnant or because there could be something wrong, or because it could be his?"

"Are you pregnant or not?" I say as calmly as I can.

"According to two home pregnancy tests, yes. And according to logic and my calendar, if I am pregnant, it's yours. But according to what is within the realm of actual possibility, I don't fucking know!"

She's getting really upset now. I don't want that.

But I'm fucking reeling here.

"Look, I know that you trusted me to take my birth control properly," she says. "And I know that I screwed up because I've been so busy lately, and maybe I haven't taken it like clockwork, and I... I thought it would be okay..."

"You thought?"

"This isn't all my fault. It takes two to make a..." She chokes out the word. "Baby."

"I can't take the pill *for you*, Quinn," I growl.

"Do I need to remind you of all the unprotected sex we had?"

"I didn't realize it was unprotected."

"You didn't wear a condom and we were both okay with that."

"I wasn't trying to get you pregnant," I grit out.

"Well, I wasn't trying to get pregnant! Believe me, the last thing I need in my life right now is a baby who needs me!"

"Then maybe you should've thought of that, before—"

"Is that what *you* were thinking about? When you said all that stuff about putting your seed in me?"

I blink at her, stunned. "That was just play. Dirty talk."

She gapes at me, appalled. "Oh, you like to play dirty?" She gets to her feet. "Is this dirty enough for you?" She dumps the salad all over the dining table and my dinner plate.

She's shaking. Trembling with emotion.

I get to my feet, meaning to pull her into my arms, but I don't. I just stand there while she trembles.

I can't fucking do this.

Fatherhood?

No.

I'd fail miserably at being a good father, just like I failed at being a good son.

We stare at each other for a long moment. She's breathing hard.

"I can't be the first one in my family to have a child," I tell her.

"That's all you have to say? You don't want to have a child before your sister or one of your brothers do?"

I barely hear her. My mind is in overdrive. "That's what you were talking to your friends about, outside."

"I was telling them I don't want you to feel obligated. And I don't need you putting any pressure on me, either."

"You talked to them first? About this?"

"Of course I did. They're my friends." She takes a deep, shaky breath and says, "I can raise this child alone if I have to. Mom did it with me. We'll be okay."

I stare at her, really trying to hear what she's saying.

She doesn't have any feelings for me. That's all I'm hearing right now.

If she did, wouldn't she be asking me for my support? Instead of going to her friends first?

Wouldn't she be wanting to do this together?

But of course she doesn't want to do this together. Any woman can see I'm not father material.

Her friends probably told her so already.

She puts her face in her hands. "I'm sorry. I'm sorry I made a mess on your table. I'll clean it up. I'm just... an emotional disaster right now."

"It's okay. The staff will take care of it."

She crumples into her chair.

I just feel numb.

I tell her the only thing I can think of that might make her feel better. "You'll be a wonderful mother, Quinn."

She starts to cry.

I've just come home from school.

I'm standing in the foyer of my family's home. I'm alone. But I can hear sounds in the distance, coming from upstairs—a door closing. Then the muffled voices of my siblings. My mom.

More than I can hear them... I can feel their sorrow.

I'm supposed to be there, with them.

I climb the stairs to the second floor, and I hear a sound that I've never heard here before.

It's the sound of a helicopter in the distance.

When I get to the top, I see the door to the room where the terrible thing is going to happen, and I know they're waiting for me.

I walk toward it.

When I finally reach it, I start to open the door.

But before I can see what's inside, I wake up in a panic, with the *whump whump whump* of helicopter blades in my head.

Chapter 22

Quinn

"Shit. It's not cooking."

I'm making breakfast when I realize the quiche I put in ten minutes ago is still cold and runny.

"The oven again?" Mom asks from the breakfast bar, where she's icing cupcakes for a client. She baked them last night, and the oven was working fine.

"Yup." I check the elements on the stovetop, but they're not working, either.

I pull the baking dish out of the oven, cover it, and slide it into the overstuffed fridge. "This place is falling apart," I mutter, digging through the fridge for other breakfast options. I'm not feeding Mom cereal. "How can we keep putting money into a home we don't even own?"

"We can't. The landlord will fix it. I'll call him today."

"I'll take care of it. Don't worry." Of course, every time he "fixes" it, it just breaks again. What we really need is for him to buy a new one, but I don't know if he ever will.

"I wasn't worried," she says, but I barely hear her as I start making a grocery list. I didn't realize we were so low on everything. And I can't even heat up leftovers, because our ancient microwave died last month. I would've replaced it already if my car wasn't in the shop again.

I feel like I'm caught in an endless cycle of barely making ends meet, and everything slowly but inevitably falling apart around me.

And now I'm pregnant.

I haven't even told Mom yet. I don't want to tell her until I feel like I have a handle on it, a solid plan, and I can convince her that I'll be okay. I can't become a source of stress for her.

What am I even going to tell her about the father?

You'll be a wonderful mother, Quinn.

That was the only nice or supportive thing Harlan said to me when I told him I was pregnant. And that was almost a week ago.

The only thing worse than the torment of stopping myself from reaching out to check on how he's doing is the fact that he's barely reached out to me. He's become even more withdrawn, and when I stopped texting him two days ago, he went silent.

I'm dying to know where we stand. I want to know what he's thinking and feeling, but I'm way too tender to ask him right now.

I feel guilty for springing this on him, as if it were solely my fault. I'm terrified of the future, and my ability to take care of Mom and the baby. And I've started getting wickedly nauseous throughout the day. If I was partially in denial that I was pregnant that first day, there's no denying it now.

I've been trying to cope by doing what I do best. Working. Taking care of my responsibilities. Which are now the baby and therefore my health, Mom and her health, my job, our business, and our home, more or less in that order.

Except for when one of them breaks down and suddenly takes priority. Like the damn oven.

"I don't know when you started thinking I was so much more fragile than I am," Mom says out of nowhere.

"What?"

"Whatever you're obsessing about, maybe you should talk about it. You keep things inside and let them just spin and spin. It's like watching a sad, obsessed little hamster on a wheel, thinking it's getting somewhere."

I scowl. "Really? I don't do that."

"Oh yes, you do. You're so like your father that way."

Am I?

Shit. It's crazy how over two decades later, it still hurts to suddenly hear him mentioned when I'm not prepared for it.

To think of my own child, growing up without a chance to really know their father? Just because I couldn't make a relationship with him work…

I mean, I'm just assuming that Harlan is the father. Because as hard as I know that road may be, I desperately don't want the baby to be Justin's. I'd honestly prefer a flat-broke Harlan to a Justin, any day. Because at least there's a chance that I could fall madly in love with Harlan.

I already know that's not happening with Justin.

But I can already feel it starting to happen with Harlan. And if we really gave it a chance…

I just don't know if I have the ability to deal with his mood swings and the turmoil it's going to cause me. I have too much on my plate already. I need a man who's emotionally stable.

I'd even take that over financial stability.

I finish making my grocery list, and check my online banking for my checking account balance. Not great. But fuck it. I can do this.

Maybe I just need to start thinking of myself as a mom-in training. If I can take care of Mom, I can take care of this baby.

I've got this.

"By the way," Mom says. "You're doing it again."

"Ugh. Stop watching me."

"Well, you're the most entertaining thing going on right now. Do you want me to put on *The Last of Us* and leave you alone?"

"Yes. I'm heading out anyway. Do you want anything from the grocery store? I'll pick up takeout on my way back."

Before Mom can answer, someone knocks on the screen door. I look up to find Harlan standing outside.

He's holding a large paper bag that looks a hell of a lot like takeout. And a tray holding three large smoothies.

"Good morning," he says stiffly.

"Uh, good morning." *Calm down, heart flutters.* I try to tell my body we don't get excited about men who ghost us after impregnating us, but too late.

"Have you had breakfast?" he asks me.

"No," I say warily.

He holds up the bag and the smoothies. "I brought breakfast. For your mom, too."

I open the door for him. "Come in."

"Thank you." He steps inside, swiping off his sunglasses. And maybe that's when he notices my mom at the breakfast bar.

She's forgotten about her cupcakes, and stares openly at the man in her kitchen.

"Do you ladies like breakfast sandwiches? I brought egg and back bacon, and an avocado one, just in case. And smoothies."

"Oh, we like meat," Mom says suggestively.

I shoot her a look that I hope conveys *I will duct tape your mouth.*

"That wasn't necessary," I tell him.

His gray eyes lock on mine. "You need to eat properly."

That bossy look on his face says, *Because you're pregnant.*

I can feel the pink creeping into my cheeks, and Mom

watching us. "Thank you." I snatch the bag from him, set it on the counter, and say, "This is my mom, Lorraine. Mom, this is my friend Harlan. He's been letting me bake in his kitchen."

He raises an eyebrow slightly at the word "friend." I ignore it, and he crosses the room to shake Mom's hand. "Pleasure to meet you, Lorraine."

Mom looks openly awestruck. "What a work of art. It's like you're chiseled out of stone."

She's really lost a filter since becoming a cougar.

Harlan cracks a smile, caught off-guard in a way I don't think I've ever seen.

"You have your daughter's charm," he tells her.

What? I'm *charming*?

"I suppose I do," Mom says. I have never seen Lorraine Monroe look so flattered.

I have no idea what's going on here, but I'm not sure I like it.

"Let's eat." I shove a bunch of junk that's piled on the kitchen table aside and start unpacking takeout boxes. "I have a shit-ton to do today."

"Do you tell her she works too hard?" Mom asks him. "Or is it just me?"

"I've told her. She doesn't like to hear it." He starts taking dishes from my hands as I pull them from the cupboards, and setting the table. "I've advised her that if she quit the waitressing job, she could really make a go of the cake business." I have a hard time even looking at him while he chats with Mom.

I'm hurt. It's been haunting me, that when I broke down crying, he didn't touch me. He didn't pull me into his arms. He just stood there.

And now that he's right here, I can feel that same ache.

The desire to be closer to him.

"But she doesn't appreciate unsolicited advice," he adds, glancing at me.

"Well, who does?" Mom says. "Though knowing what advice to take and what to leave is key."

"True."

I don't know whether to be pleased or annoyed that they seem to be bonding. Over their shared disapproval of my life choices.

Mom moves over to the table, and takes the seat Harlan pulls out for her. "Quinnie," she says disapprovingly. "You don't take business advice from someone who's wildly successful in business?"

"I don't like you like this, Lorraine," I grumble, as Harlan sits down with her.

"She doesn't like to see us getting along," she tells Harlan, like a traitor.

"Not true," I say, dumping cutlery in front of them.

"Oh, it's true. I've never liked a man she's introduced me to before." She leans in and tells him conspiratorially, "She has this terrible habit of dating down."

"We're not dating," I interject, before he can say anything.

"Well," she says, "I'd rather you brought home a fuck buddy who was a true gentleman than married a loser. Even if it doesn't give me grandkids."

"*Mom.* Jesus. Tone it down." To Harlan, I say, "I have never seen her like this. I need to get her meds checked."

"Quinn! Who raised you to be so rude?"

I roll my eyes. Mom's "who raised you" thing is always her comeback when I say or do shit she doesn't like. I never let her get away with it.

"*You* raised me, Lorraine. And isn't it 'rude' to like someone simply because you know he's a billionaire?" I claim an egg-and-bacon sandwich and sit down.

"I like that he surprised you and your mother with breakfast," she corrects me sharply. "It reveals character."

"Or psychopathy," I mutter.

Harlan just smiles in that way I've seen him do so infrequently, with his eyes, like he's truly enjoying himself.

Come to think of it, I've only seen him smile like that once before. The morning we woke up in bed together and he called me a grump.

He blinks at me. "What?"

"Why are you so happy right now?" I demand. "It's early as fuck. I haven't even had coffee."

He gives me that bossy look again and informs me, "You shouldn't be drinking coffee anymore."

I glare at him.

Mom watches us curiously.

"Mornings are great," he says lightly. "You can get a lot done before other people get in the way."

"Oh my god," I groan, as realization dawns. "You're a morning person."

"Oh, I love morning people!" Mom says, delighted.

"Don't you have work to do?" I grump. I've been denied coffee, and instead handed a rooibos tea that tastes of flowers by an extremely controlling billionaire who seems to think he can just pop in and take over my life whenever he feels like it. It's an annoying pattern. "It's Monday."

I'm in the back of Harlan's SUV with him. After he drilled me about my plans for the day, he insisted on driving me around as I ran errands. He and Manus have just taken me grocery shopping, and helped me deliver Mom's cupcakes.

Now we're driving deep into the Kitsilano neighborhood on "a little detour." I don't know why.

"I have a lot of work to do," he says. "But this is important. And time sensitive."

We pull in behind a row of commercial buildings facing West Broadway. When we park, Harlan comes around to get my door, and offers me his arm. He's been doing this all morning, as if I'm suddenly breakable now that I'm pregnant.

A man waiting by the back door shakes hands with Manus, and lets us into the building. Harlan and I enter alone, stepping into what appears to be a commercial space in mid renovation.

It's empty except for the construction tools that are still everywhere. At the front end, there's a storefront area and a big window facing the street.

"What's going on?" I ask Harlan, as he leads me into the middle of the room. "Where are we?"

"This, Quinn Monroe," he announces, "is your bakery."

I stare at him, shocked.

"Or at least it could be," he says. "It's being renovated, as you can see. It was stripped right down to the studs, and the new drywall has just gone up. It will be painted by the end of the week, and then it can be outfitted for your bakery as needed. There was a delicatessen with a full kitchen in here before, so electrical, plumbing, and exhaust fans are all in place."

I look around, still in shock.

"What do you think?" he prompts when I just gape.

"I... I don't know what to think."

He steps into my line of sight and looks me in the eyes. "I want to apologize for how I reacted when you told me you were pregnant. It wasn't my best hour."

I scrape myself together and find words. "Yeah. I noticed." Then I admit, "It wasn't mine, either."

"I want to make things right," he says seriously.

I sigh, feeling exhausted by his mood swings, and the hormonal changes that are already affecting my body.

"Honestly... I don't even know what that would look like, Harlan. I've been upset that you've been distant. But the truth is, I can hardly blame you. We barely know each other. And this was supposed to be casual." I take a deep breath and forge on. "I've had more time to think about it, and I meant what I said. I don't expect anything from you. And I really have no vision of the future right now. I'm just trying to get by, day by day. It's all I can manage."

Every word I just said is true.

But fuck, I crave his support like I crave his attention.

I'd rather try to handle this together than apart. I just don't know if he wants that, if he could ever want that, or if it would work, anyway.

"That's all understandable," he says calmly. "It's been a shock, to both of us. But I thought maybe you'd reconsider leaving the waitressing job if you had some security in your business. I can help with that."

I take this in.

I know he said he's supported start-ups before. And maybe this is a simple solution to my problems, in his eyes. It's generous.

But it's also easy for him to buy me a bakery. He bought Crave on a whim, because I worked there. I still don't understand to what end.

I really don't understand this man at all.

He keeps telling me he wants just a sexual relationship. But then he wants me to quit my job. He wants to help with my business.

It's like what he really wants, as always, is control.

He wants ownership of me, but without giving me any real part of himself, is that it?

"I hope you know that I'm serious," he says, like he's struggling to understand me, too. "I haven't bought it yet, but it's ours if you want it."

I can tell he's serious.

"Could you see yourself here, running your bakery?" he asks me.

Honestly, I don't know. It's so hard to even wrap my head around the idea that my dream, which always felt so out of reach, could suddenly come true.

But as I gradually get past the shock that he's actually offering to buy a bakery for me...

I try to take a more serious look around.

It's definitely not what I would've chosen. Parts of the walls are drywalled, while others are stark concrete. Exposed metal beams crisscross the ceiling. The only window is on the front wall. It feels like it would be perfect for a hipster coffee house with an industrial vibe. Which is really suitable to Vancouver.

But not so suitable to me.

However.

It's a bakery. Of my own. In a fairly prime location.

Not the location of my dreams. But a cool, bustling neighborhood.

I could never afford the location of my dreams, anyway. Because a storefront with a view of the water would be not only rare to find in Vancouver, it would be astronomically expensive.

Harlan is waiting for some kind of response, and he certainly deserves one.

"I can't believe you'd do this for me," is all I manage.

His reply to that is a confused, "Why not?"

Maybe to him, this is a purely logical investment. Even if it turns out not to be a financially sound one, it's an investment in the happiness of his baby's mother.

"It means a lot to me that you'd be willing to invest in my dream, and Mom's," I tell him. "I'm touched. Really."

I look around again. Maybe I could turn it into my dream bakery, with some work, and some time...

"I'm glad you feel that way," he says. "Because this isn't even the best part. There's also living space attached."

"Living space?"

"There's a generous two-bedroom apartment above. It's being renovated right now, but we can go up and take a look. There's a den with a window that can be converted into a bedroom for the baby. And even a rooftop garden area."

"I... don't know what to say."

He drifts closer to me. "I know you've enjoyed having more space to bake in. This would be even better. It would be yours."

More space. In his kitchen, he means. In his house.

Which I won't be using anymore, once I move in here, is that it?

"You'd buy it so I can work here, and live here? With Mom?"

"I thought it would be the best solution. I want to support you in raising the baby, however makes you happy."

His words are kind. But his tone is even, unemotional. Businesslike.

Detached, even.

I take a long look at him, really trying to see him, too.

Standing a short distance away from me in his black suit, studying me in return, he reminds me of the Harlan I first met. Mr. Black. Cold, closed and unknowable.

I feel so deeply unsure of where I stand with him, I barely dare ask. But I force it out.

"Harlan... do you want to be in the baby's life?"

I definitely can't bear to ask, *Do you want to be in my life?*

"Of course," he says stiffly.

I turn to look out the window, onto the bustling street, and take a breath. What are the chances he'll open up to me, want any kind of real relationship, before the baby comes?

There's only eight months until then.

How long will I be able to work? Care for the house and Mom?

Can I really do it all myself?

I try to look at this offer objectively, as the opportunity that it is. The opportunity for Mom. The truth is, our current home is becoming too much work for us both.

"It will be hard to get a business off the ground while pregnant, and then becoming a new mom," I tell him.

"That's fine. We can hire support. And you can take all the time you need," he says easily. "Don't you think it could work? It's a great space."

I turn to face him again, and I try to smile. "It's amazing. Can I have some time to think about it?"

He's so stoic, I can't even tell if he's surprised or not that I'm not jumping at the offer. "Of course. I can hold the deal off for a bit. Why don't we go take a look upstairs?"

"Okay."

I try to tell myself that this as a purely thoughtful gift. And extremely generous of him. In some ways, it's actually a serious commitment to me and the baby, right?

It's not a bunch of walls Harlan's putting up between us.

Chapter 23

Quinn

I'm crumb coating a single-tier, ten-inch round cake in Harlan's kitchen when he pops his head in and says hello. "Don't let me interrupt you. I was just checking to see if you're here."

"I'm here." It's Saturday, but I'm not working at Champagne tonight. I told him I'd be here when he came home.

He said he was meeting up with his sister this afternoon, which seems like a rarity. But it is their birthday today.

"I'm just going to shower and get ready," he says, his gaze dragging over the cute blue dress I'm wearing under my apron.

"Sounds good."

Once I've got the cake completely covered, I pop it into the fridge to let the crumb coat firm up a bit before I add more buttercream and smooth it out.

I step outside to stretch and get some fresh air. I've been in the kitchen for a few hours.

To my surprise, I find Harlan on his back patio, still in his suit, sitting on the edge of a lounge chair and stroking the black cat at his feet.

"Why do you pretend you don't love that cat?" I ask.

I think I startled him.

He gets to his feet. "I'm going for that shower." He gives me a kiss on the cheek as he passes by. "Don't let it in the house."

"You mean *her*?"

He just gives me a slightly disapproving look, and heads into the house without a word.

The cat meets my eyes.

"Yeah, I saw him loving on you," I tell her. "Are you trying to tell me he's not as cold and grumpy as he pretends?"

The cat hops daintily onto the vacated lounge chair, and stretches out in the warm spot.

I go over and stroke her soft fur for a moment. "Good girl. You make yourself right at home."

I head into the kitchen and do a bit of cleanup, then pull out the cake. As I'm piping on the buttercream and smoothing it out, Dani calls me on FaceTime.

I prop my phone up and keep working so she can see me.

"Nicole says you have tonight off," she tells me. She appears to be driving. "Does that mean you can come out and play?"

"No, unfortunately."

"But you look so fab, and it's Saturday night. Who are you all dressed up for, if not me?"

Damn. I don't love admitting that I'm dressed up for Harlan, but it is what it is.

"It's Harlan's birthday. And his twin sister's, obviously. There's a Vance family dinner."

"Oh. He invited you to his birthday dinner? That's kind of cool," she admits grudgingly.

I turn that over. "Hmm. He didn't, exactly. He just told me it's happening. But that's just how he is." At least, I think it is... "He probably doesn't love getting a bunch of attention. He's not like that. But I'm actually looking forward to another family dinner. I really like his siblings."

"Uh-huh. And would that be a birthday cake you're making right now? For the birthday dinner you weren't 'exactly' invited to?"

Damn it. How does she always make my crazy so... obvious? "Yes. Are you happy?"

"That's a whole other topic, Quinn. Don't change the subject."

"I made the cake for both him and his sister," I say defensively. "You know, to try to keep it casual."

"Right. Because making him his own cake that says *Happy Birthday, Daddy!*, while that's probably what you're dying to actually do, might be too much."

"Stop it."

"You know I'm right."

"I would. It would be cute. If it wouldn't give him a heart attack. I kind of need him alive so he can be around for you to judge his fathering skills. What fun would that be without him?"

"Good point."

"Actually, I've been meaning to call you..."

"I'm right here, babe. My number hasn't changed."

"I know. But you know me. I've been so busy, and that just makes it easier to avoid the things."

"What things?"

"Things like telling you that he took me to see a building he wants to buy for me."

"Just a minute. I need to pull over so I don't run someone down. This conversation is much too juicy for steering." She pulls over, parks, and shoves her face closer to her phone. "Did you say *building*?"

"It's just a bakery. With an apartment over it for Mom and me to live in. And the baby, of course."

"Oh. That's all." She rolls her eyes. "Are you nuts? What's wrong with you? Why didn't you call me?"

"Because I don't know what I'm doing! I'm just trying to survive this whole drama, one hour at a time. My life is turning into some lame TV movie, and I don't even know if it's the kind with a tragic ending."

"They don't cast men as hot as Harlan in movies like that," she says dismissively. "Let's circle back to this building thing. Did you say yes?"

"I didn't say anything. I just told him I need to think about it."

"Good. What are you doing tomorrow?"

"Well, it's Sunday. So, laundry and vacuuming while Lorraine listens to Mötley Crüe and Duran Duran at an ungodly volume?"

"Wrong. You're listening to Nicole and I discuss your life, and figure out what you need to do about this building thing."

"Uh—"

"I may even help you do laundry. And we'll bring samosas."

"Shit. Okay, fine. But just know that he already told me he wants to be in the baby's life. And that he wants to support me in raising it however I want to. And he's already proving that's true with his generosity. This offer is a commitment to me and the baby."

"I mean, who are you trying to convince? Me or you?"

I sigh.

"The fact is, that baby comes in eight months," she says. "So hear me out on this, okay? Your place is falling apart. And Lorraine's not getting any worse these days, thank god, but she's not really getting any better, either. So, the sooner you can get settled and comfortable before the baby comes, the better. And whatever he offers you in the way of support, just know that you deserve it."

I take that in, my chest flooding with affection. I blink back tears. I've been extra emotional lately. "Why can't I just have a baby with you?"

"Oh, no. Don't get it twisted. This is just cool aunt energy."

"I totally thought you were going in a different direction with all this."

"What direction?"

"The one where you tell me he's not good enough for me, because he didn't immediately get down on one knee and put a ring on it."

"That is true. But Quinn, you're pregnant. All that matters right now is you and that baby, and that baby's grandma. If he doesn't want to join the most beautiful family ever, it's his loss."

My eyes sting, listening to her speak. But I'm pretty sure I hear Harlan coming.

"I should really go, Dani. I'll see you tomorrow, okay?"

"Okay, babe. We'll come over around noon with those samosas."

"And Dani? I love you, you know."

"You stop it," she says, and hangs up, just as Harlan steps into the room.

He looks sharp as hell in his black suit. It's pretty much the same as he always looks, but I don't know... maybe it's just my squishy, pregnant heart and all the hormones that are making me think he looks better every time I see him.

"You look nice," I tell him.

"You, too. Too nice for someone who's been slaving in a kitchen all day." As he moves toward me, his gaze skims down my dress again. My hair is partially up, too. I even curled it a bit.

I want to look nice for his family. Especially Savannah.

I really want her to like me.

"Thank you. I'm almost ready. What time do we need to leave?"

He stops a few feet away from me, glancing at the cake. I haven't written *Happy Birthday* on it yet. I'm not sure if I'm going to.

"For what?" he says.

"For your birthday dinner."

He stares at me. And I know exactly what he's going to say.

I feel it sinking through me like an anchor.

"I... was planning to go alone."

"Oh." I blink at the cake, suddenly struggling to pipe on the pattern of yellow buttercream pearls up the side.

"Quinn."

I blink at him. "I just assumed..."

"Assumed what?"

"I thought when you told me about the dinner, that we were going."

He clears his throat. "That can't happen, Quinn."

The sinking feeling is making me kind of sick. And maybe just a bit angry.

"Why not?"

"Because," he says evenly, "my family doesn't know that we've been seeing each other, much less that you're pregnant."

I'm stunned.

"You haven't told them... anything... about me?"

"Nothing new. You were introduced to them as Darla, then I told them we broke up. You know that."

"But... we didn't break up. Did we?"

"Technically, we were never really together."

"I can't believe you're saying this to me right now."

"Quinn—"

"Regardless of how you feel about me or don't, you're telling me that you never mentioned to any of them that you've been seeing me? Or that I've been here, working out of your kitchen?"

I'm starting to tremble.

"I told you that we couldn't see each other. That it was unacceptable to them."

"Yeah, you told me. Like, before we hooked up the first time. Things have changed."

He stares at me. "What's changed?" he says gently.

It crushes me.

I don't want him to be gentle with me.

I want to be furious with him, and how can I do that when he's being gentle?

"I thought... I just assumed at some point you must've mentioned me. Told them we're seeing each other."

"Why would I do that?"

"Because things have changed! Maybe it hasn't changed for you," I say, my voice starting to quiver, "but I'm *pregnant*, Harlan. That's about as changed as I can get. I'm bloated. My boobs hurt. My hormones are all over the place—"

"Try to stay calm," he says calmly. "It's not good for the baby."

I try to keep calm, but it just frustrates me further that he's so calm. "If you don't want to tell them about the baby yet, that's okay. I know it's a lot. And it's early. I haven't even told Mom."

"It's not just that."

"Then what is it? You can't seriously expect me to be 'Darla' forever, even after I have your baby."

"As far as they're concerned," he says carefully, "you are Darla."

"But I'm *not*. Why won't you just tell them the truth? That you broke up with her, the *real* her? That she's Geneviève Blaise? And I'm *me*. And I'm someone you care about?" My voice wavers on those last words.

I feel desperate. Wounded.

Pathetic.

Harlan looks slightly frustrated, maybe. I really can't tell. He definitely doesn't admit that he cares.

It makes me really wonder what it will be like when the baby comes.

And how fucking lonely I'll be.

Of all the things I learned while being raised by my wonderful mother, my biggest takeaway was that I never wanted to end up a single mom.

And ending up a single mom because you've been rejected by the baby's father, who you're actually falling in love with?

I can't handle this.

"It's about privacy," he finally says, stiffly. "I can't expect you to understand how important—"

"Is it? Or is it about secrecy?"

I know he's keeping things from his family.

But I really have no way of knowing if he's telling me the whole truth, either.

Is he really over Geneviève? I wonder this, almost daily. Since he's lying about her identity to protect her, maybe he still cares about her. A lot.

Is he still in contact with her?

I remember how his sister said that he was "holding out for Darla."

Maybe he's still holding out for her.

I don't know what other possible reason he could have for keeping me at a distance. Other than maybe he just doesn't like me that much.

But that's even more painful to consider.

Maybe he doesn't care about me as much as I want him to. Maybe he never will.

Maybe he can't, because he's still in love with her.

Maybe he's not even capable of loving anyone.

Have I been totally delusional? About the bakery he offered to buy for me, and what it might actually mean? About us, somehow building a life and a family together?

"Maybe you just can't stand the idea of me and your siblings in the same room, and everyone asking questions," I tell him, "and the truth somehow coming out."

"We can talk more about this when I get home tonight," he says in a low voice. "I have to get going. I can't be late for a dinner that's in my honor."

I stare at him, stunned. And hurting.

He's really leaving without me.

"I'll see you later," he says.

Then he walks right out of the kitchen, to go to his birthday dinner without me.

While I stand here, decorating his surprise birthday cake, like a fool.

Home. Does he think that's what this is?

An empty mansion, where you never let anyone in to love you?

Not even a damn cat.

I told him I had the night off, but does he really expect me to just wait here for him to come home? From the birthday celebration that I'm not welcome at?

It fucking burns, this horrible, raw feeling in my chest. I knew he'd do this. I knew he'd cut right through me, if I let him.

And I did.

I stare at the cake as tears flood my eyes, until I can barely see it anymore. I set my tools down.

Then I bury my hands in the cake.

I've never smashed a cake before. It's satisfying and depressing all at once.

But I just want to erase this cake, and this giant mistake, from existence.

Because now I know the truth.

That Harlan Vance cares much more about keeping his secrets than he does about keeping me.

Chapter 24

Harlan

I come home to find Quinn gone, and her kitchen tidy. I can't help noticing there's an entire smashed cake in the trash can that's been left by the counter, where I last saw her working.

I can't be sure, but it seems like a lot of her personal things are gone.

Like her pink standing mixer.

The house feels weirdly empty without Quinn here making noise, playing music, her pretty things strewn about. I don't know when I got used to those things. She's only here a few times a week, and often I'm not even here when she is.

But when I come home and find her here... There's nothing better.

I go up to my bedroom.

Every time she stayed the night, she seemed to leave something behind. A lipgloss. A hair brush. A bra.

I was beginning to think it was on purpose.

They're all gone now.

As I look around the bedroom for any lingering sign of her, finding none, a black shape slinks in the open window, startling me. "*Jesus.*" I pluck the cat off my windowsill, and not for the first time. "You need to stop climbing on the roof. You'll get hurt."

As I carry her downstairs, she purrs in my arms.

I wonder if I should have the landscapers trim back some of the trees, so they don't reach so close to the house.

"Trust me, you don't want to get attached," I tell her as I walk her out into the backyard, and set her down. I never should've started feeding her in the first place. "What if you come back one day and no one's here?" I nudge her toward the bushes. "You're a hunter, go hunt."

I go back inside and shut the sliding glass door.

The cat just sits there on the lawn.

I send Quinn a text. *Do you want to talk tomorrow?*

She doesn't text me back.

I've just come home from school.

I'm standing in the foyer of my family's house. I'm alone. But I can hear sounds in the distance, coming from upstairs—a door closing. Then the muffled voices of my siblings. My mom.

More than I can hear them... I can feel their sorrow.

I'm supposed to be there, with them.

I can hear Mom crying.

As I climb the stairs to the second floor, I hear helicopter blades in the distance.

When I get to the top of the stairs, I see the door to the room where the terrible thing is going to happen, and I know they're waiting for me.

I hear my dad's voice, calling to me, and I start to cry.

I hear the *whump whump whump* of the helicopter blades as I walk toward the door.

When I finally reach it, I start to open it. And I hear my dad say my name, close in my ear. *Harlan*.

I wake up in a panic, with his voice still in my head.

I didn't know I could still remember the sound of his voice.

I haven't heard it in so long.

And for a long time, I just lie here in the dark, trying not to lose it again.

"Megan and I were talking about her wedding cake," Savannah tells me. "Darla's name came up. Quinn, I mean." My sister pauses dramatically, waiting for my reaction to this.

It's been three weeks since our birthday dinner, and I haven't seen Savannah since. I've barely seen Quinn, either, since she's not really speaking to me.

At least, that's how it seems.

And since's there's no one other than Quinn who I really want to speak to right now, I'm not inclined to make small talk about my brother's wedding preparations.

I've been having that old dream almost every night, and I'm not sleeping well. And every time I hear my dad say my name, I wake up, soaked in sweat and panicking all over again.

I'm on the verge of calling up one of my old therapists.

But I fucking hate therapy.

Savi is studying me like she's reading me for signals, so I do my best not to give her any. No twitching. No picking at things with my fingernails. No straightening items on my desk.

I don't keep much on my desk, so I don't have to worry about temptation. But my cell phone is sitting there, fucking crooked. I have to resist the almost irresistible urge to straighten it.

I just keep staring at my computer screen. Savannah just

walked into my office unannounced, and now she's hovering, neither of which she ever does.

"Don't you have work to do at the resort?" I say flatly.

"You make it sound like it's a vacation."

"Isn't it?"

"Very funny. I'm actually thinking I'll need a vacation after it finally opens. A long one. And you can all just call each other to fix your shit instead of communicating through me."

"Good luck with that. Graysen wouldn't last a day."

She sighs. "Isn't that the truth."

"So what have you come to say on his behalf this time?"

"Not his. Jameson's. His fiancée's, actually. You know, Megan…"

I frown. Are we back to this?

"Apparently," she goes on, "one of her bridesmaids is a close friend of Quinn's. And that cake Quinn made the night we all met her *was* exceptional. But I told Megan I should run it by you. Since she's your ex and all. So? What do you think?"

I hear the grouchy sound that comes out of me, but I don't look up. "That it would be a good idea for my ex-lover to design my brother's wedding cake? No."

Savannah helps herself to one of the uncomfortable-on-purpose chairs in my sitting area, which means this conversation isn't going to end nearly as quickly as I'd like it to.

I press my hand to my thigh under the desk, and my fingertip starts doing its thing as she talks, spelling one word over and over; for some reason, the word my mind decides to fixate on is *WEDDING*.

"You know, you remind me of Scrooge, hiding behind his piles of gold coins."

"What the hell are you talking about? I'm not hiding."

"What are you so afraid of?"

"What the hell does that mean?"

"Well, you've been even more closed-off, grumpy, secretive, and distrustful than ever lately. Way worse off than you were before you completed your challenge, correct?"

"And your point would be?"

"Was the challenge really that difficult? You had to let us in, just an inch, by introducing us to a woman you had a fling with, a woman you were severing ties with anyway, and that was so distasteful to you that now you've locked the door in our faces and tossed away the key?"

I look up at her over my screen. Is that how it seems?

Is that what I did?

"What do you want from me, Savi? An open door policy on my soul?"

She gets to her feet, studies me thoughtfully for a moment, then sighs quietly. "I don't want anything *from* you, Harlan. I just want you to be happy. But I guess that's always been a tall order."

"I'm fine."

"Yeah. You seem fine." She heads for the door, apparently deciding I'm beyond help, or whatever it is she thought her goal was in coming here. "You're invited to dinner at Graysen's tonight. I'll tell him you'll be there."

"Don't."

She gives me a disapproving look.

I sit back after she leaves, and replay what she just said.

I don't like that she seems to see things that I don't tell anyone. How does she know I'm worse off now than before I introduced them to Darla?

She's right. But it disturbs me that she can tell.

I fucking hate it whenever one of my siblings seems to know me better than I think I know myself. It's invasive and uncomfortable, like an itch I need to scratch at, but can't.

I straighten my phone, and the screen lights up with a text from a member of my security team, Lincoln.

I open it, and my heart kicks. I call Quinn immediately. "What's happening?" I demand when she answers. "Where are you?"

"I'm fine," she says calmly. "Just calm down."

"You can't just skip out on Lincoln like that. I've assigned him to you full-time. It's his job to drive you."

"Yeah, well, Dani's dropping us off."

"Where?"

She sighs. "It's just a doctor's appointment. Don't freak out."

"What's wrong?" I'm already up and out the office door.

"Nothing."

"Is it Lorraine?" I bark at Brant, "Car," as I head for the elevator.

"Mom's fine. We're not fragile, Harlan. We can take care of ourselves."

I jab the elevator button and demand, "Tell me why you're going to the doctor."

I know she thinks I'm overly controlling.

And I know I keep making it worse.

Ever since she smashed that cake in my kitchen and moved her mixer out, she keeps telling me that she needs space. Time. Room to breathe.

The very next day, she informed me that she'd be baking out of her own kitchen while she "decides what to do." It's been driving me crazy.

So I insisted on buying her a new oven.

When she started making excuses about being "too busy" to see me, I insisted she let me track her phone, so I'd know where she was in case anything happened.

When her car proved no longer worth repairing, but she

wouldn't let me buy her a new one, I assigned a driver to her. And a bodyguard. Lincoln now drives her everywhere, and reports everything she does to me. So I know she and the baby are safe.

Whether she's at home, or with a client, or sitting by the waterfront thinking, I know where she is. And who she's with. I even know, to some extent, how she's feeling.

Because I have Lincoln take pictures of her, and send me updates. Hourly.

Or every fifteen minutes, if I'm stressing out.

I barely get to see her in person. Her choice, not mine.

But that's not going to make me stop thinking about her.

Stop *wanting* her.

And I can't help worrying obsessively about her whereabouts and her safety.

The truth is, she and the baby are beyond my control. And I just need her to be safe.

Can't she understand that?

"It's just an appointment, a checkup about the baby. I'm going with Mom. You don't have to leave work early."

I lower my voice. "You told Lorraine?"

"Of course I did. I wasn't going to keep it from her forever. I need support, Harlan."

"You have support."

"Emotional support," she clarifies. "Money is not an acceptable stand-in for time and attention."

"You have my time and attention."

You seriously have no idea.

The elevator door opens. "Shit. I'm about to lose reception, but I'll call you back on my way there—"

"You don't have to come. Are you at work?"

"I'll be there as fast as I can."

It's a fucking ultrasound appointment. And she didn't tell me about it.

I don't know whether to be more angry or fucking crushed that she didn't ask me to come to this appointment with her. I also need to decide who I need to fire, because how did I not know about this?

I'm supposed to know everything. *Everything.*

Where she goes, who she sees, and what she needs.

Always.

I sit by her side, holding her hand, watching on the screen as the technician performs the ultrasound—by inserting a wand thing right up inside her. There's a sheet over her knees so I can't see it, but I grit my teeth when she squeezes my hand.

Then we actually see the tiny blob on screen, like a little bean.

I watch, mesmerized, as the technician measures the fetus. I try to listen and absorb every word as she confirms the length of time Quinn has been pregnant, and tells us the likely due date.

She shows us the little flicker on the screen that is the baby's heartbeat, and Quinn's eyes glisten.

There's a burning sensation in my throat and chest that feels like a mixture between heartburn and the kind of love that a man would go to war for.

After the technician tells us that the doctor will be in to speak to us in a moment, and leaves us alone, I tell Quinn**,** **"**I want to take you home to my place tonight. To stay."

She blinks at me for a moment. I know she's emotional right now, and all of this is a lot. And I've been trying to let her do things her way.

But no matter how I try to give her space, give her time, and not put pressure on her, I can't get around the simple fact that I want her with me.

I fucking long for her.

"I've already told you," she says, awkwardly sitting up, "I'm staying at my place. I need to be near Mom. And it's just... simpler this way."

"But you don't even own that house," I try to argue for the dozenth time. She never listens.

She's right, that I've been using money as a stand-in. She wouldn't accept anything from me unless I made it about the baby, so I keep focusing on that.

But I'm getting desperate, and wondering, again, if I should buy the house she rents for her, and fix it up. But by the time that could happen, the new place above the bakery will be ready. And she shouldn't be living in a construction site anyway. That can't be good for the pregnancy—

"Harlan. I have medical lube up my cooch and I'd really like to get cleaned up and put my pants back on."

I get up to get out of her way, but try again. "It's not a stable enough situation. You and the baby should come live with me."

She doesn't even look at me when she says, "How will that work, when your family doesn't even know about me?"

Someone clears their throat. The doctor has stepped into the room. "Perhaps I'll give you another moment alone?"

"No, thank you," Quinn says. "I have some questions for you, please. And Harlan was just clearing out, to give us a minute."

She just kicked me out of the room.

"I'll be in the waiting room," I mutter.

I go sit down next to Lorraine, who takes one look at me and shakes her head. She sets her magazine aside and pats my knee.

"Becoming a parent is terrifying," she says. "I know."

I meet her eyes, feeling like an asshole.

"We should've told you," I tell her. "Together. Getting your daughter pregnant... that's something I should've spoken to you about. Even if it wasn't planned."

She eyes me. "From what she tells me, and I know she told you the same thing, she's not entirely sure the baby is yours." She seems to be testing me a bit, which is fair. But she doesn't even try to hide her disappointment when she adds, "She said it might be Justin's."

I knew I liked this woman.

"According to what I just heard in there," I tell her, "it is mine."

"Oh?"

"Yes. Anyway, I don't see *him* here, stepping up and trying to be the father."

"Maybe he would, if she gave him the chance."

I bite back my thoughts on that.

Lorraine considers me for a moment. "She didn't invite you here today, either."

That's true. I can't deny it.

"You would've been that baby's daddy, even if it wasn't yours?" she asks me.

I don't answer right away. The truth is, if Quinn wanted me, the answer to that is yes.

But according to the dates we were just given during that ultrasound, I *am* the father. And I'm still not sure if she wants me.

"You don't have to tell me," Lorraine says. "I can see it." She leans in and adds gently, "You're a daddy already."

I don't feel like one. At least, I feel like I'm failing at being one.

"You know why?" she asks me.

"No. Why?"

"Because you're here. And you're scared."

We sit together in silence. We're the only ones in this corner of the large waiting area.

"You might not ever feel ready," she says after a moment. "Even after they're grown and gone. And people might not say this often, because it's not pleasant and it's not what you want to hear, but there are a lot of downsides to parenting. There's pain and sorrow involved."

"You don't sugarcoat, do you, Lorraine?"

She laughs dryly. "Would you want me to?"

I grunt. "No. I'd rather you didn't."

"My daughter brings the sugar to this family. You want to know what the upside is?" She leans in a bit more and nudges her shoulder against mine. "That woman in there. She's been a wonderful daughter."

Yeah. I figured.

"And I know she wants more than anything to open a bakery, and live out our shared dream," she says. "But I don't need a bakery. With all I've been through... these days, I just need my baby to be happy, healthy, and safe. Quinn is the best thing I ever did with my life. And I don't care how many billion-dollar companies you have. That baby she's carrying will be yours."

It takes me a long moment to recover from the swell of mixed emotions, and reply to that. "This kid is going to have the best grandma ever, Lorraine."

Quinn's mom smiles. But there's a hint of sadness in it. And I know she's thinking that terrible thing that plays in the back of Quinn's mind all the time.

How long will she be around to be a grandma?

When Quinn comes out, I get to my feet, blinking away the damn tears Lorraine put there with her wise mom words. I never had a mom who talked to me like that.

I make a silent promise to myself to do everything I can to be a decent father to her grandchild.

"Are you okay?" I ask Quinn.

"I'm fine." To her mom, she says, "The baby is doing great. There's a heartbeat, and everything is on track. You're going to be a grandma in July."

Lorraine gives her a big, tight hug that says more than words could. Quinn's eyes sparkle as she clings to her mom, and when our eyes meet, she buries her face in Lorraine's neck.

When I see the tears in Quinn's eyes that she's trying to hide, it hits me all at once—that this wall between us is my fault. Because this is exactly what I did to Chelsea, right? The only other woman I ever had a serious relationship with—I pushed her away, just like I'm doing to Quinn now, without meaning to.

Chelsea left me, started a family with another man.

But Quinn can't do that. This baby is mine.

She's mine.

She has to see that, doesn't she?

That we're meant to be together.

When she and Lorraine pull apart, she hands me a piece of paper. "I asked the doctor about paternity testing," she tells me. "We can do this thing called NIPT, as early as next week. It's a Non-Invasive Prenatal Test. They just take a blood sample from you and me, and they can tell if the baby is yours. That's some information about it, for you."

I look into her eyes. "I know the baby is mine. You heard what the technician said, about the date of conception."

"I know." She shifts uncomfortably. "I just want you to know for sure. That I wasn't with anyone else."

I consider that, and that she seems so concerned about it. "I trust you, Quinn."

"I'd like us to do the test, though. So you never have to question. Okay?"

"Okay. If that's what you want."

She nods. I try to put my arm around her, but she's so stiff.

"Come on," I tell them. "I'll drive you home."

Quinn gives me an uncertain look, but seems too tired to argue. "Okay. Thank you."

"And since we're all together... I think it would be a good time to show your mom the new place, above the bakery. We can swing by on the way."

Quinn glances at her mom. Lorraine remains conspicuously silent. "It's not exactly on the way, Harlan," Quinn says.

"It won't take long."

"Harlan." Her voice is gently firm in a way that scares me. "I know you may not like this. But I've made my decision. And we're not moving into that place."

Chapter 25

Quinn

"We're doing limo karaoke," drunk Dani informs me. "Every time we pick someone up, we play a song for them."

"We're not singing, though," drunk Nicole clarifies.

"So, *not* karaoke, then," I say.

The girls just laugh, because they're drunk.

I've just climbed into the back of a limo, joining Dani, Nicole, and Dani's twin sister, Danica. Dani welcomes me with a cup of sparkling apple juice.

"We need something from the eighties for Quinn," Nicole announces, scrolling through her phone, which is tethered to a panel inside the limo.

"Which will match the interior of this limo," I point out. "I've never seen so much neon in my life."

"Isn't it awesome?" drunk Danica says happily.

Honestly, I would've rather stayed home tonight, in my jammies, than gone cruising in a party limo and out to a bar. But it's four days until Christmas, everyone is in the holiday spirit, there's a big party at Champagne tonight, and Dani rented the limo for us. The girls brought the limo to my place to pick me up, so how could I say no?

They all look gorgeous, and every one of them has pink cheeks.

"I see you've already been doing shots," I remark soberly. There's an open bottle of Baileys Irish Cream and a bottle of Prosecco in a built-in bin of ice, and they're all drinking Prosecco from plastic champagne cups. "I'm not saying I'm jealous, but I'm sort of jealous. Not only can I not drink alcohol right now, I'm swelling all over, nothing fits right, and I may throw up before the night is over. Just warning you all."

"Poor girl." Nicole pats my knee.

"I can't wait to be pregnant one day," Danica says dreamily, as if I somehow made it sound enjoyable. So far, for me, it really hasn't been. But Danica is quite different from her twin, as in way sweeter, and deeply in love with her *two* men—long story—and I know she's actually happy for me.

"Well, maybe tonight's the night for one of us," Nicole says, and cackles happily when Dani gives her a disturbed look.

"No!" Dani says. "Condoms on cocks, always!"

"Yeah, I could've used that reminder a few months back," I say, and sip my apple juice.

Danica gives me a sympathetic look.

"Ooh, I know!" Nicole has finally found a song, and puts on "Don't You Want Me." "This a perfect song for you and your... situation," she shouts at me over the loud music.

"What situation?" Danica shouts.

"She met Harlan when she was waitressing," Nicole shouts back. "Listen to the lyrics."

"What's going on between you two?" Danica shouts at me. We aren't super close, but I know Dani tells her some things, even if I don't. And I think Danica is the only one of my girlfriends who thinks Harlan is a great idea. But then again, she hasn't met him yet.

Even Nicole has become real iffy about Team Harlan, ever since he knocked me up and I told her about all the mood swings. His, not mine.

"I don't even know," I say, and when I see she can't quite hear me, I shout, "I don't know!"

I'm now wondering if a night of super loud music in a bar, surrounded by drunk people, is a bad idea for the baby.

Should I even be going out tonight?

"Why are we sitting here so long?" Dani yells. She's trying to look out the windows, but they're heavily tinted. We've barely gotten rolling from my place, but she's right, we've been sitting still for a while. "We're not even at an intersection..."

The words are barely out of her mouth when the door next to her flies open. The girls all draw back, startled, and "Don't You Want Me" spills out into the night.

And there stands Harlan.

He wears his usual black suit, without a tie, and when he leans down to look into the limo, the expression on his face is murderous.

"What are *you* doing here?" Dani shouts.

"Wait!" Nicole scrambles to turn down the music, so we can all hear this. "Okay, proceed."

"This is ladies' night," Dani informs him at a more reasonable volume. "No men are allowed in this limo."

"Except the driver," Danica adds politely.

"And unless we pick them up at a bar," Nicole stage-whispers.

"I won't be picking up anyone at a bar," Danica says earnestly.

"It's standard ladies' night rules," Nicole informs Harlan. "Also, you look nice. I like your suit."

Harlan ignores them all. All the girls are staring at him, but his gaze has locked on me.

"Get out of the car, Quinn," he says evenly.

"Uh... Danica, this is Harlan," I tell her. My heart is thumping. I'm not *not* happy to see him. I slightly don't mind being rescued from this party limo right now.

But I definitely don't appreciate being abducted by my baby's father in front of my girls. Especially when he's acting like a belligerent caveman.

Danica being Danica, however, shuffles over to the open door and offers her hand. "Oh, hi! So nice to meet you, Harlan."

He doesn't even glance at her.

"Quinn," he growls warningly.

"Maybe if you asked her nicely," Dani says coolly.

He just stares at me. Danica withdraws her hand and scoots back into her seat.

"Please, get out of the car, Quinn," he says with restrained fury.

I glance at my friends. Dani gives me a look like, *Don't you dare, you crazy, horny pregnant woman.*

"Okay, I'm just gonna go." I scoot toward the door.

"Quinn!" Nicole says. "What about limo karaoke?"

"Yeah... I think my baby daddy is in a mood. I'll catch up with you girls another time."

Dani frowns.

Harlan offers me a hand. I take it and he lifts me out of the car, setting me on my feet.

I wait for him to shut the door before I smack him on the chest. "What are you doing? You can't just show up and bark orders at me in front of my friends!"

"I said please." He laces his fingers through mine and pulls me toward his SUV, which is parked directly in front of the limo, blocking it. Manus waits for us politely by the open back door, as if his boss isn't acting like a total psycho.

"You need those etiquette lessons," I mutter.

"We'll talk in the car," Harlan growls.

We climb into the back of the SUV, Manus shuts us in, and we get rolling, while I quietly fume and recover my dignity.

"That was embarrassing, you know. You need to apologize to my friends, the next time you see them."

He scoffs. "Sure. After they apologize to me."

"Are you kidding? That was hella rude. Dani paid for that limo."

"Yeah?" He pins me with a glare. "How rude is it when they talk about me, and my child, like I'm not even there?"

I balk. "When did they do that?"

"Every single time I see them."

I think about that as I gradually calm down. My girls have been around a lot, that's true. As in, pretty much every time I see him these days.

It's been weeks since I told him I wasn't moving into that apartment above the bakery space he wanted to buy for me, and the only time I really see him is when he drops in unannounced at my house. And usually, at least one of my girls is there. It's like they decided to start taking shifts to babysit me after I became pregnant—and my situation with the baby's father became such a disaster.

I don't mind the extra love from my friends. They've really rallied around me. Because that's what great friends do.

But okay, they haven't been super welcoming to Harlan. I get that.

"They're just protective of me," I tell him. Surely he can understand that.

He's protective, too.

"And yet when I'm protective of you," he says, "I get pushed away."

Maybe that's true. "Well, my girls are a little less barbaric about it. They cook for me and rub my feet and help me do the dishes. You give me orders and bodyguards and track my phone. It's stifling."

He glowers at me. He says nothing, but now my hair seems to be the focus of his anger.

"What?"

"You changed your hair," he says in a low, accusatory tone.

"That's why you showed up and dragged me away from my friends? Because I went to the salon today and didn't tell you?"

"Frankly, yes."

"What the hell, Harlan." I don't even know what to say to the man. "So, you don't like my new hair color, and this is how you choose to tell me?"

"Why did you change it?"

I can't believe how personally affronted he's behaving about this.

"Well, I colored it turquoise when I was going through a hard time earlier this year and just needed a change, because I do that sometimes. But I didn't want to keep coloring it while pregnant and breast-feeding, so now that I'm out of the first trimester, I decided to just have it colored back to my natural brown." I study him as he continues to assess my new look, which is really my natural look. "Is it bad?"

"You look beautiful," he says tightly. His gaze drifts down to my plump pregnancy boobs, which are bursting out of my dress.

"So... what is it, then? You're upset that I went to the salon with Nicole instead of you? Is that it?"

"You could've told me."

"Why would I tell you?"

"I don't know, Quinn. You never tell me anything. The only way I find out is by stalking you."

"That's not true."

"It is true. Your girlfriends know everything, because you tell them. I show up with dinner, and it's the wrong thing, but your friends know what you need to eat so you don't feel sick. They know you're experiencing morning sickness before I do—"

"That's because they're around more."

"Because you let them come around more."

That may be true.

"They've completely taken over," he says resentfully, "like I'm not needed."

"Well..."

"Don't say it," he growls.

"I *don't* need you to raise this baby, Harlan," I tell him carefully.

"I have rights."

"I'm not trying to take the baby away from you." I soften my tone. I don't want him to think I'm waging war on him. I'm really not. This whole situation has just been hard, on so many levels. "That's not what I'm saying. I just needed... air."

He takes a deep breath, and I think he's calming down.

"Are you really upset because you don't feel needed?" I ask him. "Or because you think you're not *wanted*?"

He doesn't answer, his mouth clamped shut.

"I never said I didn't want you," I say gently.

"Then why don't I ever see you?" he demands.

"I've been busy. There's a lot on my plate."

"Yes, I noticed. You quit Champagne, yet you go out to bars now as often as when you worked in one."

"First of all, that's not true. Second, I quit Champagne because you generously offered to cover my rent, for now, so that I could cut back on work."

He also bought me a new oven; that was the concession made when I refused to come back to his kitchen. And he bought me a new bed, insisting that it was important for the pregnancy.

I appreciate it all, but this never-ending power struggle is exhausting.

"I covered your rent so you didn't have to work so hard through the pregnancy," he corrects me. "So you could rest. Going out partying isn't resting."

"We're not partying. At least, I'm not. I'm just spending time with my friends."

"It's a Thursday, Quinn. You could stay home."

Oh my god. I just don't understand his possessive bullshit. If he doesn't want me to be his woman, because he "can't offer me more" and all he wants is sex, why is he so obsessed about controlling my every move?

Is this really about the baby, or my hair, or my friends?

"I don't know what you want from me," I tell him.

"I've told you what I want. I tried to buy that bakery for you. I pay for things because I'm trying to help you."

"And I appreciate it."

"Do you? You haven't slept over at my place since you became pregnant."

I stare at him.

"So *that's* the problem," I say. He isn't getting laid, so he's throwing a caveman hissy fit?

"You barely let me touch you," he growls.

"Me? You've been so cool and formal, you might as well be a stranger."

"Because I don't know what you want!"

"Don't yell at me."

He takes a breath. "I tolerate your 'I've got this and I don't need you' act—"

"It's not an act!"

"I tolerate your friends gossiping about men, including your ex, right in front of me. I even tolerate their attitude that I'm little more than a sperm donor. But it makes me wonder if that's how *you* see me."

"Of course not."

"It fucking feels like it."

"Please, don't swear. I don't want to see you upset. I'm so tired."

"Then why were you going out tonight?"

"Because my friends wanted to take me out, okay? And it's almost Christmas. And I wanted to make them happy."

He glowers at me. "And what about me? Do you want me to be happy?"

"Of course."

"Then come home with me."

I can feel his smoldering heat, and it's clear what he wants. He wants to get me naked. Right now.

Maybe he wants to spank me and tell me I've been a bad girl, until I behave for him. Until I beg for him.

And while that would be fun…

"I'm not sure that fixes anything, Harlan."

"How can I fix anything," he says in a low voice, "when I don't even understand what the problem is?"

"I feel the same way," I say, frustrated.

Neither of us says anything else. I can feel his anger, too, which I imagine is an expression of his hurt.

Or maybe it's his fear that I truly see him as nothing but a sperm donor? And not a real father to this baby?

That's not true.

I'm just hurt, too.

When I look out the window and suddenly realize where we are, that we're driving into his neighborhood and toward his house, I groan. "My god. As if your obsessive, overprotective stalking isn't enough. Now you're kidnapping me. Again."

"You didn't seem to mind last time," he says darkly.

A familiar heat washes through my body.

But I glare at him.

"You think I'm just coming up to your bedroom with you? After everything that's happened?"

"Why wouldn't you? Explain that to me."

"Because... I'm upset."

His eyes narrow. "What are you upset about, exactly?"

I take a breath. "Nicole told me, a few weeks ago, that Megan and Jameson decided to go with another wedding cake designer," I admit. "Was that your doing?"

"That's why you've been so angry with me?" he demands. "You're upset that you lost out on a cake design job, so you're lashing out at me?"

"How am I lashing out at you? I was just going out with my girlfriends, and you crashed the party and stole me like a caveman. I'm surprised you didn't just drag me away by the hair."

"I would never do that," he says stonily. Then he adds with a whiff of indignity, "You're pregnant."

"Oh! You think this is funny?"

"Nothing about this is funny." He adds in a low, chocolatey voice, "And a man can't steal what belongs to him."

"I *belong* to you? That's how you see it?"

His jaw does that crackling thing that is never a good sign. "That baby in your belly belongs to me."

I lay my hands on my belly protectively. "This baby is *ours*," I correct him calmly. "Which means Jameson and Megan are the baby's family, too."

"You can't design their wedding cake, Quinn."

I sigh in frustration. Does he really think this is about a damn cake?

When we pull into his driveway and park in front of his front door, he opens the door of the SUV, and I follow him out. He helps me down, and holds my hand as he walks me into the house.

I want to be here. I really do. I've wanted to be in his house, in his arms, for weeks.

But not like this.

Not when there's this terrible distance between us. I can feel the jagged edges of his emotions right now, and surely he can feel mine.

Fucking isn't going to make them all go away.

It would be a delicious distraction, but that's not nearly enough.

We left any possibility of having that kind of only-skin-deep sexual relationship behind the moment I found out I was pregnant.

As soon as we're alone in his foyer, I stop in my tracks and say, "I guess you're not taking me to your brother's wedding, either? You'd rather keep me hidden away from your siblings like some dirty secret."

He frowns.

"Are you ever going to introduce them to this baby? Or are you just going to hide their little niece or nephew in the closet every time they come over?"

He gives me a look that says I'm really asking for that spanking. Then says, "I can take you to the wedding if that's what you want."

I'm actually shocked he'd say that. I'll be massively pregnant when Jameson and Megan get married. "As what? Your pregnant friend?"

He gives me a long look. "We're not friends, remember?"

I'm starting to feel nauseous, and try to swallow the rising feeling. "I need to sit down."

"What's wrong?" Instantly, he grabs my arm and gets in my face. "Do you feel faint?"

"No. I just feel sick."

He walks me over to a bench and sits me down. "You're sick? Since when?"

"Not *sick* sick."

He crouches in front of me. "Are you in pain? I'll call the doctor."

"Harlan, stop. It's fine. Really. It's just morning sickness."

"It's almost ten o'clock at night."

"Yeah. It's a real misnomer. It comes on at any time of day or night it damn well pleases."

His eyebrows draw together. "Well, what fixes it?"

That's such a Harlan question, I have to smile a little. "Nothing, really. Sometimes eating a bit. Mostly I just need… comfort."

He blinks at me, and I sigh. Because clearly I just spoke to him in a language he doesn't understand.

"A bath would be nice," I interpret for him. "Followed by sleep. Lots of it."

I don't think I've ever seen Harlan Vance take anything so seriously as he does right now—when he gently picks me up in his arms, carries me upstairs and into the bathroom, sets me carefully on my feet, and tells me, "Get undressed, Quinn."

Chapter 26

Quinn

We're standing in the lady bathroom off Harlan's bedroom. When I just wrap my arms around myself and definitely don't start getting undressed, Harlan takes a deep breath, like he's holding onto his patience, and starts the bath water running.

My attention creeps over to the many beauty products on display. Including a lot of pretty, feminine-looking tubes, jars and bottles, and makeup, which clearly don't belong to Harlan. They're all over the countertop, which was stark and empty the last time I was here.

I actually feel nausea creeping up again, but this time, it's not pregnancy related.

"Has someone else been here?" The words are out of my mouth before I can stop myself. "Another woman?"

He scowls at me. "Of course not."

"Then what's all that stuff?"

He turns away, adjusting the temperature of the bath water, so I can't read his face when he says, "It's for you."

I take another look at the items, all the skin care and luxury cosmetics.

There's a basket of bathing supplies by the bathtub, too.

He got all this stuff for me? To make it more welcoming and comfortable for me, when I finally came back?

He squeezes a dollop of something that smells lovely into the bath, like lavender and vanilla.

"Don't make it too hot," I tell him. "It's not good for the baby."

"I know that," he says grumpily. "I've read the books."

"What books?"

"All of them."

I try to picture that, but can't.

He glances at me, almost self-consciously, and mumbles, "I listen to audiobooks in the car."

Somehow, that's even harder to picture. Harlan and Manus, driving around, listening to audiobooks about pregnancy.

When he approaches me, I suddenly feel shy. Like this is the first time he's going to see me naked.

"Take off your clothes, Quinn," he says gently.

"Do I have to?" I joke.

His eyelids lower as his gaze roams down my body. "It will be a much more comfortable bathing experience if you do."

The way he says *bathing experience*, I'm definitely wondering if I'm in for more than a bath here.

When I hesitate, he moves behind me. I can see him in the mirror as he starts unzipping the back of my dress with focus.

I swallow. "My body is changing," I warn him.

"I hope so. That means the baby is growing." He drops the dress to my ankles and deftly unhooks my bra.

"I feel fat," I say self-consciously as he peels it off, my breasts bouncing free. God, that feels good, though. My nipples hum, desperate for his attention.

"You're gorgeous, Quinn," he says, his voice low and rough, as he dips his fingers into my panties. They tug against my clit, making me shiver. He pulls them gently down my legs, sparking little shivers all the way down.

He undresses me like I'm the most precious thing on earth to him. Not fragile. But beloved.

It takes my breath away.

When I'm completely naked, his hooded eyes find mine in the mirror. Then they find my pussy. "Do you want help getting in the bath?"

"I'm okay."

I climb in and sink into the warm water, and he shuts off the faucet.

Then he strips off his jacket, and starts rolling his sleeves up over his strong, sexy forearms, watching me the whole time.

I try not to stare, reminding myself that I'm mad at him.

I pick up a washcloth that sits on the side of the tub, but he takes it from my hand. "Sit back."

I settle back into the bath, too tired and too thirsty for his attention to argue. He lathers up the cloth with body wash. Then he kneels by the tub and smooths the soapy cloth over my skin. Legs, feet, and toes. Then arms and hands. He's soaping each individual finger when I finally decide I'm speaking to him again.

"I just don't think you're being fair," I tell him, trying not to sound like I'm in heaven.

"It's almost cute how much you fight me," he mutters.

"As long as you win," I counter.

He gives me a look that's part dangerous and totally aroused.

But I don't want to forget that thing I'm mad about just because my body wants his so badly.

"Your brother and Megan, they would be such important clients to me. And the guests at their wedding, those are also potential clients."

At least he seems to be listening, and calmly. "I'll get you other clients."

"I didn't ask you to do that."

His eyes meet mine. "It would be my pleasure." He soaps my breasts and I sigh, kind of rolling my eyes. His gaze moves hungrily down my chest. "Your breasts are swelling."

"Yeah, I'm pregnant," I say dryly, like I'm not enjoying this at all. "All of me is swelling."

He carefully washes my hips, then my belly, which is definitely swelling a little.

Then he takes my hands and gives me a gentle tug. "Stand up."

I get to my feet with his help, then put my hands on his shoulders for balance. I'm becoming soft and rubbery, and I only sag against him more as he lathers my ass with his strong hands, massaging me with body wash.

He looks up, his gaze moving greedily over my naked breasts, then locking onto my eyes. "What did I do that hurt you, baby?" he asks me. "I'm going to fix it."

I try not to pout when I say, "You don't want me at your brother's wedding."

He says softly, "I can't have you around my family, or tell them about the baby, unless you continue to let them believe that you're Darla. Can't you do that for me?"

"That's not fair. You're trying to put this on me, like I'm the one who's in the wrong."

"I already told Savannah it's just a nickname. They can call you Quinn now. What does it matter?"

"You think this is about a name? My name, or whatever they think it is, is not the point. I don't want my relationship with my baby's aunts and uncles, your brothers and sister and sister-in-law, to be built on a lie. Do you?"

"Of course not. But that doesn't change anything."

I gently push his hands away.

He doesn't like it. But I don't care.

"So you prefer secrecy and lies to honesty and trust," I say.

"It's not what I prefer. It's the way I need it to be." He squeezes out the cloth in the bathwater and uses the warm, clean cloth to wash between my legs, his eyes darkening as he does it.

"To protect *her*," I say, my voice breaking. "You're still protecting her."

And now I've revealed the bruising truth. The source of my hurt. Now he knows that I'm still jealous of her. Geneviève Blaise.

The real Darla.

"It's not about her," he says tightly.

"Of course it's about her. It's always been about her."

"Come here." He takes my hands, and guides me as I step out of the bathtub.

I watch him warily as he dries me off with a big, plush towel, but I'm losing this battle with myself. I can't resist the pleasure of his touch.

So I just let him touch me.

My hormones have been doing crazy shit to me, and I've been horny as hell.

Horny, and wanting him.

And the way he's looking at me right now, I know he's been missing me, too.

He's down on his knees in front of me, and the way he caresses my body with the soft towel, so slowly, while carefully studies my nakedness, is maddening. He's setting me all aflame, making me burn for him. It's like my whole body has forgotten I'm already carrying his child, and is urging me to let him plant himself inside me again.

He strokes my swollen nipples with the nubbly fabric, and

asks me, "Do you like that?" His voice is low and dark with need.

"Yes," I breathe.

He moves the towel between my legs, nudging my already-swollen clit. "How about this? Does this feel good?" He caresses my pussy with the towel. If I'm wet there, it's no longer from the bathwater.

I moan wordlessly as my eyes roll closed, and I dig my fingers into his shoulders.

"Have you been playing with this pretty pussy," he whispers, "while you think about my cock?"

"You're a monster."

"So you tell me," he says, not the least bit offended. "And I'll take that as a yes."

And just when my rubbery knees are about to give out, he drops the towel, scoops me up in his strong arms, and carries me into the bedroom. He lays me down gently on his bed, on my back.

But instead of stripping off his clothes before he joins me, he just gazes down at me, like I'm some beautiful prize he can't believe he's won.

When he finally lies down beside me, he's still dressed. He's on his side, facing me. My body is still humming from his caresses with the towel. My breasts are swollen and plump, and he stares hungrily.

Then he starts placing soft, worshipful kisses on my breasts. His slight stubble is rough on my skin, making me shiver, and he takes his time... leaving sweet, sucking kisses all over. While completely ignoring my nipples, which are swollen and dark, and extra sensitive.

"Beautiful Quinn," he says softly. "Tell me how you feel. Right now."

"I'm aching," I whisper as my nipples tighten, begging for

the attention of his hot, luscious mouth. He knows exactly what he's doing when he keeps ignoring them.

"Tell me, baby. Where does it ache?"

"Please, Harlan," I beg breathlessly.

"Tell me," he demands. "Where?"

I know he knows. He just wants me to say the words.

"My nipples and my pussy."

"Mmm. Does my sweet girl want these gorgeous, achy nipples sucked?"

"Oh my god, *yes,*" I cry shamelessly.

He chuckles, driving me mad.

Finally, he flutters his tongue over one taut, eager nipple. I whimper, it feels so good.

"More," I beg.

He keeps teasing, fluttering his evil tongue over the taut peak. "More?" His fingers drift over my hip, toward my pussy, so fucking slowly I think I might die. "How about this aching pussy?" he taunts, like the beast he is. "Should I play with it?"

"Please..."

"You want me to touch your clit?"

"Fuck. I'm dying..." My heart thuds in my chest as he makes me wait for it. "*Please.*"

When his fingertips finally reach my clit, gently fluttering over it, I gasp.

He drags his teeth along my nipple, just lightly, and I cry out. His fingers are so warm as he fondles me with gentle purpose, making me pant and sweat. When I start to tense, he says softly, "Just relax for me, sweet girl. I'll take care of all your little aches."

I try. I try to take a breath and relax, but everything is quickly swirling together into one giant, aching, throbbing mass of need that's centered between my legs. And he just keeps teasing at it, so gently, with his deft fingers.

He flutters his tongue over my other nipple, then takes it into his mouth. He groans, a sound of masculine contentment, and starts sucking. Goosebumps break out all over my body, and I feel myself gush.

My body wants to be fucked by his. Hard.

But he seems to have no intention of fucking me. Just teasing me until I completely fall apart.

When I start grinding my hips a little, trying to get more pressure from his fingers, he pinches my clit. I squeal and fall still. Pleasure surges through me.

I almost come.

"Shh. Not yet," he murmurs as I struggle to catch my breath. "Nice and relaxed. That's my good girl."

I fucking melt when he calls me his good girl.

I bask in it, glowing in his approval.

He moves his mouth from one throbbing nipple to the other, and resumes teasing. "My sweet, horny girl," he taunts happily, in-between licks. "You're going to come for me, so hard, aren't you." Then he sucks me into his mouth again, deeper, and my eyes roll back.

I try harder to relax and be still, and just feel everything he wants me to be feeling right now. His hot, wet, sucking mouth. His teasing tongue. His patient fingers between my legs, gently persuading me to succumb, to surrender to him.

I lay perfectly still, the way I know he wants me to, just receiving the pleasure he gives as he stokes my arousal, higher and higher. Until the first spasm of pure ecstasy makes my hips twitch and my pussy jerk. I moan raggedly as I start to fall apart.

I can't stop it this time.

"That's it, baby," he says, a thrill in his voice. "Let go."

He bites my nipple a little, and I cry out as the climax explodes through my core. I feel it in my nipples as he suckles. I scream softly until my voice is hoarse, as he strokes me right through it, coaxing my pleasure in waves. My pussy clenches, over and over, longing for the sweet stretch of his swollen cock, filling me with his hungry thrusts.

I'm throbbing all over, aching for him to possess me. My thighs are soaked in my need for him.

Maybe this is exactly what he wants...

"Harlan," I plead.

"I know, baby," he says softly, "keep coming. Good girl." Then he sucks my throbbing nipple into his mouth again as I keep falling apart.

He coaxes and coaxes until he's lavished me with every last twitch of pleasure I can possibly feel.

Only then, when my body finally stops quivering and spasming in response to his caresses, he releases me.

He settles next to me, and pulls me against him, drawing the covers over us both. I feel boneless as he guides my head to his chest, and I collapse there, spent.

I can barely stand to move, but my fingers slide beneath the untucked hem of his shirt, seeking his warm skin.

I feel his heart beating, steady and strong, beneath my cheek.

He's silent, just holding me, and I know I'm going to fall asleep in his arms, and fast. I feel tender and raw and totally spent.

Satisfied.

And scared as hell.

I whisper brokenly, "Do you think you could ever love us like you love her?"

But if he answers me, I don't hear it.

Chapter 27

Harlan

I step outside, onto my backyard patio, feeling fucking defeated.

Do you think you could ever love us like you love her?

Quinn fell asleep before I could figure out how to answer her. Before I could explain.

But would I have explained?

No.

I walk across the patio and sit down on a chair by the pool under the moonlight.

This patio is why I bought the house. I didn't care about the rest of it, other than having some vague understanding that this is the kind of house I'm expected to live in—expensive. I don't care about furniture or square footage or views.

I just want this private spot surrounded in hedges and trees where I can be alone, breathe fresh air, and fucking think. It's not that I want to be totally disconnected from everything and everyone around me. I like going into the office, sometimes. I like having staff coming and going.

I just prefer to be alone in the middle of it all. The tight, innermost circle I've built around myself just doesn't have room for anyone in it but me.

At least it didn't until Quinn came along.

Now, the space around me feels eerily empty without her in it.

It makes me think that Damian was right. Maybe I'll die alone because I just push people away. I expect the worst of them. I just hate people in general until they somehow prove themselves worthy of my hard-won respect. And sometimes, they do.

But there's no one, outside of my family, who's ever won my love.

Maybe no one's ever wanted to before.

But with those words tonight, Quinn told me that she wants my love.

Maybe I just need to learn how to love her like she deserves. Because everything I've been doing so far to try to take care of her and show her I care isn't fucking working.

Somehow, it's doing the opposite.

I've made her feel unloved. And it fucking kills me.

I sit back in this quiet spot with the hum of the city beyond, where I've found the answers to so many of my problems over the years. And I notice a strange sound that doesn't belong. This small, indistinct mewling.

At first, I think I'm imagining it. It's just a child playing off in the distance, or a bird... but then it comes again, much clearer.

I get to my feet, adrenalin spiking.

I follow the sound, and the automatic lights come on as I circle the house, lighting my way through the dark. And right under my bedroom windows, low down under the edge of a bush, I find her.

Her green eyes shine at me when I crouch down.

I can tell that something's not right.

I reach in, and when I try to put my hands around her, she mewls again. It's a sound of fear. Or pain.

She's hurt, I think, but I can't tell where. "It's okay," I tell her gently. "I've got you."

When I pick her up as carefully as I can, her hind leg flops strangely. She makes a pained little cry.

"Shit, shit, shit." I swear at myself as I carry her into the family room and lay her down on the sofa. I think her leg is injured. And if it is... maybe she fell off the fucking roof? Just like I said she would.

I fucking knew this would happen.

I should've just let her into the house.

Would it have killed me to leave a window open for her on the first floor? Or put in a fucking cat door?

Now this sweet, small thing is in pain.

She's broken, and it's my fault.

I've just come home from school.

I'm standing in the foyer of my family's house. I'm alone. But I can hear sounds in the distance, coming from upstairs—a door closing. Then the muffled voices of my siblings. My mom.

More than I can hear them... I can feel their sorrow.

I'm supposed to be there, with them.

I can hear Mom crying.

As I climb the stairs to the second floor, I hear helicopter blades.

When I get to the top of the stairs, I see the door to the room where the terrible thing is going to happen, and I know they're waiting for me.

I hear my dad's voice, calling to me, and I start to cry.

I hear the *whump whump whump* of the helicopter blades

as I walk toward the door. The black cat runs across my path, startling me.

I'm confused.

She doesn't belong here.

When I finally reach the door, I start to open it. But I can't hear my dad's voice anymore.

I wake up in a panic.

I'm sitting in the vet's waiting room the next morning when Quinn walks in. When our eyes meet across the room, I can see her concern, and I sit up as she comes over. She sits down next to me.

"I'm okay. Everything's okay," I tell her automatically, taking her hand in mine. I'm exhausted. I barely slept. But I can see that she's worried and I don't want that.

"What's going on?"

"How did you know I was here?"

"You let me track your phone, remember?" She puts her hand on the back of my neck as I rub my face. I did. When I insisted she let me track hers. "Is everything really okay?"

"It's fine." I pull her into my arms. "Don't worry." I put a hand on her belly but I'm distracted.

"You were gone when I woke up. And I was worried."

"I'm sorry. I didn't mean to make you worry."

"It's okay. I didn't need anything. I just… I missed you."

I laugh humorlessly. "You missed my obsessive, overprotective stalking? Isn't that what you called it?"

"Yes," she says sweetly. Then her expression turns worried again. "I see I was right to be worried. I don't think I've ever seen you dressed this casually before."

She's right. I'm a mess. I'm wearing jogging pants and a

sweatshirt. I check my watch. "I didn't realize how late it is." It's almost ten in the morning already.

"You didn't go into work today?"

"No."

"I can only imagine one reason you're here." She squeezes my hand and says gently, "Something happened to your kitty?"

My eyes instantly tear up and I press my fingers into them.

"Oh, Harlan." She wraps her arm around me. "What happened?"

"I think she fell off the roof."

"Oh my gosh." She looks toward the empty reception desk, and the doors into the doctor's offices, as I've been doing for the last half hour. There's no one else here except for some guy with a golden retriever in the far corner.

"She's alive," I reassure her, realizing she might be wondering.

She sighs with relief. "I thought cats always land on their feet, though...?"

"Yeah. That doesn't mean the feet don't break."

"Shit." She puts her head on my shoulder. "I'm here, okay?"

"Okay."

Does she know how good it feels to hear her say that?

The warmth that floods me when she cuddles into me and tries to make me feel better is intense.

Maybe I've been so afraid of losing my inheritance and my place in my family, and so focused on keeping my secrets, that it snuck up on me that I've become so much more afraid of losing *her*.

I'm terrified she'll uncover the truth about Darla, and I'll lose her over all the lies.

She wants to be properly introduced to my family—as herself—and she deserves that. She's having my baby.

How can I expect her to play Darla forever to cover up my lies?

I can't.

But what else can I do? Invent another Darla to play the role of my ex-lover?

My go-to solution is to just create another lie. Because in the past, that's what I would've done. But my lies are just digging a deeper and deeper hole. It's become an impossible problem I can't solve, and I don't know how to get out unscathed.

"I should've let her into the house," I say out of nowhere.

"This is not your fault, Harlan."

"But I took her for granted. I kept pushing her out. I just didn't want to get attached to her. But now she's hurt, and maybe she will die."

"So, she's really yours? You always said she was a stray."

"I don't know. Maybe I just didn't want her to be mine. But she kept showing up, and... maybe I got attached. I didn't even want to know who owned her, because then I really would lose her." I've started picking at the seam of my pant leg, my finger incessantly spelling out the word. *ATTACHED.* "The woman working the twenty-four-hour desk when I brought her in last night said they'd contact her owners. But she isn't in today. I'm waiting for an update."

"You love her," Quinn concludes.

"She's just a cat."

"Then why are you sitting here looking like hell and fighting back tears in the middle of a workday?"

I know she's right.

And for some reason, I can't just turn off that love, even though I want to.

Fuck.

"No offense, Harlan, but you look worse than I've ever seen you."

I don't doubt it.

I don't think I was this much of a mess when Granddad died.

Actually... I don't think I've allowed myself to feel real grief or sorrow since Dad died. Nothing else has ever made me feel so helpless to my emotions. But maybe that's because his death also felt like...

My fault.

It's definitely not just the cat that's made me this much of a mess.

But I don't say so.

"Did you get any sleep last night?" Quinn asks me worriedly.

"Not much."

After driving the cat to the vet, they said I should go home and get some sleep while they took care of her and kept her overnight. I tried to sleep in a guest room so I wouldn't bother Quinn. But the bit of sleep I did get was interrupted by the old dream.

I look at Quinn, really seeing her for the first time since she walked into the vet's office. She looks *really* worried.

And so fucking precious.

"You look beautiful," I tell her. "Don't worry about me. The only ones you need to take care of right now are the baby and Lorraine."

"Is that why you had the adjustable bed delivered to the house for Mom this morning?"

"I just wanted her to be comfortable."

Quinn shakes her head in wonder. "You know how many times I've talked to her about investing in a bed like that, so she can sit up easily in it when she has those tired days, and she just wants to stay in bed and watch a movie or read a book? She says they're for old people. She wouldn't even hear of the idea from me. But when she found out the delivery was from you... Jesus. She sent me like twenty photos of it already, from every angle. I think she would've accepted a dirty diaper if you sent it."

I raise an eyebrow.

"What I'm saying is my mom thinks you're the shit, and she has reason to. Because you pay attention, and you treat us like family." She sighs. "I know how much you've been doing for us, Harlan. And I haven't thanked you enough."

But I don't want her thanks. I've never wanted that.

Maybe I've just always wanted *her*, but been too fucking terrified to admit it, to either of us.

"But you were right," I tell her. "I've been taking care of you with money and thinking that's enough. Maybe I just don't know how to be enough for someone else. Especially a child."

"I mean, who does? I have no idea how to be a mom. But I trust that I'll figure it out."

"Maybe that's because you have such a great mom."

She squeezes my hand reassuringly. "Look what you're doing for this little kitty, though. Clearly, you're trying to give her what she needs right now. Doesn't that give you even a glimmer of hope that you'll figure out the fathering thing?"

"I don't know, Quinn." I can't even look at her when I say, "What if I pass all my fucked-up flaws on to our child?" Because it's entirely possible, and that terrifies me, too. That I'll somehow fail my child, genetically, before they even get a chance to be normal.

No, not normal. Incredible, like her.

I know she probably thinks I mean my obsessive nature. My OCD. But that's only part of it.

"Then you'll be understanding, because you know exactly what it's like," she says easily. "Who better than you to help and support them? You'll teach them how to be amazingly successful. Just like you've been."

Maybe she's right.

Maybe my mom could've been more supportive. And maybe my dad should've helped me more, protected me, like I'm trying so hard to do for my kid, before I even meet them.

Maybe part of the reason I've been pushing Quinn away is because I've been trying to protect her and the baby *from me*. Because I'm afraid that I'm not good enough. That I *won't* figure it out in time to be a decent father.

Maybe all my obsessive behavior toward Quinn—trying to keep her safe and protected and *mine*—are all because I'm afraid of losing her and the baby, but I'm self-sabotaging, too. Because I'm just pushing her further away.

What she needs is to know that I love her. That I'll be her emotional support.

That was what I needed from my parents the most, but didn't get.

Or maybe I need it so badly *because* I didn't get it?

I don't fucking know.

"It's okay to be afraid," Quinn says. "My mom said to me the other day that becoming a parent is terrifying."

"Yeah. She told me the same thing."

"Well, I think she's right. Because how can you bring someone into the world that you know you're going to love beyond all else, and one day, one way or another, you're going to have to say goodbye to them? Nothing is forever." She looks into my eyes with a tender hope that makes my heart burn. "But don't you want to love someone with everything you've got, while you can? Even if it's 'just a cat'?"

A door opens, and I manage to tear my eyes away from Quinn long enough to register that the vet's assistant is walking toward us. She smiles.

"Good news," she says. "We got a hold of Darla's owners. They're coming to take her home."

Chapter 28

Quinn

I stand over a luxurious pet bed in Harlan's sunroom, where the black cat reclines on a blanket like a little queen. Her wounded leg is in a cast, a little heart on it made out of red medical tape.

"I can't believe that's Darla," I say.

Harlan crouches next to me, fussing over the pet-gate wall that he had his staff set up posthaste to keep the cat secure while she recuperates. She won't be wandering freely until the cast is off.

"I mean, yes, her name is Darla," he says distractedly. "But no, she was never my lover."

"Gee, thanks for clarifying."

He nudges her food bowl closer to her, then steps over the gate.

I shake my head. "Worse... I can't believe they abandoned her like that."

The couple who came to collect Darla, her owners, refused to pay the vet bill when they found out how much it was. They actually got irate about it and told the vet to keep her.

Jerks. They were driving a Jaguar.

Harlan paid and brought Darla home.

"Explain, Harlan. Please. She's safe and comfy now, I promise."

I have to actually take him by the arm and tug him over to the sofa in the adjoining family room. He comes, but he doesn't sit down. The guilt runs deep.

I seriously think he blames himself for her falling off the roof.

"Climbing is just what cats do," I assure him, as I already did so many times on the ride home. I'm not sure he fully heard me. "You won't be able to stop her from climbing in the future."

His eyebrows are all twisted together as he watches her lick her belly fur. "Maybe she'll just be an indoor cat from now on. I have a large house."

My god. I can literally see how loving he is.

He adores that cute little broken cat.

I'd be jealous, except it's just so freaking beautiful.

I just wish he could see it.

But I'm distracted, too. I'm still processing that there really is no Darla. At least, no human Darla.

Which means that his ex-lover Darla, the woman I built up obsessively in my head, isn't real. She never was.

I sit down on the sofa, watching him pace. "So... Geneviève Blaise. She's not Darla, then?"

"She's not my ex at all. She dated Jamie, not me."

"Oh my god. You have no idea…"

He finally looks at me. "How mad you are that I lied to you?" he fills in.

"How relieved am I that you didn't sleep with that woman," I counter. "She's beyond gorgeous! How can I compete with a freaking movie star?"

He stops pacing, and his eyes burn into me. "You don't have to compete with anyone."

Oh, *wow*. My insides turn to molten muck when he looks at me like that.

But if he thinks I'm letting him distract me with those bedroom eyes of his, fuck that.

"Were you ever planning to tell me that the cat is named Darla, though? If I hadn't found out like this?"

"If you want the honest answer—"

"Yes, please."

"Then, no." He frowns worriedly. "Probably not."

I sigh. "Well, the cat's out of the bag now, right? Can I please have the explanation that I've been waiting for? I am not going to be patient on this. And you're killing me here."

He sits down on the sofa, takes a deep breath, and says basically the last thing I'm prepared to hear.

"I thought I was having a baby once before."

"Oh. Uh..."

"But I was wrong," he adds quickly. "The woman's name was Chelsea. She was my most serious girlfriend. I mean, maybe she was my only serious girlfriend. This was years ago. She became pregnant, but within twenty-four hours of me finding out, someone tipped off my brother Graysen that she was sleeping with her golf instructor. It turns out the baby was his."

"Oh, god. Harlan. That's awful."

"I mean, it wasn't fun. It didn't really sell me on the idea of falling in love and living happily-ever-after. Chelsea and her golf instructor ended up there, but I ended up kind of shutting down. More than I already was. I don't think I really loved her like she wanted me to. I didn't want to fall in love."

He pauses, looking at me almost guiltily, like he's worried how I'll take this. But I'm just so glad he's letting me into something from his past. Something that feels *true*.

"And then," he goes on, "things just got worse after she left me for that other guy. My family made such a giant deal out of the whole mess, wanting to talk about it all the time. They wanted *me* to talk about it, but I didn't want to. I just wanted to move on."

"I guess that's understandable..." I'm trying to be supportive. And I can understand not wanting to dwell on such a thing, for sure. "But you have to talk about it sometime, with someone, right?"

He stares at me for a beat. "You sound just like Savannah."

"She must be a wise woman."

He kind of grumbles in agreement. At least, I think it's agreement.

"Either way," he continues, "my siblings definitely didn't let the topic of my love life rest. They became nosy as hell, like I now needed their help or something. I guess their idea of supporting me in moving on was asking me at regular intervals if I was seeing anyone. Over and fucking over again. For a while, I just said no, whether I was or not. I just decided that I was never going to tell them yes. Because then they'd pry for more details. But after a few years, they weren't really taking no for an answer anymore. They knew I was lying. And that just made them poke at me more."

"I hate to say it," I interject gently, "but I think they were just doing that because they care about you."

"Incessantly prying into my personal business is caring?"

"I mean..." I blink at him. "Isn't that what you do to me because you care, more or less?"

He glares at me. "Hardly," he mutters, but I know he can see my point.

"Look. If I treated my girlfriends and my mom the way you just said you treated your siblings, whenever they asked if I was seeing anyone... I can tell you, they'd pry. They'd be concerned about me. And, as people who love me, they'd feel a right to know who I was dating."

Harlan's nostrils flare as he takes that in. I know he doesn't like it.

But how can he argue my logic on this?

"This is what relationships are, Harlan. Sharing. Transparency. Building trust."

His jaw does that crackling thing that tells me he doesn't love what he's hearing.

Too bad.

"So, what happened? After they figured out you were lying to them about not seeing anyone for like, years?" I prompt.

I watch his chest rise and fall as maybe he digs deep for what he's about to say.

"I lied to them again."

Color me not surprised.

"I see. How?"

"I made up a woman named Darla, who didn't exist."

And there it is. The truth.

Finally.

"And how did that come about? You were already in love with the cat, so it just made sense?" Okay, maybe I'm provoking him now, but come on.

I want the truth behind the truth. I want all of him. I want to know how that crazy, giant brain of his works, and why he does what he does.

I'm starving for his truth.

He glowers at me. "No, Quinn. I was not in love with the cat. I'd had a particularly annoying argument with Savannah about my personal life. I hated her prying, being all concerned about me. But I also hated to disappoint her or upset her. It was becoming a problem. So I did what I do whenever I have a problem. I looked for a solution. And that was the day I met the cat."

He gazes over at the little black ball of fur, napping in her new bed, the leg with the cast poking out.

"She wandered onto my patio out of the shadows as I was sitting there, thinking. Then she just kept showing up, every day, for almost a week. I had Manus drive her to the vet, to see if she had a microchip and they could find her owners. It turned out she had a chip, and he told me the vet said her name was Darla. It wasn't a conscious decision ahead of time, but the next time my sister asked about my love life, I told her I'd met someone named Darla."

I shake my head a little. "Evil."

"Maybe so. But it worked. From then on, whenever the subject of my love life came up, I told my siblings that I was 'holding out for Darla.' I guess it was just interesting enough for them to believe, and just vague enough that I could string them along for a while, keep them buying into the intrigue of it."

He rubs his face like he's exhausted.

"And they just kept buying into it? And you were okay with that?"

"It's not like it made me happy, Quinn. But over time... I guess the myth of Darla became like a security blanket. I was able to keep the walls shut tight around myself, the way I wanted them. I know I shouldn't have lied to them. It just seemed like a solution to the problem at the time."

"But how was a lie like that going to hold, forever?"

"It probably wasn't."

"So, you were just going to keep telling it, until it became another problem to solve?"

"Yes," he says, like this is perfectly reasonable.

I guess if you're him, it seems reasonable somehow.

I'm really trying to understand this.

"Well, I think it goes without saying that I don't think it's a great idea to lie to your siblings about something like that. But it seems like you did it because at the end of the day, you just didn't want to disappoint them."

"You don't have to sugarcoat it," he says.

I frown. "They wanted to know you were okay, and maybe that you would end up in a good relationship one day. I get that. But you wanted privacy and they wouldn't respect that. And maybe you just wanted them to think you were okay... even if you weren't."

He stares at me for a long moment, and I can tell I'm right about that.

"I know how I dealt with it was wrong," he says quietly. "I never actually thought it was right." He shifts closer to me. "But I hope being honest with you about this now is the right move. I don't want to lose you because of something like this." He looks into my eyes. "I did warn you that I'm a liar."

Ugh. Those eyes of his.

I used to see them as switchblades. Now I see them for what they are; a beautiful gateway into fathomless depths from which I may never escape.

The way he looks at me makes me weak.

I take a deep breath, and a moment to collect my thoughts.

"But you didn't just lie to them about one thing, Harlan. You also asked me to lie to your family for you, to pretend to be Darla. Actually, you forced me to. With blackmail. Why?"

"Because, like I told you back then," he says simply, "they wanted me to introduce them to Darla."

"But you didn't. Are you ever going to?"

"I can't. Because there is no Darla. Then they'd know I lied." He takes my hands in his and looks deep into my eyes. "You can't tell them, either, Quinn. I'm telling you all this in confidence. I'm trusting you."

With those words, I can feel the wall he's still got up between us. This whole confession about Darla, the cat, and the lies he told his siblings might seem like he's letting me in, but suddenly, it doesn't *feel* like it.

"But why can't you just tell them the truth now?"

"It doesn't matter anymore. You know the truth."

"I don't, though. You told me why you lied to them. But you haven't told me *why* they suddenly wanted to meet Darla."

He hesitates, and I know he's holding something back, for sure. "I can't tell you the reason. What does it matter?"

"Because, Harlan. All of this... these lies you tell your siblings, and whatever it is you're keeping from me... You're still lying."

He's still lying to *me*, and our baby is coming in six months. How much more time do we have to get this right?

To become a real family? One that doesn't keep secrets from one another?

A family that's built on a solid foundation of trust.

The kind of family me and this baby need.

"I'm being honest with you," he says. "Right now."

"So, you're being honest with me, but you still won't ever introduce me to your family as Quinn? Just Quinn? Not Quinn-who-we-also-know-as-Darla?"

He takes a breath. Exhales. "I can't tell them that Darla doesn't exist, Quinn. Darla has to be *someone*."

Fuck me. I can't believe what I'm hearing.

What I'm *still* hearing.

I get to my feet. I tell him, "Then introduce them to the damn cat, Harlan." I'm so exasperated, I don't even know if I'm more frustrated or hurt. "Can't you see that the solution to your problem is literally staring you in the face?"

He stares at me for a long moment.

Then he looks over at the cat. She's awake now, like she knows we've been talking about her.

She stretches a little, and her green eyes meet Harlan's.

Then he looks up at me again. And for the first time, I see true fear in his eyes. "What if I can't?"

I sigh, my heart aching, for both of us. "You can trust me, Harlan. But I just don't think we have a hope in hell as a couple if that only goes one way."

Chapter 29

Harlan

"So, what's the big emergency?" Damian asks.

"Yeah. You seem so calm," Jameson says suspiciously, eying me. "Where's the body?"

"If he wanted us to help him hide a body," Damian quips, "I doubt we'd be doing it in his house."

My siblings have gathered around me in my family room. A room I never invite them into. Savannah's wandering around, looking at the family photos on the otherwise empty bookshelves. It's making me uncomfortable.

I've called them all over to my house for "an emergency meeting," which I've never done before. The last time I invited them all over, I lied to them.

I cheated in Granddad's game.

But when Quinn left here today, after telling me our relationship would never work if she couldn't trust me, and I realized she was right, I came to the conclusion that I need to come clean.

I need to tell my family the truth.

Granddad wouldn't want me to win his game based on a lie.

My grandma once told me, *Losing people you love makes*

you break or it makes you hard. And maybe she was right. But the part I didn't know then was that she was the hard one. She'd let herself grow hard, over many years of marriage to a man who was in love with another woman.

And by the time she said those words to me, just before she died, I was already broken.

I've been broken for a long time.

I never wanted to end up as soft as my mom, because I saw firsthand how badly it ruined her when my dad died. How it changed her, made her desperate and needy for her new husband's approval.

But I also don't want to end up so hard that I settle for a loveless life.

Maybe the only way to start putting my broken pieces back together is to be honest with the people I love about what I've done—and let them love me as I am.

Or leave me if they can't forgive me.

Maybe it's not up to me to decide for them. And it's wrong of me to deceive them just to try to keep them in a relationship based on lies.

I guess I don't want to be like Granddad anymore, either.

"You might want to sit down for this," I tell my siblings.

None of them sit down.

"Could you be more dramatic?" Jamie says irritably. "What is it?"

"I have something to tell you all." I take a breath and dive right in. "The truth is that when I had you all over for dinner and introduced you to Darla, I lied to you. The woman I brought to dinner, Quinn, was never Darla. That was a lie."

The silence in the room is beyond uncomfortable. I'm just waiting for someone to start yelling.

"Harlan." Savannah speaks first, but she's not yelling. "How could you do that?"

I guess I'm flattered that she actually seems shocked. And disappointed.

I suppose she thought better of me.

"Because I felt I had to. I'd already lied to you all, repeatedly, when I told you there was a woman named Darla I was after. So, when I received my challenge, I asked an employee, Quinn, to pretend to be Darla. Actually, I didn't ask her. I made her do it. Basically... I blackmailed her."

"Jesus Christ," Graysen mutters.

"So now we have to worry about this woman coming back and suing us?" Damian says. "Not smart, Harlan."

"No. I promise you, you don't have to worry about that."

"Yeah, because your promises are so trustworthy," Jamie mutters.

"You're missing the point. This is not about her. The point is I made her lie for me to cover up my lie."

"So, you didn't complete your challenge three months ago like we thought you did," Graysen concludes.

"You just lied to us, over and over?" Savannah still looks disappointed.

"That's what he just said," Jamie says. "And are we really pretending to be surprised? This is *so* Harlan."

"I don't understand," Savi says. "Was there ever any Darla? Or did you just make her up?"

I clear my throat. I'm actually shocked no one's yelling. Graysen isn't even freaking out. Yet.

"There is a Darla, actually," I say. "She's sitting in the sunroom, if you want to meet her."

Damian and Graysen, who can see into the sunroom from where they're standing, look that way. There's a moment of confused silence before I see it on their faces, when they put two and two together.

"It's a cat," Graysen says, unimpressed.

Damian chuckles under his breath.

Jameson has joined them, and now Savannah, frowning, goes over to look.

"You have serious issues, brother," Jamie says.

"Since when do you have a cat?" Savi demands. "And what's wrong with its leg?"

"Her."

They all look at me like they've never met me before.

"She fell off the roof."

"Oh. Poor girl." Savannah drifts into the sunroom to look closer.

Jamie rolls his eyes. "Please tell me we're not forgetting that Harlan's lied to us for months just because we suddenly found proof that he's human."

"He can be human and still fucking with us," Damian points out. "Witches have cats, don't they?" He smirks at me.

Great. More people who think I'm a witch. This cat just had to be black.

"This one's way too cute to be a witch's cat," Savi provides helpfully.

"Let's stay on track here," Graysen grouches.

"There's really nothing left to say about it," I tell them. "I've told you the truth now. You guys can go ahead and decide if I failed my challenge. That's how the game works."

Honestly, I'm more concerned about losing Quinn right now. Keeping my inheritance isn't nearly as important as keeping her and the baby she's carrying.

I'm so afraid that maybe I'm going to lose them, that maybe I've already lost them, I'm feeling somewhat numb to this whole moment—putting my fate in my siblings' hands.

I'm really not sure what they'll decide. I've spent hours upon hours over the past several weeks obsessively analyzing, from every possible angle, trying to figure out how I can fix this whole mess, dig myself out of this hole, if the shit hits the fan. How I can get rehired by Vance Industries and make it all okay, and continue to take care of Quinn and the baby. Even if she never forgives me.

There has to be a way I can earn my siblings' trust back, if not their love, even if it takes the rest of my life.

But living without her is not an option.

Quinn and the baby are what really matters.

"What's to decide?" Damian says. "This shit is hilarious. We all know Granddad would be loving this."

Graysen frowns deeply.

"Come on," Damian prompts, looking around at our siblings. "Old Stodd would be laughing if he were here right now, and we all know it. As far as he'd be concerned, Harlan completed his challenge."

"You're right about Granddad," Savi says tentatively. "He'd be loving this twist. He'd probably adopt the cat."

"The cat isn't up for adoption," I mutter.

"It's true that Granddad would find this amusing," Jamie admits, grudgingly. "But the fact is, Harlan lied to us."

"What Harlan did," Damian counters, "technically, was introduce us to two Darlas. A woman *and* a cat."

"He introduced us to a *fake* Darla and lied to us," Jamie says. "He cheated at Granddad's game. And the deadline on his challenge passed months ago."

"Be fair, Jamie," Savannah says. "We have a year in total for all of us to complete our challenges. That's the official rule of the game. We were the ones who decided Harlan had one month. He took longer than that to come around, but now he's introduced us to the real Darla. His challenge was 'Introduce us to Darla,' and he's done that. For real this time."

"But it's a fucking cat."

"I don't care if Darla is a cockroach," Damian says dryly. "We're done here."

They all look at Graysen, who's been staring at the cat with a frown and listening to the rest of us argue.

He slowly shakes his head, then sets his gray eyes on me. I see disappointment, disapproval, and extreme annoyance in his gaze.

But I think I see grudging acceptance, too.

"If it helps," I offer, "I have a large veterinarian's bill with the name of the cat on it, should you need some evidence. The vet will corroborate that the cat has been named Darla all her life, and that her birth predates the challenge. She is the real Darla."

Graysen rolls his eyes.

"Congratulations." Damian shakes my hand with a smirk. "Well played. I have places to be."

Jameson shakes my hand next, reluctantly. "Congratulations, Harlan. You're even more of a freak than I took you for. But I hope your cat heals."

"Thank you."

"Harlan." Graysen comes to give me a stiff handshake. I know he's pissed at me. "Next time, save us all the trouble and just tell us the truth."

"I'll work on that."

"Don't make me any promises you won't keep."

"I won't."

Irritated but apparently satisfied, he nods.

I pull him in for a hug. "Thank you."

He takes a moment to recover from the surprise, but he pats me on the back.

My brothers leave all at once, Jameson complaining that he's late for a date with Megan because of me.

Then it's just me and Savannah and the cat in the sunroom,

staring at each other. Savannah's wearing Chanel, but she's down on the floor, stroking the cat. It kind of warms my heart.

I try to absorb this moment, and the feeling of being safe and warm, with family. It's a feeling I wish I had more of in my life.

My siblings may let me get away with this grand fuck-up, but I know it's going to be a long road rebuilding what I've broken.

It wasn't one or two lies that did it.

It's been years of shutting them out that I'll have to atone for. And repair. One truth at a time.

My twin sister eyes me, and I know she's a little pissed at me, too.

"She's sweet," she says. Her tone says, *Maybe too sweet for you.*

"I know. I think I'm going to keep her."

She gives me a dry look. "I meant Quinn."

"Oh." I clear my throat, uncomfortable. I hate disappointing Savannah the most. And lying to her.

"I think you like her more than you let on before," she says.

"How do you know that?"

"It was obvious when you mentioned her just now. I don't know. Something in your eyes. It's like you're not as shut down as before."

"Yeah. Maybe."

"Maybe it's time for some sweetness in your life. You've been bitter for so long."

I sigh.

"You know," she says, "when you lie to people, you rob them of the opportunity to really know you."

"That sounds like a quote. Grandma?"

"That one was Mom, believe it or not. She said that to me when I was about ten and I stole something of yours. Candy of some sort. It was Halloween. I lied because I already ate the whole thing, so I couldn't give it back, and I felt so guilty. And maybe she wasn't used to me lying. She called me 'Miss Savannah Vance' in that tone that told you you'd better listen. She didn't get stern with me like that very often."

I snort. "Must've been nice."

She tilts her head, studying me. It reminds me of me, actually, when she looks at me like that. "You look like me when you do that," I inform her.

"Because I'm calculating right now," she says. "I think that's why our brothers feel cheated. It's not that you cheated the game. It's that you robbed them of the chance to know the truth. You didn't trust them with it."

"Since when do they want to know me?" I push back. "We've never been close like you are with them. I don't give a fuck about hockey, or Damian's sex kinks, or whatever the fuck Graysen's into."

"Who says you have to be? I spend more time with them than you do, sure, but I'm not into those things, either. I just make an effort. I find the common ground. It isn't always easy, you know."

I decide to go pour her a drink, because apparently she's not leaving anytime soon, and she shakes her head at me.

"Seriously, Harlan." Her voice follows me into the family room. "Why didn't you just tell us the truth when you first received your challenge? That there was no woman named Darla? That you made her up? We would've been annoyed with you, but what else is new?"

"How could I know that you'd have my back?"

"Jesus Christ, Harlan. Because we're family."

I step back into the sunroom and put a glass of Merlot in her hand. "I didn't know that. I had no idea how you guys would react."

"Then maybe you should pay better attention. You're good at that, when you want to be." She takes a sip of her wine, considering me. "We're not out to get you."

I sit down in an armchair, facing her and the cat.

"If you lost your challenge," she says, "or if any of us lost our challenge, we'd *all* suffer. It would affect our business and our family. And maybe we could all just make a deal that we all completed our challenges whether we actually did or not, but that would be cheating Granddad's game. And there has to be some integrity to it. That's the whole point."

"I know."

"We're in this together. But you have to do your part."

"Okay."

"Then why did you cheat?"

"Because. *Fuck.* I was scared."

Savannah sighs. Maybe she's taking pity on me. "I do believe that is literally the first time I've ever heard those words out of your mouth in my entire life."

"Yeah." I toss back most of my Manhattan. "First time for everything."

Savannah eyes me, maybe pulling together all the pieces in her head. "And what about Quinn? Did she know about... all this?" She waves her manicured fingers in the direction of the cat.

"She does now."

"I see."

"And also..." I take a breath. "She's pregnant."

My sister blinks at me, looking about as confused as she should.

"I really should've prefaced that," I add, "by telling you that I've been seeing her ever since I told you that I broke up with her."

I wait for her to tell me I'm an asshole for lying to her yet again. But instead, she gasps a little. "I'm going to be an aunt?"

"Yes. I believe that's how it works."

"Oh, shit. I love that for me!" She gets up and comes to give me a hug.

I pat her awkwardly on the back. "Yeah. Congratulations."

"Congratulations, you!" She pushes me away. "Why aren't you excited?" she demands.

"I'm just trying to figure this out, day by day."

"Oh, god. The mental computing you must be doing. The hard drives must be overheating up there." She knocks a knuckle lightly on my skull.

"Funny."

"But true." She settles into the armchair next to mine. "I demand, as your twin and the auntie of your unborn child, that you tell me everything. Right now."

"Unfortunately for you, that kind of demand doesn't work on me. But anyway, there's nothing to tell. Quinn is amazing. End of story."

"Amazing, how? I want words, brother."

I groan. Honesty is a bitch.

"Fine. In a nutshell... she's been working her ass off for years to take care of her mom, Lorraine, who's battling cancer and raised her as a single mom. They live in a shitty old rental house, and Quinn is literally holding that place together with duct tape and a positive attitude. She's been through so much. I'm just trying to make the pregnancy as easy on her as possible. But honestly, I've never felt so powerless."

Savannah waves her hand in the air dismissively. "You have money, though. You get a bunch of nannies, and you take care of her mom. You'll be fine."

"I don't think I want that. I mean, sure we can get a nanny, to help us. But I don't want my children to be raised by strangers."

"Children?" Savannah raises an eyebrow.

I ignore it. "You know what I mean. I don't want them to be raised the way we were. I want to be accessible to my children."

"You said children again."

I frown at her.

She's looking at me with a kind of awe. This is new to me, and I don't know how to take it. "Well, then. If you've already thought about stuff like that, you're a giant step ahead of Mom and Dad already."

"Yeah. I guess."

"So why didn't you just tell everyone about the baby when they were here? Graysen's going to be so excited."

"Graysen doesn't get excited."

"Over this, he will. Why didn't you tell us all together?"

"Because I don't know what I'm doing, Savannah," I admit, frustrated. "Quinn is pissed at me every other day, and she has reason to be."

"I take it she isn't living here with you?"

"No."

"Why not?"

"Because she doesn't want to."

"But why?"

"Because," I growl, "look at me. How do I be a good father when my relationship with my own father was so messed up?"

I twitch uncomfortably in the long silence that follows that, as my sister studies me. I'm spelling with my fingernail on the arm of the chair, incessantly. That old standby, *BEAUTIFUL*. I don't even know when I started doing it.

Finally, Savannah says, "So that's it. You're afraid of being a father. Or rather, being a shitty one."

"That's a big 'it,' Savi."

She does that dismissive thing in the air with her hand. "None of that matters. I know you, Harlan. Possibly better than any other human on earth. We already lost Dad. And I know that in some ways, you lost him most, before he even died. Are you seriously going to allow yourself to lose the chance to be the father you always wanted?"

"I'm trying *not* to lose anything," I argue.

"Then succeed. You're capable of way more than you think when it comes to this stuff."

"But how do you know that? I've never had someone who needed me before. Chelsea didn't need me. She needed something I couldn't give her, so she went and got it from someone else. That's the truth."

"No, what she did was she cheated on you and got knocked up by someone else. Don't make that your fault."

"Maybe it was. At least partly."

"Well, Quinn is having *your* baby, right? And maybe she loves you, or will love you. Don't you think you're ready for that? I mean, isn't it about time?"

I don't even know what to say to that, except "I don't know."

"Well, when is the baby due?"

"Six months," I say tightly.

"Okay. So, in six months, ready or not, you're going to be a father. Which means you need to step up. Like, yesterday."

"I am stepping up. Quinn and the baby will have everything they need."

"Sure." She reaches over and presses a hand gently to my chest, right over my heart. "Except *this*."

I'm up late that night, lying on the sofa. Drinking Manhattans and watching Darla the cat sleep in the next room.

When I finally nod off, I dream.

I'm having sex with Quinn on the sofa.

Then I hear my dad calling, in the distance. By the time I get to my feet, Quinn is gone.

I walk into the foyer, and it's the foyer of my own house. I hear a sound in the distance, coming from upstairs—a door closing.

I call out to my dad.

No one answers.

As I climb the stairs to the second floor, I hear helicopter blades.

When I get to the top of the stairs, it's not my house anymore. It's my childhood home. I see the door to the room where the terrible thing is going to happen, and I hear my dad's voice, calling to me.

I start to tremble and cry.

I hear the *whump whump whump* of the helicopter blades as I walk toward the door.

The black cat is lying on the floor against the wall, her hind leg in a cast.

She's wounded, and it's all my fault.

When I finally reach the door, I'm shaking. I start to open it.

It opens all the way—into nothing. I plummet into the roar of the helicopter, and wake up in terror, my heart pounding.

The cat lies on her bed, watching me, green eyes alert. I think I startled her awake.

I'm still lying on the sofa.

I get up to make myself another drink, and I don't sleep again that night.

I just think about all the things I need to say to Quinn, if I'm going to be honest with her.

And if I have the courage to say them.

Chapter 30

Harlan

It's raining and dark when I show up at Quinn's house. Lights are on inside, and Christmas lights twinkle around the windows.

As I approach the screen door, I can see Quinn in the kitchen, decorating a round cake. She's spinning it on a turntable, scraping the pink icing on the sides to make it perfectly smooth.

I knock lightly on the old door frame, rattling the screen.

When she looks up, a lock of chocolate-brown hair falls over her face. I never would've thought she could get any prettier than she already was with that crazy turquoise hair, but I'm looking at her right now, and she's fucking beautiful. I don't know if it's the pregnancy or the fact that she's just meant to be a brunette, but she's glowing.

She looks surprised to see me, standing out here in the rain. "Harlan." She walks over to the screen door. "What are you doing here?"

"Well, sitting at home on a rainy night watching a cat heal is fairly boring."

"If you're trying to be adorably pathetic, it's totally working." She opens the door and tugs me in out of the rain.

The next thing I know she's ladling apple cider from a pot on the stove into a mug for me and dusting it with cinnamon. The whole place smells like apples and cinnamon, Christmas decorations have been hung everywhere, and music is playing softly somewhere down the hall to the bedrooms. Not Christmas music. The eighties stuff Quinn and her mom love.

We take our mugs into the living room, where there's a small Christmas tree twinkling, and boxes and piles of... stuff. Literally everywhere. I watch in awe as Quinn manages to clear a few piles from the sofa to balance precariously on other piles, so that we can sit down.

The mess doesn't even stress me out as much as I'd think it would, I'm just so glad to be with her.

"We've been clearing out Mom's everything room to make room for the baby," she explains. "It's been a process, as you can see."

"Everything room?"

"Yeah." Quinn blows on her hot cider. "That's what we call it. It's the room where Mom puts everything she can't bear to part with. And believe me, there's a lot of it. There isn't a hobby that woman hasn't tried over the last six years."

Six years. I wonder if that's how long Lorraine's been living with cancer, and unable to work as much.

I'm trying to get a look at the photos in a photo album that lies open on the coffee table, without being obvious about it. "I'm seeing knitting, jigsaw puzzles, what appears to be decades worth of birthday cards... and what looks like a mild pottery obsession? And I don't even know what else."

"No one but Lorraine really does," Quinn teases as her mom comes in, wearing a South Park T-shirt and pajama pants, and carrying a fluffy pink blanket.

"Harlan," Lorraine says happily, "I thought I heard your voice! It's quite sexy, you know."

I think Quinn almost chokes on her cider. "Mom. Take it easy."

"We're having a little trouble with the old heater in here," Lorraine says to me, as she wraps me in the blanket, tucking me in like I'm her child. "Sorry for the chaos. It's all for the greater good, and a home for that baby."

"No apology needed," I tell her. "This is what a home feels like."

Lorraine smiles, delighted, and wraps Quinn in another blanket she pulls off the back of the sofa. Quinn looks mildly put out as her mom fusses over her, but doesn't complain. *Cozy* isn't even a strong enough word for this feeling. It's cozy chaos in here, for sure. But moments like this are what the word *heartwarming* was invented for.

Quinn's eyes meet mine, and her lips quirk as I take a sip of cider, wrapped in the fluffy pink blanket. It is chilly in here without it. Maybe I can see now, though, how living in a drafty house with sketchy electrical and appliances that are always breaking down is tolerable when you have a mom like Lorraine to share it with.

I can suddenly picture birthdays and Christmases and anniversaries, snuggled together under fluffy blankets, drinking cider while a cake bakes in the oven, and I'm understanding more and more what *family* can really mean.

When Lorraine leaves the room, I say to Quinn, "You've been avoiding me today."

"Yeah," she admits.

"You turned off your location tracking."

"Are you the only one who deserves privacy? Can't I have any?"

"Of course you can," I tell her, but it sticks in my throat. I hate giving her space.

These last two months—ever since finding out she's pregnant, and everything becoming so tense between us, so fraught with uncertainty—have been two of the hardest of my entire life.

I've wanted her right next to me, the whole damn time.

"I understand why you'd want to keep living here and not move in with me," I tell her, and she softens. "I may have been wrong about this old house. This may be the greatest place on earth."

"I'm sorry I disappeared yesterday. After our conversation about Darla. The cat, I mean, and... everything. I needed time to think."

"Quinn, I don't think I've ever felt so cared for."

She seems perplexed by this, but touched. "Your family must be really cold..." she jokes.

"Not cold. Just... not this, either."

Lorraine comes in again. "I found this baby picture of Quinn." She hands it to me. "Isn't she the cutest, fattest little thing you've ever seen? She had such a big head! I used to call her my little bowling-ball-headed baby."

"Nice, Mom," Quinn says, unimpressed.

"She was just the roundest little thing—"

"Mom. Don't you have something to organize in the other room?"

"Okay, okay. I can take a hint." Lorraine gives Quinn a look and says suggestively, "I'll leave you two alone."

"It's always nice to see you, Lorraine," I tell her as she leaves. "Thanks for the photo of baby Quinn."

Quinn rolls her eyes. "Stop kissing up. She already adores you."

I grin.

Then I study the photo of the happy baby Quinn, smiling at something off camera.

"What?" she says.

"Lorraine is going to be the best grandma. Better than both of mine were, for sure."

Quinn tears up, but tries to hide it as she sips her cider. "She's looking so forward to it."

"I know that's a hard topic for you..."

She lowers her voice. "The hardest thing is imagining my child not getting to meet their amazing grandma."

"That's not going to happen."

"I've just never felt like I can trust that. So I just take each day, one at a time. And do my best to appreciate it, no matter how good or bad it is."

"I feel a little sad, too," I admit, "when I think about the baby not getting to meet my dad. Though he wasn't always so amazing."

Quinn wipes away her unshed tears. She looks keenly interested. "You've never really told me anything about your parents."

"Maybe I should."

"Yes, please."

"What, right now?"

"Yes?" She blinks at me hopefully.

Shit. Honesty, right?

I prepared myself for this.

I didn't know I'd have to face it so soon. But Savannah was right. The clock is ticking, and I really should've stepped up with this. Like, yesterday. Or any of the days before, ever since I met Quinn and had chance after chance to let her really know me.

"Okay... if you want to hear it. I guess there's a lot to say, actually."

Quinn sips her cider and waits patiently. "I'm listening."

I set my cider aside. "Well, probably the most important things I can tell you about my parents and my relationship with them all relate back to the fact that I'm dyslexic."

She takes that in.

"Oh. Okay," she says gently. I can tell she's surprised. Maybe she had no idea.

I hope she's not hurt that I never mentioned it before.

"I should add a caveat to that, that my dyslexia is undiagnosed. It's just something I figured out about myself over time. Savannah helped me figure it out, actually. She's the only one who knows."

"I see. Go on."

I take a deep breath and consider where to go from there.

"We grew up here, in Vancouver, in the house that Graysen still owns. As the only girl, Savannah was sort of favored by my mom. And I think I always felt like the misfit in the family. I got frustrated in school a lot, and acted out. My teachers would say things like, 'he's so capable, he's just not applying himself' or 'he isn't trying hard enough.' It took me a long time to understand that I was able to memorize things, like how words looked, instead of actually learning how to spell."

I pause, to let myself go back to that time, and try to remember things I really tried to forget over the years. So I can explain something, to her, that I've never really had to explain before.

"When I'd try to read, the words would move around on the page, and I'd have to focus really hard. It was exhausting. So I'd read comic books, because the small bits of text were so much easier to ingest. But when I'd try to write book reports on them, I'd get in trouble. I was told I was lazy. I just didn't know how to explain what was happening when I tried to spell or read, because I didn't know that other people learned differently than I did."

"That sounds really frustrating," Quinn says sympathetically.

"Yeah. I kind of hated school because of it. I had this one teacher who was super strict about spelling. I spelled the word 'beautiful' wrong on a quiz, and he made me stay after class and write it on the chalkboard, over and over. I can still spell it, but not because I actually *learned* how to spell. Because I can see it on that chalkboard in my head."

"Huh," she says, like she's trying to picture it. "I don't know if I understand the difference. If you see it, you see it, don't you?"

"But I only see it because of that memory. If you asked me to write down the word beautiful, and I didn't have that memory, I wouldn't be able to sound it out and figure it out. I can't 'sound out' words."

I can see she's trying to understand, but it's hard for her to grasp.

"It's really hard to explain. But I still write words like that in my head, over and over, and I don't even know why. I think it's like this overlap between the dyslexia and my OCD, this compulsive way of seeking control, putting the letters into place, over and over again. I write words with my fingertip constantly, but it'll be one word over and over. A lot of the time, I don't even know I'm doing it."

"I've seen you do that, I think. Your fingertip moves. Sometimes when we're lying together in bed, your hand is on me, and I think you're asleep, but then your fingertip starts twitching."

"Yeah. I can imagine it's pretty annoying."

I wish I could say I'd stop doing it, but I don't know if that will ever be true. I'm not even sure I want to stop doing it, it's such a part of me. And it is soothing, in a weird way, even though it doesn't exactly soothe me. It's something to focus my mind on when I'm otherwise stressing out. A false sense of control.

"It's not annoying," she says. "But you said no one knows? Your brothers don't know? Your staff? People who work with you?"

"My brothers, no. They've always just poked at me about being lazy because my writing is sloppy. Some of my staff might suspect. But I've always found ways to work around it. And now I have so many people working under me who can take care of anything I need them to, it's easy enough to cover the fact that I can't spell worth shit. And spell check only goes so far. If I wrote an actual email to a business associate without one of my assistants or my secretary cleaning it up, people would think I was stupid."

"They wouldn't think that," she says. "They'd just think you're in a hurry, or you used dictation and it screwed up—"

"Seriously, Quinn. People judge. When you suck at math, no one blinks an eye. But if you can't spell common words, believe me, people think it's a direct sign of lack of intelligence."

She considers that. "And you never talked to anyone about this? Had it properly diagnosed?"

"No. I don't feel like I need to. The writing's on the wall. And it's terrible."

"Wow. Did you just make a self-deprecating joke?"

"I believe I did."

She gazes at me, looking charmed. "Harlan Vance, who are you?"

"If you keep looking at me like that," I flirt, "I'll be anyone you want me to be."

"Don't flirt," she says, but I know she likes it. "This is a serious conversation."

"Well, there's not much else to say about the dyslexia thing.

I even told Savannah to stop sending me articles about it. I'm sort of over it."

"But why? It's not something to be ashamed of."

I swallow. There's that sharp shard feeling in my throat, the one that lodges there when I'm truly uncomfortable, and I know she's hit a wound.

I *am* ashamed of it.

"Because it was the source of all my struggles and frustrations in school, and the frustrations with my dad. We'd argue about it all the time."

Quinn's eyebrows pinch. "He was hard on you because you struggled in school?"

"Always." I take a breath, then dive right in. "Our last conversation, before he died, was an argument. He was angry with me for skipping classes, and I accused him of being harder on me than all my siblings. I truly thought I was his least favorite child, and I told him so. And he really seemed upset. The last thing he said to me was, 'I have a harder time being your father than anyone else's, because you're so much like me.' And then he told me that he loved me. That wasn't something he normally said, at least not to me." I hesitate before telling Quinn the full truth. "I didn't say it back."

"Oh, shit," she says softly.

Then she sets her cider aside, unwraps herself from her blanket, and comes over. I open my blanket to let her in. She snuggles against me, wrapping her arm around my waist, and putting her head on my chest.

She just holds me for a long moment as it sinks in how much I needed her to.

It's like she's telling me, without words, that everything will be okay.

"What happened after that conversation?" she asks me gently, after a few minutes.

I just hold her and breathe for a few more moments, until I think I can get it all out.

"The next day, I was late coming home from school. I'd skipped English class again, so I knew I was in trouble, and I'd avoided coming home for dinner. I knew Dad was going to ream me out again. We'd argue, I'd get sent to my room, and then I'd sneak out later anyway." I really don't want to think about what happened next. But I promised myself I'd face it. For her. "But that wasn't what happened."

"You don't have to tell me," she says.

"I do."

I rub my hand over my face, reliving those next few minutes. Not warped memories in an old, repeating dream. But real minutes that I actually lived. The worst in my life.

"When I got home, the house was quiet. One of the staff told me that my family was waiting for me up in my dad's room. And I just got this terrible feeling. I went upstairs. My parents had separate bedrooms, and when I walked into my dad's room, all my siblings and my mom were there, but Dad wasn't. Mom was crying in Graysen's arms. And they told me that Dad had died that morning, with two of his friends, in a helicopter crash."

"Harlan... I'm so sorry. That's just heartbreaking." Quinn's arm tightens around me. She looks up into my eyes; hers are watery and so blue. "I can tell that you feel guilty about it. But what happened, and the way things ended, were in no way your fault."

"But maybe if I wasn't making things so difficult for him at home, he would've been around more. Maybe, that morning, he wouldn't have taken off in that helicopter."

"No. That had nothing to do with you. You were a kid, and you were struggling. I'm sure your dad knew you loved him."

"Maybe."

"What about your mom?" she asks me.

I sigh. "I'd love to tell you that my relationship with my mom was much better, but I kind of swore to myself I wouldn't lie to you anymore. So the truth is, I didn't have a great relationship with her, either. After Dad died, she remarried one of his business associates, and she moved me, Savannah and Jameson with her to France, to live with our new stepdad and his kids."

"Oh. That's… a lot."

"Yeah. I think she wanted a whole new life as her way of getting over what happened, but I wasn't ready for that. To me, it felt like everything that was important to me got ripped away, so suddenly. I was struggling with grief and guilt, and in the middle of it all, my grandparents, my older brothers, they all let Mom take me away to another country. And even then, when I told Mom I wanted to live with her, she said boarding school was the best place for me to be. But maybe it was the best place for me to be *for her*."

"I don't get it," Quinn says. "I don't understand why she wouldn't want you around. Especially after losing your dad."

"She didn't seem to want any of us around. I spent the next few years struggling to know where I fit in, and not belonging anywhere. Back home, Damian and Graysen got closer, and I drifted further away. And when Savi and I came back to Vancouver as adults, things were just never the same."

"But maybe they could be," she says. "Maybe you can get closer again. I'm sure your family loves you."

"Then I guess I don't really know what love is." This is a brutal thing to say to a woman I'm hoping will love me. I know that. But I have to say it anyway. "But maybe that's because I never really had any role models to show me what love is. For me, love was agony. Love was loss and abandonment and rejection. I couldn't even understand why women I dated always wanted to get *closer*. It repelled me. I kept all my relationships surface-level. Even the girlfriend who left me because another man got her pregnant. I thought we might get married one day, because maybe I thought that's all a marriage was; picking someone who you went through the motions of a life with. And after she betrayed me, I think I fucking gave up."

"You didn't, though," Quinn says.

"I really did. I decided love wasn't for me. There would be more agony and no more loss, because I'd keep nothing worth losing. I'd be stronger on my own." I look into her blue eyes. "But you know what I learned last night, while watching a cat with a broken leg sleep?"

She smiles sadly. "What?"

"I'm really not as strong or hard or self-sufficient as I pretend. I like having someone to come home to. Someone who needs me, like I need them. The truth is, I get lonely sometimes, with only my grumpy-ass self for company. I just kept telling myself I'm not good with people, so I don't feel like I need them." I study her pretty face.

"But then this ridiculous, frustrating, incredible woman with turquoise hair came along. And you were right. I became a monster, for you. Overprotective, possessive, controlling. And when I got you pregnant, for a few minutes, I actually thought it was the worst thing that could happen. It was like my worst fear happening all over again. The baby might be someone else's. And worse, if it wasn't... I was terrified of fatherhood. But by then, I think I was already way more terrified of losing you."

"It doesn't have to be like that," she says. "You don't have to lose me. There can be other endings to our story, Harlan."

"Yeah. I'm starting to see that." I pull her closer, right into my lap. "I've been so afraid to let people in. But you're already in. I'm crazy about you. And I'll do anything it takes to fight for you, and win." I take a deep breath, and promise her, "Except lie to you. Because more than anything, I want you to trust me. I want a family. I want *you*."

"Of course you do," she says easily, wrapping her arms around my neck. "I never believed that grumpy act for a minute."

I consider that. I think she's half teasing. But also, half serious.

"You know, it really was an act, in some ways," I admit. "I think I've worked really hard to present this version of myself that seems perfectly in control all the time, to overcompensate for my shortcomings."

"But your dyslexia is not a shortcoming. In some ways, I bet it's even become your superpower. You had to find ways to work around it, right? You ran into problems, you learned how to find creative solutions. You figured out how to excel. Maybe that wouldn't have happened if you weren't dyslexic. Because it makes you see the world in a different way, and maybe that way is beautiful."

I take that in, and I can't refute it. "You have a beautiful way of making sense of things, Quinn Monroe."

"Thank you." She blows out a breath. "But believe me, I'm scared, too. Why do you think I work so hard? And I'm so fiercely independent? I've always feared being left alone. I don't have siblings. It's just me and Mom. And if Mom…"

"You don't have to think like that," I tell her. I place my hand gently on her little belly. "We're all here right now. All four us. Together. Well, five, if you include the cat."

She smiles at me. "Five of us. I like that." She kisses me on the cheek.

"Jesus. How did I suddenly get a family of five?" I mutter. "Ten seconds ago, I was a bachelor."

Quinn narrows her eyes at me. "Please. You haven't been a bachelor since the moment you laid eyes on me."

I gaze at her. "That's weirdly true," I admit.

"And you should really give yourself credit where it's due.

Because you're already a great father. You're doing it by showing up, taking care of me and the baby. And I hope our child is just like you, in so many ways."

"I'd much rather they be like you."

"I don't think we get to pick…"

"It's okay. It's going to work out either way."

"How do you know that?" she asks me softly, and I know she's looking for reassurance.

So I tug her a little closer, and answer her as honestly as I can. "Because I think this is the first time in my life that I've ever felt like I have everything I need. And if that's true, then no matter how imperfect I am, I know I'll have a lot to give."

She smiles thoughtfully.

"What?"

"This is what gives me hope for us, Harlan. Alone, each of us is a bit of a hot mess, in our own way—"

"A bit?" I tease.

She narrows her pretty eyes at me. "But together, we somehow work, don't you think?"

"I hope so."

"Good. Then let's be perfectly imperfect together. We're family now, Harlan, no matter what happens. You'll always be the father of my baby."

I brush her soft hair from her cheek with my fingers, and cup her jaw. "There are going to be so many more cakes," I promise her. "So many reasons for celebrating, together. Including Lorraine's next birthday."

She sniffles, fighting back tears. "I hope so."

"And I know you like it here. But I was wondering if you and Lorraine would move into my house with me. You'd really be helping me out. It could really use a woman's touch. I don't even have a Christmas tree up. It's sad."

She swipes a tear from her eye. "I noticed."

"Lorraine can have her own suite. She can even have an everything room. And we can make a nice room for the baby."

"When were you thinking?"

"Yesterday."

She laughs.

"If that's too soon, sometime before the baby is born would be ideal. So we can bring him or her home, together."

Her smile fades, and she chews on the side of her lip. "Shit. Now I feel bad."

"Why?"

"Because, that cake I was decorating..." She gestures in the direction of the kitchen. "It's a baby shower cake," she says guiltily. "The girls are throwing me a shower next month, and I've been working on a practice cake. I thought I might also make it a gender reveal cake."

"So, why would that make you feel bad?"

"Because, I didn't tell you... You know that blood draw we did, for the paternity test?"

"Sure..." We both got the test results. Which confirmed that I'm the baby's father.

"Well, with that same blood sample—my blood, I mean—they can look at the baby's sex chromosomes. So, they can tell the baby's gender." She gazes at me with her open blue eyes.

"You know our baby's gender?"

"Don't be mad."

"Why would I be mad?" I'm thrilled, actually.

"Because I asked them to email the result to me?" she says. "And I got the email yesterday. But I didn't look, I swear. I was so mad at you, I considered peeking today. But I couldn't do it. It felt wrong, like I'd be meeting our baby for the first time, and you weren't there."

"Oh." I don't know what to say. I'm really not mad. "Wait, though. I saw pink icing on that cake."

"Yeah. I was going to do the whole thing pink *and* blue. And then maybe when we cut into it, everyone gets to see the reveal?"

"That could be cute…"

She blinks at me. She's practically buzzing with excitement. "You don't know how hard it's been not to open that email."

"So, then… we could open it together?"

"We could."

"Like… right now?"

Quinn bites her lip again and pulls out her phone.

She opens the email, and we read it together.

Chapter 31

Quinn

I wake up in Harlan's bed, to Harlan kissing my neck and chest.

"I'm so sleepy," I mumble.

"I know, but it's time to go."

"Nooo," I moan softly as he kisses his way up my throat.

"Oh, yes. We have an appointment and we can't be late."

I groan as he lifts me off the bed. "But I love it in your bed," I protest weakly, trying to wake up, and he chuckles. *I love you.* The words almost fall from my lips, but don't.

He puts me on my feet, and pulls on his jacket. "You'll be back in my bed in a few hours," he assures me.

I pout.

It's just after dinnertime; we ate, then I got dressed for this meeting he set up with some "very important" potential clients. But then I fell asleep on his bed, fully clothed.

After he showed up at my place last night and we had that big, emotional talk, he brought me back here and we spent the night making love. I didn't get nearly enough sleep. But then we spent the morning sleeping in, and having sex all over again.

Then again in the shower.

Then he was on the phone making secret plans, while I hustled in the kitchen, stressing over the array of baking samples he told me I suddenly needed to make—samples which he had whisked away while we ate dinner, to be set up by whoever, wherever, for this mysterious client presentation.

Since it's Christmas Eve, I really have to wonder what kind of client would want to meet us now, and if this is all some trick.

But Harlan won't tell me a thing.

I can only hope that whoever is in charge of setting up my pretties gets all my instructions right. I'm used to presenting my baking to clients myself, whether in person or online, and fussing over every detail. All this mystery is killing me.

"Why can't you just tell me who we're meeting?" I complain as I slip into my shoes. "It would make it so much less stressful for me."

"Where's the fun in that?" Harlan's eyes twinkle with mischief.

"You look like your brother Damian when you do that," I inform him.

He frowns, then slides his hand up my skirt—and gently squeezes between my legs. "Don't stress, baby. I've got you."

"Oh my god, your hand is so warm." I almost melt back onto the bed as he kisses my neck, his slight stubble making me shiver.

"I fucking love it when you're all sleepy and soft..." He groans against my skin, squeezing again.

I moan.

I almost think he's going to take me down. He's been insatiable today. Ever since he asked me to move in last night, it's felt different between us. More solid. Real.

Something to hold onto.

I've been picturing a future with both of us in it, and our little family around us.

I've been letting hope expand in my chest like a balloon, lifting me up.

"Come on, baby," he purrs. "You can do this." He scoops an arm around my lower back and propels me toward the door as I groan in protest. "This could be the meeting of your life."

"Are we getting Quinn's Cakes into Whole Foods?" I quip. "Trader Joe's? Walmart?"

"I'm not sure why you think that's so funny, but no."

"I half thought maybe you were getting me the wedding cake gig for Jameson's wedding after all," I tell him suspiciously. "But when you asked for sample cupcakes too, I was thrown." I made seven different flavors this afternoon, between Mom's cupcake recipes and my cake samples. It was hard to decide what to focus on when Harlan would literally tell me nothing except *I need you to make some of your best samples for some VIPs.* "I don't even know if these are potential cake clients, or clients for *your* business, or what," I complain. "You've told me nothing."

"Have I mentioned that you're super cute when you're impatient?" he asks as he leads me down the stairs to the foyer, where Manus is waiting.

"Yes," I grump. "I must be adorable right now."

We drive into the underground lot beneath the Vance Bayshore resort on Bayshore Drive, mere blocks away from Vance Tower, on the waterfront. I've never been here before. The resort isn't finished yet; it's undergoing a major renovation and expansion since the Vance family bought the property. So Harlan tells me as we park and get out of the car.

Then he takes my hand and leads me through a fire exit door to the outside, and up a set of concrete steps. We emerge onto a stretch of grass on the northeast side of the resort, facing the harbour and the public Seawall, a gorgeous walkway along the water.

"Um, Harlan? Where the heck are we going?" When we pulled into the resort, I assumed we were meeting these very special potential clients inside. Now that I see the people strolling with dogs and jogging along the Seawall in athleisure wear, I'm worrying I might've overdressed for whatever is about to happen. "Are we meeting with these people on a boat or something? Or having a picnic? Should I have brought a swimsuit?"

I wore high heels, which are now sinking into the grass.

Harlan gives me his solid arm and helps me along. He wore a suit, but he always wears a suit. "Patience," he says, the corners of his eyes crinkling.

"You're maddening when you're happy at my expense."

"There are more elegant ways to get here, I promise. When the resort lobby is finished, there's a grand hallway that'll lead straight through and out the back of the building, to access the water side. But right now, it's all under construction."

When we reach the Seawall, we follow it around the corner of the building. There, what will obviously be a restaurant and a couple of commercial storefronts face the water. The sun is just starting to go down beyond Stanley Park to the west, and the dusk light gleams on the glass facades.

"This is going to be a wine bar," Harlan says as we pass the first storefront.

"Nice. What a great location." We pass the large restaurant in the middle. "What kind of restaurant will this be?"

"West coast fusion and seafood."

"Yum. And what's this one?" We reach the final storefront. It's right on the corner, with an epic view of the mountains and Stanley Park.

"You'll see," he says, as he opens the door for me.

I step into the shop.

It's been freshly painted a soft cream. It's empty, except for some twinkly lights that have been strung around the room, giving it a romantic, fairy-tale glow. There are glass cases along the front counters, like you'd see in a café or deli.

Or a bakery.

"You know how sometimes the perfect thing is right under your nose, but you don't see it?" Harlan says meaningfully, close behind me.

My nose is starting to tingle. I don't dare dream that he's about to say what I think he might be about to say, but my baking samples have been laid out on a single banquet table in the middle of the room. Presented beautifully, I can only imagine, by the resort staff.

I turn to him. "Are you talking about me?"

"Yes," he says seriously. "But also..." He looks around. "Your dream bakery."

"Harlan..."

"It's perfect, right? I don't think I understood until I walked in here how wrong that other space was for you. But I get it now."

When I don't respond, because I'm too overcome with emotion, he takes my hand again and starts showing me around.

"Picture it... The displays filled with your delicious creations. The tables arranged over here, with the velvet chairs you wanted..."

Oh, wow. *He listened.*

When I droned on and on about my bakery dream to him, describing what I envisioned, while we ate dinner one night, many weeks ago... He totally listened.

And it has a view of the water.

He leads me in a daze behind the counter and into the

kitchen, which is three times the size of the tiny work space I had at Crave.

"The kitchen is fully installed. You just need to pick all the finishes. That's the fun part, right?"

He watches as I turn in a slow circle, trying to take it all in. I have to blink away the moisture in my eyes to see straight.

"We can put in window seats, like you wanted. It's really a blank slate. You can make it as beautiful as you envisioned. Your baby daddy might even throw in a generous decorating budget so you can make it extra pretty."

When I'm still too blown away to respond, he asks, "What do you think?"

"I think when you say 'baby daddy,' it sounds extra ridiculous. And far too much like 'sugar daddy' for my liking."

"About the bakery, Quinn," he says, and squeezes my ass like it's a warning that I'm being naughty.

"I think... it's truly magical," I admit, my voice all choked up.

He looks deep in my eyes. "It's for you."

I take a deep breath. Are we going down this road again? The one where he thinks he can just fix everything with his money?

"It's very nice, Harlan. But—"

"The best part is, you won't have to deal with a lease or a boss, and I don't even have to buy it. Because we already own it."

"We?"

"Hello?" a woman's voice calls out from the front.

Harlan offers me his hand again, and I take it hesitantly. "Oh, good. They're here," he says.

"Harlan," I whisper, "what are you up to...?"

He leads me back out into the storefront—to find his sister coming in the front door, followed by all three of his brothers.

These are the extremely important clients he wanted me to impress?

"Oh, man," I breathe. "You could've warned me."

"I did." Harlan glances at my red wool dress. "You look great. Very festive."

I poke him in the back. From the look on his face, I think he's genuinely confused about why I'm mildly panicking right now.

I may never truly understand this man.

But maybe that's half the attraction.

I cling to his hand.

"Thank you for coming," he greets his siblings, as I stand here, awkwardly.

"How could we not?" Jameson says sarcastically. "Top-secret, super last-minute meeting on Christmas Eve, and my fiancée isn't invited? Sounds fun." He eyes the single table decorated with cakes suspiciously, while the rest of them eye Harlan. And me.

Not one of his siblings can possibly miss that I'm holding his hand. I wonder if they can tell I'm rocking a little baby bump in this dress.

"Hello," I say, giving them a little wave. Here I am again, the girl with the turquoise hair, but now I'm a brunette. Do they recognize me?

"This is Quinn," Harlan says. "My girlfriend. And she's pregnant."

I just about die right there.

"He didn't warn me he was doing this," I say, my face heating. "I would've asked him not to blindside you."

Savannah recovers first. "Quinn, it's so lovely to see you again." She strides forward to offer me a hug. "Congratulations! I'm *so* thrilled."

Then Harlan's brothers greet me in turn. They seem utterly

shocked. But they congratulate me, and Harlan. A little warily, maybe.

I can't blame them.

"Forgive us if we seem surprised," Graysen says. "I didn't know Harlan was seeing anyone. And I definitely didn't expect this when he insisted we come down here tonight." He gives Harlan a sharp look.

"I wanted to tell you all at once, in person," Harlan says coolly. "We're having a baby girl."

"Oh my gosh. Yes!" Savannah hugs me again. "Another girl in the family. It's about time!"

I laugh, elated that she's so happy. "I suppose it is good news." I look at Harlan's brothers, and I can see this all sinking in for them, a little more slowly. "You're all going to have a little niece in a few months."

"When is the baby due?" Graysen asks.

"July," I say, smoothing my slight belly.

"I also wanted to discuss something else," Harlan says, and his siblings all look at him. "You all tasted a cake Quinn made, when you met her last time. Remember?"

"The vanilla cake with the fruit," Savannah says. "I remember."

"Quinn's a fantastic baker and cake designer," Harlan tells them. "I was just showing her this space. I already talked to Savannah," he tells his brothers, "and she agrees that a bakery would be perfect here."

Oh, shit. This is so uncomfortable.

I don't see any of them jumping for joy at the idea.

"A bakery?" Graysen says. "I thought this was going to be a café."

"But a bakery would be so much more... cozy," Harlan says.

Jameson looks confused. "I'm sorry, did you just say *cozy*?" I can tell by the looks on his brothers' faces that this isn't a word they've probably ever heard out of Harlan's mouth before.

Harlan ignores him, telling Graysen, "It will be cakes *and* coffee." He shows them all to the lovely table displaying samples of my best work. "Come, have a taste. Quinn's desserts speak for themselves."

"Oh, these are your cakes, Quinn?" Savannah immediately zeroes in on the cupcakes and scoops up a decadent dulce de leche. "I loved that cake you made for us."

"Thank you so much."

"Tell them about your vision for your bakery, Quinn." Harlan shoves a sample of funfetti cake into Jameson's hand.

"Well... my plan is to open an artisan bakery, to be the home of Quinn's Cakes, my custom cake business. It would be like a café, but elevated. Beautiful front windows featuring gorgeous, colorful cakes each week, like works of art. And an array of cakes in the interior displays, including on-trend, seasonal, and classic flavors and designs. We'll have a curated array of daily cupcakes and cakes by the slice as well, flavors that I know, from my experience working in several bakeries over the years, are crowd pleasers. And we'll serve locally roasted coffee."

"You said, 'we,'" Savannah says. "Do you have partners?"

"My mom is my business partner. She's the queen of cupcakes."

"Well, I can attest to that," she says, after biting into her cupcake.

"She'll be thrilled to hear it."

"Your mom made all these, Quinn?" Graysen asks, tasting a red velvet cupcake.

"The cupcakes are all from the recipes of Lorraine Monroe," I say proudly, "my mom. All cake samples are mine."

"You make quite a team," Damian says, sounding impressed.

To Graysen, he says, "We should be selling these in our restaurants."

"Feel free to keep tasting," Harlan says. "I just wanted you all to have a chance to see and taste more of Quinn's hard work. And to be here when I showed the place to her, and told her..." He turns to me. "If you love the space, Quinn, and can see yourself being happy here running the bakery of your dreams, it's yours."

None of his siblings say anything. But there does seem to be an air of uncertainty in the room, like they're all waiting to see how this plays out.

I admit, I am, too.

"But... you own it, though," I point out.

Harlan comes closer to me and takes my hands. "Well, you'll own it, too. Once you co-own the whole resort as a member of the Vance family." You could definitely hear a crumb drop when he adds, "As my wife."

"Oh. Fuck." That's Jameson, I think, and I'm vaguely aware of one of the other brothers elbowing him in the ribs.

I think I hear Savannah gasp.

But I'm too stunned and simultaneously breathless to say a word.

"You were right that I was keeping you from my family," Harlan says, "because I was afraid of the truth about Darla coming out. I was wrong to ever ask you to lie for me."

"Blackmail," Jameson coughs.

"I was wrong to blackmail you," Harlan amends, casting Jameson a dark look. "As you may have gleaned from my brother's rude interruption, I told my siblings the truth about Darla. And the truth about you. But I didn't tell them everything."

I swallow nervously, my heart thrumming a mile a minute.

"The whole truth, Quinn Monroe," he says devoutly, "is that I love you."

I sniffle, starting to cry.

"I love the way you pour your heart into every single cake you make. You care so much about making your clients happy, and about your friends, and your mom. I love that you and Lorraine have so much love in your home, and you've welcomed me there. I love how determined you are to raise this baby well, and take care of everyone around you. And I love the way you leave your little messes around my house, and you forget where you put things, and you sneak food to my cat, and you make the whole place feel like a home. It's not home anymore when you're not there, Quinn."

"I know," I say shakily. "My home doesn't feel that way anymore, either, because you're not there."

"So, I want to build a life with you, and our baby, and Lorraine. I want to start every morning with you, watching you grump around and then perk up over your morning coffee."

I laugh, and he wipes the single tear from my cheek as he talks.

"And I want to come home to each other every night," he says. "I want to watch you build your dream, and support you every way I can. I want us to raise our daughter together, and I want to pick her up after school every day, even if it means Graysen has to get used to me working from home."

I glance at Graysen, who kind of rolls his eyes.

"And I want to have more kids with you, Quinn," Harlan vows, "in a home that smells like your baking. I want you to be my wife. And I promise you that I'll work every day to make sure you feel loved and cared for. Because you have the biggest heart of anyone I know. You make people feel loved. Even me. And you deserve to feel that kind of love back, tenfold."

He gets down on one knee in front of me, and I tremble with emotion.

"Please, will you marry me? I promise to be a wonderful

father to our little girl." Now he's crying, and it totally does me in.

"Yes. I'll marry you. Please don't cry."

He swipes the tears from his eyes as Jameson leans sideways to try to see his face—and Harlan's tears, which maybe he's never seen.

Then Harlan pulls out a ring box.

"I forgot to present you with the ring." He laughs nervously. I've never seen him this way, such a mix of naked emotions. His fingers even shake opening the box.

Then he slides the ring onto my finger.

"Oh my god," I gasp when I get a look at it.

Harlan looks up into my eyes again. "Do you like it? Lorraine thought you would."

"Of course! I love it." He gets to his feet and pulls me to him. Our kiss is wet with salty tears. "I'm a disaster right now," I breathe when we pull apart. "You talked to my mom about this?"

"Of course," he says.

"Can I hug my new sister?" Savannah asks. "I'm trying to be patient over here."

Harlan steps back so Savannah can hug me, and Harlan's brothers congratulate him. "It's my mom's ring," I tell her, showing her the modest diamond ring. "The one my dad gave her when he proposed. I know it's simple, but Harlan couldn't have picked a more perfect ring for me."

"He pays attention," she says softly. "That's how he shows you he cares. That focus of his."

"Yeah." I wipe the tears from my cheeks. "He does."

I get a round of hugs from Harlan's brothers. Then Graysen says, "Well, what a great way to start the holiday season. Can we take you both for a drink, to celebrate?"

Harlan looks to me before answering. "Quinn?"

"I would love that." I lay a hand on my belly. "Non-alcoholic for me, of course."

"I'll arrange a table at Velvet." Damian pulls out his phone and steps away.

"I'll call Megan, to join us," Jameson says. "She'll be thrilled," he tells me, then steps outside to make the call to his fiancée.

"How fitting," I muse as Harlan takes me in his arms, and everyone else seems to fade away. He pulls me close, wrapping me up in his body, as if sharing this moment has been a real ordeal, and he needs me all to himself now. "Celebrating our engagement, right where we first met."

"It's strange to think that that night at Velvet was the first time we met," he says. "I feel like I already knew you that night."

I roll my eyes a little, teasing. "You can't count stalking me as knowing me."

"You're right. You're much more lovely up close than I could ever have imagined."

"I love you, Harlan Vance," I tell him, standing on my tiptoes to wrap my arms around his neck, and bring my lips closer to his.

"You have no idea how much I adore you," he says, his lips brushing mine. "I'm going to give you and our little girl everything I've got, and then some. I'll never stop working to deserve you, Quinn."

I kiss him softly, and promise him right back, "I'm going to spoil you rotten with my love. You'll be incorrigible. An absolute monster."

"Yes," he agrees. "I'll be your monster. Forever."

Epilogue

Harlan

New Year's Eve...

"That's it, kitten," I groan. "I can feel you about to come on me."

I'm deep inside my fiancée as warm water rains down on us. I have her backed up against a wall in her shower. We're supposed to be getting ready for the party tonight, but we're definitely taking our time.

As soon as Quinn came in here and got the water running, I followed her in—and it started steaming up, as I put my hands and mouth all over her.

Her soft cries now fill the shower. She has one foot propped up on the bench seat, her thighs spread open for me. Her hands grip my ass as I fuck her, deep and slow, and my thumb massages her swollen clit.

I can feel her bearing down on me as her breaths come shorter and harder, and my cock swells. "Harlan," she gasps, clinging to me.

I suck on her earlobe and murmur, "I'm going to come in you so hard."

She moans in anticipation and sucks on my neck, making my cock impossibly harder inside her. I feel halfway delirious as I fuck her, a little faster now.

"When you come for me," I growl, "I'm going to plant my seed inside you."

"It's... already been planted," she pants. But I hear the smile in her voice.

"Mmm." Our eyes connect for a thrilling heartbeat before I kiss her deeply. Her fingers dig into my ass as I work her clit—and her hips buck wildly against me.

I feel her go off, her pussy convulsing, squeezing the length of my cock.

I keep fucking her, keep kissing her through her orgasm, as she shudders against me, little cries caught in her throat.

And when her movements slow, her climax mellowing and fading, I bury my face in her neck and come, hard. I groan against her throat as she clutches my ass and holds me tight, and as always, I feel *pulled*.

Into her. Into *us*.

Closer and deeper and *forever*.

When I finally come up for air, we're both panting softly. We kiss and kiss as the warm water rains down. And eventually, reluctantly, we slide apart.

She's pinned her hair up to keep it dry, so I forego the pleasure of washing it and instead lather her with body wash, slowly, watching her from hooded eyes.

She watches me just the same, like she's drunk on me.

I feel the ridiculous smile that spreads slowly across my face.

"What?" she whispers, smiling back.

"We should name her Rain." It occurs to me in the same instant it comes right out my mouth.

She tilts her head, considering. "Our daughter?"

"Yes."

"That's adorable."

"She's from Vancouver, and it rains here a lot. And I happen to like the rain. And besides... it's part of 'Lorraine.'"

Quinn's lips part as her eyes mist over. "That's... so beautiful, Harlan." She slides her arms around my waist and gives me the sweetest hug, pressing herself against me. We just hold each other for a long moment.

I can feel her heart beating against mine, know our daughter's heart is beating inside of her, too, and it's everything. Everything I ever could've wanted for myself, but never really thought I'd have.

"I love you, Quinn," I whisper against her hair, and she hugs me tighter.

"I love you more than words," she whispers back.

We've only been engaged for a week, but it's been the best week of my life. By miles. I love her more every single day.

We've spent the week getting her and Lorraine moved in. We celebrated Christmas together. We've had endless sex. And some more serious talks, that have just strengthened our bond. Which I think we owe to the little girl we're bringing into the world; to make sure her family has the most solid foundation possible when she enters into it.

We've even negotiated living together in a way that will work best for all of us. She's agreed to limit her chaotic style of "organizing" her things to her own spaces; her bathroom and the family kitchen where she'll bake with Lorraine. And I've agreed to work on accepting that children are messy.

Quinn and her mom have agreed to respect my need for cleanliness, and to do their best to be considerate of our shared spaces. And if living with people who don't put things away exactly as I want them to becomes too much, I've agreed to go back to therapy.

Quinn gazes up at me and says dreamily, "I guess I should get out and start getting dressed."

"If you must." My hands roam down to her ass and squeeze.

She kisses me, then reluctantly pulls away. She rinses off and slips out of the shower, and starts toweling off as I rinse.

"Shit!" she cries, startling me. She's looking at my watch on the bathroom counter. "I didn't realize what time it is!" She flies out of the bathroom, naked, as I turn off the shower. "We need to get ready!" she shouts from the direction of the walk-in closet

I step out and dry off with a sigh of contentment. We're throwing a New Year's Eve party at the house. *Our house.* We have the staff and caterers taking care of everything downstairs. There's no reason to worry about a thing, but it's adorable how seriously Quinn is taking it all.

She's been excited about the party all day, and keeps fussing over her playlist, and the cake she made, and the drinks she wants to have served—even though she can't drink.

"Don't worry," I tell her, as I stroll into the walk-in. "You're going to be an incredible hostess."

She's digging through a drawer filled with panties, messing up the neatly folded rows. I try not to watch. "I feel like I'm going to puke, I'm so nervous," she says.

"You just need to get used to the beauty of having staff," I try to reassure her. "They'll do the work. We just show up and enjoy."

She pulls on a pair of lacy black panties. "Easy for you to say. You just put on the same black suit you always do and you're good to go." She looks entirely jealous of the fact that I'm totally relaxed. "I have so many directions I could take my dress choice, and I have hair and makeup to do..." I stroll toward her as she rambles. "And I made that extravagant cake that took most of the day—"

"Of course you did." I come up behind her and wrap my

arms around her. Making her stay still, tucked in against me. I give her a kiss on the top of the head, smelling her hair. It's like lavender shampoo and cupcakes. "Just breathe."

She takes a deep breath.

"I just need everything to be perfect," she says.

"Now you sound like me." I release her and pull out some underwear to slide on as she races around, pulling out bras and jewelry and whatever.

My Christmas gift to her was a little moving-in shopping spree. She was hesitant to buy too many clothes while pregnant and not her usual size, but we managed to fill her half of the closet pretty decently, and I made sure we got plenty of lingerie.

"It's crazy," she says, laughing a little. "I feel like this is my debut into high society or something, and I don't know what the hell I'm doing."

I snicker. "You give my brothers way too much credit. And the guest list is literally them, my sister, Megan, and your mom. It's low pressure." We decided to make our first official party as a couple in our home family-only. And I'm really looking forward to it.

To starting off a fresh new year with my family—all of them.

"I know. I just really like everyone you just mentioned," she says, "and I've never had siblings before. I feel so lucky to have your family becoming mine."

"Baby. We're the lucky ones."

Our eyes catch across the room, and she gives me a sweet look that tells me she fucking adores me.

The feeling is mutual.

I choose a suit—easy—as she searches through her new dresses. She pulls out a long black one and a short blue one, holding them up for me. "Decide, please? I need to get dressed, asap."

It's tough, but not that tough. Blue always looks fire on her.

"Blue," I tell her.

"You're so right," she says, and promptly stuffs the black one back, dashing off to the bathroom with the blue one.

As soon as I've pulled on my pants, I go into the bedroom and grab my phone, to check for progress updates from Carlisle. I want to make sure preparations are rolling along perfectly downstairs, for Quinn. If anything's not perfect, I want to make sure it's taken care of, so she doesn't need to worry about a thing tonight.

But I see I've missed calls from Savannah. Seven of them.

And a text message that says, *Call me*.

I call her back right away.

"Harlan," she says breathlessly. "I've been trying to reach you."

"I see that. What's going on?"

"I just wanted to get you on the phone. To tell you, rather than just text you..."

"Tell me what?"

She groans a little. "I'm so sorry, okay? But I'm not going to be able to make it to your party tonight."

"Are you serious?"

"I know it'll be a great party. I'm sorry," she repeats.

Quinn struts out of her bathroom, looking much calmer—and absolutely gorgeous—in the off-shoulder blue dress that makes her eyes glow.

I drop my jaw, and she does a little spin.

"Savi, I'm putting you on speaker," I tell my sister. "Quinn's here."

"Oh, hey Savannah!" Quinn calls out as I put the call on speaker.

"Oh, hi Quinn," Savannah says. "Is anyone else there?"

"Nope! Just me."

"How can you miss the party?" I demand, and Quinn's face

falls. "It's New Year's Eve, Savi. You know, bringing in the new year with those you love? How can you not be with your family?"

"Uh..."

Quinn pouts exaggeratedly, and there's a long pause on the other end of the line. I go over to her, wrap an arm around her shoulders, and kiss her on the forehead.

Finally, Savannah says, "Damn. I feel bad here, you guys."

I meet Quinn's eyes. She gives me a worried look. And mouths *What's going on?*

I'm getting kind of worried myself. "Savi, are you okay?"

"Yes. I'm okay. I'm very okay." She adds, sounding a bit nervous, "Don't be mad, Harlan, okay?"

My sister is never this evasive.

"Savannah," I say seriously, "what the hell is going on?"

"I got married," she blurts.

Quinn gasps. I see the surprise on her face, but it's not even close to the shock I feel.

I struggle to collect myself, and utter the only two words that make sense right now. "To *who*?"

THANK YOU FOR READING!

The next book in the Bayshore Billionaires series
—Savannah's story!—
is coming soon.

***

What to read next in the Dirtyverse…

If you want more of Dani, and her twin sister Danica's steamy,
mistaken-identity romance, dive into **Hot Mess** (*Players* #1).
Turn to the end of this book for a yummy preview…

Or, start where it all began,
with rock star Jesse Mayes and sweet Katie Bloom's
fake dating romance, **Dirty Like Me** (*Dirty* #1).

Scan the QR code to see Jaine's books on Amazon:

Note to Readers & Acknowledgments

I adore a grumpy/sunshine pairing, but even better if the sunshiny one has their grumpy moments and the grump can evolve to have sunshiny moments, too. As with anything I write, I really strive not to put characters into boxes but let them come to life as real people in my head. Some characters spring forth from the depths of my creative soul almost instantly, fully formed, as was the case with Harlan when he graced the very first page of his brother Jameson's book, *Charming Deception*. Other characters are much, much harder, and for whatever reason, it sometimes felt like Quinn was taking forever to reveal herself fully to me—which is really my fault, not hers. But once she did, I was just so delighted to know her! I am so in love with this couple, and I hope you are, too!

I also love a strong girl squad like Quinn's, and I do hope to right books for Dani and Nicole in the future. If you want more of their story so far, the wonderfully boy-crazy Nicole was briefly introduced in *Hot Mess*, and also appeared in *Charming Deception*; Dani has appeared in many other books in her role as alpha female supporting character, mainly *Hot Mess* and *Irresistible Rogue*.

I now have such a wonderful team of people helping to support me, and spreading the word about my books. Thank you to Valentine, Josette, Ratula and the rest of the team at Valentine PR. My PA and Queen of Fandom, Alyssa Giselbach. Jackie Dubray, and all the book-loving influencers who tell the world about my books. The passionate members of Jaine

Diamond's VIPs and Jaine Diamond's Spoiler Room. To Emma Shelford, thank you for all the book chats. And to all my lovely author friends around the world, thank you for your ongoing support.

To Mr. Diamond, my partner in love and publishing, I couldn't have gotten through this book without you. Harlan really wouldn't exist without you, either. Thank you for your endless dedication and support, and for being my forever.

And finally, a massive, heartfelt THANK YOU to YOU, for reading this book!

If you've enjoyed Harlan and Quinn's story, please consider posting a review and telling your friends about this book; your ongoing support means the world to me.

With love and immense gratitude,
Jaine

Playlist

Find links to the full playlist on Spotify and Apple Music at
jainediamond.com/darling-obsession
or scan the QR code:

If I Look Fine—Roet
Nightmares—Two Feet
Make You Mine—Madison Beer
New Girl Now—Honeymoon Suite
You?—Two Feet
Love Is a Battlefield—Pat Benatar
Kiss Me Slowly—Jon Dix & Beck Goldsmith
Figure It Out—Royal Blood

Playlist

Black Cars—Gino Vannelli
Obsession—Beds and Beats
Turn Me Loose—Loverboy
I Want It—Two Feet
i like the way you kiss me (burnt)—Artemas
Hungry Like the Wolf—Duran Duran
if u think I'm pretty—Artemas
Love Is a Bitch—Two Feet
Head Over Heels—Tears for Fears
Let's Dance—David Bowie
Feather—Sabrina Carpenter
The Beach—The Neighbourhood
Every Time You Leave—The Black Keys
obsessed—Olivia Rodrigo
Put It on Me—Matt Maeson
Every Breath You Take—The Police
All Goes Wrong (feat. Tom Grennan)—Chase & Status
how could u love somebody like me?—Artemas
Don't You Want Me—The Human League
Love You Like I Do—Vancouver Sleep Clinic
PDA—Allan Rayman
Sink or Swim—Artemas
Lost the Game—Two Feet
True—Spandau Ballet
By Your Side (feat. Tom Grennan) [Acoustic]—Calvin Harris
Lips On You—Maroon 5

About the Author

Jaine Diamond is a Top 5 international bestselling author. She writes contemporary romance featuring badass, swoon-worthy heroes endowed with massive hearts, strong heroines armed with sweetness and sass, and explosive, page-turning chemistry.

She lives on the beautiful west coast of Canada with her real-life romantic hero and daughter, where she reads, writes and makes extensive playlists for her books while binge drinking tea.

For the most up-to-date list of Jaine's published books and reading order please go to: jainediamond.com/books

Get the Diamond Club Newsletter at jainediamond.com for new release info, insider updates, giveaways and bonus content.

Join the private readers' group to connect with Jaine and other readers: facebook.com/groups/jainediamondsVIPs

- goodreads.com/jainediamond
- bookbub.com/authors/jaine-diamond
- instagram.com/jainediamond
- tiktok.com/@jainediamond
- facebook.com/JaineDiamond

Preview of Hot Mess

Don't miss the first book in the Players series,
Hot Mess, Ash and Danica's story!

*Hot Mess is a steamy, swoony second-chance romance
—with a twist—featuring a mistaken identity,
an embarrassing tattoo, a broken, irresistible bad boy,
and the woman who's destined to be his.*

PROLOGUE

Ash

I'd never believed there was any kind of grand purpose to my life, or to the relationships that came and went from it.

I'd never believed in fate, or karma, or any of that shit.

With all the bullshit I'd been through, why would I?

I definitely wasn't feeling any kind of manifest destiny that day.

I couldn't feel much at all.

Then I got off the chairlift at the top of the mountain, the edge of my snowboard caught in the ice and I went down, hard, twisting the shit out of my knee.

It had been three days since I'd broken up with my girlfriend, Summer. Three days since I'd had my heart smashed.

Three days since I'd started partying.

It was a gorgeous, clear morning. Bluebird day; fresh powder, perfect conditions. I'd planned to spend all fucking day on my board, sweating out the alcohol.

Then, you know, start drinking again.

But then I fell getting off the fucking chairlift.

I was barely able to crawl out of the way in time before the guys getting off the chair behind me ended up on top of me. It was two of my bandmates, Pepper and Janner, who pretty much pissed themselves laughing at me. Zero sympathy.

I could've boarded circles around either of these guys, hungover or not, but in that moment, they weren't the ones on their asses in the snow.

At least Johnny, who'd been on my chair with me, gave me a hand up.

It was our first run of the day. The four of us had just dragged our asses out of the hotel, and my day of boarding was already done. Couldn't put much weight on my knee, couldn't even coast my ass down the hill. Had to sit down in the snow and wait for help, while Janner sat with me—and laughed at me.

Guess that's what you get after staying up most of the night, drinking way too much tequila with a bunch of rock stars.

And circus freaks.

And a bachelorette party.

Long story.

The medics had to collect me and give me a ride down the hill on a snowmobile. They took a look at my knee and wrapped it up, told me to go easy on it for a few days. I passed when they asked for photos; I wasn't in the mood to play rock star. But I signed their skis before I limped on my way.

By the time I got back to the hotel, it was a ghost town. Everyone was on the slopes. So I got changed and did the only thing there was to do: start drinking. I hit up the empty lounge, sat at the bar, ordered a beer and chatted a bit with the bartender.

Johnny came back to the hotel not long after I did.

I was alone at the bar when he found me. Said he was too hungover to board and ordered himself a drink.

"Shot of bourbon," he told the bartender. "And one for my wounded friend here."

I looked at Johnny then. Really looked.

I didn't know Johnny O'Reilly well. I didn't know we were friends.

I'd only met him a few times before. We were both rock stars on the rise, both from Vancouver, spent a lot of time in L.A.. Ran in the same circles, hit the same parties.

Two days before, he'd come to my breakup party in L.A., and here we were.

In Alaska.

Alone in some bar.

And he'd sat down pretty damn close to me.

Johnny had that striking combo of a deep tan, bleach-blond hair and blue-green eyes. The tattoo over his shoulder climbed out of his thermal shirt and up one side of his neck—the shirt that clung to his sculpted chest and arms. He had a guitarist's callused fingers and clean, square fingernails. Nice hands, white teeth, slow to smile.

And dark, serious eyebrows that made it look like he was always thinking, like he cared about something, about you, even when he didn't.

... And that air of fucking calculated recklessness. The one that told you he was always in control.

Thing was, I kinda had a weakness for guys like Johnny O.

Bad boys.

Not exactly my type, but... tempting.

The shots came and he slid one over to me.

And that was it.

I clinked my shot glass to Johnny's, and when I looked into his eyes, my fate was sealed.

Granted, I sealed it myself.

Maybe I was still kinda drunk from the night before and just getting drunker, but I knew what I was doing. No one forced that shot down my throat.

If I hadn't done that first shot with Johnny that day, no fucking doubt, things would've gone down differently than they did that night.

But then maybe, just maybe, I never would've met *her*.

Printed in Great Britain
by Amazon